PRAISE FOR M. L. BU̲ ̲ ̲ ̲ ̲

Top 10 Romance of 2012, 2015, and 2016.

— BOOKLIST: THE NIGHT IS MINE, HOT POINT,
HEART STRIKE

One of our favorite authors.

— RT BOOK REVIEWS

Buchman has catapulted his way to the top tier of my favorite authors.

— FRESH FICTION

A favorite author of mine. I'll read anything that carries his name, no questions asked. Meet your new favorite author!

— THE SASSY BOOKSTER, FLASH OF FIRE

M.L. Buchman is guaranteed to get me lost in a good story.

— THE READING CAFE, WAY OF THE WARRIOR:
NSDQ

I love Buchman's writing. His vivid descriptions bring everything to life in an unforgettable way.

— PURE JONEL, HOT POINT

THE IDES OF MATT 2017

A SHORT STORY COLLECTION

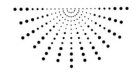

M. L. BUCHMAN

Buchman Bookworks

Receive a free book and discover more by this author at: www.mlbuchman.com

Cover images:

Two silhouette of a soldier on a beautiful background © Santiaga

Leaving Earth © Philcold

Romantic couple riding © bezikus

Man and Woman Couple in Romantic Embrace On Beach © Darren Baker

MH-6 Little Bird © San Andreas

Soldier On Patrol © rudall30

Couple in love © yanlev

CH-47 Chinook Helicopter © Michael Fitzsimmons

Desert © Subbotina

Moon and Helicopter over Citi Field © slgckgc

Beautiful weeping willow in a park © Smileus

U.S. Army UH-60 Black Hawk helicopter © Michael Kaplan

Silhouette of a soldier and a dog © Prazisss

US soldier © zabelin

Rudolph red nose reindeer © Mirage3

Christmas vacation on tropical beach © pashapixel

MH-47E Special Operations Chinook Helicopter © USASOC News Service

SIGN UP FOR M. L. BUCHMAN'S NEWSLETTER TODAY

and receive:
Release News
Free Short Stories
a Free book

Get your free book today. Do it now.
free-book.mlbuchman.com

Other works by M. L. Buchman:

The Night Stalkers

MAIN FLIGHT

The Night Is Mine
I Own the Dawn
Wait Until Dark
Take Over at Midnight
Light Up the Night
Bring On the Dusk
By Break of Day

WHITE HOUSE HOLIDAY

Daniel's Christmas
Frank's Independence Day
Peter's Christmas
Zachary's Christmas
Roy's Independence Day
Damien's Christmas

AND THE NAVY

Christmas at Steel Beach
Christmas at Peleliu Cove

5E

Target of the Heart
Target Lock on Love
Target of Mine

Firehawks

MAIN FLIGHT

Pure Heat
Full Blaze
Hot Point
Flash of Fire
Wild Fire

SMOKEJUMPERS

Wildfire at Dawn
Wildfire at Larch Creek
Wildfire on the Skagit

Delta Force

Target Engaged
Heart Strike
Wild Justice

Where Dreams

Where Dreams are Born
Where Dreams Reside
Where Dreams Are of Christmas
Where Dreams Unfold
Where Dreams Are Written

Eagle Cove

Return to Eagle Cove
Recipe for Eagle Cove
Longing for Eagle Cove
Keepsake for Eagle Cove

Henderson's Ranch

Nathan's Big Sky

Love Abroad

Heart of the Cotswolds: England

Dead Chef Thrillers

Swap Out!
One Chef!
Two Chef!

Deities Anonymous

Cookbook from Hell: Reheated
Saviors 101

SF/F Titles

The Nara Reaction
Monk's Maze
the Me and Elsie Chronicles

Strategies for Success (NF)

Managing Your Inner Artist/Writer
Estate Planning for Authors

CONTENTS

Also by M. L. Buchman   vi
Welcome to 2017   ix

Love's Second Chance   1
Heart's Refuge   45
Circle 'Round   85
Welcome at Henderson's Ranch   121
Flying Over the Waves   155
Sound of Her Warrior Heart   193
Since the First Day   235
Love in a Copper Light   275
Her Heart and the "Friend" Command   311
First Day, Every Day   373
Love in the Drop Zone   415
Delta Mission: Operation Rudolph   455
The Christmas Lights Objective   505
Thanks for reading along!   543
Don't miss these prior great collections!   545

About the Author   547
Also by M. L. Buchman   549

WELCOME TO 2017

2017 has been a good year for Delta Force and The Night Stalkers in my "Ides of Matt" stories. As a matter of fact, with only one exception out of this baker's dozen, they're *all* Delta Force and Night Stalkers. (The sole exception is *Welcome at Henderson's Ranch*. As the ranch is now run by my former Night Stalkers Emily and Mark, I suppose that it too belongs in this world.)

None of this wasn't planned.

With only rare exceptions, it is typically only the month before that I start thinking about what the next month's "Ides of Matt" story will be. I look for inspiration in the news, in novels I'm working on, serendipity, or even snippets of a conversation. Sometimes it stems from older novels I happened to pick up when verifying a fact (or simply enjoying some time with favorite characters).

That last of these inspirations is one of the fun yet challenging parts of being a writer who loves working in series. Both of the Delta and Night Stalker worlds have become large and complex. The Night Stalkers alone is now six or seven separate series. And I'm often having to dig back through older books to make sure I get my facts and characters right. Of course, I love these characters. I *miss* these characters. So I'll often go to check a fact and end up rereading half a book before I catch myself. A dangerous time trap.

I wasn't even conscious of this "theme" for 2017 until I began assembling this volume. Out of curiosity, I went back and peeked at 2016. I had: hotshots and lookout towers from my Firehawks world, my first Delta Force short stories, Henderson's Ranch, Night Stalkers, and even one for my small town Oregon Coast contemporary romances in Eagle Cove.

Then with some trepidation, I looked at this year's tales again. I feared they might have a sameness, a commonality that might somehow diminish this volume.

Not even close.

I have Delta snipers with hard pasts and surreal missions. I have stories of war dogs and refugees, of combat search-and-rescue teams and drug lords. Settings range from a Montana ranch to Mexican drug wars to riding through ocean storms off Scotland and Panama. One takes us to a swampy river bed in the Ukraine and another into outer space.

Characters ranged from the hardened warrior to the eternal optimist to... Well, you get the idea.

My wife just shakes her head. Yes, the myriad shades of these stories is *exactly* what it's like inside my head.

So, in this remarkably divisive year of 2017—both at home (the US for me) and abroad—I looked for what was the common theme of the stories I've chosen to tell.

Romance, of course. I *love* romances. And with only one real exception, these are all pure romances. In *Circle 'Round* I wanted to check in on how Lola Maloney was doing after she took over command of the 5D from Emily and Mark.

But there are other themes that run deep in these tales and I am encouraged by them. They are themes that give me hope for the future when I'm feeling down and they encourage me to work harder to capture them on the page.

Whether my heroes and heroines are infiltrating deep into foreign countries or chasing after one of Santa's lost reindeer, there are two things they never lose:

Hope and Optimism.

To me as an author, these are the essential ingredients not only of my stories, but of my life. I always seek the bright side. I firmly believe that we will eventually triumph as people over all of the socio-religious-economic-political-gender turmoil that we face.

Some call me naive, but I don't think so. Perhaps it is because I have a daughter and I wish a better world for her to live in. But I think the reason is much more rooted in all of the wonderful people I've met and all of the ones I have yet to meet. They are the ones who make me feel the way I do.

Meanwhile, my year's stories are sent out in the sincere desire that they will help spread those three cornerstones of my writing: hope, optimism, and (of course) love.

For you, my readers, with all my heart.

M. L. Buchman

-Oregon Coast, 2018

M.L. BUCHMAN

3-TIME BOOKLIST TOP 10 ROMANCE AUTHOR OF THE YEAR

"Buchman's Best Yet!"
Target Engaged, Booklist

Love's
Second Chance

A DELTA FORCE ROMANCE STORY

LOVE'S SECOND CHANCE

*D*elta Force operator **Hector Garcia's** mission as scout for the take-down of a Mexican cartel leads him straight into a gun battle.

Hired gun Alejandra Martinez prowls at the heart of it. The woman who told him to leave town five years ago looks and fights even better than back then.

Only together can they hope to find *Love's Second Chance*.

INTRODUCTION

This story is not about Mexican cartels and Delta Force snipers.

They are setting elements ripped from the news. The Mexican-US border wall was in the headlines as this was written shortly before President Trump's inauguration. And sex-trafficking is one of the most horrific crimes against women that is still slow to be recognized.

But again, that was setting, and not what the story was about.

For me this was a story about regrets.

Twenty years ago I found my soulmate. Seriously. I could not have asked for the gift of a more amazing woman to walk into my life and, for reasons that continue to mystify me, she's chosen to stay. There is not a moment of that decision to be together that I have regretted. Even though I didn't believe in the word soulmate until I met her.

However, there were some incredible women before that as well. Over the years with my wife, I've come to understand how a few of those relationships could have ended very differently, or not ended at all, but for a few different words being said. Would those words have made a difference—sometimes on their parts, sometimes on mine? I don't know, but I'm left to wonder.

I didn't seek to redeem these characters' past love for myself. But the writer in me wanted to somehow offer that gift of a second chance at love to the memories of those fine women who agreed to walk the same path with me for a short while.

CHAPTER ONE

 "ou really stepped in some shit this time, Alejandra Martinez." She didn't even know where to direct her fire. Or if she should fire at all.

Lying prone on the roof of the highest building in the area, a whole two stories, gave her the best vantage of the cesspool that had been her hometown for over twenty-five years. US-Mexican border towns sucked, especially when they were on the Mexican side. But she'd never found a way to leave it.

If she started shooting over the low parapet of aged adobe, they'd know she was up here and that could start to suck really fast. Of course another couple of hours up here in the midday sun baking her butt on an adobe grill and maybe she would be ready to shoot all of the assholes who had conspired to trap her up here. They'd gotten blood on her new jeans and sneakers, which was really pissing her off. At least it wasn't hers.

"Next time you're stuck in a street war and trying to survive, remember to bring milk and cookies. Or at least some water." Good reminder, if she ever got out of this one. A six of cold beer sounded good too.

Life had been so much simpler twenty-four hours ago. She'd had a lover, a lousy-as-shit job—making it only a little better than her lover—and something that sort of resembled a place to be.

Now she had a cartel war surrounding the building she lay on top of, and her job was dead—her former employer had owned most of the blood she was wearing. Too bad her job had been to protect his stupid ass. He'd not only been stupid enough to piss off the Alvarado cartel that controlled all the contraband traffic through this town, he'd neglected to tell her he was also setting up the street gangs for a hard fall. They'd found out. Everyone wanted him dead and it was hard to blame them.

The steady crack of automatic gunfire and the hard thwaps of bullets impacting on stone and metal echoed up and down the streets below. These guys were using ammo like it was free. As far as she could tell they were either fighting over who got to claim taking the idiot down, or they were having a gunfight just for the hell of it.

"This town is really going down the toilet."

"Wasn't all that impressive to begin with," a deep voice resonated from close behind her.

As she swung around, a big hand grabbed the barrel of her rifle, stopping it halfway to its new target.

There'd been no sound.

No warning. Not a creak or shift of the rotten roof timbers.

A big *muchacho* knelt close behind her on the roof. He was loaded for action. He held a combat rifle in one hand and her rifle barrel in the other as calmly as if it was the other end of an umbrella or something. Despite his light jacket she could see a pair of Glock 19s in twin shoulder holsters and would wager he had more ammo and another hidden carry or two on him.

A glance past him—the roof access hatch was still closed and latched.

"How the hell did you—" But then she recognized him and knew. "Hector Garcia? Haven't seen your pretty face since Marina was still a virgin." Which was close enough to never. Her little sister had probably seduced her first boy from side-by-side bassinets at the hospital and hadn't slowed down since. At times it was hard to tell if she was a whore or just a slut.

Actually, Hector's wasn't a pretty face, not even the part that wasn't covered by his wrap-around shades and a scruff of three-day beard that looked good on him. He'd broken his nose twice that she knew of, and now maybe a third time by the look of it. She still remembered the knife fight that had earned him the wavering scar from jawline to temple. His dark hair was long, the way he'd worn it ever since he'd lost an ear during a street brawl. He might be a mess, but Hector also looked really good. He used to be one of those slender and dangerous types. Now he was a powerfully wide and dangerous type.

And at the moment...she must look like shit. *Just perfect.*

She'd been riding *guarda* on a candidate for congress presently bleeding out in the middle of the plaza. What *idiota* campaigned in favor of building a wall on the Mexican side of the border to stop drugs and illegal emigration? That was American-style craziness. But he'd paid her more than she could make anywhere else even marginally legal—which meant he was also on the take in a dozen different ways and worried about it. She could have defended him against one or two shooters. But the two gangs duking it out on the streets below had brought them to his speech by the truckload. She'd dropped four before her sense of self-preservation kicked in.

Now Alejandra was really pissed about the blood on her. She'd also crawled through a shattered luncheon buffet on her way up to the roof. Total mess.

Not usual at all for her to think about how she looked in the middle of a gunfight, but she and Hector had a past—even if it was a long-ago past—and her last shred of vanity had been drowned in reeking mole sauce and blood.

He let go of the barrel and she sat up to get a better look at him.

"Shit, woman!" He placed a big hand on top of her head and shoved her back down onto the roof.

Moments later a single bullet cracked by overhead. She'd drawn exactly the kind of attention she hadn't wanted.

Hector rose quickly onto one knee, then swung his rifle up so fast she could barely follow it. No time to aim. No time for anything. He just fired: two shots, a hesitation with a slight shift upward, then a third. He dropped back down. "That should take care of that."

She'd been a shooter of one form or another ever since she was little: possum as a kid, armadillos to put meat on the table after Dad had bugged out, and bad guys as a policewoman—until the drug lords made that too dangerous a beat. But she'd never seen anything even close to what Hector had just done. He'd barely even looked for the target. Maybe the sound of the bullet had been enough. Maybe for him. And she knew if she tracked down the corpse—for she had no doubt that's all it was now—it would have two holes close together in the chest and one more in the head.

There was certainly no return shot whistling aloft from below.

"Sorry," she should have stayed down.

"*De nada!* So," Hector lay on the roof beside her. "You busy much?"

"You saw the body in the plaza?"

"Yeah."

"That was my meal ticket. No major loss—wasn't much of a lover either."

Hector's face darkened at her second statement.

She swung the butt of her rifle into his gut, aiming between a pouch of ammo and a Glock 19. She caught him hard enough to earn her an angry grunt.

"You been gone, hombre. You don't get to judge shit."

He shrugged one shoulder in agreement, but didn't look much happier about it.

Well, neither was she. Especially not with Hector Garcia lying just inches away to remind her of how good her best lover ever had been.

The gunfire down on the plaza was dying down. Probably running out of ammo at the rate they were using it.

"Why? You got any bright ideas on how to keep me busy?"

"More than few," his easy leer said plenty. But she still knew him well enough to know that sex wasn't the only thing he had on his mind.

CHAPTER TWO

*H*ector had remembered Alejandra Rosa Martinez as a total knock-out, but that was nothing compared to what he'd found up on the roof.

He'd come back to his shithole of a hometown for a mission, not looking for her. Not really. In five years his life had totally changed—no reason to assume that hers had stayed the same. Or that she'd be real interested in seeing him. But a few questions about her had led him to the plaza, just as all hell had broken loose.

He hadn't expected to walk into a gunfight, though four years in the US Rangers and another year as a Delta Force operator had let him see the patterns quickly. There was an obvious hole in the battle running from door to door.

The *policia* were wisely hanging back a couple blocks and waiting it out—though they needed a real lesson about how bullets skipped along concrete walls and he hoped they didn't catch one. It was the reason that war zone photos always showed the US military walking up the center of a street rather than hugging the buildings.

But whatever sides were fighting around the plaza and up on

the low roofs, the lack of action from the best vantage point spoke volumes. Somebody held the high ground, which meant they were defending it, but there was no sign they were using it. Someone smart—maybe like Alejandra. He got up to the second story inside the building, leaving only a few broken bones behind him. Not a one of them understood that it would hurt less if they'd just let go of their gun when he was ripping it out of their hands.

At a rear, second-story window, he'd managed to reach up high enough to loop his rifle's sling over a protruding outside timber and used his rifle as a ladder to haul himself onto the roof. There he'd been confronted by one of the finest asses he'd ever seen.

How Alejandra had gotten even better looking in the years he'd been gone, he'd never know. It shouldn't be possible, but it was true.

"You done here?" he nodded toward the plaza.

"Shit, you think?" her sarcastic tongue hadn't changed one bit.

"Good. Got a job I could use some help on."

"You show up out of the blue after five years and you suddenly need help from me? Hector, you're an asshole. You know that, right?"

"Sure."

She snarled at him.

"Never argue with a lady when she's right," he threw one of her favorite sayings back in her face.

Her growl went deep and feline, but when he belly-crawled to the roof access, she followed.

He unsnapped the latch without making a sound. She had her rifle ready to aim down when he opened the hatch. With a shake of his head, he warned her off.

He flipped the release and threw the hatch wide.

They both rolled away from it. Moments later, a half dozen wild shots cut upward through the hatch. One shooter. Off center to the right.

He aimed through the roof itself and laid down a short line of fire. Crawling across it earlier, it was clear that it wasn't much of a roof. The rounds punched through easily.

Alejandra did the same from the other side and her angle looked good.

Hector rolled back and dove through.

The shooter was down.

Alejandra dropped in beside him, so close it was hard not to just grab her. With a toe of her boot, she kicked the shooter over. He'd been hit both front and back. She'd always been good, but somewhere along the way, she'd gotten even better.

"Alvarado's eldest. They were both really pissed when I wouldn't marry him. His dad, Miguel, is *not* going to be happy about this." She nudged a boot against him again, hard to believe he was finally dead.

"Good," Hector offered her a smile. "You can tell Miguel yourself when he finds you in his bed tonight."

"That's part of your plan for...whatever?"

It wasn't, but he'd forgotten how much fun it was to tease her. For a second he thought she might try aiming her rifle at him again and he was ready for that.

Instead she kicked him in the shins. Hard.

CHAPTER THREE

*W*hatever Hector was into, Alejandra wasn't interested.

But she was.

They scrounged lunch in the deserted first floor café while the gun battle finished dying off around them. They sat side by side in the cool darkness of the kitchen, their backs against the steel door of the walk-in refrigerator and good visibility of both approaches —each with their rifle across their lap. They'd found cold beer, but Hector had opted for water so she'd done the same.

"Where the hell did you go, Hector?"

"North." The only thing north was the US.

"Why?"

His frown said he didn't like that question. Not a bit.

She finished her empanada then nudged his ribs with the butt of her rifle.

"You told me to go. Said you'd kill me if you ever saw me again," his face said that his second empanada tasted like bitter sand. He chucked it under the sink.

Alejandra thought back to the day he'd gone. She'd been furious with him for something, then he'd bugged out and she never had a chance to take it back. What was...

Marina! Her slut of a sister had bragged about taking down Hector.

"You weren't supposed fuck my sister while you were with me."

"Didn't."

She opened her mouth, then shut it again. One thing about Hector, he never lied. He might keep his trap shut, but he never lied.

"Pissed her off some that I wouldn't."

Whereas her little sister lied about everything—and Alejandra always fell for it. Big sisters were supposed to trust their little sisters. But she'd described certain things about Hector that only a lover would know...or someone who'd spied on him making love. "Shit! I'm gonna strangle the little bitch."

Again Hector's indifferent shrug.

"So I tell you to go and you just do? No argument?"

"You had a .357 revolver aimed at my crotch. I'm not gonna argue with that. I know how good a shot you are."

"And you don't even try to come back?"

Hector looked over at her with those sad, puppy-dog eyes of his. She'd never been able to resist those. Six foot of tough hombre was not supposed to have window-to-his-soul kind of eyes, but he always had. "Without you, I had nothing here."

And he hadn't. His family made hers look like all the good bits of a Thalía telenovela.

"Five years." Somehow they'd lost five years. "Five goddamn years."

CHAPTER FOUR

*H*ector leaned his head back against the refrigerator door and closed his eyes. Yeah, he'd abandoned her to this hell for five years. If she'd done it to him, he'd never forgive her. Shit.

Closing his eyes didn't help.

Now he wasn't seeing her long flow of softly curling black hair with just a hint of her grandmother's dark gold, framing that perfect face. He couldn't see the proud curves above her slender waist that he had so loved to bury his face in. But he could smell her: rich, dark, spicy—overlaid with drying mole sauce on her tight jeans. Like a mix of the lush bounty of the goddess Mayahuel and the fierce and deadly earth goddess Tlaltecuhtli. She had seemed that way ever since they'd sat side by side in *primaria* school desks and learned about the ancient Aztecs.

And she was still that even now, squatting in a darkened kitchen waiting out the stupid shit going on outside: lush, dangerous, and so goddamn good to look at.

He'd landed his fair share of bar babes over the years. His ugly excuse for a face drew in as many as it put off. Not a one had been worth even half of Alejandra Rosa Martinez.

He shouldn't have tracked her down; it was just messing with his head. She wasn't essential to the mission—though it was a better angle than the one he'd thought up while planning back at Fort Bragg. His assignment was to investigate and assess, then call for what assets he needed. If he shifted his plan to include Alejandra, he had all he needed right here.

Reading the profile on cartel boss Miguel Alvarado had brought up too many memories, too much anger. He shouldn't have taken the assignment.

Missions can never be personal. The commanders of Delta Force had beat that into his head again and again. Yet this time it was. His hometown. His family that had been destroyed. And now, in a file handed to him like a random draw, he knew why.

But he *had* tracked her down.

He thumped his head back against the refrigerator door.

Just walk away, Hector. You did it to her before, you can do it again. It's safer that way. Better for her. Sucks totally for you. But since when was that anything new?

Even knowing the right course of action, Hector knew he didn't have the strength to do it again. She was all the past he had. There was no way she could fit into his current life—she wasn't exactly the patient housewife sort—but there was no way he could stand to pry her back out of his heart now that he'd found her. Not that he'd ever been able to.

"So, what's Alvarado up to this time—other than gunning down my meal ticket? And why you?" Even her voice—he'd even missed the sound of her voice. He remembered it like yesterday.

Hector sighed. There was no way to resist having her by his side, so he should just give in. Even if it would only be on a mission.

"Miguel Alvarado is known for moving drugs and immigrants

across the border. Pain in the ass, but the US has had plenty of bigger fish to fry."

He could feel her shrug as a movement through the cool metal against his back.

"He's gone a whole lot lower—human trafficking for the sex trade—and it's time to shut his ass down."

"Shit!" Her sound of utter disgust said that was news to her. "Why *you?*"

That was actually a hell of a good question. What he'd seen in the file back at Fort Bragg, intel and his commanders had certainly seen as well. His hometown—giving him the best knowledge on the ground. His family—he'd told the stories to the psychologists during induction testing into Delta. That had to be in his files. It didn't take a genius to connect Alvarado and his own family. His family had worked as Miguel's guns until they were picked off one by one. He'd probably have been in the family trade and dead by now too, if not for Alejandra threatening to shoot his balls off. Just him left now.

There was only one thing he'd never told the psychs about, one piece that had remained for him alone.

He opened his eyes and looked at her.

"Because, I'm the best bastard for the job."

CHAPTER FIVE

*T*he best bastard she'd ever known.

And now he was going to be a *dead* bastard if she ever got her hands back on him.

Tonight's plan had sounded so simple as they'd hashed it out. No unconsidered twists and turns. Whatever training Hector had gotten in the US, Alejandra saw it shine out of him. He brought up scenarios and variables like it was fact, not guesswork. His easy confidence had made it comfortable to believe and trust him despite his five-year absence.

She tugged against the heavy ropes tied around her wrists, but all it did was abrade her already sore wrists. His plan had been great—right up to the moment she'd stepped off plan and everything had gone to hell.

"I was *not* supposed to end up in Miguel Alvarado's bed, Hector. That was supposed to be a goddamn joke." But she had. The bedroom in Alvarado's hacienda was lush. Dark wallpaper, leather and mahogany furniture, a massive California king bed with satin sheets…and a tie-down ring at each corner.

She still had her clothes on, but it was a good bet that wasn't going to last.

Hector had been careful not to say anything about his life in America, but she'd listened to what he hadn't said. No mention of wife or kids. No mention of anything except "work". That's all he called it: work. Not like it took magic powers to figure out what that meant.

The US didn't send Border Patrol hombres south of the line. They were tough bastards, but they were strictly by-the-book types. The US military didn't invade friendly countries. He'd shrugged off Miguel Alvarado's drug trafficking the way no DEA agent would and she suspected that if Hector was CIA, he'd feel creepier.

He didn't. Hector cut a solid, steady hole in the world gone to shit.

US Special Operations Forces. Green Beret, Ranger...one of those types. Except they'd sent him in on his own. A true specialist. Now she knew how he shot the way he had. Delta Force. No one else operated alone, could do what he did, and made it look so goddamn easy.

He hadn't just gotten out...he'd gotten *way* out and done good besides.

Alejandra fought back the burning in her eyes. For some brief fantasy moment, she'd thought there might suddenly be a way out for her as well.

She tugged at the rope, knowing it was futile.

Today had also offered a lousy as shit lesson about revenge.

Hector had gone for some supplies he'd stashed out of town— and she'd gone for Marina. If she'd laid low, like he'd said, she wouldn't be here.

Instead, slamming open her sister's door without knocking, Alejandra had found her with a man, of course. Except this one had Marina gagged and was holding a gun on her. The wide terror of her sister's eyes had made Alejandra hesitate for the wrong second.

Someone grabbed her from behind, and before she could fight him off, Marina's captor had simply cocked the hammer of his pistol and put the barrel against Marina's temple. Then he'd smiled at Alejandra.

Hector had told her what Miguel Alvarado was now into, cross-border human trafficking for the sex trade. She wasn't a damn bit pleased that she and her sister were getting to see that first hand.

The two of them had been herded into an underground holding area with two dozen others. By the light of the lone dim bulb, Alejandra could see enough of their coloring and features to tell that most were Guatemalan or Oaxacan—at least half were underage. Refugees no one would ever miss except for the families back home waiting for news that would never come. In the stuffy, crowded cell, Marina had told her that the man who had captured them had been a pissed off ex-lover, one of Alvarado's men, who she'd dumped for being too rough.

They were the only locals waiting to be shipped off.

"My timing seriously sucks," Alejandra looked once more at her reflection in the mirrored ceiling above the bed. Miguel Alvarado was a kinky bastard.

He'd come to survey his "cargo" earlier. He'd merely grunted when he spotted Marina. But when he'd seen Alejandra, his smile had gone evil. That was how she'd ended up tied to his bed.

So much for hope.

Now it was just a question of how awful the ending was going to be.

Any time in the last five years, death wasn't that unexpected. She'd known her life expectancy in Mexico stank.

But for one brief afternoon, there'd been hope. The loss of that was now doubly devastating.

CHAPTER SIX

*I*t had taken Hector six hours through the sweltering afternoon and until well past sunset to track Alejandra. He'd lost ten years off his life when someone had finally dared to tell him that she and her sister had been taken away—bound. That had cost him half the time, finding that first step.

No other Delta Force assets in the area, nor any that could be in place fast enough.

He got on the radio with the intel boys, but this wasn't America —security cameras didn't hover above every street corner. However, they had been tracking a pending shipment of women. The challenge was not only to rescue the shipment, but to nail Miguel Alvarado red-handed.

Hector's plan had been to screw up the night's logistics badly enough to force Miguel to take a personal and very visible hand. He was too well connected to turn him over to the Mexican authorities, but once across the border, there were other ways to deal with him. They needed him alive, at least long enough to reveal his whole network.

But now Alejandra was gone and the paths had all led here—

the massive hacienda several miles out of town. He'd dumped his beater vehicle in a handy arroyo and run the last few miles overland. The adobe wall around the massive compound was topped with glass shard and razor wire. Miguel had always been a rich bastard, but clearly he'd reached new depths that he'd needed to turn his home into a fortress.

Hector slid into the compound, only having to leave two guards down for the count. No dogs, which was a mistake, though there were ways of dealing with them. Just made his job easier. Miguel used to keep pit bulls, until they'd mauled one of his sons.

Hard floodlights blinded guards and cast hard shadows.

The security cameras within Miguel's compound weren't well placed—there were plenty of blank spots where they could be avoided. But they acted as excellent signposts guiding him on which way to go—the more cameras, the more important the area was to Miguel.

Inside the garage, Hector found a trio of hot sports cars (all red) —including a Ferrari that looked like it would be an awesome ride. Further in were a half dozen heavy pickups and SUVs appropriate for transporting a personal militia, and a battered American school bus.

Even as he watched, he saw a line of women and children being led up to it from some underground cellar, but not onto it. Instead, hatches in the yellow sides were opened up and the women were made to crawl inside.

Everyone knew that school buses weren't set up to carry luggage underneath like a Greyhound. To any but the most careful inspection, it would appear empty except for the driver who was bound to have some "legitimate" excuse for crossing the border.

They loaded the right side first. Just before she crawled into the rearmost compartment, he recognized Marina Martinez. The years had been far less kind to her than they had to her sister. There was still a beauty there, but now it looked hard and strained. She also looked terrified. He didn't recognize anyone else.

When the guards finished and moved around to load the other side, he slipped up and unlocked the rear hatch.

"Where's Alejandra?"

"Hector?"

He clasped a hand over her mouth to silence her, then repeated his question.

"Miguel took her," she whispered carefully. "You have to save us. You must—"

"Shh. Too many guards here. I'll come for you later." Before she could protest, he lowered the hatch and relocked it.

And there wasn't time to stop the shipment—he had another priority now.

A quick drop-and-roll beneath a black Chevy Suburban was all that saved him from discovery.

He had the beginnings of an idea and began putting it in place as he slipped deeper into the shadows.

CHAPTER SEVEN

iguel seemed disappointed that she wouldn't scream. His hard slaps only served to piss her off and make her jaw hurt. Fine, as long as he didn't break it—so that she could chew off his face if she got the chance.

He made all sorts of threats and boasts—most having to do with fucking her to death just to teach her a lesson. Apparently rejecting his now-dead son, as well as his job offer to be a shooter for Miguel's illegal operations had really pissed him off. It was hard to tell which had made him angrier.

Too smart to risk freeing her hands or ankles, Miguel used a steak knife to slice away her clothes.

"First me. Then the knife," he wielded it down near her waist. "Don't worry, Alejandra. It will be fast. I have other business to see to tonight as well."

He stripped and knelt above her. Alejandra braced herself for the worst. She wasn't going to cry or beg, not for Miguel's benefit. There had to be more horrid ways to die, she just couldn't think of what they were. She wouldn't cry for him, but inside, where her heart ached, she would cry for what she and Hector might have had.

She closed her eyes as his hot breath landed between her breasts.

"First, I'm going to—" then he squeaked.

Alejandra opened her eyes and couldn't make sense of what she was seeing.

Miguel's eyes were wide with shock.

In the mirror above the bed, she had a bird's eye view of the baddest, angriest warrior she'd ever seen.

She'd thought Hector had looked heavily armed and badass this afternoon. Now he was something else. A pair of night-vision goggles had been pulled up onto his forehead. He wore a vest that hung with two pistols, dozens of magazines of ammo for both pistols and rifles, as well as grenades and flashbangs. His puppy-dog eyes now belonged to a full-grown Doberman—a really pissed one.

And she couldn't see his rifle, not all of it anyway. The muzzle appeared to be jammed well into Miguel's ass. The angle was such that if Hector fired, the round would miss her, traveling up through Miguel's body and out the top of his head. She might get splattered with his brains.

She was fine with that.

"Lose the knife."

She thought she knew all the moods of Hector Garcia, but she'd never seen him so angry, so focused in her entire life.

Apparently, neither had Miguel. The blade clattered to the floor.

"Sideways, slowly, until you're lying facedown on the bed. You so much as brush against Alejandra and you're a dead man."

Miguel edged carefully away. The rifle moved with him.

"You okay, Alej?"

Ah-lay. A name she hadn't heard in far too long. She couldn't say all of the things that welled up inside her, didn't dare let them out in the world yet. Digging deep, she found something else. "Could do without the goddamn ropes."

Keeping his rifle shoved someplace dark and nasty, he pulled out a big military knife and slashed her bonds.

Her clothes were in tatters. She went and found some others stashed in a dresser: women's, a wide variety, some close enough to her size. *Bastard.*

She came back and picked up the knife Miguel had dropped to the floor and shifted around until he could see her holding it close by his nose.

"How would you like to fuck a knife, Miguel? Be glad to hold it for you. I'll put you down just like I did your rabid dog of a son."

CHAPTER EIGHT

"*I* need information first," Hector had to slow her down. Not that he could blame her. He felt the same way.

To find Alejandra after all these years and then to come so close to losing her again made him sick. What Miguel had planned for her...the fury rose in a wave that threatened to choke him.

But the 75th Rangers had taught him how to rechannel fury, saving it to focus on the battle moment. Then Delta had taught him how to turn hot fury into cold, until it was a finely-honed weapon.

It didn't take long to get Miguel to spill everything: hierarchy, contacts, combinations to safes, and passwords to his computer. He'd tossed Alejandra a recorder and she'd held it close to his mouth to make sure they didn't miss a thing. How she didn't rip his face off in the process was one of the most impressive displays of restraint he'd ever seen.

Before he let Miguel get dressed, he yanked his rifle free, and shoved a small breaching charge for blowing open locked doors up the guy's ass.

"See this?" he held the remote up close for Miguel to see. "One press of the button and you explode from the inside out. We clear?"

Miguel nodded hurriedly.

Hector tossed the control to Alejandra who caught it one-handed, then looked at him thoughtfully but didn't say anything.

On their way back to the garage, the three of them walked as if everything was okay, Miguel imperiously waving guards aside. They made a few stops along the way. A small knapsack was soon filled with the contents of Miguel's safe, though Hector didn't bother with the cash. Instead he left an incendiary for whoever opened it next. They picked up Miguel's laptop and smartphone along the way, dropping them into foil bags to avoid anyone tracking them.

In the garage, the bus and most of the SUVs were gone.

"Tell me you have a plan, Hector," Alejandra had picked up several weapons along the way until she was almost as heavily armed as he was. It looked damned good on her. "My sister's out there somewhere."

Hector loaded Miguel and his files into the trunk of the Ferrari —thankfully he wasn't a big man. Then Hector hit him with enough morphine from his Delta med kit to keep a horse down for a day.

He and Alejandra slid down into the soft, black leather of the bucket seats.

Yes, he had a plan. But he had a mission to finish first.

CHAPTER NINE

From the start, Alejandra decided that she was really glad that she was on the same side as Hector. He definitely put the bad in badass. And then he kept getting better.

In the Ferrari—which was one of the coolest rides she'd ever had (it grabbed low and yanked her ahead like a sexual shot)— they'd caught up to the bus and the escorting SUVs close to the border station.

Hector had simply waved a hand out the window as they passed, for the SUVs to keep following the bus. He'd slipped in ahead of them all just at the border.

Whatever ID he showed the border guard had certainly gotten his attention. After a few whispered instructions, the guard let the Ferrari and the school bus roll through.

Hector stopped the car before the bus was fully out of the border crossing control lane, trapping it there.

The SUVs had hung back at the last moment, truckloads of armed guards didn't just roll through border crossings.

Hector pulled out a remote control just like the one he'd tossed to her earlier. He had trusted her—trusted her to not kill Miguel unless they needed to, and to do it in an instant if it became necessary. He'd been right on both counts. No one had ever known her as well as he did.

"I didn't want to risk getting them mixed up," then he flipped up the cover on the activation switch of the one he held, offered her an evil grin, and pressed down on it with his thumb.

The three SUVs still on the other side of the border thumped hard, brilliant light shining out all of their windows. Remote control flashbangs.

In moments, the Mexican border patrol, rifles raised, had everyone out of the vehicles and lying on the asphalt, along with a big enough stack of weapons to make sure they spent a long time in prison.

The next moment, their own vehicle and the bus were surrounded by the US Border Patrol.

INS agents gathered up all of the women and children. A very small team in an unmarked black SUV emptied the still-unconscious Miguel and his files out of the Ferrari's trunk. Their eyes had gone a little wide when she handed over the remote trigger on the breaching charge, and told them exactly where it could be found. Then they were gone.

She and Hector turned to watch as the INS began reassuring the frightened women and children. One was handing out blankets, another with water bottles, and even a few stuffed animals for the youngest to cling to.

"Should I give your sister a contact number? Though I'm not sure if someone that sexy should be allowed into the US."

"You *are* a bastard, Hector. I'm the one you're supposed to be calling sexy." But it was hard to put any real heat behind it with the way he was smiling down at her.

Then she thought about it.

Hector was offering to give a contact number to Marina. It would be *his* contact number, to call if Marina wanted to reach *Alejandra.* That meant that whatever happened next, she herself would be with Hector. Discovering that the tiny shred of hope that had nearly died during the evening wasn't so tiny after all just blew her away. That was way better than being called sexy.

"Sure," Alejandra managed after a deep breath to make sure her voice was steady. "She is my sister after all."

He pulled out a slip of paper, wrote his name and a phone number on it and then handed it to her. At his nod, Alejandra stepped into the crowd of women being corralled onto the bus by the INS agents, this time into the seats rather than the hidden compartments.

She couldn't think of anything to say. Some fit of Marina-jealousy had cost her five years of being with Hector. But it would have been five years in the hell that was a Mexican town on the wrong side of the border. Now she was on the north side of the border next to a top US military soldier. It wasn't up to her to understand how this screwed-up world worked, but she would absolutely make the best of it.

Alejandra handed the slip of paper to her sister. Marina might be a sex-crazed maniac, but she immediately understood what it meant for both of them.

Marina's "Sorry" was the only word that passed between them as they hugged, but it was a long hug and her little sister's smile wished her joy.

Alejandra waited until they were loaded and gone, waving as the bus disappeared into the night.

She turned and saw Hector leaning against the hood of the Ferrari, his big arms crossed over his chest. He'd shed his weapons into the trunk. The black t-shirt that had been under his vest showed just how wonderful his chest had become over the years.

Alejandra stepped up until she was standing between his wide-braced feet.

"What's next?"

"East or west? Your choice, Alej." His deep voice was as soft as the darkness.

"What's waiting for us?" He didn't flinch at the *us*. Instead he unfolded his arms and slipped his hands onto her waist. It was the first time they'd touched in five years and it felt as if they'd never been apart.

"To the east about a day's drive is Fort Bragg, North Carolina. If you're interested, my unit is starting a testing course for new inductees in a couple days. I already called in and got you clearance while you and your sister were talking. I swore up and down that you're a shoo-in. Which is a safe bet because you are. The test is brutal, but I got no doubts."

Alejandra leaned up against him and his arms came up around her. It was the best place she'd ever been.

"And to the west?" she could barely speak past how tightly he was holding her.

"About a ten-hour drive out of our way is Las Vegas. They've got these twenty-four hour wedding chapels. Again, if you're interested." She couldn't see his smile because she had her nose buried against his chest, but she could hear it.

Once more that surge of everything she wanted to say to him shot through her. She dug down and sought for something that would keep his ego in line. That would let him know that she wasn't that easy. That he couldn't just sweep back into her life after five years and change everything in a day.

Except he already had. A job, the best lover, a team to belong to. A home. He *had* changed things; he'd made a dream she hadn't even known about come true.

"One question."

"Uh-huh?"

She looked up into his beautiful eyes, knowing now it was something she'd get to do for the rest of her life.

"Ten-hour drive?"

"Uh-huh," he sounded pretty damned pleased with himself at her response pointing them west.

"But isn't that in, like, a normal car? That *is* a Ferrari you're leaning against."

This time he smiled along with his grunt of satisfaction.

She didn't bother answering yes before she pulled his face down and kissed him.

Their love was so big that it didn't need to be said.

IF YOU ENJOYED THIS, YOU MIGHT ALSO ENJOY:

3-TIME BOOKLIST TOP 10 ROMANCE OF THE YEAR

M.L. BUCHMAN

Heart's
REFUGE

A NIGHT STALKERS 2352 A.D. ROMANCE STORY

HEART'S REFUGE

*B**rody Jones* *flies Lifter Rescue—diving down into the hazards of Low Earth Orbit. There he saves who he can of Earth's last refugees.*

Captain Karina Rostov *of the Future Night Stalkers can't understand Brody's career choice—neither his commitment to Lifter Rescue nor his refusal to fly with her.*

When a rescue flight forces them both to confront their pasts, each must finally face their own Heart's Refuge.

INTRODUCTION

When I reread this story, I find myself inclined to think that it has a similar theme to the prior one—it totally *doesn't.*

For this story, I reread the year's first story, Love's Second Chance, *to see if there was another story wrapped in there I wanted to tell. I thought I'd try the same theme, simply placing it in a new setting to see what I learned this time. Writing is always exploration and discovery and I'd thought to plumb these depths further. However, all I did was carry over the theme of regrets and atoning for the past as a starting point for the next story.*

The core of this story lies in the much broader theme of the on-going global refugee crises. I've read a lot about it but didn't want to write about the geo-political ramifications (which are vast and are addressed in Peter Zeihan's books and especially his 2017 newsletters). What interested me was the people. The ones who climbed onto marginal craft to leave Cuba. The ones who spent weeks in sealed cargo containers to escape China. Those who hoped for the promised land by leaving their homes in Syria, Afghanistan, and Northern Africa, and risking everything to reach Greek or Italian beaches.

How that must change a person.

How even being exposed to it in the miniscule ways I have, has shifted my thinking about home and the desperation that forces someone to leave all they know in trust for the unknown future. I have **huge** *admiration for their courage. And I wanted to think about how they've chosen to stand up in the future of their new homes.*

That was the core of this story.

As an aside (nerd alert), I spent nearly as long getting the orbital mechanics and range of fire of the IndiaBeam correct as I did writing the story itself.

CHAPTER ONE

*B*rody Jones worked his way around the Mod18 ship, checking her over in case there was a rescue mission today. Fifty meters of spacecraft that had seen too many flights but, like a beater truck in the old vids, was always game for another round. He liked its tenacity even if he felt sorry for it sitting in this particular hangar.

His ship was parked in a narrow space at the end of the Number Four hangar—thankfully inside Brit Habitat One rather than out on an umbilical space-dock on the outer hull. It let him do inspection and service without a spacesuit which was a major plus. However, it also meant that his old Mod18 was parked alongside five sleek, military Stinger-60s that belonged to the Night Stalkers. They were beautiful, lethal craft.

The white finish on his Mod18 was tinged from a partial reentry burn which she'd never been designed for. The massive NAS logo—Non-Aligned Ship—was nearly obliterated with solar bleaching. In space, paint cheap enough to afford didn't last long. He and a few likeminded had scraped together enough to run the one ship and keep her maintained. "Pretty" was outside their budget.

Non-Aligned Ship, as if his old Mod18 was somehow crooked. Lifter Rescue wasn't associated with any government. In fact, if they hadn't been given hangar space at Brit Habitat One—parked out at the Lagrange 2 point beyond Luna—there wouldn't be any Lifter Rescue operation at all. However, with the Brits' stamp of approval, the other remaining governments of deep space were forced to cooperate as well.

The thruster nozzles showed no signs of cracking. The primary and secondary cooling fins weren't so fortunate, but they were still serviceable—for a few more flights at least. He came around the nose cone and spotted a woman leaning against the closed airlock.

It wasn't Felice, his Number Two. She never hauled herself out of her rack this early unless there was a rescue alarm.

When he saw who waited for him, with her arms crossed and her glorious dark hair flowing to her shoulders, he was torn between irritation and being seriously pleased.

"Hey there, Karina." Night Stalker Captain of Stinger-60 Number One-Four-Alpha—the toughest bitch in space, by her own proclamation. That was the irritating part about her.

"Hi, asshole," but over the years her standard greeting had almost become affectionate...or at least kind of friendly.

"Well, at least some things never change." She was also one of the best pilots in the entire system; only the very top ones made the Night Stalkers. A challenge that he'd never even wanted to try. Still, he had liked piloting beside Karina in flight school and still missed that, five years later.

"Some things never do," she sounded particularly grumpy. "Like you going out again in this flying hazard." The *seriously pleased* part was that she actually spoke to him, listened to him, occasionally drank with him—though they'd hardly gone past that. There'd only ever been one night between them. Not a night actually, really just a moment, but he'd never forgotten it. No matter who he'd bedded over the years, and there'd been some incredible women, it wasn't enough to erase that memory.

He also appreciated the contact because almost everyone else socially plas-walled the people who flew for Lifter Rescue, as if what he did was worthy of contempt. She was perhaps his sole champion among the most powerful military in space—even if there wasn't much she could do for him there. At least she didn't revile his chosen career in public, only to his face.

Brody shrugged. It was an old argument. They'd agreed to disagree long ago and even that hadn't stopped it entirely. He leaned back against her Stinger-60, garaged by some weird fate next to his Mod18. There were twenty of these ships stationed at Brit Habitat One all the time, in addition to an equal number on upsystem patrols. The likelihood of his ending up beside her craft seemed beyond chance. For whatever reason it had happened and he liked the opportunity to see her more often—even when they exchanged little more than friendly snarls.

Lift Rescue had been a point of contention between them, ever since graduation day from flight school. She hadn't spoken to him for at least a year after that. There were fewer missions every year, but he didn't care.

Earth still had the occasional Lifters, people so desperate to leave that they built their own ships to climb the gravity well. And almost every one needed some help to make it out. That's where he and his Mod18 came in—a role that hadn't even existed in the first three phases of humankind's climb to space.

First had come The Exploration—brave lunatics atop chemical-filled bombs.

The Expansion had been far safer—mag-lev rail launches that had delivered settlements from the Senegalese on Mercury to the Swiss out on Pluto. There were rumors of some settlements all of the way out in the deep Kuiper Belt, but if they survived, they weren't talking. No surprise really as it would take a serious dose of paranoia to climb so far.

Even during The Exodus, most of the craft had been purpose-built or were salvaged from Expansion-era craft.

But toward the end of the Exodus, they began running out of ships and Lifters had gotten creative. They'd even salvaged the ancient chemical rockets from The Exploration. Nobody had the power or the skills to climb out to Luna anymore—most didn't make it into orbit. Lifter Rescue tried to help those who didn't disintegrate at launch or punch a brief hole into the ocean after a failed lift.

"One of these days, I'm *not* going to come down and save your ass," Karina didn't move from where she leaned against his closed airlock in her space-black jumpsuit. She'd looked incredible in flight school. She looked even better now. His brain went there, even though experience had taught him not to bother hoping.

"Never asked you to." Besides, there'd only been the two times. One, when he got in beyond his ship's abilities—the reason he'd replaced his first copilot with Felice. And the other when he'd faked an emergency because, in a rare, massive lift, there were more people to rescue than his one ship could handle.

No one could agree on what to call this latest phase. The official term was The Aftermath. Felice's vote had been The Exhaustion—as the last of free Earth tried to climb the gravity well. His personal favorite was The Expectoration, the last of humankind being spit out of the planet with nowhere to go except up.

Brody sighed.

Everything seemed to be a battle with Karina. A challenge to be faced down or a tally to be accounted for. Other than their ships being berthed side by side, he wasn't even sure why she kept talking to him.

"So, your new plan is to block my airlock for the rest of your life?" Yet he wasn't sure he'd mind. His life would be far less if she wasn't a part of it—no matter how small a part that was. Over the years he'd tried for a bigger part, but the answer had consistently been an evasive *no*—as if she hadn't even heard him.

"Maybe it is, at least until I figure out what to do about you." Karina Rostov was a tough-as-plas pilot and had a dark-eyed beauty that he could never ignore.

She was also a fifth-generation Expansionist. Her people had spaced long before the Russo-German-Turk War had erased all three countries in one bloody week, along with most of Europe. Back when humanity's entire future hung beyond the sky.

His family hadn't been so fortunate. When he was a kid, they'd spaced aboard an old Minuteman VI missile they'd found in a Montana silo and converted for The Lift. Three families, four years of work, and he'd never forget the raw terror—or the man who had plucked the few survivors out of the sky before the missile ballistically reentered Earth's atmo. He was retired now from his cargo hauling business, but still one of Lift Rescue's main benefactors.

With Karina's pre-Exodus heritage and his family being just… Aftermathers (Expectorants sounded a little vile even for him), there were even higher barriers between them.

"What are you doing here, Karina?" He couldn't enter his ship until she moved away from his airlock and she didn't appear to be in any mood to do so. While he'd be glad to look at her all day, she always had an agenda. It wasn't like her not to state it and move on.

"I don't even know why I'd care if you died rescuing the useless," like he was an idiot for doing so.

"You mean the *hopeful?*"

She shrugged uncomfortably.

Maybe he finally needed to let go of his Karina Rostov fantasies. How could she think about people that way? It was hope that drove them aloft despite the horrific odds.

CHAPTER TWO

U *seless.* There were times Karina would like to cut out her tongue.

Her parents were old-school Ukrainians—a distinction that had been meaningless even before her great-great-grandparents had lifted during The Expansion. It was an isolationist distinction that Mom and Pop had brought back to life in reaction to The Aftermath. It made her first responses dour and the ones after that worse.

And for some reason, Brody Jones brought out the truly horrid in her. But she couldn't seem to stay away from him either. He was everything she wasn't: blond, blue-eyed, and popular despite his chosen profession, a choice she'd never understood.

Her own Night Stalkers commanders and crew only tolerated her because she could outfly any of them. She'd been born to fly a Stinger-60; it was in her blood. Yet her one great weakness, she couldn't resist poking at this particular Mod18 pilot.

"What is it about you?"

"Me? What about me?"

Karina tried to formulate some kind of a rational answer. Her mind was excellent at analysis—of everything except Brody Jones. She could master the most complex operation: deliver troops to Saturn's Titan and extract another team off Jupiter's Europa all with a minimum fuel burn rate and exact timing.

But understanding Brody was completely beyond her.

Launch detection! The alert blared out of both of the sleevepads in their flightsuits. It echoed around the hangar as well as over the PA system.

They tapped in unison and a quick holo of Earth formed above each of their raised arms with a first-approximation orbital track rising from the surface.

"Kourou, French Guiana," Brody identified it faster than she could. Northeastern South America. "The old European Space Agency site."

"Threat or Lifters?"

"Lifters," Brody declared without hesitation. "Minimal military there before The Exodus. Most of it is underwater since The Melt and the sea-level rise, but someone found a way to lift."

No threat. Stand down alert, her sleevepad announced. For a decision to be made that fast, the launch must not have been big enough to escape Earth's orbit. If it couldn't reach them, it was no longer her concern.

"Out of my way, Karina. I've got to fly." But it most certainly was Brody's.

For reasons that eluded her, she didn't move, forcing him to push her aside. The globe projecting above his sleevepad came straight at her head and she flinched away.

"Oh, sorry," Brody pulled back, tapped his sleeve, and the globe went away. He tapped again, "Felice where are you? We have a run."

This time a big red cross projected above his arm for a moment before it switched to her face. "Hey, Brody! How are you, buddy?"

She sounded toasted. Actually, the hospital logo flash said drugged not drunk.

Felice raised a bound arm into the image area. "The Skyball game last night rocked. Too bad I'm sidelined until the bone reknits. You shoulda been there. Where were you? Probably off doing your usual: getting drunk and mooning over Queen Bitch Rosto—"Jones slapped the disconnect.

"Crap!" He looked about the hanger helplessly.

Karina could only blink in surprise. Not about the "Queen Bitch"—that one she'd heard a thousand variations on. But Brody Jones was attracted to her? Really? How had she missed that?

Before she could collect her thoughts into a question, the other two members of his crew came racing down the hangar past the long line of Stinger spacecraft.

"I need a copilot," he declared to no one in particular. His arriving crew shrugged—Vetch and Warwick were a med and a gearhead, not flyers.

Was Brody too hyped to react to the end of Felice's comment? No, he was blushing. First time for everything.

His eyes swung to her. His blush slowly turned into a smile.

"No way, Brody."

"Are you on the first-call list?"

She wasn't. Though a Night Stalker was always ready, she wasn't on the alpha-alert team today. "There's no way I'm going to copilot your crap Mod18 to go help a bunch of suicidal Aftermathers."

Even as she complained, Brody wrapped a big hand around her arm and was easing her aside.

"But..." he ignored her protests, punched in the airlock code, and hustled her past the outer and inner hatches.

Once they were both resealed, he let go of her to tap his sleevepad. Moments later, a copilot's pre-flight checklist popped up on her own.

"I'm not flying with you."

"Sure you are," his easy grin was infectious. "Do you have something better to do on a Thursday morning than go flying?"

"On a Mod18? Sure!" She hadn't flown a Mod18 since basic training, and hadn't flown copilot since very early in her career.

"Go," he gave her a shove toward the engine inspection port.

For reasons she couldn't unravel, rather than flattening him and departing back through the airlock, she went. It was only as she was signing off on the last items on the list that she spotted the date—it was Sunday, not Thursday—technically her day off, as much as a Night Stalker ever had one.

Karina watched Brody as he slid into the command chair and began systems startup. Thursday? Why had he said that? He had to know the day. Then she almost laughed. Brody had always been the one with the sense of humor—a skill she totally lacked. He'd said Thursday because it was the most boring-sounding day of the week—not mid-week and still too far from the weekend. Anything was more interesting than a Thursday and he was using everything he could to coax her into going along.

Well, Jones was right about one thing: there wasn't anything better than flying.

CHAPTER THREE

"NAS-LR1 entering LEO. This is NAS-LR1 entering LEO." Brody made sure that the transmission was on automatic repeat. "Non-Aligned Ship, Lifter Rescue One entering Low Earth Orbit." They were only halfway down from Luna, but it was always best to give a clear warning to prevent a preemptive strike from the surface.

"That and a Stinger-60 gunship will keep us in business," Karina muttered. "Except we don't have a Stinger do we, Brody?"

"No, we've got a group of civilians in trouble. Find them, Karina." Felice was good, but the whole ship felt different with Karina beside him. There was a sudden rightness to his world that he wished he had more time to enjoy.

"This part of space give me the creeps," but she started working the problem while he focused on finding a safe orbit.

"Creeps me out, too. No matter how often I fly into it." Most of Low Earth Orbit was a blind spot courtesy of the IndiaBeam. Coming anywhere near the I-Beam Zone was bad news, really bad news.

There were only a few groups remaining in any semblance of

power down on the dirt. The biggest was India. They hadn't joined The Exodus. Instead, they lofted a satellite that had opened into a big mirror. Using a ground-based destructive beam, they'd laid down scorched earth for a thousand kilometers around their borders—which just happened to include Pakistan, a swath of China, and several other irritant nations. After that was done, they'd proved their willingness to burn anything out of the sky that they could spot, which had included all the eyes-in-the-sky above the Eastern Hemisphere.

Even doing an overflight at two hundred kilometers in an NAS-declared ship on a rescue mission was a dicey proposition. Bottom line: if an Earther lifted anywhere within the I-Beam's range, they were on their own. Very few who did ever crossed out of it. In Low Earth Orbit, India's range was two-thousand kilometers in every direction. Basically overflights anywhere between Saudi Arabia, the Philippines, and Mongolia were screwed.

"Got them!" Karina put up a projection.

Brody saw that it would take three orbits to match speed. And it was going to happen directly over the I-Beam.

CHAPTER FOUR

"*N*o! I didn't come out here to die, Brody Jones. Not for you. Definitely not for—" Karina could feel her parents' bitter epithet striving to surface, *Aftermathers*. By sheer will, she managed to suppress it. "—people I've never met."

She *wasn't* her parents—who were parochial even by modern isolationist standards. She refused to hold their system-view. But she wasn't going to die for unknown Lifters either.

"I've followed your missions. Since when did you, a Night Stalker, shy away from risk?"

"There's a difference between calculated risk and suicide."

He'd followed her missions?

"Do you follow all the Night Stalkers?" They weren't exactly public record—hell, most of her missions were extremely classified. But there was a fraternity among pilots that Brody did a better job of fitting into than she did. He'd be able to get the stories if he tried.

"Just yours," it was barely a gruff mumble.

"Why do you do this?" She waved toward Earth because she wasn't comfortable pursuing why he followed her missions.

He tapped for a full orbital display which filled the space between them. It made his face hard to read and any continuing conversation awkward. He didn't speak, though she could see his jaw working hard.

"They're on a decaying ballistic arc." Instead of reaching true orbit, their trajectory was off. They were going to make three orbits, then... The reality caught in her throat.

"Early in the fourth orbit they'll reenter and burn up," Brody concluded softly.

"We *can't* cross through the I-Beam Zone!"

"Even if they don't fire off the I-Beam, these Lifters will already be in reentry by then. We have to find a way to catch them sooner."

Karina checked the fuel load and ran some rough calcs in her head. They were going to have to catch them in their second orbit to have time to get the Lifters offloaded before the I-Beam came over the horizon.

"How about this?" She tapped out a course.

"That places us inside the Aussie protection dome."

She spun the projection and saw that it did. The only other big Eastern Hemi player—the Australia-New Zealand dome—wasn't playing at all. They'd put up an energy field and disappeared behind it three decades ago. No one had heard from them since. The dome was huge, reaching well beyond the atmosphere. Anything that hit its silvered surface disappeared in a flash of static discharge and was never seen again—no debris, nothing. Broken down to component molecules and no one knew how they did it. They weren't telling either.

Karina studied the problem again. Angle of insertion, delta-vee, the I-Beam Zone, the dome...the factors swirled about her. She looked out at the Earth, like a perfect blue-and-white Skyball, glittering among the stars. They were directly above the sunlit, daytime sky and the old planet glittered. There was no way to see the problems from up here: the disease, the political and religious rifts, the pollution, the radiation.

And then she superimposed all the factors and obstacles in her mind on the actual Earth. It was one of those tricks that she'd concluded made her such an exceptional pilot. Others relied completely on the virtual projections, but she could see the multiple orbits in her head, superimposed on the real world.

She finally saw one, and only one possibility. She keyed it in without looking.

CHAPTER FIVE

"Oh my god, you've totally lost it!" Brody looked at the shift in the projection. It broke a hundred safety rules. Maybe two hundred. He'd never have thought of that in a million years. The stress factors on the Mod18's structure began rolling up the screen: a lot of yellow but, surprisingly, no red. Even factoring in her present condition, it should be okay.

"But that's..." he ran out of words. It was elegant. Risky, wild, and wholly unorthodox, but there was a beauty to it that told him it would work. There was no time to decide, but he didn't need any. If Karina said it was good—

He rammed his thumb down and print-authorized the course change into the flight computer.

"Hang on! We're—" his warnings to Vetch and Warwick in the rear were chopped off by the hard burn.

A muttered curse was all that came over the intercom.

Maybe he should have given them a little more warning. It didn't really matter; the intercept wasn't the hard part. It was the escape that was going to get interesting.

They caught up with the Lifters over the remains of Canmerica

East. The Melt had drowned most of the coastal cities, except New York which had built a skyscraper-high dike wall. Then in a final fit of isolationist paranoia, they'd dropped an asteroid on the Isthmus of Panama to cut apart the two continents—as if nations in South America didn't have a navy or a space force.

Brazil had collapsed early on, which hadn't surprised anyone. But Argentina and Chile had joined together and retaliated with a line of meteor strikes from Quebec to Atlanta. Canmerica East had no longer existed by the time of The Exodus.

He and Karina caught up to the Lifter halfway through their second orbit.

"That was beautiful, Karina."

"Thanks," she kept her head down, studying the controls.

Brody temporarily cleared the nav projection and looked right at her over the much simpler docking control layout they'd need in a few minutes. "Seriously, Karina. I wouldn't have come up with that in a decade."

"Actually, Brody, you already did. Last semester of flight school, Advanced Orbital Mechanics. There was a problem in the seventh chapter I couldn't get."

He vaguely remembered her tracking him down one night with a flight problem. It was the one time she'd come to his room—which was what he really remembered.

"I was so afraid I was going to flunk out if I missed it."

"It was only one problem, Karina. You always worried too much. You were the top of the entire class. And the way you flew, there wasn't a chance of them failing you."

"I'd spent two days on it. You said you hadn't looked at it yet, but you cracked it in under an hour."

Impressing Karina Rostov had been plenty of motivation. He didn't even remember the problem now. But he could picture her electric smile the moment she'd understood his approach on it. Her kiss had been no mere peck of thanks. It hadn't been romantic either, but it had sizzled in his mind for all of the years since. His "one big moment" with her—how utterly pitiful.

A squawk from the computer forced him to focus on the docking procedure. Mating up with the old Ariane rockets was always a challenge. They'd never been engineered for human transport, so the fabricated ship-mating collars were often a challenge. More than one Lifter hadn't thought it through beforehand. Open-space transfer without spacesuits had a very low survival rate. One Lifter ship hadn't had a hatch at all and there'd been no way to cut one in time before they fell and burned up during reentry. That one had been hardest—their radio had worked most of the way down.

Thankfully, these people had installed a universal docking collar on the side of the instrument delivery shell. He let Karina bring the ships together. Letting his hands ride on their linked controls, he could feel the incredible subtlety of skill she achieved as if it was second nature.

There was a hard *clang* as the hulls came together, but the connection showed all green and was holding pressure. He left the problem of station-keeping to hold the ships together with the flight computer.

"Come on," he signaled Karina to unbuckle as he did the same. "This can be the hard part, but it can also be *so* good. And just in case…" he tapped his sidearm.

Karina checked her own then nodded her understanding.

They floated back to the belly hatch where Warwick waited. Vetch had the medical station warmed up.

"Do it," he gave the command to proceed.

CHAPTER SIX

*K*arina forgot to breathe while the hatches were opened.

How could Brody not remember that night? It had shaped so much of her flying ever since. He'd shown her a new way of conceptualizing orbits that had rocked her mental world. With a simple screen of calcs, he had revealed a level of mastery behind his easy-going exterior that had humbled her. He had made her a different pilot, a better one.

She stole a glance over at him, but he wasn't watching the hatch, he was watching her. He looked aside quickly.

Felice had said that Brody was mooning over Queen Bitch Rostov. What possible reason...

Then she remembered something else about that long-ago night. She'd kissed him in thanks. It had been an unthinking gesture that she'd felt mostly embarrassed about. A senior pilot had been waiting for her that night and yet she'd kissed another man. Now, she couldn't even remember the pilot's name.

She'd also forgotten that kiss. Apparently Brody Jones hadn't.

What sort of a woman was she that she'd blocked all that out?

Easy answer: Queen Bitch Rostov. Yet somehow Brody always saw past that. She now knew that was part of why she kept being drawn back to him. Because only Brody Jones saw her differently than everyone else did—even herself.

"I—" she turned to him, but his attention was now riveted on the first of the Lifters emerging awkwardly from the hatch that joined the two ships—unused to the zero-gee of space. A man, a woman, two teenage girls, a small boy. They were emaciated and weeping. They kept touching Brody's crewmates as if to make sure they were real. They arrived in a cloud of smells she couldn't separate. Salt tears, body odors, and something she didn't recognize that reminded her of the hydroponic farms but was a hundred times more powerful. It made her wonder what humanity had lost in leaving Earth.

More people followed and the ritual was the same. A broken arm was routed over to Vetch's med station. There were any number of black-and-blue marks that they'd feel later. Soon there were forty people crowded in the Mod18's bay. No more followed.

"Stay here," Brody told her before leveraging himself down into the Lifter's hatch.

She ignored him and pulled herself through the hatch too.

The odors were different in here. The sharp tang of fear and human waste—released in fear or...

A woman stared at her from a mattress on a steel deck floor. Her eyes were wide and her jaw slack. She looked as if she'd died while screaming.

Brody was checking each body. Occasionally, he'd nudge one free and float it toward her. In the zero gravity, it didn't take much for her to push them up toward Warwick waiting on the Mod18. Some were merely unconscious, others conscious but immobile with shock.

She looked around. The Ariane's equipment bay was barely three meters across and five tall. In that space they'd built mattressed tiers that had impossibly held fifty people. She counted seven of them who would never leave.

Brody was grim as he double-checked each one left behind.

"I had no idea," her whisper sounded overloud in the cramped space.

He nodded. "Out of choices, they take the only chance they can get."

She waited for him in the ill-lit stinking confines of the pod while he arranged a young boy's body so that he almost looked natural.

"He could have been my brother. Was almost me," Brody's voice was a whisper as he brushed the boy's hair gently into place. "An ICBM was never meant to carry people. We didn't know how hard the Minuteman missiles boosted. Three families totaling twenty people. I begged to ride at the top of the cone—I so wanted to be the first one into space—it was the only thing that saved my life. Dad built a small platform at the nose, just big enough for me. Everyone else packed in below, with only room to stand during the launch. They crushed one another under that awful acceleration. The only other survivors were an aunt, who ended up raising me, and the technician's wife who killed herself just a month after losing her whole family—that was all out of twenty people. This is how I pay back."

His voice was even, calm, steady, though she could feel the pain surging from him into the close air.

Karina wondered if she'd ever really known Brody Jones.

She had always thought of him as a slacker. He'd been a top flyer at school. Not as good as she was on the actual piloting, but truly exceptional in the mechanics, and an outstanding leader. Then, when she'd suggested that they go military together—with some lame image of the two of them blazing paths of glory throughout the system—he'd just shaken his head.

"Lift Rescue," was all he'd said. That was a flyer level below Patrol, Cargo, or even Salvage.

It hadn't made any sense. But she'd been so hyped on the chance of a highly prestigious future that she'd been afraid to ask. His blue eyes had been so sad that she'd backed away rather than stepping forward. Was that what had kept drawing her back to him all these years?

Hope that she would change his mind?

Or the unanswered question of why he never would?

Now she knew the answer. And as she slowly eased from the small pod, which was now just a coffin, she knew why she'd been afraid to ask. Her own life suddenly looked trivial and privileged compared to this.

CHAPTER SEVEN

*A*fter kicking loose the Ariane, they rode in silence down the gravitational slope: thermosphere, mesosphere, stratosphere. He had double-checked that the Lifters were quiet and safely strapped into acceleration hammocks before he'd aimed the Mod18 down the path of Karina's flight plan. They slid within fifty klicks of the Aussie dome: the shining silver that shrouded any view of the nations within and meant instant death to any who approached.

Brody had never told that story of his own Lift to anyone. Only his aunt and the man who'd rescued them with his cargo vessel, flying well into range of the I-Beam to pull them out, knew the whole awful truth.

The Mod18 skipped off the upper atmosphere at barely fifty kilometers above ground. At this low of an altitude—due to the curve of the horizon—they were flying below the I-Beam Zone. Barely.

The mass of the northern Himalayas lay spread beneath them. He'd never thought he would see them in his lifetime, especially not so close. The jagged peaks, holding some of the world's last few glaciers, glittered like corridor signs guiding their way.

The Mod18 was never designed for an Earth reentry and definitely not a landing. He kept the spacecraft in a slow roll so that no one area took the brunt of the massive overheating. Alarms were triggering every few seconds. It took both of them working as fast as they could to deal with them.

Overheated nose plate, he rolled slower across the back to give it a few more seconds of cooling.

Primary computer core shut down, Karina force-fed the flight plan into the backup.

At the bottom of their passage, they were little more than a meteor across the Tibetan night, a herald in a land where no one and nothing survived to interpret their passage.

Forever and nineteen minutes later they clawed back up into Low Earth Orbit over the Hawaiian volcano that had finally made sure there was no more Hawaii.

He checked in with the crew and passengers. They hadn't lost anyone in the blazing passage.

Karina didn't speak once on the long flight back up to Luna's L2 and the British habitat can. Medical and immigration took the passengers from them: shock, limping, tearful thanks.

Soon it was just the two of them and Mod18 at the end of the long, quiet row of Stinger-60s.

"She's a good old girl. She's fits in better now," Karina patted the nose of the Mod18. She had a soft smile that he barely recognized. He turned away because it hurt to see it, knowing it would never be for him.

Brody looked down the row. Five immaculate, well-maintained, stealth-black Stinger-60s. And his reentry-scorched Mod18. The NAS logo was long gone and the last of the white paint showed through the char only in a few well-protected spots.

He nodded in agreement, not sure of what to say next. What to do. Karina the Queen Bitch who had started on the flight with him wasn't the woman who now stood close beside him. A lot of crews had quit before he'd learned that he had to be the only one to go down through a Lifter's hatch—there were some things that were too hard to ask others to face.

Yet Karina hadn't hesitated. But neither had she spoken afterward. She hadn't been his to lose, but still he wondered if he'd lost her anyway.

"I've been thinking," Karina's voice was soft and he couldn't read anything in her dark eyes when he risked looking at her once more.

"I suppose that's better than running away from me as fast as you can," which is what he'd been waiting for. He leaned back against his ship because it grounded him in what was important. If she ran, he might just run after her, all the way to the Night Stalkers, and Lifters be damned. He crossed his arms over his chest, the only thing that kept him from reaching out for the impossible.

CHAPTER EIGHT

*I*s that what she'd always done? Run away? Maybe it was. Unable to face his choices, his hidden sorrow, his eyes that hid so few of his thoughts now that she knew how to look.

Yet she had kept coming back. Now she truly knew why.

Whatever Brody had done, he'd done with a single reason and a single passion more pure than she'd imagined possible. Certainly better than any of her own motivations had ever been.

"I was thinking about the Night Stalkers."

"I like my job just fine. Same answer I gave you after flight school, Karina. Lift Rescue," and again she saw the sadness in his eyes. But it was different from the sadness she'd seen in the Ariane's capsule. That had been about the Lifters who hadn't survived their dream; this was personal.

"I know that, Brody. You'd be less than who you are if you did anything other than LR. I get that now."

"So, why are you thinking about the Night Stalkers? If you're suddenly talking about leaving them, I'll never speak to you again."

"You're not getting off that easy." But actually, she had thought about that for a big piece of the flight back. What it would be like to fly with Brody? There was an immediacy to what he did. He saw the deaths, but she could still see the damp places where the men and women who he had saved had wept their thanks onto his shoulders. Lives he had changed, including his own.

"Then…what?"

"I thought about the similarities of what we do. There are a lot of soldiers who are alive because of what I do."

"Damn glad you see that."

"I'm not stupid, Brody."

"Nope," he still leaned back against the Mod18. No qualifications, just simple agreement. As if he simply *knew* things about her that she sometimes doubted so deeply.

"So, here's the deal."

"There's a deal? Like I said, if you're thinking of leaving the—"

"Shut up, Brody."

He harrumphed and shut up.

"The deal is: you ever need a backup pilot, I'm your first call. I'm going to talk to my commanders and make sure they know. I'm also going to take a couple weeks leave until Felice's arm heals. After that, unless I'm on an active mission, I'm your Number One call. Clear?"

He studied her for a long moment, then hit her with one of those big smiles of his.

She didn't know how a man who'd seen so much could smile like that, but she'd like to find out. Very much.

"That's huge, Karina. Do you have any idea how huge?" In his excitement, he grabbed her hands, squeezed, let them go, grabbed them again. "You were always the best pilot I ever flew with. And I can't afford a permanent backup. Every time any of my team gets so much as a stubbed toe I break out in a cold sweat. It's such important work. I can't let anything—"

"I know," she freed a hand and rested it on his arm to stop him. "I know." She liked the way it felt to touch him. And oddly, that simple contact was enough for her to now remember the kiss that he'd never forgotten. After that kiss, she'd made myriad post-graduation plans—all based on the assumption that, of course, he'd fly with her. But when he'd chosen Lift Rescue, she had backed away, unable to understand why a man with his skills would ever make such a "low" choice. Worse, she had locked her heart away—safe from everyone...including herself.

Now she knew.

It was because she'd never met a better man than Brody Jones. She also understood that she never would. Maybe it was finally safe to let her heart back out.

"There is something else we need to talk about," she freed both hands and stepped back. She needed some distance from him if she wanted to get this right.

He eyed her cautiously.

"A little comm told me that you spend a lot of time mooning over some Queen Bitch named Rostov."

Brody groaned, "I'm going to kill Felice as soon as her arm is better."

"Your option. But what if I gave you an excuse to stop mooning?"

"Like what?"

"What's your operational base, Brody Jones?"

He shrugged those nice big shoulders of his, "Same as yours, Brit Habitat One."

"Same as mine," she nodded. "Let's go." She slipped an arm through his to tug him off where he was still leaning on the Mod18.

"Where're we going?" The back of his flightsuit was black with the char from the Mod18. There was a marginally cleaner imprint of his body on the hull. It made it very easy to imagine what imprint he'd leave upon her body.

"We have to check something, very carefully."

"You've lost me, Karina."

No. No, she hadn't. She had found him. She'd found him long ago, but her eyes hadn't been open to see that. They were now.

Karina had always simply flown, being best was all that mattered. But now she knew why she flew. The best man she'd ever known had taught her. Brody helped Lifters arrive—she made sure the place they'd given everything to reach was safe once they made it.

"What are we checking out?"

"We need to know whose quarters, especially whose bed, is more comfortable. We need to test them both very thoroughly because I'm planning on us using whichever one we choose for a long time."

Brody looked down at her with those smiling blue eyes as they walked from the Mod18 and down the line of Stinger-60s. It was a walk she was looking forward to taking together—for all the years to come.

IF YOU ENJOYED THIS, YOU MIGHT
ALSO ENJOY:

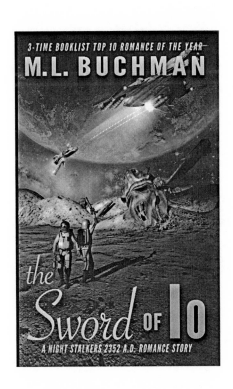

M.L. BUCHMAN

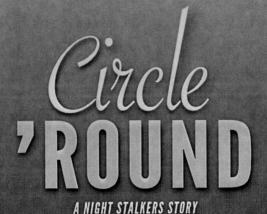

Circle 'ROUND

A NIGHT STALKERS STORY

CIRCLE 'ROUND

*C*hief Warrant Officer Lola Maloney *never expected to lead the Night Stalkers of 5th Battalion D Company. But when Beale and Henderson left, they put her in charge.*

Now the 5D's first mission under her command is going all to hell. Only she can salvage it—her team's very lives depend on her.

Lola reaches back to every trick they ever taught her and finds the answer in a most unexpected place, as they Circle 'Round.

INTRODUCTION

Leaving heavy themes behind for now, my third tale of the year was a revisiting of old friends.

In late 2013, my heroes Emily Beale and Mark Henderson departed the Night Stalkers 5th Battalion D Company. For the reason why, you'll have to read Take Over at Midnight.

They placed the 5D in Lola LaRue's hands but we never quite saw that transition of power. I wanted to see that for myself. I also wanted check in and see how she was doing as a commander. This story was originally written shortly after Take Over at Midnight *but saw only a very limited release in* Fiction River: Last Stand.

It was roughly two years from sale to publication. I reread the story after the rights finally reverted to me and I was very pleased that the story's interest to me as a reader hadn't diminished at all with the passage of time. I still love checking in with my characters. I love the contrast between Lola and any other character I had written to that time. She was more dynamic and, in many ways, freer than any prior character of mine. I so enjoy that about her and I'm still proud to include this fun tale.

CHAPTER ONE

*C*hief Warrant 3 Lola Maloney stared at the tactical display of the DAP Hawk helicopter *Vengeance* projected on the inside of her helmet visor. Against the pitch dark of night outside the windshield and the soft glow of console instruments, the display revealed the rough terrain of the southern Ukraine and her broken flight formation.

The commander always knows what to do.

She tried it again as a mantra, *The commander always knows what to do.*

Along with a thousand plus hours of officer training, none of it meant shit at the moment—she didn't have a goddamned clue what came next.

"Kara," she called to the drone operator tucked three hundred miles away on the USS *Peleliu* helicopter carrier, though her drone was circling somewhere six miles above *Vengeance*. "You're my eyes."

"Roger. All clear."

"Everybody else get down and land now."

At her radioed command, the three other birds descended to

gather around the pair of already grounded heavy-lift Mil-17 Hind helicopters. One a shattered wreck and the other one was trying to salvage the bodies of the fallen.

Lola had "borrowed" both of them from the Iraqis for this mission. She hadn't been intending to return either one, but she hadn't planned on one being shot down either. Two bodies had been blown out through the fuselage, but there were still three bodies—she'd just think of them as bodies at the moment, not guys she'd handpicked and trained for this mission—trapped in there.

One thing Lola knew to the core of her being, she'd see the whole flight dead before she'd leave a body behind. Too much history had drilled that lesson into her head.

She had watched too much "News at 11" as captured pilots were tortured, raped, and even burned alive for "the cause"— whatever the cause of the week was. Had seen the old tapes of the bodies of dead pilots and Delta Force operators being dragged naked through the streets of Mogadishu.

That was not going to happen to her people.

If the ground team from the second Hind needed time to extract the casualties from the wreckage, she'd find it for them.

But on this flight, time was not their ally.

No one was.

The U.S. Army's 160th Special Operations Aviation Regiment drew the missions no one was supposed to know about, ever. And this one wasn't only supposed to be top secret, it could never be known that U.S. forces had been involved. The political ramifications would be horrendous. So they hadn't merely called SOAR, they'd called the edgiest company of all, the 5th Battalion D Company.

And the secret nature of the mission was why Lola had chosen the mix of craft that she had.

The Russian Mil-17 Hind transports—from the Iraqis but now sporting Ukrainian markings—and the three Kamov K-52 "Alligator" gunships—that the Georgian Air Force would be missing soon, repainted with Russian markings—had been the mask. The Alligators were supposed to pretend they were escorting the Hinds, or vice versa depending on which force they ran into...if they were unfortunate enough to run into anyone.

They were the working craft.

And her stealth-rigged, all black U.S. Army DAP Hawk, by far the most dangerous of them all, was the fist.

Once they were all parked on the bank alongside the river, she turned to Tim. Her husband—one of the unique features of the 5D that she'd never really understood was that married couples could fly together—had jumped to the front seat—from crew chief to copilot—earlier this year, and proved that he'd absolutely deserved the promotion.

"Keep the engines warm."

He nodded as she slid her helmet's visor up and disconnected the umbilical that tied her into the DAP Hawk's systems.

Her world, which had been a multi-layered tactical display across the inside of her visor, blinked out and left her blind in the total dark of a moonless night. Fumbling a bit, she pulled her night-vision gear out of its pocket on the inside of her door, snapped it into the helmet mount, and flicked it on. The world returned, in a hundred shades of bright green seen through the tunnel vision of infrared night-vision goggles.

Shedding her harness, she stepped down to the ground, which squelched under her feet. The first thing she checked was that her carbine rifle, with its stock folded neatly into place, still hung across her chest. The second thing was her helo's wheels. They'd sunk about a foot into the muck, but stopped there. They were parked in the bottomlands of the Kalmius River in the Eastern Ukraine.

The three Kamovs had landed, each just one rotor away, and appeared stable. Pilots measured small distances in rotor diameters, one rotor away meant they weren't going to engage each other's blades by accident. In combat, distances were often down to a half-rotor off some cliff face or power pole.

Rumor said that Major Emily Beale had once flown down to two feet off her rotor tips—on both sides at once—in combat. Lola still didn't know whether or not to believe that one, though with Emily...

The Kamov pilots opened their distinctive flat-paned canopy windows, but remained in their seats with the rotors at a bare idle. The fuel for this mission had been marginal at best, hovering over the delta during the entire recovery operation had not been an option, even if it turned them into sitting ducks.

She slogged to the downed Hind.

The sharp screech of battery-powered cutting tools hacking through the helo's aluminum and steel framework had her cringing, both the fingernails-on-a-chalkboard aspect and the way the sound seemed to echo into the night, as if rushing directly to the nearest enemy listening post.

A lone Ukrainian with an RPG had taken down the Hind as they'd been returning from their mission. One moment flying along in tight formation, and the next the Rocket-Propelled Grenade had turned the Hind helicopter into a tumbling ball of flame. She'd seen the track on her threat detector, clear as a laser across the inside of her visor.

She had dived onto that spot and, before they could reload, Big John had punched them down with two hundred rounds from the starboard side minigun. A matter of three seconds.

Three seconds that still echoed through the valley.

"Why can't the superpowers fight at home?" Trisha O'Malley strode up beside her.

"You're supposed to stay in your heli—" she shouldn't bother. Trisha never followed such orders, figuring they applied to the rest of the universe, but not her.

"But why?"

"How the hell am I supposed to know?"

The superpowers had been duking it out on other people's terrain since World War II had taught them battles at home were too expensive. America versus China in Korea, then Vietnam. Russia versus China in the Soviet War in Afghanistan.

And now the Ukraine.

But the Americans weren't here.

They couldn't be, neither officially nor even by rumor, or it would be the start of America versus Russia, and nobody was ready for that.

Lola remembered the day the Majors had told her they were handing over command of the SOAR 5th Battalion D Company to her.

CHAPTER TWO

"*Y*ou're shitting me!"

"We've told Command that you were the best qualified, and they agreed." Mark and Emily had taken her out for a lunchtime sail on the Chesapeake Bay that cloudless September day for "the talk."

She *hated* sailing, lunchtime or otherwise. Though she was feeling a sudden antipathy for Major Mark Henderson that threatened to make that feeling trivial by comparison.

"W'all," Henderson pulled out that horrid fake Texas accent that he was dumb enough to think was cute and funny. "All y'all have ta do is—"

"Throw you overboard! Have you lost it, Henderson?"

He gave her one of *those* looks, raised eyebrows of mock surprise over his mirrored Ray Ban sunglasses.

"Sir!" she amended with a snarl.

His grin was electric, and if Emily hadn't been seated just to Mark's other side, Lola would have pushed him overboard. And then? She'd have figured out how to keep the sailboat going, leaving him to sink or swim in her wake.

"I'm the newest pilot on the team," her rage was turning into a knot in her stomach. "How the hell am I supposed to know what to do?"

Mark opened his mouth, and by the set of his smile Lola knew she really was going to dump his ass overboard this time—whether or not Emily was in the way.

Before she could lash out, Emily rested a hand on Mark's arm, "Remember that I told you there were times to shut up?" She didn't wait for his acknowledgement. "This is one of them."

And just like that, Major Mark "Viper" Henderson was quelled. Damn, but Lola could use some tactical training on how to do that with her Tim.

CHAPTER THREE

"*E*mily told me to always protect my people," Lola looked down at Trisha. So close that she was a blinding green in the night vision—so bright it was almost as if she was an angel, which she so wasn't. "I suppose that means you as well."

"I don't need protecting. I need to not be an American soldier parked in the middle of an eastern Ukraine war zone with a lot of stolen Russian military equipment."

"Don't we all. You also need to be back in your Kamov."

Trisha opened her mouth.

"Now, O'Malley."

She snarled, but she went, which was about as pleasant as Trisha's mood ever was during a mission.

They pulled Jefferson out of the wreckage and lowered him into one of the body bags.

Don't think! she ordered herself. *Time for that later.*

They zipped up the bag and moved it to the intact Mil-17.

Lola edged in closer to assess the situation.

Ten tons of helicopter made one hell of a mess when it blew up and then crashed. The tail section lay twisted ninety degrees to the side, chunks of rotor blade scattered every which way. The external fuel tanks had done their job and broken free on impact. Though they scented the air with the sharp bite of leaking kerosene, they'd landed far enough aside that it was safe to use cutting tools inside the cockpit and not worry about a stray spark blowing them to kingdom come.

The fuselage had shredded; the rear cabin exploded from the inside. The RPG had either entered through a window or penetrated the skin before going off. Sections of sheet metal were scattered far and wide.

The bulkhead between cabin and cockpit had blown forward, driving the pilot and copilot seats up against the forward consoles, pinning them in place.

They finished extracting the copilot. He too headed for a body bag.

One of the team recognized her and paused on their way back in to say, "Twenty minutes."

"Ten," was her automatic answer.

He nodded uncertainly, so she called after him, "Eight would be better."

She stepped out into the dark night. Checked that Trisha was back where she belonged. Good, at least one thing was going right.

Then she looked over at the open cargo bay of the surviving Hind. The three main honchos behind the rebel leadership of the breakaway, Russian-backed, Donetsk People's Republic were still safely under the watchful eyes of the Delta Force squad that had snatched them.

These men couldn't be safely assassinated, not by the CIA, Mossad, or anyone else she didn't want to know about. The powers-that-be feared that would make them martyrs to the cause. *But*, if they "apparently" defected, perhaps were occasionally photographed with high-ranking NATO officials, the blow to the rebel government would be significant. Or at least that's what the CIA analysts had spouted at her during the briefing.

They hadn't said a thing about what to do if some idiot rebel farmer with an RPG shot down a helicopter simply because he could—with no way to know if it was friend or foe—and killed five people and a much needed heli-asset.

She checked her watch. Thirty-four seconds had passed since she'd called eight minutes. She closed her eyes and tried to visualize everyone else flying out of here alive.

The image wasn't really coming together very well.

CHAPTER FOUR

"If you protect your people," Emily had said that day as the sun shone off her blond hair, "as your number one priority, you will be amazed at what they will do for you."

One of the sails cracked almost as sharply as a gunshot as the forty-foot boat crested a wave and dropped off the other side. She flinched in alarm, but Henderson appeared to be in smooth control.

"I'm not you," Lola had pointed out. There wasn't a person in the 5D that wouldn't take a bullet for Emily Beale. There were only a half-dozen who could even tolerate Lola as far as she could tell...and she was married to one of them. That left five.

Emily, of course, did one of those answer-without-answering things and simply waited for Lola to put it together herself.

"Okay, not an idiot. Protect my people at all costs, and they'll learn to trust me."

Emily had nodded in that sage professorial way she had.

Lola had refused to ask the next question, though it was easy to see Emily waiting for it.

CHAPTER FIVE

"If they trust me," she muttered to herself, "then who do I—"

"Five minutes."

For a moment Lola thought it was the recovery crew with good news, but they were both still deep in the bowels of the shattered helicopter working frantically and she was halfway to the other Mil to check on the prisoners.

Then she connected that it was Kara's voice on the radio relay from the drone up at thirty-thousand feet.

"Crap! I need more time."

"Tell that to the Russians. You have three choppers and a fast mover out of Donetsk."

Lola really did not need to be fighting off a Russian jet with a bunch of stolen helicopters.

"Make that four minutes. Two more whirlybirds coming up out of Sevastapol in Crimea to the south."

"That was supposed to be our escape route. Shit!"

If Kara replied, Lola didn't bother listening. She sprinted back to the Mil-17, circling around the nose. The dead pilot's feet were sticking out where the lower front windshield had been. His head and upper body were out the main windshield. He must be trapped at the thighs by the way his body had been unnaturally folded.

A quick assessment of the metal still in the way and she knew that the estimate of twenty minutes had been an optimistic one.

Lola had traded in a career with Combat Search and Rescue to take a shot at SOAR. She'd made it. And you didn't do things like CSAR without knowing when to get drastic.

"Give me the saw!" she shouted at one of the ground crew.

CHAPTER SIX

"*A*nyone who's a decent commander can get someone to trust them, that's not the issue," Emily had handed her a crab salad sandwich, and Lola had managed not to throw it back in her face.

Mark was wisely keeping his mouth shut and paying attention to the boat. But she wondered if he was purposely using his mirrored lenses to reflect the sun into her eyes so that he looked like a dazzle-eyed star lord, a terribly handsome one, but still. He was on the verge of having his sunglasses smeared with crab salad moving at high velocity when he appeared to think better of it and looked aside.

"The issue—" Emily very smoothly reached up and dropped an ice cube down the back of Mark's t-shirt.

His yelp made Lola feel much better.

"—is finding someone who can both command and think outside the box. Lola, you don't even see the box. That is your greatest strength."

CHAPTER SEVEN

*S*eventeen seconds later—when she was done with the saw—one of the ground crew had retched out his guts, but the last body bag was on the move. The results of the crash would have necessitated a closed-coffin funeral anyway, so whether he was in one part or—

Lola raced for her helicopter.

"Wind 'em up!" she called over the general frequency. She needn't have bothered, all of the helos were cranking their engines back up to speed as fast as they could once they saw her in motion.

Lola unharnessed her carbine as she slammed into her seat, reattached the data umbilical, and snapped on her harness. Just as she was about to pull off the night vision gear, she spotted the empty Mil-17 still sitting there, straight ahead. She should have dropped a couple of thermite grenades inside to make sure it was destroyed.

"Damn it!"

Tim, like the outstanding mind reader he was, must have noticed where her attention was. Two Hydra 70 rockets roared out of the right-hand pod of the DAP Hawk. Four-point-six pounds of high explosive blew into the Mil-17 at the speed of sound, along with a great deal of unspent propellant because the bird was so close. Then the spilled fuel lit off as well.

The fireball was impressive.

With her left hand she rammed the collective down to hold the DAP Hawk in place as the shock wave rolled over them. With the right, she shed her goggles and slid her visor back into place.

And on the tactical display saw that she was in hell.

She was the last one on the ground, so she yanked up for max lift, tipped her nose down as soon as she was aloft to gain speed and carved a climbing turn.

To the north, three helos, all Kamov KA-52s, and a fast mover jet.

To the south, two helos, both now identified as Mil-28 Havocs.

To the east, a pair of fast movers out of Berdyans'k.

Five of Russia's most advanced attack helicopters and three fighter jets. The way her luck was running…

Kara managed to ID the jets from her drone's feed: two Sukhoi Su-27s and an Su-30.

Would asking for a couple of nice thirty-year old MiG-21s fighter jets really be asking too much?

She had an overloaded Mil-17, three Kamov gunships, the DAP Hawk, and a drone.

They didn't stand a chance in hell.

This wasn't some stupid Hollywood tale where the good guys would eventually triumph. Or the noble few of the *Magnificent Seven*, who would survive to ride another day.

Even if this wasn't *A Nightmare on Elm Street*, Freddy Krueger was going to plant his axe in the end zone.

She and the rest of her crew were about to get their asses kicked straight into their graves.

CHAPTER EIGHT

"he thing you don't appreciate, Lola," Mark was finally out of his snotty lecture mode, and was speaking as the commander...*former* commander of the most successful SOAR company in the regiment's history. A company he had built from the ground up.

This was a man she respected almost as much as his wife, if such things were possible. Which they weren't, but he did pretty well despite that handicap.

"You have a strategic mind. The 5D can't be commanded by a tactician. Tacticians always get thrashed when it gets really ugly. Keep your people at the forefront of your priorities. That's always the way through the problem."

Then he'd cracked that megawatt smile of his. "A'sides, worst that cain happ'n is y'all end up down a six-foot hole."

She'd already finished her sandwich, but the mug of ice tea had still been full enough to serve her purpose.

CHAPTER NINE

"*Y*ou want out-of-the-box, Mark?" she said between gritted teeth and hauled up on the DAP Hawk's collective, pouring every trick she had into gaining max climb rate.

"What?" Tim asked from beside her.

She ignored him.

"You want stupid frickin' Hollywood? Fine, I'll give you stupid frickin' Hollywood!"

Tim, being a good copilot and a wise husband, kept his mouth shut.

The helicopters were a problem, but the jets were a disaster. They could move at Mach 2 and maneuver better than a BMW Mini. Even the DAP Hawk could only go one-fifth the speed of a Sukhoi.

"Okay, folks," she got on the general frequency. "It is time to do what we do so well. Flight level is one hundred feet," though she kept climbing for all she was worth. "I want you to form up in a circle."

One thing Mark Henderson had always done a great job of was

give the perfect amount of direction. A royal pain in the ass on the ground, but he was the master of the air. He never left a need for questions. But he also never said too much, thus trapping the flyers' actions into narrow boundaries.

"You are going to circle at one hundred feet above ground level as fast as you can go. Topography goes down, you go down. It goes up, you climb. If they come at you from above, Kara and I will take them." *Or do our damnedest.* "They come at you from the side, don't break formation to chase them. Your main firepower is facing forward. You shoot dead ahead as you circle. When they're out of your sights, they'll be in the sights of the helo circling right behind you. Trisha."

"Here, boss."

"You're my chaos demon," which was definitely what the woman was. "I want everyone on her tail. She circles more to the east, you shift with her. She circles to the south, you follow. Trisha keep that circle moving back and forth so they can't get a fix on you."

"Roger that."

Already Lola could see them setting up a four-helo spinning top; one Hind and three Kamovs. When they fired their weapons they'd be like a spinning buzz saw of rockets and flying lead.

Her tactical display said less than thirty seconds until bad news arrived. And the Russians had set up the pincer well, they'd be arriving from three directions at once; no chance of escape.

"Tighten it up. Keep close together. I want your gap under one rotor between helos."

Even as she said it, they tightened up. They were now moving fast and began rolling back and forth over the river valley and the steep banks. Every ten to twelve seconds they made a full spin, shifting back and forth along the river like the circle itself was alive.

Nobody but a SOAR team could fly like that.

CHAPTER TEN

One of the Sukhoi fast movers came in fast and low, thinking the four helos spinning over the landscape like a psychotic, whirling dervish were an easy target.

Trisha fed it a Russian Vympel R-73 air-to-air missile from her KA-52's spread of weaponry before it knew what was happening.

Dennis killed the first enemy Kamov attack helicopter, and Lola didn't have time to spare to see what happened to the other three attack helos that came in low, but there was a hell of a lot of fire being exchanged in her peripheral vision—enough to light up the wide river valley in brilliant stroboscopic splashes that wreaked havoc on her helmet's night-vision display.

Her real concern was up high and she kept climbing for the DAP Hawk's service ceiling and to hell with the fuel reserve as she clawed for altitude.

Lola was trying to set up the sleight-of-hand, knowing the most dangerous attack would be coming down from high above, if only she could get up into position in time. She had dealt the game for the bad guys to see, four cards face up along the river valley and spinning in their circle.

But she'd kept two cards hidden up her sleeve.

The apparently easy target was the circling helos...to anyone at their altitude. Viewed from above they were an easy and, more importantly, an obvious target.

Two of the jets and one of the massive Mil-28 Havoc gunships came in high to do just that.

The stealth DAP Hawk had been built for only one reason, to shoot better than anything else on the planet. Only SOAR had the Direct Action Penetrators and as far as Lola knew, the *Vengeance* was the only surviving stealth model—after the loss of one in bin Laden's compound, and the other that had almost killed the now-retired Majors.

Of the two jets who'd thought to attack from above, the first one had come in very high.

Kara's drone carried four Hellfire missiles and she launched them all.

Two of them tore up the Sukhoi Su-23.

That left a jet and a helo attacking from above, and Lola had a single drone with no more ammunition and her own DAP Hawk.

The formidable Su-30 jet rolled into a dive, aimed straight down at the spinning circle of helicopters from above. That was the reason Lola had Trisha shifting them side-to-side, to make them a harder target in case Lola's plan didn't work. Not that it would buy them more than a few seconds of life, but it might be all she needed.

The second jet flew right past the DAP Hawk never realizing it was there. Tim sent a phalanx of six Hydra 70s into the belly of the beast as it plunged downward.

Three connected and blew off its wing, sending the jet into a death spiral.

The Mil-28 Havoc pilot who had come in high was good, very good. The Havoc dodged hard when he saw the Su-30 get shredded.

But Lola's bird cast almost no radar image and regrettably for

him, he guessed wrong about her location. The Russian helo ate a
barrage from Tim's Vulcan 20mm cannon.

But before he died, the Russian pilot managed to launch an
Igla-1V missile straight down at the buzz saw of helos still alight
with their own battle.

Lola put herself between the missile and her people. She
couldn't risk flares or chaff, because if the missile decided to
ignore the distractors, it would hit her team circling below.

She couldn't force the nose of her helo to bear on the missile in
time. So she rolled the DAP Hawk onto its side, exposing herself
broadside to the missile.

Lying on her back in the crew-chief's seat behind Lola, with her
minigun pointed straight up and firing six thousand rounds a
minute, Connie killed the missile only a few rotors before it would
have slammed into the *Vengeance.*

The heat blast was intense. The shockwave of the exploding
missile flipped them out of the sky like they were a swatted fly.

Engines flamed out.

She and Tim fought to restart them.

Hydraulic systems failed as shrapnel sliced through crucial
lines.

Backups kicked in. Stabilized. Held.

It took her fifteen thousand feet of tumbling freefall to recover.
No time for fear. She leveled out only moments before she would
have augered in—right through the center of her team's spinning
circle.

Lola achieved a stable hover less than two rotors above Trisha's
dervish and scanned the tactical display.

The other helos still whirled at top speed, rolling back and
forth over the landscape. And, thank god—there were still four
of them.

Scattered far and wide across the river valley there were fires
and, Lola's night vision revealed, piles of overheated wreckage. No
one was moving. No parachutes had deployed. There would be no

witnesses to the bloodbath that had occurred on the bottomlands of the Kalmius River this night. No one to report who had actually been here.

"Status?" she managed—against a very dry throat—to ask those circling below her.

Two of her crewmembers were hit but alive. One of their prisoners had been killed when a 30mm round passed through the cabin of the Hind right where his head had been, but the others were alive.

Kara reported the airspace clear from her view high above.

Lola lined them up, gave a big sigh, and they turned once more for the coast, moving fast and low.

She would raise her next glass of beer in a toast westward, where the Majors had retired to fight forest fires in Oregon and raise their daughter in safety. That was in her and Tim's future, but not yet.

Lola now knew that Mark and Emily were absolutely right. The way through any problem? Protect your people, no matter what the personal cost. And against all odds it had worked; they'd survived.

"How did you think of that buzz saw thing anyway?" Trisha's radio call broke in on Lola's train of thought.

She blew out a long, slow breath and made sure she kept the adrenaline shakes out of her voice as she did her best to imitate Major Mark Henderson's notoriously bad fake Texas accent.

"W'all…"

Everyone recognized it right away and laughed, some more shakily than others.

"I jes had y'all pull them wagons inta a circle, don'cha know."

IF YOU ENJOYED THIS, YOU MIGHT ALSO ENJOY:

M. L. BUCHMAN

3-TIME BOOKLIST TOP 10 ROMANCE AUTHOR OF THE YEAR

WELCOME AT
HENDERSON'S RANCH

A HENDERSON'S RANCH ROMANCE

WELCOME AT HENDERSON'S RANCH

reelance journalist **Colleen McMurphy** *finds her Irish penname far more professional than the Kurva Baisotei her Japanese parents perpetrated upon her at birth. Her "itinerant writer" role fit her deliciously single lifestyle, until an assignment sent her to Montana's Big Sky Country to write an article about Henderson's Ranch.*

    Raymond Esterling, *summertime cowboy, gratefully forgets his life beyond the prairie, at least for those precious months beneath the Big Sky. But when he meets Colleen, he can't help but make her Welcome at Henderson's Ranch.*

INTRODUCTION

This story has an amusing origin. I was just about to release my first full novel set at Henderson's Ranch, Nathan's Big Sky. *Emily Beale and Mark Henderson had their second child at the end of the Firehawks series in 2016's* Wild Fire *and were finally coming home.*

*I'd first visited Henderson's Ranch in a pair of stories (*Christmas at Henderson's Ranch *and* Reaching Out at Henderson's Ranch*). Those were written to see if retiring Mark and Emily to his family ranch would have any fun stories in it.*

Oh my goodness! Absolutely!

So, I plunged in and wrote Nathan's Big Sky *that was about the start of Mark's and Emily's transition out of military life. Of course you'll want to catch the second novel,* Big Sky, Loyal Heart, *if you want to really follow how they're doing. (Some days better than others.)*

To help promote that first novel, I wanted to write a story of introduction to the ranch, but from completely fresh eyes. I wanted a way to capture the nature and feel of the ranch, so sending a reporter seemed like a good start.

But who was she or he? I wanted someone who would be a complete fish out of water. Someone who...

I'm an East Coast refugee who put his life in his car after college graduation and drove from Maine to Seattle. The Pacific Northwest is definitely its own thing as much as the various states of New England that I grew up in.

So, I thought to place my reporter in Seattle, sent to the "wilds" of Montana on assignment.

Again the question of who was...

And then I remembered. Years before, in 2011, I had published the first book in my Seattle Pike Place Market series, Where Dreams Are Born. *I liked the common tie to the Pacific Northwest shared with Henderson's Ranch.*

In Where Dreams Are Born, *there is a brief scene, almost a nothing moment, in which the hero and his best friend go into a bar. (The real J&M was half a block from the theater where I worked as a prop man and electrician shortly after my arrival in Seattle.) Because the hero is in a foul mood, he ignores all of the come-on-over signals from two very pretty women. One of those women, for reasons unknown, stuck in my mind. Perhaps because she was a unique and interesting character who had never reappeared throughout the five novels and three short stories of that series.*

She had finally found a purpose all these years later and Colleen McMurphy grabbed it with both hands.

CHAPTER ONE

Dateline: August 15, Henderson's Ranch,
Bloody Nowhere, Montana

olleen McMurphy could write this article in her sleep, with her keyboard tied behind her back, and...

"The wife and I had such a splendid time there. You simply must go and write us an article about it." For some reason Larry always went old-school English whenever he got excited—which coming from her Puerto Rican boss who lived in Seattle seemed to be almost normal for Colleen's life.

He, of course, was too busy being Mr. Hotshot Editor to write it himself. That and he couldn't write his way out of a martini glass. He was one of the best editors she'd ever worked for—and as a freelancer that had included a suckload of them—but his twelve-year-old daughter could write new material better than he could. Hillary was named for Sir Edmund of Mt. Everest fame and just might follow her namesake at the rate she was being amazing. She was a precocious little twerp who was so delightful that she made

Colleen feel grossly inadequate half the time and totally charmed the other three-quarters.

So, off to Montana it was. Magazine feature article—she was on it.

The most recent in a cascade of ever-shrinking planes banged onto the runway in Great Falls, Montana clicking all Colleen's vertebrae together with a whip-like snap that surprisingly failed to paralyze her. A Japan Airlines 747 had lofted her from the family home in Tokyo to LAX. The smallest 737 ever made hopped her up to Salt Lake, and a wing-flapping 18-seater express fluttered as hopelessly as a just-fledged swallow to Great Falls. If there'd been another plane that was any smaller, they were going to have to put her in a bento box.

But finally she was here in…major sigh…Nowhere, Montana.

She'd used this job as an excuse to cut the two-week trip home in half. Two weeks! *With her family?* What *had* she been thinking? She was going to have a serious talk with her sense of filial duty before it dragged her from Seattle back to Japan again.

Outside the miniature plane's windows the airport stretched away pancake-flat and dusty. Four whole jetways, the place was *smaller* than a bento box. But their plane didn't pull up to any of them—because it was too short to reach. Instead, it stopped near the terminal and the copilot dropped the door open, filling the cabin with the familiar bite of spent engine fumes and slowing propeller roar. She'd spent the whole final flight glaring out at the spinning blades directly outside her window, waiting for one to break off, punch through the window, and slice her in two like one of Larry's martini olives.

"Enough!" she told herself so loudly that it made the fat-boy businessman—who'd made the near-fatal mistake of trying to chat her up across the tiny aisle—jump in alarm. Twenty hours and nine minutes in flight didn't usually make her this grouchy. Her parents did though.

"Why did you change your name?" *Because everyone in America would laugh their faces off calling her* Kurva—*for the Hokkaido mulberry tree you conceived me under, much too much information by the way. It especially doesn't translate so well for a girl who is Japanese flat. Besides there isn't an American alive who can say* Baisotei *properly.* Kurva Baisotei was not a moneymaking byline.

Then, not "When are you going to get married?" but rather "Why do you not give us grandchildren like your sister?" *My sister has three. How insatiable are you as grandparents?*

"Why do you not return home?" *Because you live here.*

"Ma'am?" Fat-boy was waiting for her to get out of her seat first. Maybe because he needed the full width of the tiny plane, or maybe he was just being nice. She was about to step back on American soil—even if it was Montana—so she gave him the benefit of the doubt and offered a "Thanks" with a smile that hopefully he didn't read as encouraging.

The air outside the airport smelled strange. It definitely wasn't Seattle, which had an evergreen scent that wrapped itself around you like a warm, though often damp, welcome home. Her best girl Ruth Ann always met her when she landed from trips to Japan to drag her to their favorite dive, the J&M in Pioneer Square, and make sure that she got safely drunk within an hour of landing. It was doubly strange to arrive somewhere else without Ruth Ann's patiently sympathetic ear.

Montana was dry and, despite the warm afternoon, somehow crisp. In Seattle there were a gazillion things sharing the air with her: Douglas firs, seagulls, dogs playing in the park, ferry boats— the list went on and on. Here it tasted more rarified. More…special.

Also high on the *special* list was the guy leaning comfortably on a helicopter with "Henderson's Ranch" emblazoned down the side like it had been branded there with a flaming iron. He already had one beaming couple beside him with Los Angeles cowboy written all over their Gucci. He towered above them: six-two of dark tan, right-out-of-a-romance-novel square jaw, and mirrored shades for a touch of mystery. His t-shirt was tight and his jeans weren't bad either. And—crap!—ring on his finger. Fantasy cowboys weren't supposed to have rings on their fingers, but she wasn't going to complain about this piece of the Montana scenery just because of the "Back Off" sign.

Another couple joined them. First-timers by their lost look.

"Hi!" He even had a nice deep voice to go with that big frame. "I'm Mark Henderson. Climb on aboard," and he was helping the two couples into the back seats.

Handsome guy who flies a helicopter. Sweet! Maybe Montana wasn't going to be so bad. Ruth Ann was gonna be wicked jealous. She snapped a photo of him just for that purpose.

"Looks like you're up front with me, beautiful," he aimed a lethal smile directly at her.

She returned the smile, feeling pleased. Then lost it when she realized the implications.

Two happy couples in the back.

Handsome married dude in the front.

And that's when the background research she'd done on their website finally made a horrible kind of sense. Weddings this. Couples that. Family horseback rides the other. Larry should have sent Colleen's perfect sister's family, not her.

She was a single Japanese chick, with an Irish name she'd taken from the old TV show *China Beach*. (She'd always liked the main character—strong woman back when that wasn't a very popular thing to be.)

Be strong now!

She was going to a couples' paradise. This was going to be worse than the parental purgatory.

She'd be pleasant. Polite.

And as soon as she got home, Larry was a dead man.

CHAPTER TWO

Dateline: Day Two, Henderson's Ranch,
   Montana Front Range

Montana greets visitors who fly in with the dullest landscape imaginable.
Rulers are tested here for an accurate straight edge by laying them on the
ground.

   But fifty miles to the west, the Rocky Mountains soar aloft, forcing
the eye to constantly scan upward to the bluest sky imaginable.
Henderson's Ranch lies nestled in the softly rolling country at the base of
these majestic peaks.

A night's sleep and Colleen felt much more human this
morning, even if she couldn't make sense of what lay
outside her cabin window. To the south and east, the land
stretched so far away that she felt as if she was perched atop an
infinite cliff and at the least misstep might tumble down forever. A
person could get vertigo here just sitting still.

To the west, the mountains punched aloft in bold, jagged

strokes with little of the softness that Washington's forests provided to Seattle's peaks.

There was a wildness that confronted her every time she looked at these mountains. Her inner city Tokyo childhood, her rebellious escape to the community of fifty-thousand students at the University of Washington, Seattle's million people—none of it prepared her for this stark emptiness.

Here along the Front Range, aside from a few dozen guests and another dozen ranch hands, there might not be a soul for twenty miles. It felt like a thousand.

Down the slope, a tall woman stepped out of the back door of the main lodge and rang a giant steel triangle just like in an Old West movie: *clangety-clangety-clangety-clang.*

Families and couples streamed out of the other cabins and headed downhill toward the massive two-story log cabin structure that looked like one of those Depression-era lodges. Huge, powerful, unmoving.

A quick survey showed that she was the only singleton—if she didn't count kids, and even they seemed to come in packs. Almost everyone was dressed in K-Mart Western, or some designer version that looked no more likely.

There were breakfast fixings in her cabin, and she was tempted to retreat there, but she was here to write a travelogue article. For that she had to experience the experience.

She was last down the trail to the big house. The guests were all guided along the wrap-around porch to the front entrance into the big dining room she'd seen on last night's welcome tour. Thirty people could eat communal style at the long table.

However, a few others were coming around to the kitchen door. They were dressed far more casually, and far more authentically. Cowboy boots, dusty jeans, a variety of hats—some battered cowboy, some baseball-cap redneck. The women were dressed much the same.

Not really paying attention to what her feet were doing, she fell in with the ranch hands and found herself in a massive and beautiful kitchen. The hands were making use of one of the sinks before gathering at a smaller version of the big communal table out front.

"Mornin', Colleen. Not up for our 'Happy Couples' breakfast?" Mark the pilot greeted her with an understanding smile, reading her too easily.

Time to gear up the pleasant-reporter face.

He wasn't any less handsome this morning, but a stunning blonde kissed him on the cheek as she topped up his coffee, confirming that the ring wasn't just for show.

"Not so much, if that's okay."

"Take a seat. Dad's this one, Mom's the other end, when she bothers to sit down. The rest are up for grabs."

She took a seat almost, but not quite, at the middle of the table on the far side. It gave her the best view of what was going on and would let her hear most of the conversations without being the center of them. No one so much as blinked an eye as she joined them. A pretty redhead gave her a South California, "Hey!" Her husband was more the quiet-nod type.

Another long blonde gave her a very authentic sounding, "Howdy!" just as the male cook (with a Brooklyn-tinged "Hello and welcome") came and set a plate in front of the blonde, then kissed her on top of the head.

Shit! She was in Couplandia here as well. Finally some more guys came in until there was a fair balance of single men. More what she'd expected.

Her goal of keeping track of the conversations went out the window in the first ten seconds. They were talking about the day to come and what they knew about the guests, but doing it in a handful of simultaneous discussions: "Most of this lot we won't get out of the corral for a couple days." "Did you see that absolute babe from England? Never saw a woman sit a horse so *purty.* She'll ride far and hard." His companion—alike enough to be his twin—gave him a knowing smile that was all about the woman and not so much about how she sat.

Colleen stayed focused on her meal and her article. The food was incredibly good despite how basic a hash brown-and-ham scramble with a biscuit buried in gravy sounded. Article ideas were perking up as she enjoyed the camaraderie around the table. These people liked each other. Liked working together. And whatever else they were saying about the guests, none of it was bitter or caustic. She'd expected some derision of "city cowboys" but nothing even remotely like that came up in any of the several threads she was able to follow.

She wondered what they'd be saying about *her* behind her back.

"I like the way you listen."

It took her a moment to rewind the comment because it was only the last word that actually caught her attention. She finally traced it (nearly accentless) to the man across the table. He wasn't a big man—Colleen had an absolute weak spot for big men, who thankfully often had a weak spot for petite Japanese women—but he had a nice smile so she wouldn't hold his normalness of height and build against him.

"Uh-huh," her cordial-meter was still running below normal, but then no one was supposed to see through her pleasant-reporter face. She really needed another mug of tea.

"Heard you just arrived from Japan. Family there?"

"Uh-huh," her cordial-meter bottomed out. That was a reminder that she didn't need.

"Apparently the wrong question."

"Uh-huh," she dialed up her emphatic-sarcasm mode to full.

"Do you ride?"

Her first temptation was to go to "uh-uh" but she already was being subverbal far beyond her norm. Besides, it was the easiest response. Like writing, the easiest word (the first word she thought of) was rarely the most precise or evocative one. Good writing required avoiding the obvious while still telling the story—

whether it encapsulated what it was like to work on the Boeing manufacturing line like her last article or the current purgatory of Couplandia.

Her interlocuter (yes! her vocabulary was finally coming back online) looked like a nice enough guy. Cowboy lean with a pleasant smile. She supposed that she'd have to ride a horse to get the full "Henderson's Ranch" experience and a private lesson sounded far better than shaming herself in public.

"Not yet," she added a smile which she knew was one of her strengths. The guy returned with a powerful one of his own.

It was only then that she noticed Mr. Handsome-with-a-ring Henderson rolling his eyes at her—at least that's what she assumed he was doing behind his ever-present shades.

Okay, maybe she could have been a little more subtle. But he said he liked the way she listened—one of the skills she was most proud of. That bit of insightfulness was going to earn him a lot of leeway.

CHAPTER THREE

Dateline, Day Four—

*C*olleen turned on a light against the fading day and flipped back through her notes again. Where had Day Three gone? Where had Day Two gone for that matter?

She finally found Day Two.

Mac Henderson, technically Mark Henderson, Sr. and almost as handsome as his son, had been thrilled to have her on the ranch. Apparently she was their first journalist, so their resort had a lot riding on making her happy—though he acted as if he was simply glad *she* was here, not several million readers AAA magazine would be sending this out to. Which was sweet of him to pretend.

On Day Two, he'd toured her about: cabins, yurts, cooking classes, weaving classes, horseback riding, even a military dog trainer named Stan—a big, gruff man with a hook prosthetic on one arm who only spoke to his dogs.

As the day had progressed, Mac had grown more and more excited about showing her around his ranch until he was as wound up as one of Stan's puppies. A former Navy SEAL in his sixties who almost wriggled with delight. She'd always thought SEALs were supposed to be broody and stoic, but Mac was a thoroughly pleasant guy who clearly loved this land with a passion.

What she'd found truly unbelievable was the amount of work it took to run the place, and Mac made sure that she had a chance to meet and chat with every person of the staff. The redhead who ran the barn was so voluble that Colleen couldn't have gotten down one word in ten no matter how fast she took notes—and she was fast. Her husband, the ranch manager, was laconic to the point where Colleen wondered if people catnapped between his sentences.

It took her a while to catch on that he was teasing her with it.

Day Two afternoon: Mark's wife Emily took her on a solo helicopter flight over the ranch that was stunning in both its expansiveness and its variety. The softly rolling landscape around the buildings gave way to rugged prairie, patches of pine forest, and even waterfalls along a small river that ran down out of the hills. A group of horses out at a remote fishing cabin revealed that at least some riders had made it past the corral.

The cook wasn't a cook at all—he was a dropout New York chef...one she'd actually heard of.

She was getting why Larry and his family had gone nuts over the place, but that didn't explain what had happened to her notes. She was sure she taken more of them.

Day Three's notes were definitely not here. Then she remembered...

Raymond Esterling, her Day One breakfast companion.

Who liked the way she listened.

That's what had happened to Day Three.

...and most of Day Four.

Colleen sat down abruptly on the bed in her small cabin. She ran a hand over the bedspread: Cheyenne weaving done by the owner's wife. She was one of those tall, majestic Native American women that never actually existed in real life. The blanket's geometric reds and golds were as warm as the campfire they'd all sat around while burgers were cooked over open flame on a heavy iron grill earlier this evening—some of the best beef she'd ever tasted.

Whatever in the wide, wide world of Montana was happening to her? A good girl's education in being Japanese hadn't prepared her for this place. Nor a journalist's.

Her ears rang in the silence. No cars at night, no planes. Not even the ocean when she vacationed down at Cannon Beach, Oregon and could pretend the waves were actually the low rumble of I-5 that was never silent in Seattle—easily audible from her apartment on the other side of Lake Union.

A soft whinny drew her back to her feet and out onto the cabin's porch.

Raymond sat astride a big roan—as she'd learned to call his cream-colored mount with dark legs and mane. The sunset lit his gentle face.

He'd "happened" to more than her notes. He was happening to her and none of her training, neither as Kurva Baisotei nor Colleen McMurphy, was ready for it. Not even the city pickup bars had prepared her for him—not even the good ones (if there was such a thing).

Worse, Raymond hadn't resisted her journalistic inquisitiveness.

(*Anta, sensakuzuki,* her sister would curse under her breath—*you are always so nosy,* with the *anta* insult thrown in.)

Raymond hadn't resisted it because she hadn't unleashed it on him. Which was totally unlike her. But he had impressive listening skills as well.

To his credit, after his horseback riding lessons yesterday and today—in between the lessons he was giving to others—she had a good feel for riding. This afternoon she'd joined a trail ride for beginners and even cantered once; which had been both exhilarating *and* nearly scared her back into the womb.

But she knew so little about him.

He didn't seem to mind talking—he wasn't a reclusive *hikikomori* or even a male jerk "not in touch with his feelings." But it was as if his life beyond the boundaries of the ranch stretched as empty as the scrub prairie.

She knew that was total crap—he was a summer instructor and trail guide, no more. But every time she got ready to pin him down on what he did the other eight months of the year he'd smile at her, adjust her "seat" position, point out an eagle soaring on a thermal, anything to distract her...without appearing to distract her.

Now he sat astride his horse not five feet from the porch of her cabin, looking the quintessential "cowboy in the sunset."

"You can't be some mystic cowboy forever, you know?"

"Evening to you too, Kurva." Somehow he'd gotten that out of her. He also managed to say it like it wasn't a comment on her figure, or rather lack of one, so she let him use it. Instead, he turned her name into a tease, a friendly nickname that didn't chide her for choosing another.

"Evening to you, Raymond. What are you doing up on a horse at this hour?"

"Hoping to take you on an evening ride and see the stars. It's a warm night, but you might want a jacket." Never quite a question, yet not a statement either. As if coaxing her along like a reluctant horse. She didn't appreciate the metaphor but couldn't find the urge to fight it either.

Her own mount, a patient bay named Gumdrop of all silliness, trailed behind him on a lead. Colleen was really getting the vernacular down. She wanted to do a little horse-words rap there on the porch but resisted it. Instead she grabbed a polar fleece off a hook inside the door and climbed up into the saddle.

Seattle girl in the saddle girl
Astride some rawhide like a way cool—bri—No!

Her mind nearly strangled itself when her inner rap artist cast up "bride" for worst-rhyming-word-choice-of-the-century award. Definitely not!

The vertiginous Big Sky of Montana expanded even more as they rode up past the cabins and over the rise at a lazy, side-by-side plod. Gumdrop's head bobbed easily, no longer nearly jerking Colleen out of the saddle each time the horse leaned down to crop some grass as they went along.

In the sky, golds found reds.

Reds hinted at impending purples.

Soon Raymond reined to a halt and pointed to the west, "Venus."

Colleen didn't know where to look.

Raymond pulled his mount close beside her so that she could easily follow the line of his pointing arm.

It took her a moment to pick the sparkling point of light out of the red-gold sky, then she had it. It hung above the silhouetted-black mountains like a diamond.

"Planet light, planet bright, First planet I see tonight, I wish I may, I wish I might, Have this wish I wish tonight." Ray's voice was as soft as the call of a passing bird. "Meadowlark," he filled in for her.

"This seems to be the sort of place that wishes come true." It really was. The pale dry grass lay in golden waves over the rolling prairie. Far below—she didn't realize they'd wandered so far as she had watched the shifting light—lay the cozy cluster of ranch buildings: lodge, barns, and cabins. The next farm over, a big-spread cattle ranch, was just barely visible and looked homey as well.

"What do you wish for, Colleen Baisotei?" He said it right. It was as if he couldn't quite leave her names alone but had to play with them like cat toys. It seemed to make him happy to do so and, curiously, it didn't bother her. Words were her toys as well. She liked that in a man.

"What do I wish for? Not this."

"You don't?"

"Not really. The beauty here is like a drug. Perhaps in small doses, but I'd miss the city too much as well."

"I know," his voice was as soft as the night. "I come here for the summers, retreat to my city in the fall. But I don't think about that now. Now, I am simply here."

"A cowboy."

"They let me play at being one."

Colleen liked that about him, too. He knew what he himself was, even if she didn't know what he was in the real world. And now she understood why. Whereas she— "Huh!"

"What?"

"I'm...not sure what to wish for." Peace with her parents? There was a greater chance of a forest fire in Antarctica. Finding... Colleen didn't know what to plug in there. That bothered her. She really should know.

Sure, she was doing fine. She had good friends in Seattle, whether for a quiet dinner or to go out dancing: square dancing at the Tractor, Britpop Thursday at the Lo-Fi, or bottom-trawling at the J&M. Her job sent her traipsing up and down the Northwest until she knew it like the back of her hand, but kept discovering new things there anyway. Men were pleasant and easy. She knew there was a type of man who looked at her and melted, and she didn't mind that either. Slim-Japanese-with-dark-hair-well-down-her-back slayed them...another advantage to America over Japan where she was just another potential housewife. Dressing in a tight tube-top at least doubled her yield.

But what to spend an actual wish on...

She turned to him, "What's yours?"

"I would think that was obvious from the moment you walked into the ranch kitchen, Ms. McMurphy."

And when he said it, it was.

She turned from the diamond light of Venus to inspect

Raymond Esterling, itinerant horse guide and otherwise unknown. He was what she wasn't. Melting-pot American versus pure-blood Japanese. Sandy blond and fair skinned. Easygoing to her own hyper tendencies—though those seemed to go quiet around him.

"I didn't come here looking to be a summer cowboy fling." Yet he'd grown on her enough over these last days to make it a reasonable consideration.

"Can't say that I've ever been much for flings myself. Every time I try them, I get burned."

"But you're willing to try me? I burn men baaaad! Just warning you."

"I expect, despite my mortal fear of fire, that you are well worth the risk." He also knew how to slay her with a simple piece of flattery. It might be a line, but it was a good one.

"Let's find out."

CHAPTER FOUR

Dateline...uh...unknown.

Lying naked in the bed, the cool Montana morning washes in the open window and over my body raising goosebumps. The crickets called through the night, singing a chorus of heat that had indeed scorched between the two highly-compatible humans. Now the siren call of the rising sun drags me back to the present.

For five more fun-filled days, and five enchantingly rigorous nights, Henderson's Ranch had delivered. She'd fished, learned to cook her trout on a heated rock by a wilderness campfire (though she'd passed on learning how to gut and clean the fish), gone horseback on a wildlife photo safari (she'd bagged a fox, two elk, and a rare bobcat with her camera), and even discovered some skill with a bow and arrow.

She'd also unearthed a bottomless need for how Raymond Esterling could make her feel.

Feel?

Dear gods, it was like she hadn't known the meaning of the word. Her body had responded to his in ways she'd never imagined. His hand on her calf as he checked her stirrup was enough to wrap her entire body in a warm heat. Even now it burned through her memory despite his having left her bed to start his morning chores.

And what she felt inside was equally foreign.

Demanding that her journalistic objectiveness chronicle what was happening to her resulted in—no answers.

Instead, like the splash of cold water that sent her scrabbling for the covers, she was reminded that her idyll was done. This was Last Day, Departure Day.

By this evening she'd be at SeaTac airport, waiting for her best friend Ruth Ann to pick her up and get her good and drunk. Except she didn't feel the need to. Ray had somehow purged her soul of her parents far more than the most exotic cocktail. Going trawling for a bedmate at the J&M, after she'd had a taste of what Ray could make her feel, would be beyond pointless.

Yes, he could make her feel. And by his desperate groans and happy sighs, she knew she did the same in return.

They'd started their final night together with another sunset ride. This time he'd brought a blanket and they'd made love together under the stars. Once before, she'd done it outdoors, fast and desperate on Golden Gardens beach at a college bonfire party, the fear of imminent discovery adding to the hurry.

Last night had been a slow, languid adventure under a brilliant canopy of starlight. When the half moon rose, it had turned the prairie pale yellow and was more than bright enough for them to appreciate each other visually as well as physically. She'd come to like the way Ray looked, a great deal. He was lean but strong. And only six inches taller meant that instead of her face being crushed to a man's chest when they embraced, she could lay her head on his shoulder and nestle against his neck.

She was a journalist because she loved learning new things.

The things Ray had taught her she could place in no article, but they'd been written indelibly upon her skin and emotions.

But now it was time to go. Showered and packed, she was surprised at the hugs she received after breakfast. The women in particular made a point of saying how glad they were to have met her. It felt genuine.

There! That was the hook on her travelogue about this place.

It didn't feel genuine—it *really was* genuine.

She might have become closer to the staff than the tourists, but as they all gathered together for departure, there were many warm farewells.

Colleen stood in the midday-flight time group, waiting for the helicopter to return from the morning-flight group. New arrivals were inbound for their own adventures, welcomed, and were escorted to their freshly cleaned cabins.

Then Ray arrived and cut her out of the herd. She went willingly until they were alone with the horses in the barn.

"Kurva Colleen. May I see you again?"

"Gods, please, yes. But I'll be in Seattle."

"So you said. I'll come looking for you there when I'm done being a cowboy."

"You'd better."

His kiss made that promise as the distant thrum of the helicopter approached to whisk her away.

CHAPTER FIVE

Dateline, done.

*L*arry loved the piece. For the first time, it passed beneath his evil editor's pen without a single tick-mark or correction. Her next assignment started tomorrow, learning about building boat sails. There were several premier sail lofts in Seattle and she had a very nice contract to write a multi-page marketing-promo article about them for one of the glossy magazines.

But she didn't care about any of that.

She cared about the simple text message, "J&M, 8pm. R"

It would be good to just sit with Ruth Ann, drink a Mai Tai or a Mango Daiquiri, and catch up. She'd been back two weeks. Back? As if time was now measured in distance from Montana.

Out of habit and the lingering Seattle summer heat—rather than thinking about attracting men—she wore a clingy tube-top, short shorts, and sandals, and brushed her hair out long. For once it wasn't about torturing men or even finding one.

She'd already found one, and was discovering that she wasn't getting over him as she'd expected. Her sometimes-cowboy was persevering in her thoughts—like a good story that was hard to forget. Somehow, she couldn't quite remember how, she'd let him slip away without any way to contact him. He was always good at using distraction. Perhaps he hadn't wanted to keep in touch.

Colleen had considered calling the ranch, but he would be gone soon. The short Montana summer was ending. With the start of school, their number of guests would plummet and the extra hands wouldn't be needed. Yet some part of her waited.

She went with the familiar J&M daiquiri for coolness. She also managed to snag her and Ruth Ann's favorite table. It was small, but close by the door. It offered a good view of the male wildlife down the long bar as well as at the small streetside tables outside the windows. A hundred-and-thirty years of drinking had happened here (with a one-year hiccup in '09 that had been devastating until a new owner was found), and she could feel the history every time. It was deep and solid.

The band in the back was just getting rolling. Country-rock tonight. In another hour, conversation would approach the impossible and everyone would move onto the dance floor. For now, shouting was only necessary in the deeper sections of the bar, and the dancers still had room to do some moves.

The parade of men and women through the door barely registered on her. She could see that she was registering on them, but that was the point. Dates were having to poke their men in the ribs, some of them sharply, to keep them moving.

Then one man arrived by himself—which wasn't unusual.

Dressed in typical Seattle: sneakers, jeans, and a UW Huskies t-shirt.

But his gait was odd.

As if he'd just…gotten off a horse.

Ray smiled down at her as he strode up to the table like he was still roaming the prairie.

"You're not 'R.'" But he was. Not Ruth Ann. Raymond. She hadn't even looked at the sender on the message.

"You told me you liked this place."

"I do," then she caught herself and patted the seat beside her. "Now I really do."

"And I thought you were dressed that way for me." He sat beside her.

"No, just to torment passing strangers."

"I'm hurt. But it definitely works. You're absolutely killing me."

"What are you...?" His t-shirt registered. "Huskies? You're an alum?"

"Not exactly."

She knew there were adult students, but he didn't act like a student.

He cleared his throat as if preparing to lecture.

He worked there!

"UW Professor Raymond Esterling, specializing in advanced robotics, particularly communication protocols with natural language. That means how robots and people speak to each other."

"You like the way I listen," she recalled the very first thing he'd ever said to her. Of course he would appreciate that.

His nod was easy as he ordered a beer from a passing waitress, as if it was as natural as could be. Of course, she liked the way he communicated too. Except when he evaded her.

"You knew all that time that I was from Seattle and you didn't say anything?" A part of her that had been strangely quiescent over the last two weeks stirred to life. Like one of the Front Range's hibernating bears starting to wake up. She didn't know yet if she was of the angry variety.

"That's a separate part of my life. My days in this life are pretty intense. All indoors, a lot of computer code, with some mechanics and theory stirred in. For three months every year I get to ride horses and look at the horizon."

"And snare willing ranch guests."

"Tally of one so far. But based on that narrow statistical sample, I'd say it was absolutely worth the risk. Don't you agree?"

The last, gentle words were so soft they barely cleared the noise level that the J&M was pumping itself up to.

Raymond Esterling. Robots and horses. He took her hand and the warmth ran up her arm and wrapped around her. Not just her limbs, but that strange place inside where no man had ever belonged.

Belonged.

Something she'd never done. Not in Japan, not really in Seattle. Always a barfly never a...she let the next word come after only briefly shying away. Never a bride.

Yet whether enjoying each other's bodies, riding through the sunset together, or just sitting here knowing they'd be on the dance floor soon, she now knew what the belonging meant.

For outsiders, Henderson's Ranch was about welcome—maybe having a place for a week, or a summer. But with Ray, he made it easy to imagine so much more. There was an absolute rightness that was undeniable.

She leaned in to kiss him. Just before their lips met, she whispered.

"Now I know what to wish for. And yes, absolutely worth it."

IF YOU ENJOYED THIS, YOU MIGHT ALSO ENJOY:

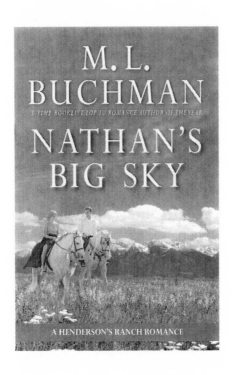

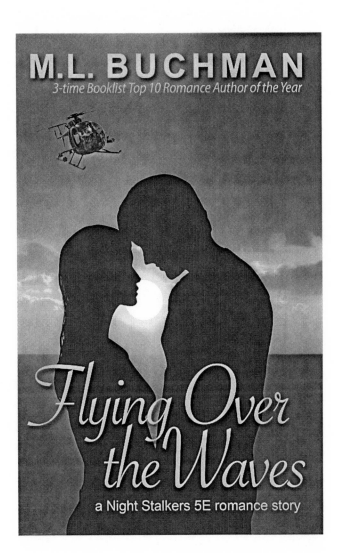

M.L. BUCHMAN

3-time Booklist Top 10 Romance Author of the Year

Flying Over the Waves

a Night Stalkers 5E romance story

FLYING OVER THE WAVES

*N*o one gets shot down during a training mission.
   Except **Chief Warrant Officers Debbie Rosenthal** and **Silvan Exeter.** *Their Little Bird helicopter plummets toward the North Sea during a Force 9 severe gale.*

   With no hope in sight, they must struggle together to survive Flying Over the Waves.

INTRODUCTION

This was the first of 2017's Night Stalker stories.

This story was a combination of a challenge I wanted to try, mixed with a coastal storm.

The Oregon Coast is not a timid one, nor is the mighty Pacific Ocean actually pacific—ever. Storms blast ashore so regularly that we don't even really pay attention until it reaches sixty miles an hour. Hurricane force winds are not strangers to the coast either.

After these storms, we often go to watch the big waves come in. (Unlike suicidal tourists, we locals know to do this from the headlands rather than the beaches.) Thirty-foot breakers appear and slam into the sand in an endless succession. They come in with such heavy impact, that the sound strikes your chest like a physical blow. It is a powerful, primal, and rather humbling experience.

Driftwood logs forty-feet long and five feet in diameter are tossed across parking lots and rammed into buildings. The power of the sea along the beaches is nothing compared to what it is farther from shore.

I wanted to capture some of this wildness on the page.

The challenge I wanted to try was isolating my Night Stalkers out of their element. Military helicopter pilots travel in teams with an immense amount of support. They fly in pairs at a minimum in some of the most sophisticated and complex vehicles ever designed, short of a spaceship.

That was when I had the idea to strip away their technology, taking them from the vagaries of the air to plunge them into the violence of the sea.

CHAPTER ONE

"Since when do people get shot down on training missions?"

"At the moment I'm more worried about the North Sea," her copilot shot back.

Night Stalkers Chief Warrant 3 Debbie Rosenthal decided that he had a point.

Tonight the North Sea was being thrashed by a mid-December Force 9 severe gale—that felt like a Force 12 hurricane the way it shook her helicopter. It slammed them around in all three dimensions with the ease of a beach ball. Command had decided that gale force winds in the fifty mile-an-hour range was a good excuse for training.

Debbie hadn't argued.

First off, Command wouldn't care what a mere CW3 said any more than her father had. He'd disowned her the day she'd joined the Army rather than marrying a good Jewish boy.

Second, such an on-the-edge flight fit her own idea of a good skills freshener, well, other than being slammed about the sky. The Night Stalkers of the US Army's 160th SOAR 5th Battalion E

Company were tasked with flying their helicopters through every form of ugly and it was great practice—when they weren't shooting at you.

When they weren't *supposed* to be shooting at you.

From a thousand feet up, flying over the North Sea in the middle of the night had merely been a good ride. From a thousand feet up over freezing waves two-to-three stories tall, breaking in huge sheets of slashing spray—with no engine—it was far less amusing.

The external cameras were good enough to paint the picture across the inside of her visor in horrifying detail despite the darkness.

"Are you sure we were shot?" It was a dumb question, but it came out anyway.

Chief Warrant 2 Silvan Exeter just pointed at the hole in their windshield that was currently shooting a stream of cold rainwater between them. The radio and engine had vanished at the same moment as their engine. The miracle was that neither of them had been hurt.

The other Little Bird in their flight hadn't been so lucky, but she couldn't think about Junker and Tank at the moment.

Their two-helicopter flight had passed above a fishing trawler seventy miles off Aberdeen, Scotland. At the time (all of sixty seconds ago) it had seemed like a good idea to do hover practice over a clear reference point. Could they hold position, in formation, directly above the trawler no matter what the wind and waves were doing? The trawler probably wouldn't even know they were there, testing hover skills in the night.

Thirty seconds ago, the trawler had unveiled a Soviet ZU-23mm anti-aircraft gun.

Not fishing trawler.

Russian *spy* trawler.

Her aircraft was damaged first. Then the ship had swung fire against the other Little Bird and held it there. The second aircraft had plummeted out of the sky, no attempt at control or recovery. They were swinging back to finish her off as well, but it took too long. By then Silvan had fired a trio of Hydra 70 rockets into the trawler.

Debbie felt the billow of the massive explosion despite the gale-level wind. Everything above sea level was erased—gun, gunner, the entire trawler. In her infrared night vision—which was still working by some miracle—she could see the remains of the hull were awash and would sink soon. Even if it was an act of idiocy, it was also an act of war. There was going to be hell to pay if anyone lived to report it.

There were only two of them left out here in the middle of the North Sea and the odds didn't look good.

Per protocol, Silvan kept calling out the engine restart procedures while going through the emergency checklist...not that anything was likely to work.

Any further disbelief that her subconscious was tossing out upon the waters would have to wait until later. After she didn't die.

Debbie could feel the heavy weight of the wind shuddering through the controls.

No hydraulic assist in a MH-6M Little Bird.

No crew chiefs in back performing some miracle, like fabricating a new engine out of old bullet casings in the sixty seconds she'd be able to keep them aloft. That was the land of Black Hawks and Chinooks. In the Little Bird, it was just the two of them.

Autorotation was dicey at the best of times. Autorotation with winds gusting past fifty and nowhere to land just wasn't going to work.

"Can you reach the raft?"

Silvan hesitated in mid-"Ignition-test on, negative indicators, Ignition-start press and hold, negative start." She'd already lost half her altitude and was descending through five hundred feet. They were at max glide time, minus a factor of extra speed so that the storm didn't flip them too easily. Better faster with less flight time than upside down with only seconds to go. Head-on into the wind to get maximum lift…it didn't matter where they went, so she wasn't worried about distance.

No one ever survived bailing out of a crashing helicopter, so the requirement to carry the small raft on long crossings was silly, but it was on the books. Ditching was something you only survived if balanced perfectly with no rotors catching the water—and in dead calm weather. And then only if you were lucky. Actually, there were survivors during storm ditchings, but they were very rare—more statistical anomaly than fact. A Little Bird wasn't some old-style US Coast Guard HH-3F Pelican designed to float. They were going to sink so fast that hitting the water was barely going to slow them down.

"I can only reach the raft if I go outside," he sounded grim. A Little Bird had a cockpit small enough that Debbie had never understood how two men could fly one. At least her shoulders were narrow enough that they only bumped together half the time they were aloft. The back two seats were even smaller. "Outside" meant stepping out onto the skid, shuffling backward in a roaring wind, and yanking the rear door open—all while she was busy pitching and yawing like a drunkard on a bender.

"Three hundred feet," was the only answer she had for Silvan.

CHAPTER TWO

"Silvan? Like Tolkien's elves? You're tall enough to be one." Debbie leaned back against the nose of her Little Bird, warm in the April afternoon. She looked up at the new guy—six-one, maybe six-two, a long way up. The sun caught his blond hair and made it shine. He was also slender like an elf, except for a very nice set of soldier's shoulders.

"Mom was a fan. And with our last name being Exeter... Exeter College was Tolkien's alma mater. I never stood a chance," new guy shrugged. *Very* nice shoulders. Good smile too. Debbie liked good smiles.

"I didn't know there were elves in the Army. Something's wrong with your ears though."

He fell for it and actually reached up to touch them, before he sighed. "Not pointed. Right. Maybe I'm a deformed elf."

"Or a reformed one." Not one bit deformed from where she was watching. Hide his ears and he'd make a very fair Legolas in the Lord of the Rings movies. His hair was still Army-short, but maybe she could corrupt him. Her own was down to her shoulders. Very un-Army, but very Night Stalkers.

The Night Stalkers' customers—Delta Force especially—let their hair go long to help them blend in when infiltrating undercover. And there wasn't a Delta operator who didn't also glory in the chance to say "up yours" to the military hierarchy that they'd voluntarily sworn to serve to the death. A lot of the fliers in the 160th SOAR took their close association with Delta and SEAL Team 6 as an excuse to let their own hair get long.

"Let it grow out. That'll hide the defect." Because otherwise he was damn near perfect. Not gorgeous, though not homely by a long stretch, but rather cute, strong, and funny. "Besides, you'd look good in long hair."

He squatted down, flexing arms and clenching fists, and grimaced horribly.

"What's wrong?"

He looked like he was holding himself back from pummeling something.

Or maybe trying to give birth right there on the runway in front of her helicopter.

"Is it working?" His voice little more than a grunt.

"Is what working?"

He stopped whatever it was he was doing and patted the top of his head. "Crap!"

"What?"

"A beautiful woman tells me to grow my hair long, I wondered if I could hurry up the process. You know, like the Incredible Hulk." When he resumed the hunched, grimace-riddled stance—she recognized it, right out of the movies.

"An angry roar and you've got it nailed."

And he roared! Right there in the middle of Fort Rucker, Alabama airfield. Other crews were turning startled looks in their direction, but Silvan didn't seem to care.

When he finished, he stood up normally, as if nothing had happened and half the field wasn't watching him, and patted the top of his head again.

Then he whispered a soft, "Damn! No change."

Debbie would have burst out laughing at that moment if she could have, he was awfully cute.

But she couldn't.

Because she knew that in that instant, whether or not she was his commander, she was gone on him.

CHAPTER THREE

*S*ilvan popped loose his harness then turned to her.

"Remember, jump into the top of a wave. If you jump into a trough from a height, you're going to fall that extra thirty feet."

They were crossing down through the two-hundred-foot mark and the difference from crest to trough was looking more like five stories than three. These waves were huge.

"After I get the raft, we jump together, from opposite sides," he shouted for emphasis.

"Roger that. Go!"

And he *was* gone: yanking free the data-and-communications umbilical cord to his helmet, jamming open the door with a shoulder, then leveraging his way out onto the bucking skid. The wind roared and swirled about her for a moment before the wind slammed it closed.

She should have said something.

Something to show that she cared.

That he was important.

That even though they'd never had a chance, she wished they had.

A vicious gust slapped them hard. She managed to lean her side of the Little Bird into it. It cost her some altitude, but it would spare Silvan the worst of it.

She was way too busy to look to see if he was still there, clinging to the outside of the helo.

One-fifty.

The wind's roar in the cabin returned with double the volume.

The rear door was open. Silvan was still with her.

"I've got the raft!" Debbie could barely hear his shout.

"Keep growing your hair!" *Stupid! Stupid! Stupid!*

That was going to be the last thing she ever said to him?

CHAPTER FOUR

"*K*eep trying," Debbie managed past a constricted throat, trying not to make their first meeting too awkward. "Six months tops and it should cover those awkward ears."

"Mom would like you."

"She doesn't like the kind of trollops you normally drag home?" Maybe it was the Alabama heat shimmering off the airfield that melted what little manners she normally maintained.

Silvan had the decency to laugh despite her catty remark. "Not much. Would you believe that some of them haven't even read *The Hobbit?*"

"Horrors!"

"Indeed," he agreed.

And that had set the tone for their entire first meeting. They'd shared stories of trainings and missions, of joining the military and that they were each nearing their first decade of service.

She'd felt bad about not sharing her past, but Silvan made it easy with stories of his own. His family life wasn't some picture postcard, but it wasn't a dysfunctional TV sitcom either. Engineer mom, professor dad, older sister lawyer with one kid and a divorce.

For eight months they'd flown together, laughed together, and survived every mission thrown at them.

In eight months he'd never done a single thing to reverse her initial impression.

Silvan was a seriously decent guy who easily kept up with her quirky sense of humor. Even better, together they forced each other to become better fliers.

It seemed they'd done everything together—except one.

CHAPTER FIVE

*W*ell, two things. They'd also never died together but, odds on, they were about to.

She didn't dare take a hand off either of the controls, so she couldn't do anything to prepare for the jump except rehearse the steps in her head: release controls, punch harness release with one hand, then yank out the helmet's umbilical cord while opening the door with the other. Thankfully, she and Silvan were already wearing inflatable life vests on top of their standard gear.

With her left thumb she flicked the landing light switch on the end of the collective control. The sudden glare revealed a nightmare landscape of sheeting spray and breaking waves covered with foaming spindrift.

A wave crested fifty feet below her.

No time to grab anything, just enough to—

Down in the trough was what remained of the spy trawler's hull.

A flat structure. The lowest deck had survived the blast. Now just barely awash.

If she could land there, even for a moment, their chances of survival were going to skyrocket.

CHAPTER SIX

"*W*hy don't you have a past?"

Debbie sat slouched beside Silvan after a brutally long mission deep into Libya to take part in wiping out an al-Qaeda camp. They'd made it back to the USS *Harry S. Truman* aircraft carrier with the first of the predawn light. By unspoken mutual consent, they'd found a corner of the hangar deck with a view out over the ship's wake. There they'd collapsed and settled in to watch the sunrise over the Mediterranean.

For a long time—from dark blue to soft pink—Debbie just let the waves hold her attention. She felt their beat in her aching body. Little Birds were meant for two-hour out-and-back operations. Muhammad Ali's "Sting like a bee"—that was a Little Bird's sweet spot. Which fit her perfectly, as her full name, Deborah, meant "bee" in Hebrew. Long missions took their toll. Ones long enough to require multiple refueling stops really took the honey right out of her mood.

Silvan waited her out. He was good at that, sensing her mood and letting her have that space. There was so much to appreciate about him aside from his skills as a flier.

"You weren't born the day you joined the Army." He was also good at calling her on her own bullshit avoidance, even if she didn't appreciate it.

"I'm a bad Jewish daughter. I didn't marry a Jew. I didn't even go into business or law. Except my family isn't just Jewish, they're Orthodox Haredi. It means we aren't supposed to even mingle with non-Jewish cultures."

"So the Army ticked them off. Is that why you joined?"

Debbie had to smile, "Can't say that I minded that aspect of it, but no. There was a boy at our *yeshiva*—think Jewish high school that only reluctantly allows girls—Moshe. He was by far the best of us all. But he was in the wrong place at the wrong time—a mugging that escalated badly. Anyway, he was dead before they got him to the hospital. That was the moment I truly became aware of the outside world. The more I learned..." she couldn't finish the sentence.

"The more you felt a need to fix it?"

She could only nod. She didn't even mind Silvan's habit of being able to finish her sentences because he was always right when he did. The waves of her life kept flowing by like the sunlit wake of the aircraft carrier as she watched—no way to ever hold onto them. No way to ever bring them back.

CHAPTER SEVEN

"*H*ull!" Debbie shouted as loudly as she could.

By the wind's roar—now augmented by the breaking waves—she knew the rear door was still open and Silvan was still with her.

If he responded, she couldn't hear it. But the roar filled her ears —they'd jump together.

She flew so close above the next crest that she could have stepped out onto the wavetop. A second later, she was over the yawning chasm of a trough. But the hull had survived or at least a piece of it.

Forty.

Thirty.

At twenty she reefed back on the cyclic hard, a final flare to dump speed and trade it in for a momentary, unsustainable hover.

A last kick of the rudder pedals.

Impact!

More of a crash than a landing onto the trawler, but it had worked.

Now all her years of training kicked in.

Not turning to Silvan—not even hesitating to be surprised that she was still alive—she slapped, pulled, opened, and leapt out.

She dove into the freezing sea and slammed against the two feet of the trawler's outer wooden hull, then collapsed onto the flat deck. She ate a mouthful of saltwater as she groaned at the abuse. A glance up revealed the Little Bird's rotors still windmilling at lethal speed.

The next wave began to lift the hull and the helo fell, tipping toward her. Nowhere to dive. Her life vest—which had auto-inflated on contact with the water—kept her pinned to the surface like a bug about to be squashed.

Through the driving sleet and icy spray, she saw the blades slash into the water less than an arm's length past her position. Without the engine driving them, they stopped almost immediately.

She felt like a lion in a carbon-fiber blade cage: the body of her helo behind her and the blades driven down into the sea in front.

Then the wave's face went near enough to vertical for the helicopter to roll off the hull. She actually banged her helmet on some part of the helo as it tumbled by—driving her face once more into the frigid wash of water now two feet deep over the sinking deck. Her helo disappeared beneath the waves.

Just because the boat's hull was wallowing so deeply, didn't abate the wave's vehemence. In a cloud of slashing spray and biting wind, it flipped the hull over this time. Catapulting her aside with the ease of a rag doll, she landed clear of its tumbling mass.

Too much for the remains of the trawler, it finally plunged for the depths. Caught in its vortex rush of sinking water, she was dragged deep beneath the surface.

She swam hard, letting the life vest tell her which way was up and broke the surface just before her lungs burst from holding her breath so hard. She slid down the back of the wave.

A light blinked in the darkness.
Silvan.
Just going over the crest of the next wave over.
He might as well be a mile away.

CHAPTER EIGHT

*S*ilvan wiped the water out of his eyes for the hundredth time since he'd plunged into the icy North Sea. Alone, he rode over the wave and down the far side, bobbing as lightly as a cork.

If ever there was a pilot to fly with, it was Chief Warrant Deborah Rosenthal.

Which was exactly how he felt every time he got close to her. He'd like to have gotten much closer, but the Army wasn't the only one against that. Their rank wasn't an issue, but the fact that she was his superior officer was. He hadn't wanted to risk not flying with her in the future.

There was also something within her. Something...torn. It had kept him pushed to a distance and he'd done his best to respect that.

And now he didn't know if he'd ever have a chance to see past whatever that was, or even to thank her for saving him.

Had she died in that final act?

There was no way he should be alive, but she'd been masterful.

Landing for those crucial few seconds on the hull had absolutely saved his life.

He'd felt the skid hit the boat's hull through the heels of his boots. The next instant he had kicked backward as hard as he could, flinging himself clear. With the two-foot-long life raft bag clutched hard to his chest, he hadn't sunk more than a few feet.

Then he'd watched in horror as first the helicopter and then the entire boat hull flipped over on where she would have jumped clear. If she even survived the landing.

He wiped his face again and tried to kick himself in a circle, hoping against hope that he'd spot the light from her life vest.

Night.

Screaming wind.

Pitch-black, overcast night.

Yet, he could see shades of the gale's madness—the waves as they ripped past him.

No thought to grab the night-vision goggles that he kept stowed under the console. When attached to the helicopter, everything he needed was projected on the inside of his visor.

Next time, if there was a next time, he'd remember to grab his goddamn NVGs.

A glimmer?

He watched closely over the next wave crest.

Definitely a brightness beyond the next wave. The only light in the night, he'd take hope from that.

He hooked the uninflated life raft to his belt on a short tether so that it would trail behind him and began swimming.

CHAPTER NINE

*D*ebbie had lost sight of Silvan. No matter how hard she
swam, he seemed to slip farther and farther away.

She made sure that her emergency radio beacon was blinking,
indicating it was crying for help, but how long was rescue going to
take to reach her? She was fifty miles from land in every direction
in the midst of a brutal winter storm. The first shot had killed the
helo's radios and there'd been no time to try the handhelds.

Now, to hear her little beacon, it would take a very lucky
satellite or someone flying directly over her and listening for her
signal. How long before Search and Rescue came looking?
Too long.

It was just her and Silvan.

No, it was just her.

That thought slammed in with a punch harder than the icy
ocean seeping into her foul-weather flight gear. Next time she
flew, she'd wear a goddamn dry suit.

No Silvan. She hadn't let him get too close to her because...

A wave crest slapped and tumbled her. Rather than burying her
under, the wind ripping at the water was enough to blow her

through the air for a short distance and bury her face-first into the water, again. She resurfaced.

Because she was an idiot.

Silvan Exeter was the best man she was never going to meet again. Impossibly, even better than Moshe who had been swept backward by the tide of time as well.

She'd lost all sense of direction when the wave had tossed her.

She treaded water, slowly turning in a circle, searching for any sign of hope. Deborah the Prophetess had led the biblical legions against the oppression of King Jabin and his military general Sisera. The latter had fallen to a woman pounding a tent peg through his temple while he rested. Well, Debbie didn't have a tent peg, a mallet, or the knowledge of a prophetess of the Lord God.

All she had was—

A shining beacon in the distance. A tiny flashing light.

Attached to a man plunging down a wave face easily five stories tall.

As he swam *in her direction.*

A rescue swimmer? Already?

No!

Leaving the chill that had threatened to encase her behind a solid wall, she dug into the waves, speeding toward Silvan.

CHAPTER TEN

*B*oth cold, gasping for breath from the hard swim necessary to fight their way together, and lost in the North Sea—the first thing they had done was kiss.

It had been sloppy, hurried, freezing, and in moments they were battered apart except for the death grip on the front ring of each others' vests.

But it changed Silvan's world.

It hadn't been a kiss of "so glad to see you."

Their coming together had been an "Oh my god, I thought you were dead!"

It took a coordinated effort, but they deployed the raft and managed to climb in before it blew away. It was small comfort in the heavy storm—it didn't stay dry, but at least it remained upright. Between judicious bailing and unfurling the canopy, they finally were reasonably secure.

The only way they could keep from being slammed together was by holding tightly to each other. It was something that Silvan had wanted to do for so long that it was hard to believe it was finally happening. Not how he'd imagined it, but holding her tight might just be the best thing to ever happen to him.

"You aren't going to die!" Debbie shook him by her hold on his vest.

It seemed an odd statement as this was perhaps the safest they'd been in over an hour.

"You aren't!" She shook him again.

"You're awfully strong for someone who isn't an elf."

She shook him again, though not as hard. As if she could anchor her words in his chest.

If they hadn't been deep in the comparative calm inside the high-sided raft, he wouldn't have heard her next statement.

"I'm not wrong this time. I can't be. You're going to live." Then she buried her face against his shoulder and simply hung on.

There, with the waves raging by dozens of feet above them, he knew he had found the missing piece, the tear in her world.

Moshe. He wasn't "some boy" who had died and changed the course of Debbie Rosenthal's life.

She'd been there. Held him while he died, telling him he was going to live. Her boyfriend? Her lover?

"Did he save you?"

Her nod told him the rest of the story. Moshe had died to protect her and she was repaying him by protecting everyone else that she could.

Silvan held her tightly, and she let him.

An eternity of howling winds and bailing out icy seawater later, a big C-130 Hercules turboprop roared by close overhead, soaring through the first light of day. It had sniffed out the track of their emergency locators.

The satellite phone had been useless, the wave troughs too deep to allow even the time to place a call. Their handheld radios were only good for line-of-sight communications. But now with the big plane circling above, he pulled out the radio and told them they were safe and uninjured...and that there was no point searching for the other two pilots. The rest of the report would be for the company commander's ears alone. He could decide who to contact about the spy trawler.

Within the hour, a helo and a rescue swimmer would arrive to hoist them off the waves. The plane promised to stay on station despite the turbulence their crew must be suffering.

CHAPTER ELEVEN

*D*ebbie lay quiet now, comfortable inside the circle of Silvan's arms while they awaited the rescue team that would pluck them from the sea. Their helmets kept the worst of the howling wind at bay.

"You don't need to worry about protecting me."

Silvan's shouted words were like a benediction. He might not understand that she hadn't had a single thought of her own survival during the crash landing—she'd been shocked when she'd survived. But she'd known without a doubt that getting down on that hull had improved Silvan's chances of survival. That was all that had mattered.

But maybe he was right. She didn't need to protect him as if he could be erased from existence at any moment. He'd survived the gunfire and crash just as they'd survived dozens of missions.

When it was their time, like Junker and Tank, it would be their time.

Until then—

Debbie sat up as much as the pitching raft would allow and

studied Silvan's face. A few strands of his beautiful blond hair were finally long enough peek out from under the edge of his helmet.

"I've got an idea."

His frown said that he couldn't hear her.

She braced herself against his shoulders by curling her fists around his vest's armholes. Then she leaned in and repeated her shout between his right cheek and the edge of his helmet.

"Bring it on, lady. If it's a good one, I'll put in a good word for you with the elf king." His breath was warm against her chilled cheek.

"How about we just worry about protecting each other?"

"Sounds like a good plan." Then Silvan's face sobered, "How long were you thinking?" He had to repeat that more loudly.

When he did, Debbie couldn't help but feel the warmth in her heart despite the hail and spray currently battering at them. "How long have you got?"

Silvan's easy smile started slow but built big and then disappeared from view when he kissed her to seal the bargain.

Debbie let her heart ride the wave as it lifted the two of them out of the trough and over the top together.

She hoped they had a long, long time.

IF YOU ENJOYED THIS, YOU MIGHT
ALSO ENJOY:

M.L. BUCHMAN

3-TIME BOOKLIST TOP 10 ROMANCE AUTHOR OF THE YEAR

"Buchman's Best Yet!"

Target Engaged, Booklist

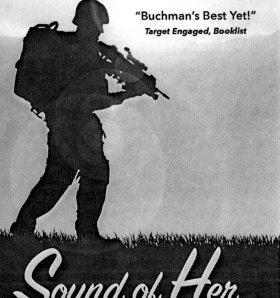

Sound of Her Warrior Heart

A DELTA FORCE ROMANCE STORY

SOUND OF HER WARRIOR HEART

*D*elta Force operator **Katrina Melman's** *hearing goes missing when her mission gets blown away. But she's Delta, the Army doesn't pay her to fail.*

Sergeant Tomas Gallagher, *the best soldier she's ever met, only speaks to her in sharp commanding tones. Now she can't hear him at all.*

Only together can they complete the mission if they hope to find the Sound of Her Warrior Heart.

INTRODUCTION

There are so many things we take for granted: good health, functioning senses, and (for the bulk of humanity) living in a relatively safe society.

Then I was rewatching the movie Black Hawk Down. *One of the soldiers (both in the movie and in real life) was temporarily deafened by being blown up followed by heavy gunfire too close to his ears.*

That started me thinking. As I'm hard of hearing and have partial colorblindness (just enough to kill my childhood dream of being an airline pilot, though I did get my private license), I've given a fair amount of thought to what it would be like to lose a sense.

I sometimes wonder if I became a writer because of these shortcomings. Perhaps they leave me a little insulated from the world around me, thereby allowing me to so enjoy the stories in my head.

Whatever it is, that was what lies at the core of this story.

Take away one sense and see-taste-smell so much more. More of the world around the heroine. More of the hero.

But they are Delta, so of course they are still committed to doing what is called for—no matter the challenges. Even if it means falling in love.

CHAPTER ONE

*P*urple.

A purple so deep that it made her think of the purest fresh-pressed grape juice.

Purple grapes. Round globes of color so dark that they ate the brilliant sunlight until they were almost black.

Green leaves. Impossibly blue sky.

Katrina knew something was wrong, but it took her a moment to identify what was missing.

Birds. There should be birdsong. Her family's vineyard was never quiet when the grapes were so close to harvest. This late in the season the bees had moved on to more flowery pastures, but the birds should be singing, arguing, playing.

Funny, she didn't recognize this row of vines, she thought she knew them all.

It was hard to care, though. She'd always loved to lie on the rich soil between the rows of vines and stare at the deeply blue sky. She rarely spent that time thinking about the future or the past. In her memories it hadn't been about some boy either. Of course when the boys came along, she'd spent less time alone in the vineyard watching the sky. No, the vineyard was always about the present moment.

A thread of black smoke slid across the blue sky. Burning a slash pile? To early in the season for that. The summer was still hot and dry.

She reached a hand up through the silence to pluck a grape. They looked ripe enough that half the cluster might fall into her palm at the lightest touch.

Except she didn't recognize the hand. They weren't her slender teenage fingers. Where was the silver thumb ring that Granny had given her at twelve that had finally moved to her middle finger at fourteen?

This hand was strong, with a shooter's callus on the webbing between thumb and forefinger. And why was the hand, *her hand* covered in red, sticky...blood?

A face intervened between her and her view of sky, grape leaves, hand...blood?

It was a hard, male face.

One that needed a shave.

It should have alarmed her that he was so close, but she knew him. Or thought she should. He wore a close-fitting military helmet and anti-glare glasses. She flexed her jaw and could feel the familiar pressure of the strap of her own helmet. Squinching her nose revealed that she too wore sunglasses.

Why did they need helmets to lie in the vineyard to watch the grapes ripen in the sunshine? She didn't like sunglasses, they changed the color of the blue sky. She tried looking around the edges, but they were wrap-around, just like his.

He was familiar.

Very familiar.

But never from this close. That wasn't normal.

His lips were moving, but she couldn't hear a thing.

"What?"

He clamped a hard hand over her mouth and his lips made a "Shh!" shape, but she couldn't hear anything.

She studied his lips.

Words. They were forming words.

Kat! Are you okay? Not Katrina. Kat wasn't a family nickname. Always her full name in the Melman family. Miss Katrina to the Mexican field hands as if her family were lords and ladies rather than third-generation Oregon vineyard owners.

Sure she was okay. Though it was weird to have the face asking it silently, especially that face. She associated it with a cold, emotionless tone that could slice concrete.

But why wouldn't she be okay? She was lying in a lovely vineyard, the sun warming her face while she watched purple grapes, blue sky, and black smoke from a slash pile fire. It was expanding though. Maybe the fire was out of control.

The bloody hand was still bothering her.

And the silence.

Maybe she wasn't okay.

Maybe she'd been—

The memory slammed in like the blast of a mortar.

Which was exactly what had happened.

CHAPTER TWO

Sergeant Katrina Melman suddenly remembered the feeling of flying.

There had been the high whistle of an incoming mortar round. She and Tomas—who she always teased about abandoning his poor H somewhere along the way, cruelly leaving it to wander the world on its own—had dropped flat in the vineyard and offered up a quick prayer for the round to land somewhere else.

It had partially worked. Rather than a direct hit, the force of the blast had merely thrown her aside, slamming her into a line of grape vines. The burnt sulfur smell of exploded TNT overwhelmed the sweet grapes and rich soil.

Pain was starting to report in. Abused muscles, the nasty gash on her hand, but nothing felt broken.

"I think I'm okay."

Tomas shushed her again. Again she had to concentrate on his lips to figure out which words he was speaking silently. *You're shouting.*

"I am?"

Again the hand clamped over her mouth.

The silence. The echoing silence. The world hadn't gone quiet. Her hearing had gone instead.

Deaf.

When she nodded her understanding, Tomas eased off his hold on her. He mouthed out some long sentence that she had no hope of unraveling, especially as he kept looking away to scan the vineyard, hiding his mouth in the process.

"I can't hear you," she tried to make it a whisper.

Tomas spun back to face her and winced.

Unable to hear herself, she'd lost all calibration of her volume.

You can't? Tomas' lips moved, but she heard nothing—not even the proverbial pin. At least she was fairly sure that's what he'd said. Lipreading was something they taught undercover types. She was a shooter.

Katrina stuck with just shaking her head.

Shit! No problem reading that. With quick rough hands he began inspecting her.

She slapped his hands aside then sat up, and wished she hadn't. Every muscle screamed—silently—in protest. She began inspecting herself. Everything moved when she tried it. A quick pat-down revealed no sources of blood other than her hand.

Tomas bound that quickly enough, using the medkit that hung from his vest.

Armored vest.

Field.

Mortar.

She looked around and spotted her rifle tangled in one of the grapevines. She slid it out and it appeared none the worse for having been blown up.

"That makes one of us who's okay," she whispered to her baby. The MK21 Precision Sniper Rifle was fifty-two inches and eighteen pounds of silent death that let her "reach out and touch someone" over a mile away. It was her reason for being—her role in Delta Force. Her role in—

Moldova. She and her rifle had been blown up in a vineyard in the Eastern European country sandwiched between Ukraine and Romania. Except no one was supposed to know they were here. They—

Tomas slammed her down to the ground and lay on top of her and her rifle. She could feel by the rigidity of his body that he wasn't dead. He was bracing over her like a human shield. For half a moment she thought she finally saw a bird flying across the sky. A falcon swooping on its prey. An...incoming round!

She felt the ground buck against her back from the explosion. The air blast hit against the far side of the vines, peppering the two of them with hundreds of grapes blown off the vines. The vintner was going to be furious.

Tomas pushed back to kneeling beside her.

We've... but Tomas turned away and she missed the rest of his sentence. It was as if he didn't want to look at her after lying full length upon her a moment before. They were both wearing combat vests, making it one of the unsexiest moments ever, but she got the feeling he was still embarrassed by it.

Sitting up, she grabbed the helmet straps on either side of his jaw and turned him back to face her.

"What did you say?" Katrina struggled to keep it soft. Tomas didn't reprimand her so she must have succeeded. "I'm deaf."

His eyes widened briefly. Then he grabbed her head, his powerful hands strong but gentle along her cheeks, and turned it to either side to inspect her ears.

No blood, his lips formed the words quickly, but she hoped she got it right.

She heaved out a sigh of relief at his words. Good. That was good. No dribbling blood meant that maybe her eardrums were still intact.

He made a sharp slicing motion to the west with a flat hand. Right. They needed to get moving. He signaled reminders to stay low and go down the center of the path—jostling a vine might give away their changing position.

At her nod, he led off.

Stepping out, she walked straight into a grapevine.

She scooted to the middle of the path and tried again.

This time she plunged into the grapes the next row over.

It wasn't vertigo, she'd had that induced during training and learned how to fire through it. Besides, vertigo always made you spin in the same direction. With her ears out of operation, her balance was off.

Tomas grabbed her arm and, though it felt like he was pulling her hard to the right, they progressed straight down the aisle of dirt between two rows of green leaves with her weaving like a drunkard.

Fifteen seconds later she felt the air thump against her back as a mortar killed the poor grapevines she'd stumbled into. Whoever was firing at them was good.

CHAPTER THREE

*B*y the end of the row, she began to get a feel for how to counteract her balance problems.

Tomas yanked her down to the soil, scanning the terrain ahead. He might be a hardcore pain in the ass, but she couldn't ask for a better soldier to be at her side. There was no better man to be in a tight situation with in Delta. She'd tried to talk to him in camp, but he always gave her the cold shoulder, with a voice that could be used to chill a meat locker. However, on assignment, he guarded her like a mother hen or big brother. He was the best soldier, and she'd always been drawn to the best, but for some reason he wouldn't even give her the time of day once they were back in a green zone.

That green zone felt awfully far away at the moment.

They lay together at the edge of the lush vineyard. Looking back she could see that it swooped down into a valley and up the next hill in neat and orderly rows. She'd never had a Moldovan wine and wondered if they were any good. Simply by the size of the field, they were successful. She plucked a grape. Blue-purple. Thick skin that resisted her bite before it popped, flooding her mouth with a high sugar content. Merlot probably. Or maybe a Zinfandel, they tasted a lot alike while still in the grape. She could be lying in the hills of Oregon's Willamette Valley…if it weren't for someone firing a mortar at them. Very few mortars being fired in the Willamette Valley in her experience.

Right! Time to start thinking like a soldier again.

Ahead lay a five-meter strip of rough dirt thick with tractor tire tracks. Beyond it lay a field of thin brown stalks chopped off at one meter high. It was a no-man's land in which they'd be completely exposed. Past several hundred meters of stalks, a line of trees.

Tomas tapped her arm and pointed to the right.

Katrina had to scoot forward to see around him. A large red combine was parked in the middle of the field, at the edge of the tall stubble. Beyond it stood sunflowers—acres of sunflowers. Their heads were dried to a gray-brown and the combine would soon be harvesting them. Except the cab was empty and the door hung open. The machine still vibrated and smoke swirled up out of its exhaust stack. The farmer had abandoned his vehicle when the shelling had started.

"I hate working with foreign military."

Tomas nodded his agreement.

That's what must have happened. Moldova was way down the list on the international index of governmental corruption—their score was in the bottom third and falling fast. You could buy the entire parliament for the price of a Super Bowl commercial. Throw in a signed football and you could probably buy the military as well. The US must have dutifully informed someone of their planned operation on Moldovan soil, who had then reported it directly to the Russians who coveted Moldovan territory. Or perhaps she and Tomas were still alive because some faction of the local military had decided to take care of the problem themselves —it wasn't like the Russians to miss quite so many times.

Well, killing a pair of Delta Force operators wasn't all that easy either.

"Where are they?" she asked Tomas quietly. There were two scenarios: the people firing the mortar could see their position, or the mortar crew were hunkered down, out of sight, but had a spotter who could. Either way she and Tomas had to find them.

Tomas pulled out a small radio scanner. In moments he had a lock on the enemy's frequency. She could see by the indicator light that they were real talkers, either locals or overconfident Russians. He hooked up a small DF loop and began rotating it to get their direction.

She tried to remember how she'd been lying on the ground when she'd seen the incoming round. It had come from...the line of trees to the west.

Tomas pointed in two places: one toward the trees, one...in the direction of the combine.

Katrina slid the caps off the ends of her rifle's scope. She tapped Tomas' shoulder. He turned to her and she made as if to press her hand flat against the ground, then repeated the motion on his shoulder.

He lay flat, braced his elbows wide so that he was steadier than the Rock of Gibraltar. Then he rested his head on his folded hands, but turned toward her rather than the combine. Dark eyes. She could feel his dark eyes watching her despite the lenses he wore. They have always watched her, the sole woman on their squad. Every time she turned, Tomas' eyes were tracking her.

Ignoring that, she unfolded the bipod on the front of her weapon and rested it against the small of his back. The combine was parked a thousand meters away and upslope from them so she needed the extra height to brace her weapon. She lined up with a break in the vines and began inspecting the combine at high magnification.

The main harvester bar was set a meter high and she could see its cutters still working. The high cab was indeed empty. The unloading pipe was swung back out of the way. The...

She swung back to inspect the cab. It was empty. But through the double layer of glass, windshield and side window, she could just make out a man standing behind the cab. It was an almost impossible shot, especially for a single shooter. She would have to break the windshield, then the side window, and then might have a chance of hitting the target if he hadn't already moved. Two shots minimum, probably three.

Tracking upward, seeking any way in, she spotted just what she needed. Between the top of the cab and some other piece of gear, a pair of binoculars inspected the vineyard. She flipped off the safety, glanced at the grapevines to estimate the wind—it was so strange not to hear it rustling the leaves—and compensated for the bullet's fall and a thousand meters of windage.

The MK21 had a silencer, but there was always some noise. Now, for her, it was truly silent as it kicked her in the shoulder. A half second later, the binoculars were gone. Between the combine's tires she could see a body plummet onto the field. She worked the bolt and fed another round into the downed spotter just to be sure, not that a .338 Lapua Magnum round would have left much of his head. Even at over a half-mile out, the body twitched from the massive kinetic impact of the bullet. No question that the spotter for the mortar team was permanently out of commission.

There was a whiff of burnt gunpowder as she chambered another round.

She glanced at Tomas and nodded that it was done, but froze halfway through.

He was smiling at her. It was gone the moment she'd caught him at it, but she knew she'd seen it. Tomas didn't smile at anybody for any reason.

No. That wasn't right. She'd seen his smile before—never directed at her, of course—but she'd seen it. But his face, when he smiled, made it possible to imagine Tomas speaking to her in a warm and gentle tone. *That* was too strange for words so she kept her silence.

CHAPTER FOUR

*C*learing out the mortar team didn't take long. Idiot One sprang up to go check on the shooter. Idiot Two raced away in plain view and earned himself a shot in the back though he was closer to a mile away by the time Tomas pointed him out.

Katrina busted up the mortar tube and defused the remaining ammo while Tomas hid the bodies. He showed her the spotter's arm tattoo—a black bat hovering over a blue circle meant to represent the Earth. It was a Spetsnaz tat, Russian Special Forces. So, their enemies this morning were one Russian and two locals, because a Spetsnaz would never run from a fight. Spetsnaz. It was a surprise that she and Tomas survived. Definitely time to go.

Her feet were now steady enough that she probably could have navigated on her own, but Tomas showed no inclination to let go of his grip on her upper arm and she wasn't complaining.

There was a steadiness to him. Not merely his gait, but his reliability. His grip never varied, except to tighten briefly when she stumbled on a particularly gnarly root. He scanned ahead as they moved through the woods.

Last night's insertion into Moldova had been screwed up in a bazillion different ways. The mortar attack counted as a bazillion-and-one.

First, the transport helo had a mechanical failure. A team of mechanics had raced to fix it deep into the night. So, their launch window at dusk had, well, gone out the window. They'd finally hit the ground in eastern Moldova at two a.m. But their ride had long since given up and vanished into the darkness. No option left but to cover the ground on foot, dressed in full US military gear, with much of the transit in broad daylight.

That's why they'd ducked into the vineyard in the first place, good cover. Into a vineyard—and straight into a trap.

Tomas set a ground-eating pace through the woods that they could both maintain for hours with only minimal breaks. Once they were deep in the woods and several kilometers from the dead mortar team, they made quick work of cutting down some wild cherry branches and creating a small lean-to using the massive trunk of a fallen oak. It was several feet larger around than the Willamette oaks, it must be an English oak. She'd always wanted to go walking among the Cotswolds of England and see some of them. Now she was being hunted across the Moldovan countryside. It sure wasn't the same.

Inside their shelter, Tomas called up to Command during a satellite overflight. She couldn't lipread a word because he held the radio so close to his mouth. Whatever their conversation was, it was short.

Katrina focused on picking the small wild cherries off the roof of their bower for them to eat. Tart! But good.

That's when the fact of her deafness slammed home and stole her breath away. What if it wasn't temporary? At first she hadn't had time to think about it, then she'd shoved aside her fear by convincing herself it was just a TTS, a temporary threshold shift. But what if it wasn't? What if—

Tomas tapped her on the shoulder and she almost cried out in shock.

He eyed her carefully, making a point to mouth his question slowly, *You okay?*

So not. But she gave him a nod that was a total lie.

He snapped his fingers close by her ears.

She could only shake her head.

In answer, Tomas reached out and pulled her against his chest. It was awkward; all of the gear on their vests kept it from being close and she had a fistful of cherries, but still she appreciated it. For a moment she lay her cheek against the cool metal of the emergency lifting ring on the front of his vest, and let herself be held.

Making sense of that was no easier than making sense of her deafness.

A woman in Delta Force did *not* let herself be held. She didn't dare let herself be seen as weak, not for a millisecond. Women were too rare a breed in Special Operations and especially in the heavy-duty combat units.

Beyond that, the last person on the planet she'd ever expect to have empathy was Sergeant Tomas Gallagher—the toughest damn bastard in anyone's army. It was easy to remember his cold, hard voice. But she couldn't reconcile that with the way he was taking care of her.

He held her until she felt some sense of control come back. Not relief. Not hope. But at least the sense that somehow or other she'd get through this and that maybe, just maybe, she wasn't going to be alone in that effort.

She sat up and patted his arm in thanks. It was a good arm, thick with muscle, honed with thousands of hours of training and hundreds of missions. She realized she needed to make herself stop patting him.

Distraction needed.

Katrina passed him a handful of the tart cherries after making clear he had to spit out the cherry pits—they were naturally laced with cyanide. Then she pointed at the sky, to where the satellite antenna had been aimed and made a questioning face.

You can talk, Tomas admonished her. *Soft-ly.* He was over-accentuating his lip movement which helped. Tomas Gallagher being thoughtful was still a shock.

She shrugged at her descent into sign language. Not being able to hear immersed her into a strange world of silence that she felt reluctant to break. Also, her own voice was wrong—foreign, muted to silence by whatever was happening in her ears. She could feel that she was speaking, but couldn't hear it, neither volume nor tone.

He tapped the lapel of his shirt, pointed again to the west, tapped his watch, and gave a thumbs up. Command had reported that their targets, a Russian general and a Moldovan one, were still expected to be in position at the time previously reported.

Good news. The mission wasn't blown yet despite the problems they'd encountered.

He pointed upward, held up three fingers, then placed his hands palm to palm against his own cheek before closing his eyes.

She didn't get it.

He began slapping his pockets but pencil and paper weren't something you carried on a self-contained mission into a "friendly" foreign country. He looked around again, then spotted something.

He held his hand palm up and moved it until he was almost touching her breast. He did it fast enough that she jolted back against the log.

Tomas held up a hand in apology and, if she didn't know better, she'd say he blushed.

This time he moved his palm more slowly until it was suddenly filled with the bright light of a sunbeam that had found its way down through the forest canopy and into their hastily assembled hideout. It had been shining against her ribcage. He tapped his palm, then pointed upward.

"Oh, the sun."

He nodded. This time the three fingers, a tap of his watch, and a sign to sleep made sense. Three hours to sunset when it would be time to move out; she *should* get some sleep.

Tapping his own chest, he made the signal for lookout—a hand shading his eyes.

She held up two fingers, then bent one in half.

Oh, she could speak.

"Hour and a half, then it's my turn to watch."

He nodded and she settled herself more comfortably against the log. A Special Ops soldier could sleep anywhere: a roaring plane flight, inside a bunker during a firefight—didn't matter. Their small shelter was cozy. It smelled of fresh cherries that matched the vivid taste on her tongue and crispy-dry oak leaves. And was very, very quiet.

She sighed.

Then she remembered what it had felt like to be held by Tomas. They were shoulder to shoulder. He had good shoulders.

After a night and a day on the go, she was exhausted.

She leaned her head onto his shoulder and felt him jolt in surprise. It was a long time before his arm settled as lightly as the sunlight on her shoulders. She didn't stay awake long enough to feel whether or not his fingers wrapped around her arm.

CHAPTER FIVE

*K*atrina awoke with a start. It was soft twilight. She listened carefully, but didn't hear a thing...because, shit, she was deaf. This was definitely going to take some getting used to.

She was also warm and comfortable inside the curve of a man's arm. Of Tomas Gallagher's arm. For a moment she let herself revel in the feel of it, the security of being held, of lying against a man she trusted with her very life.

Except they were both soldiers.

As she pushed herself upright, he eased his arm off her shoulders.

"You didn't wake me for my half of the watch."

He shrugged.

She thumped the side of a fist against his shoulder.

He tapped his ear and then hers with a soft touch.

Oh right, she couldn't listen. "Sorry. I hope you didn't mind me sleeping on you."

He clamped both hands around his own throat and pretended he was gagging.

She clamped a hand over her mouth to suppress the laugh and wondered where the hell Sergeant Tomas Gallagher had gone. The man she knew had absolutely no sense of humor.

"You're being nice to me."

He shrugged and looked down to rummage through his kit for some energy bars. She didn't take the one he offered.

"Why?"

He turned away but stopped when she rested a palm on his cheek. Without his sunglasses, his dark eyes bored into hers. She tried to say something, she truly did, but her throat was suddenly dry.

"Why, Tomas?" finally creaked out of her throat.

He rested one of his big hands over where hers still touched his cheek.

The light was making it harder to see, but he might have said, *I'm an idiot.*

A moment later he leaned forward and kissed her. It wasn't some tentative little peck. It wasn't a question either. It was a kiss that demanded attention. It was hard, fast, and deep. He grabbed either side of her armored vest by the armholes and hauled her into his lap.

Tomas' strength was overwhelming, pinning her against him. She knew that at the least hesitation on her part, he'd let her go, but no hesitation came from anywhere inside her.

Surprise? *Hell yeah!*

Hesitation? *Hell no!* Not from a kiss like the one he was delivering.

In the same unit? *Don't give a shit!*

On a mission? The mission could wait just a goddamn minute —she was busy here. Busy having her rocketing heartrate pound against her chest, if not her ears.

He let her go at last and some small bit of her sanity returned. She was straddling his lap, her arms locked around his neck. One of his hands had slipped down between her armor and butt.

And he was grinning like the big bad wolf.

"You're not a bit sorry, are you?"

He patted his free hand downward to remind her to watch her voice. His other hand was still occupied elsewhere. He shook his head.

"Odd. Neither am I."

She couldn't hear his groan, but she could feel it conducting through her fingertips. He said something that she couldn't begin to follow, especially with the last of the light.

Katrina could only shrug.

He dug his fingers hard into her bottom one last time, pulling her tight against him, vest to vest.

Yep! Her body was screaming for it too, but…

"Mission time," she kept it soft.

He nodded and they tried to disentangle themselves. Somehow one of her pockets of .338 Lapua Magnum magazines got hooked on his spare 7.62mm magazines for the HK416 combat rifle he carried and it took them a moment to move apart.

Once separated, she became terribly self conscious. They *were* on a mission. They *were* in the same squad. And Tomas Gallagher hated having a woman in The Unit—that much she was sure of. Except now she wasn't.

Had he been avoiding her for other reasons than she'd thought?

Duh! So if *why* wasn't the right question, the next question was…"How long?" She tapped his chest then hers to make it clear what she was asking.

He held up a single finger.

"One hour? One day?"

He made a flipping motion.

"Day One?"

He nodded.

"You wanted to kiss me since the first day I joined The Unit? Why?" *Now* "why" was the right question.

He rolled his eyes at her. He tapped her on the chest and held up a single finger again.

"Because I'm the only woman on the team?"

No. He tapped her chest—directly on the sniper rifle magazines that had just tangled them up. Then on the MK21 before he tried a double thumbs up. *You best. Very sexy,* he mouthed carefully. He ran his hand down her vest's side plates, over her ribs, waist, and hips to make his point.

"Because I shoot well? That's exactly what every woman wants to be admired for," despite her words it *did* mean a lot.

In answer he ran a knuckle over her cheek so gently that she couldn't help closing her eyes.

"Okay, not just because I shoot well."

He nodded with a grin. Then he dug out his night-vision goggles and clipped them onto his helmet.

"You are a mystery to me, Mr. Tomas Gallagher."

He gave her a thumbs up and another one of those killer smiles once she had her own NVGs in place and turned on.

CHAPTER SIX

*S*even hours hard hiking to reach their target point and three more hours to investigate possible hides.

Command had, of course, done their usual head game. That told them that the CIA was calling the shots on this one because they never did anything straightforward if they could do it bass-ackwards instead.

Katrina decided that it was a good thing she'd been in the Army for long enough to know that they *always* did that. At least it made it so that she was only royally pissed rather than in a murderous rage when the truth came out.

When Tomas reported that they were on site, Command informed them that it was the *Moldovan* general who was their target. He was the only person who'd been told about their mission at all. The fact that they'd been attacked by Russian Special Forces had served to confirm that he could be easily bought.

The Moldovan prime minister himself had told his general that the secrecy of this operation was a matter of Moldovan National

Security. Yet here that general was, meeting with a Russian general at a base just over the Moldovan border in Transnistria.

Transnistria was a breakaway region of Moldova, aligned with the Russians rather than the US, NATO, and the EU. Only four other nations recognized it, though it had been a splinter nation since 1992. A splinter the Russians wanted to exploit. Re-annexing Moldova, just as they had the Crimea, would help secure the Russian frontier against an attack by land forces.

Nobody in the West was in favor of that, except the purchased general. The prime minister of Moldova couldn't be seen to act against his own military despite his general's other war crimes, but it was time for a message to be sent.

And apparently it was up to her and Tomas to send it.

As part of the plan, she'd brought a second barrel and bolt for her rifle, and ammunition to match. In less than two minutes she'd changed from the far-reaching hammer of .338 Lapua to an odd cartridge only ever used in Russia, a 5.45x39mm. It fired only half the distance forcing them to find a location that was both well hidden and close to the meeting site.

Tiraspol airport was technically non-operational, despite being the only airport in the splinter country and housing all five planes of their air force. No one was sure if they could fly, or survive taking off on the aged runway even if they did work.

But helicopters could land here just fine.

It was finding suitable cover that was the issue. They had to get close, preferably well under five hundred meters with such small caliber ammunition, and yet not be found after she took the shot.

Tomas led her in. The airport was unlit except for a single streetlight near the entrance. The runway itself was open to the surrounding farmland, making it easy to walk onto the airfield. They lay in the unmown grass at one end of the runway and inspected the structures carefully.

He tapped his radio, then pointed at the only decent building left standing.

"Command says that's where the meeting will be?"

Tomas nodded.

She studied it through her rifle's night scope and shook her head. Not a chance from here.

Tomas grinned and tapped his temple.

Katrina gestured for him to lead on.

Sticking to a dry drainage ditch behind the buildings, they crossed behind the old terminal and slipped up to the remains of the Transnistrian Air Force. Five Antonov transport planes, all with flat tires—none operational. A dozen helicopters, only two of which looked serviceable, and a pair of Yak two-seat trainers that must date back to World War II. One was clearly being scrapped for parts, but the other one looked serviceable. It was long, an olive-drab green, and had one of those humped glass canopies.

She shook her head.

He tapped the side of the plane.

She shook her head again.

Tomas pointed at the office building.

Three hundred meters away, an ideal shot.

"This is your idea of an exfiltration plan after we're done here? An ancient airplane that may not fly? I'd like to survive this mission."

In answer, he leaned in and kissed her lightly. Apparently he wanted to survive it as well. How was she supposed to argue with how his lightest touch could make her feel?

CHAPTER SEVEN

*K*atrina awaited her moment. She was slouched in the front seat of the Yak-18. It smelled of old pilot sweat, gasoline, and sausages. At the moment she was not appreciating her heightened awareness of her sense of smell since going deaf.

Tomas—presently in the pilot's seat behind her—had inspected and prepped the plane, encouraged at finding the gas tanks full. Then they'd nudged the tail around until she had a perfect shot through the partially open canopy. There would be no sign of where the shot had come from. No one would look in the middle of the airfield. And if someone did, Tomas was confident he could get the plane moving quickly.

The meeting happened as planned. At noon, a brand-new Kamov Ka-62 Executive transport helicopter flew in and landed exactly where expected. It was met within minutes by two cars that had swept in through the front gate.

Tomas knew that if he needed her attention, he could thump a fist on the side of the airframe from his position in the rear pilot's seat well behind her. But for now, her attention was narrowing. It was Tomas' job to make sure that she stayed safe. It was her job to erase the man who had set a trap for her and betrayed his prime minister.

She couldn't kill the Moldovan general outright, or they'd know there was a sniper on the field, but she had a plan.

First to emerge were a half-dozen guards from either side. Then the two generals climbed out of their respective craft at the same moment and approached each other. A Transnistrian official, also resplendent in his uniform, accompanied the Moldovan. It was too perfect.

The guards formed a wide circle facing outwards, thankfully none quite facing their aircraft—even with the flash suppressor, her shot would not be invisible.

The windsock was rippling hard, ten mile-an-hour crosswind, gusting to twenty. Thankfully, she had fired a few thousand rounds of the 5.45mm ammunition at the Fort Bragg firing range to familiarize herself with its flight characteristics—the wind was going to drag this round a long way sideways in three hundred meters. It would make her shot look as if it was coming from well to the west of their current position if someone noticed the angle of attack.

The two generals approached one another, with the Moldovan facing her but not yet blocked by the Russian.

Three shots. If she was shooting as a Delta, she'd use four, but the Russians fought differently.

When they were two steps apart, she fired a single round into the Moldovan general's heart. Delta would have placed two there.

On her next heartbeat—in his face. It caught him before he was over the surprise of the first shot.

For the last shot, she picked a Russian guard standing behind the Russian general and put a round through the meat of his thigh.

At his scream, the Russian general yanked out his sidearm as he spun. He then shot the first Transnistrian guard he spotted. In moments, all of the Transnitrian locals were gunned down—including the high-ranking official.

Someone must have forewarned the police—at least enough so as to make them station a team nearby. They swarmed out of the office building and had the Russian general, his troops, and the helicopter pilot under arrest within moments.

Katrina eased her weapon back in through the plane's canopy and waited, but no one so much as looked in their direction. Who would attack from the middle of their own airfield when the perpetrator was so obviously caught red-handed?

The Russians were going to have very poor relations with Transnistria for some time to come.

And Delta? They'd never been here at all.

CHAPTER EIGHT

"Can't we just walk out?" Katrina waved past the canopy at the deserted airfield. Darkness had come and shrouded the only signs of what had happened today: bloodstains on the sun-bleached pavement and an abandoned Russian helicopter.

It was awkward, twisting in her seat to see Tomas' lips with her NVGs. He said something that she couldn't follow.

"What?"

Trust me, accompanied by one of his smiles. She'd learned about them. They were full of promises—ones that she hoped, no, that she *knew* he would keep. It made him impossible to argue with. She just wished that she could imagine his voice as anything other than harsh and cold, but it was all she'd ever heard from him.

She turned back in her seat and tightened the cross-shoulder harness.

"Why walk when you can fly?" She finally worked out that was what he'd said.

She'd had the mandatory basic training and could survive as pilot in a half-dozen different aircraft—*survive.* Her only hope was that his skills were far more practiced than her own. Thankfully, the Yah-18 was a trainer: pilot in the rear, student in the front. It meant she didn't have to touch anything.

No one bothered them as the engine caught and spun to life on the darkened airfield. It shook the plane, momentarily filling the cabin with the acrid bite of exhaust fumes but, at least to her, it was painfully silent.

Tomas taxied them to the blacked-out runway. Then, unleashing a mighty vibration that she assumed was accompanied by a massive roar, the single engine awoke and pulled them down the abandoned runway. The plane jounced and wobbled, but they were aloft before it could shatter her spine.

Once in the air, Tomas turned them south with a confidence she knew she lacked. Safe in his care. Safe in his arms.

The irony wasn't lost on her for a moment. Tomas' very careful attempts to not treat her differently, to not show her his feelings, had only served to enhance them.

She now understood his prior silences. And those in turn had made her more aware of him. It had made her notice what a standout soldier he was. And their distance had probably driven him even harder to excel, which had only made her notice him all the more.

Yet she'd already been deaf the first time he demonstrated his feelings. Even if the damage was permanent, there was no questioning the truth of them—not of the man who had thrown himself over her so that the mortar might somehow kill him but spare her, and not of the man who now flew the old Yak from close behind her.

A half hour later, they slid out of the sky and landed on a long sandy beach. The plane jolted, but not too badly. As always, Tomas knew exactly what he was doing.

They sat together on the sandy shore of a Romanian park along the Black Sea. Small waves broke on the sand in clean white lines as they watched the night together. Tomas had radioed for a helicopter from an American helicopter carrier that was cruising offshore. It would pick them up soon—and drag the old plane out to sink in the depths of the Black Sea erasing the last evidence of anyone interfering at Tiraspol. Now it would just be a plane gone missing on a much more newsworthy day.

They sat close, hip to hip on the sand.

"What if my hearing doesn't come back?" Their NVGs were pushed back on their helmets, so she might as well have been talking to herself. She wouldn't be able to read any reply on his lips.

But she wasn't alone. He pulled her tight against his side and kissed her on the temple.

Not alone.

She'd always been alone. The family's black sheep, the first one *ever* to enter military service. One of the first women to qualify for front-line combat. Again one of the first into Delta Force. Delta had accepted her, even welcomed her, but she'd been the only woman on her team. It was a lonely existence.

Tomas continued to hold her close. Rather than going for the kiss, that she would have gladly welcomed, he somehow knew she needed something else even more. Instead, he just held her.

The fear began to slide away.

The fear of the mission—always there during but already fading fast, as usual.

The fear of not being good enough to be a woman in Delta. Even if it was her final mission today, she'd proven that she belonged.

The unrealized terror that she'd always be an outsider, always alone. All she had to do was breathe in the warm, earthy, and slightly sweet smell of Tomas Gallagher that reminded her of lying in a vineyard beneath the ripening grapes.

One fear remained. A fear worse than never hearing again. A fear that—

Then she became aware of something. It was so foreign that

she couldn't make sense of it for a moment. It had been going on for a while.

"Hey!"

She could feel Tomas twist to look at where she lay tucked inside the curve of his arm.

"I can hear the waves on the sand." Whatever her body had done to protect her during the explosion had released its hold on her hearing.

"Really?" Now she would forever know what his voice could sound like—soft, kind, and filled with wonder.

"Really." And then her last fear slid into the night. The fear that she'd never get to hear Tomas Gallagher say, "I love you."

IF YOU ENJOYED THIS, YOU MIGHT ALSO ENJOY:

M. L. BUCHMAN

3-time Booklist Top 10 Romance Author of the Year

Since the First Day

a Night Stalkers 5E romance story

SINCE THE FIRST DAY

*C*o-pilot **Danny Corvo** *accepts his role as straight man on the jovial crew aboard the Night Stalkers' helicopter* Calamity Jane II. *Ignoring his attraction to the wildly vivacious* **Crew Chief Carmen Parker** *proves to be much more difficult.*

Racing through the tail end of a hurricane off the Panamanian coast —what a crazy time to declare his feelings.

But this stormy night must be the one to tell her how he's felt Since the First Day.

INTRODUCTION

This is another story with a funny origin.

There I was, happily writing away on the third novel in my Delta Force romance series, Wild Justice. *One of the things that I love including in my stories is cool tech, and to launch and recover high-speed Special Operations Zodiac boats out the back of the big Chinook helicopters is seriously* cool.

But, even though it fit the story well, I had used it in the first Night Stalkers 5E romance, Target of the Heart. *So, I knew I had to do something more. I decided to play with the situation: Delta Force, all geared up for battle, and sitting in their rubber boat—while it's parked in the back of a helicopter flying through a storm.*

And who better to fly through the storm than some characters I hadn't checked in on in far too long. My last flight with the crew of the Calamity Jane had been in By Break of Day *in early 2016. I knew that with Kara's and Justin's relationship a fact, something else was bound to be going on with this fun crew.*

So, I made them my transport team for the Delta Force team.

I didn't give any real thought to the musically-minded crew's song selection while writing the novel. I just kept it peculiar as a running joke against the background of the Delta Force planning mission.

Then I thought...why were they singing those songs?

And there was my story!

CHAPTER ONE

*P*resent Day, June 13, 2300 Hours (11 p.m. Panama
Local Time)

"It was a dark and stormy night!" Danny Corvo declared over
the intercom as he fought the big helo's controls.

"Ho-ly crap!" Carmen's words were jarred out of her by the
Calamity Jane II slamming into another squall line as if it was a
solid wall. "Did Danny just make a jo-ke?"

He should have kept his mouth shut and just flown the damn
helicopter.

The massive Chinook twin-rotor helicopter was getting
battered by the tail end of a tropical storm they were using for
cover on this training mission. The last thing to do under those
conditions was to encourage Carmen.

"He did?" "What did I miss?" The other two gunners, probably
woken up by Carmen's initial shout, chimed in like it was some
special event they didn't want to miss. The Night Stalkers of the
160th Special Operations Aviation Regiment—SOAR—could sleep
through almost anything. Except one of Carmen's cheery blasts.

"Do another one, Danny. Do another one," Carmen pleaded like

241

a toddler rather than being a definitely grown up, way hot redhead.

Captain Justin Roberts just grinned over at him from the pilot's seat. *You've stepped in it now,* written clear across what little Danny could see of his face. From the nose up, his features, like Danny's, were covered by his visor and helmet. It was an odd habit that made them turn to each other for a joke, but not during anything to do with flying. It wasn't as if they could see much. Most of his vision was blocked by the tactical view projected on the inside of his visor. The captain was a pale version of himself set beyond the display. He would have been invisible if they were over land, but at the moment they were beating ass toward an unsuspecting ship at sea with a team of Delta Force in the back. They had a Zodiac boat and were doing some exercise about taking down a cruise ship. Even storm-whipped, the sea didn't paint much on the tactical display.

Danny refocused on the inside of his visor. The weather was painted in large swaths of "don't go here" lying exactly in their path. Of course they'd just flown through a whole section just like it over the last half hour, so that didn't worry him. The horizon was a pale line across the center of his view with altitude, airspeed, and other critical readouts down the left. Dead ahead lay four symbols for ships: cargo and container carriers whose jobs were not being fun at the moment with the thirty-foot seas. And over the horizon, a small red rectangle pinpointing their target—a disabled luxury cruise liner, empty and under tow. Justin's wife Kara Moretti was back aboard the USS *Peleliu* and had the ship pinpointed for observation with her Gray Eagle drone quietly circling far above.

At least the Delta Force team was on their own circuit, so they'd still be able to sleep. It wasn't like Delta ever spoke to anyone else—ever—anyway. And not even to each other much that he'd seen.

"Please, please, please," Carmen wasn't going to let him go.

"Carmen. Begging. I like it," he took another run at being brave.

A fist thumped down on his shoulder which told him Carmen had shifted forward to the observer seat close behind the side-by-side pilots' seats. She was a very physical gal—which sent his thoughts in entirely the wrong direction. He supposed he was lucky, she'd probably have done it much harder if she'd known where his thoughts went so often.

"Picking on your pilot-in-command. Very dangerous, Carmen. *Picking* on the *PIC*," he emphasized the play on words, too late realizing that was probably too obvious.

"Why dangerous, Danny? It's just you."

"Maybe you're in the mood for a swim." Mission profile said stay low, the storm said stay high, he was a Night Stalker so he'd climbed a hundred feet above the waves, rather than the five thousand any rational Army pilot would have. The Night Stalkers flew at the edge of what he liked to call rational insanity. He'd become very comfortable with that over his five years with the 160th.

"Swim with the dashing Danny Corvo? Be sti-ill my heart." A microburst bounced them up fifty feet before he could compensate. Maybe staying a *little* farther from the waves would be a good idea. He took it as a sign from Mother Nature and stayed where she'd just bounced them to. They'd now be visible from farther away, not that radar would pick them out in this crap. The rain lashed so hard against the windshield and hull at their hundred-and-fifty-mile-an-hour speed, plus an obnoxious amount of wind velocity, that he could hear it despite his helmet. It was louder than the beastly big rotors of his Chinook.

"Swimming with you? That *totally* works for me."

A couple of the guys hooted encouragement. It was rare for anyone to banter with Carmen past the first round or two. Her wit was faster than an RPG and not much less dangerous.

He glanced at the engine readouts, even though that was Justin's job at the moment, with Carmen as a backup. The temperatures looked good, so the rain wasn't enough to drown the twin, five-thousand horsepower Lycoming engines. He turned his attention back to keeping them in the air.

And to picturing Carmen in a dark red bikini that matched her hair. Her fair skin and blue-green eyes the color of the tropical sea. Which at the moment was pitch black because it was almost midnight in a bitch of a storm a hundred-and-sixty miles off Panama. Almost midnight. It was hard to not smile even if it didn't really mean anything, except to him. He checked the dash clock, 2304 and counting.

"No, none of you mugs will *ever* see me in a bikini, so just stop thinking about that."

"Which plants the image firmly in my brain," Danny heaved on the thrust control along the left side of his seat to compensate for a sudden downdraft, but managed to stabilize at eighty feet above the waves before climbing back up.

"Ho-ly crap!" There was no air pocket to jar her words this time, so she did it herself. Damn but she was funny. "You guys heard that? You!" She poked him in the arm. "What did you do with our quiet and shy Danny Corvo?"

"I put him out to pasture where he belongs."

"Whoa!" "You were right, Carm." Vinnie and Raymond chimed in from the back.

"This *is* a passel of strange, ain't it," the captain agreed, his Texan accent far thicker than normal.

Danny liked flying with Justin Roberts. He was always cheery— even when everything was going to hell. Justin also gave him plenty of pilot-in-command time. He'd flown with a lot of commanders who just wanted you to sit your ass in the seat and leave them alone. However, egging Carmen on wasn't going to help anyth—

"Crazy weird," Carmen agreed. "It *sounds* like Danny. And I can see his cute little chin."

Just how every Army Special Operations guy wanted to be described by a hot soldier woman.

"Where oh where has our Danny gone?" The captain broke into song as he was apt to do at the drop of his cowboy hat.

Danny did his best to ignore it as they mangled the verse. At least until Carmen joined in with that sweet alto of hers for the refrain, *"Aliens done took him away."*

Images of sticklike green men bearing rectal probes—and a particularly hard slam by the storm—definitely knocked the bikini-clad redhead out of his thoughts. Too bad. If his imagination was worth shit, she'd be damn cute in one.

CHAPTER TWO

resent Day, June 13, 2310 Hours (Panama Local Time)

Danny had never joined in the singing aboard the *Calamity Jane II.* Carmen had teased him about that any number of times, to no avail. At least he'd stopped complaining about their choices of music, mostly.

He was such a quiet guy that he was hard to read. Even his laughs were quiet and his looks thoughtful. Though she could never tell quite what was going on behind those steady eyes.

"Why are you always such a serious guy?" The question was out before she could stop herself.

"Am I? I thought I was a happy-go-lucky leprechaun. Damn, and I was so close to finding me a pot of gold."

"Thought you said you were Portuguese." He looked it with those deep brown eyes, black hair, and sun-dark skin. He was also too handsome for words.

"That was the other Danny Corvo."

The others laughed, but Carmen was actually a little worried and found it hard to join in. This *wasn't* the Danny that she knew.

He wasn't the kind of guy to crack under the stress of a flight no matter how horrid—to emphasize the point, her teeth clacked together sharply as the seat's shocks bottomed out hard in the next air pocket. But she couldn't imagine what was up with him.

She spent a few moments on the HUMS interface—as she'd been doing every five minutes or less of their ride through the storm. The helo's Health and Usage Monitoring Systems was reporting no problems, though she often *heard* problems before HUMS reported them. After nine years in Chinooks, the last two as a Night Stalker crew chief, the aircraft was in her blood. And no matter what the pilots thought, this was *her* bird. She was responsible for every nut, bolt, and signoff. The pilots just climbed aboard on occasion to do some flying.

She rested her hand against the inside of the hull and could feel it vibrating with the controlled violence of the twin Lycoming turbines spinning at fifteen thousand RPM and the uncontrolled violence of the storm. She could also feel every little shift in attitude and speed. It was unreal how fast Danny compensated for everything the storm could throw at him. Maybe he *was* some alternate version of himself.

For a while she simply rode along, enjoying the connection between them. The motion of the helo tied to the constant tiny corrections Danny made on the cyclic and thrust control. She couldn't see his feet on the rudder pedals in the dim light, but she could imagine the expert dance he used to keep fifteen tons of helicopter and crew headed toward their destination.

But she couldn't explain the sudden surfacing of a sense of humor. She liked knowing exactly what was going on with *all* of her equipment, and having a copilot suddenly develop a sense of humor was definitely throwing her.

Not that Danny was *hers.* He was actually the only one on the crew who hadn't at least made a pass at her. Of course Justin's had been after he was happily married to the lethal Kara Moretti, so it had been pure tease that she'd happily returned in kind.

But for her there'd always been something special about Danny.

She remembered her first day as a Night Stalker...which had been a night much like this one.

CHAPTER THREE

Two Years Ago, June 14, 2320 Hours (Alabama Local Time)
The downgraded hurricane had been beating the shit out of southern Alabama as a tropical storm when she'd gotten off the plane at Fort Rucker. It was a real "sicker" of a flight, everyone who wasn't a seasoned flier had been puking their guts out for the entire second half. Even some of the old hands lost it just from listening to all the others.

Carmen would admit that she'd regretted the gut bomb bacon-cheeseburger she'd had just before flight, but refused to be humiliated by seeing it again quite so soon.

She was a Night Stalker crew chief—at long last Fully Mission Qualified. And FMQ Night Stalkers didn't lose their shit because of a little lumpy air. Nonetheless glad to be on the ground, she shouldered her duffle, yanked on her helmet against the last of the six new inches of rain Alabama had gotten that day, and stepped off the flight squarely into a seriously handsome man's chest.

She flattened him right onto his ass.

"Boy, you sure are a pushover," she managed to keep her feet, barely. The rest of the flight began unloading to either side of them as the man she'd plowed into continued to lay in a puddle on the tarmac looking up at her. The storm cracked with lightning, revealing his bewildered expression, as fast-following thunder said the latest weather wasn't done with them yet.

"Sergeant Carmen Parker?"

She nodded and offered a hand, not that she was all that steady yet from the rough flight, but it seemed the least she could do.

He shook his head, either trying to clear it or to say no.

But before she could withdraw her hand, he'd taken it and let her help him to his feet.

"Thanks."

"This is your definition of personal space?" The man stood just inches away, their clasped hands the only thing keeping them apart. So close that it was hard to tell, even in the light spilling out of a nearby hangar, if he was really as handsome as her first impression.

"Not really," he took a step back, then another. He was mighty slow about letting go of her hand though, which was kind of sweet. No complaints from her: muscled, Latino, five-ten to her five-six, and one of those guys who was surprisingly handsome but probably didn't realize it. His easy smile lit his face without doing anything more than saying, "Hi!" No "Hey, baby!" or "Nice to meet you, hot stuff!"

She'd never minded guys flirting with her—especially because she could kick the ass of anyone who overstepped the bounds. But Danny was like the perfect straight man for her teasing. Maybe even too straight because it didn't seem to phase him in the slightest.

"I'm Danny Corvo, the copilot on your new assignment." Then he shook the hand he'd still been holding and let go. One more step back and "proper personal space" was reestablished.

"Lead on and I will follow," she put a lot of sass into it just to test him.

"This way," he waved toward an electric golf cart of all things.

Truly a straight man, unless he was gay. No, she'd seen where his eyes had traveled, however briefly. Then he turned and she saw that he was soaked from butt to brain because of his dunk in the puddle. Yet he made no complaints, no tease. Not even a decent grumble. Weird.

CHAPTER FOUR

*P*resent Day, *June 13, 2330 Hours (Panama Local Time)*
Even after two years, Danny never quite understood what had hit him that day. The shock of Carmen striding down the flight's ramp like she owned Fort Rucker had been visceral. When she'd slammed into him it had become physical as well. He'd had no extra attention span to even try to recover—he'd simply toppled over.

He'd looked up at the vision of Woman standing over him. Serious curves under a black t-shirt and camo pants. The finer qualities of her figure only emphasized by the heavy duffle she wore backpack-style, pulling her shoulders back. Topped off by a Night Stalkers helmet painted with a flamenco dancer in a flirty red skirt on the side.

Carmen from the opera by Bizet.

It had unquestionably been the new crew member he'd come to fetch from the transport flight, but all he'd been able to do was lie in the puddle and stare as she sassed him.

Real smooth.

In two years, he also hadn't figured out what he should have done differently. You didn't just grab a woman like Carmen Parker, her inner strength showed as clearly as her figure from the first moment. In the way she walked, in the way she carried herself, in the way she held focus on what mattered to the exclusion of all else. If she had to walk out into a hail of gunfire to help an injured aboard, she did it without a cringe. If some meathead tried to grab her, she laid him out flat, then dusted her hands of him and went back to whatever she'd been doing. Nothing touched her when turned on that laser focus—which was pretty much all the time.

A particularly heavy squall line in the storm had him climbing up to five hundred feet before they hit it. Sure enough, the solid wall of water that this tropical storm called "rain" took ten percent out of his engines—water just didn't burn very well no matter how much Jet-A fuel you let loose with the throttle.

He kept an eye on the engines as he came out the other side. The Lycomings only took a few seconds to clear their throats and climb back to full power. Damn but he loved this bird. Almost as much as he loved—

Useless thought. Carmen Parker wasn't for the likes of him.

But he couldn't think of anything other than her strength. And her boundless joy and humor—she was funny enough for any five other people combined. That was one of the main reasons he kept his mouth shut. Anything he came up with was going to sound lame next to the cool shit Carmen could deliver on no notice.

Once the engine temperatures had restabilized at fifteen-hundred degrees, he descended back onto profile. Their target ship was well out of the storm now, shifting into the calmer waters close under Panama's mountainous coastline, but he angled in a little deeper into the storm to get them as close as possible while under its cover. Night Stalkers method: push every training opportunity to the limit and maybe, just maybe, you'll have the chance to survive the real thing.

Danny remembered the day things had changed between them. It had nothing to do with mud puddles that had almost earned him a "Danny the Duck" nickname or his soaking flightsuit.

At least not one soaked with water.

CHAPTER FIVE

One year ago, June 13, 2340 Hours (Yemen Local Time)
        Justin was flying right-seat as usual. But a new copilot flew in Danny's seat—out for an indoctrination run. He was FMQ in the tiny MH-6M Little Bird helicopters. A Little Bird had four seats, but you didn't want to be one of the folks in the back seat, compared to the fifty-plus troops that his Chinook could carry in addition to her five crew. Weighing in at less than a ton apiece, a Chinook could lift fifteen Little Birds without breaking a sweat. But the company commander wanted every one of their pilots to at least have a feel for the capabilities of each airframe type that SOAR flew. And what Pete Napier ordered, nobody messed with.

So, while the copilot had stretched his flight legs over the nighttime Gulf of Aden, Danny had been relegated to the back to see what the crew chiefs did for a living.

"We do all kinds of cool shit back here," Carmen had set them to Intercom Channel 4 so that they wouldn't bother anyone else as she gave him the tour.

"Such as?"

She pointed to Vinnie and Raymond sacked out on the hard steel deck.

"You sleep?"

"You guys up there are just giving us a rocking cradle ride—"

The trainee was slamming the Chinook through a turn worthy of an F-35 Lightning II fighter jet, forcing both of them to hang on so that they didn't tumble about the cargo bay like pinballs.

"No hostiles around," Carmen didn't even break her speech as the helo slid to a halt in mid-air and did a full spin—not an easy trick in a Chinook, which he flubbed the first couple times. "No gunnery practice to do. We might as well grab some shuteye back here. I can run this whole sweet bird by myself."

"Except for flying it," Danny tried to carve out some territory for his role.

"Pilots! Feh!" Carmen wiggled her fingers at him. Then she started guiding him through an in-flight systems check. Every five minutes this, every ten that, and a full tour of the bird's interior along with a dozen systems checks every half hour. She waved the checklists at him, though it was clear she didn't need them. They were at least as long as the pilot's set. "Then when we're on the ground..." she'd pulled out an even bigger set of checklists.

Carmen had always humbled him. Now he was discovering that she was more daunting than he'd thought. If he could just somehow—

"Alert Status One! Alert Status One!" slammed in over the primary intercom channel. Vinnie and Raymond bolted to their feet as if electroshocked.

"You!" Carmen had jabbed a finger against his arm. "You stay attached to my hip or you'll get run over."

"I should—" he pointed forward, but knew he wasn't needed. All through Carmen's tour he'd been aware of the rapidly growing competence of the new pilot as Justin ran him through the paces. A Chinook was no Black Hawk and trading positions in mid-flight was actually possible. But Justin didn't call him forward and he supposed he agreed. Nothing like being at the helm during action to really learn what it took. And Justin Roberts could handle almost anything solo if he had to.

Their little training sortie became a crash-priority evac for a mixed team of the 75th Rangers and Delta. By the time they hit the Yemeni shoreline, a heavily-armed DAP Black Hawk and a Combat Search and Rescue Hawk had joined them as well.

Carmen and Vinnie each shot a few test rounds out of their side-facing miniguns then began checking their personal weapons. He did the same. Raymond went to the rear of the cargo bay and began rigging his ramp gun, even though the ramp was still closed tightly, shutting out the night.

They came in on the terrorist camp low and fast.

Danny presently had the crews' tactical feed on his visor rather than his normal pilot's version. Far more information about the engines and systems performance—next to nothing about the terrain except in the broadest strokes. The threat monitors were soon piecing together the situation. Small arms fire raking along the ground in a vast, back-and-forth interplay of flying death.

The DAP Hawk climbed above the camp and answered back hard.

It was so disorienting when their missile slammed down on one of the compounds—he hadn't known it was coming like he normally would have.

The DAP Hawk gun platform was raining down hell. The CSAR bird was hanging back in case it was needed, and their Chinook was head-on into the fray. On the ground, one Black Hawk was burning fiercely and another was being protected by more soldiers than the one bird could carry out. No...soldiers and several rescued hostages.

Justin—Danny could feel the familiar flight control of the captain taking control—eased the *Calamity Jane II* toward the men on the ground surrounding the beleaguered Black Hawk.

More and more of the fire was directed upward at the DAP

Hawk dancing and spinning overhead, which eased the burden here on the ground. Justin got them landed close beside the waiting troops.

The instant the ramp was down, troops stormed aboard. Not all of them were soldiers. Three hostages, two clearly American and the third sounding Japanese, looked battered, confused, and disbelieving at their sudden rescue. There were no hostiles as prisoners. Some operations just didn't call for that.

Several soldiers came aboard with a rifle in one hand and an arm over a buddy's shoulders. Most of those hit the relative safety of the cargo bay and collapsed.

Carmen's station was on the side away from the action—whereas Vinnie's side gun was unleashing a near constant roar of four thousand rounds a minute—so the two of them grabbed med kits and began helping the worst of the wounded.

The hull rattled with small arms fire. Sometimes a double-smack as a bullet penetrated one side and splatted against the other. Soldiers were hitting the deck as the windows were shot out.

He'd strapped off two legs with tight bandages and was pressing down on a shoulder wound as they lifted. Less than twenty feet in the air, the helo...flinched. Forty thousand pounds of helo wasn't supposed to flinch.

Critical system failure or—

"Corvo!" Justin's voice called him forward. But if he let go on this guy's wound, he'd bleed out before anyone else could get to him.

"You!" Danny shouted a nearby soldier. "Pressure! Here!"

The man was injured himself. "Can't you get the medic?"

Danny tapped the downed man's armband—a red cross bathed in blood. "He *is* your medic."

The guy looked positively green, but placed his hands onto the wounded medic's shoulder.

"If you're gonna be sick, turn to the side so that you aren't sick on him." Then Danny scrambled forward over the bodies of both the wounded and exhausted. The helo was wavering, making him stagger like a drunk on his way forward.

There was no question about what the problem was when he got to the front. The forward windscreen was shattered and the trainee copilot hung limply in his harness.

"Carmen!" Danny shouted out and hoped they still had their private intercom set up.

"Can't see shit!" Justin complained.

Danny saw why. There was blood trickling down his face and it had covered both his eyes. It wasn't gushing, but it wasn't good. The captain couldn't wipe it away because he needed both hands on the controls.

In moments Carmen was at his shoulder.

He gave the blinded Justin moment-by-moment directions on the flight controls while Carmen helped him lever the trainee out of the copilot's seat. He tried not to be too squeamish as he slid in to sit in another man's blood. Finally buckled into the seat's harness, he shouted out, "I have control."

Justin slumped down—having kept them aloft and steady on sheer nerve—and cursed. "Hell of a way to run a rodeo."

Danny flipped to the pilot's view and the full tactical hell of the situation slammed in. Much of the camp was burning. Men were down everywhere, though he didn't see any American bodies—no telltale infrared tabs that would have glowed like searchlights in his night-vision display.

Three soldiers ran from the second Black Hawk—now also burning brightly—toward the back of the Chinook. Danny eased the tail back down. One stumbled and fell—and didn't get up.

From the copilot's raised seat, he spotted the problem. Someone had picked up an AK-47 from a fallen Yemeni and shot the Delta Force operator at least a dozen times from behind, mostly in the leg.

Danny snapped the position lock on the thrust control to free up his left hand. Yanking out his Glock sidearm, he shot twice. Once to blow out his side window, and once to shoot the Yemeni with the AK-47 in the heart.

The shooter collapsed.

Danny slapped the sidearm back in his holster and began easing back down for the wounded Delta.

"CSAR 1. We've got him," a woman's voice. Someone jumped out of the medevac bird and rushed over to the fallen soldier crawling along and dragging one leg.

"Roger. *Calamity Jane II* aloft."

He pulled up and back to clear the CSAR bird and the two grounded and burning Black Hawks. Then got them the hell out of Dodge as soon as the CSAR bird was aloft.

As he was pulling away, he finally got perspective on the shooter he'd just downed and the man he'd taken the AK-47 from in the first place. The shooter was half the size of the dead man.

"I just shot a kid." Probably dropped him on his dad's body.

Carmen, who'd been treating Justin now collapsed in his seat, spun to face him.

He remembered the feel of her comforting hand on his shoulder for a long time after she'd turned back to bandaging the captain.

No one else had heard. He also left that part out of the after-action debriefing.

CHAPTER SIX

Present Day, June 13, 2350 Hours (Panama Local Time)

Carmen did a full inspection and systems check as Danny continued to fight them through the storm. A couple of the Deltas were awake. It was a strange team. Three women, four men. She'd never seen a female Delta before and here was a whole clump of them. A gaggle of geese. A flock of ewes. An incoming disaster of Deltas? What would it be like to be a woman who kicked butt at a Delta level? She'd miss her Chinook too much, but the three women looked beyond cool.

One of the guy Deltas called her over.

"Oh. My. God!" Carmen slapped a hand to her chest and put her wrist to her forehead. "I'm gonna faint. It only took four hours for one of the silent warriors to acknowledge that they weren't the only people on this flight." Then she collapsed onto one of the Zodiac's pontoons and fell upside down into the bottom of the boat to sprawl at his feet.

Several of the Deltas startled awake, inspected her strangely for a moment, then went back to sleep.

"Got a question for you, once you're done playing the lead role from a Bizet opera."

"What are you talking about?" She continued laying upside down, but raised her head to inspect him. He was handsome, but she was feeling oddly self-conscious about teasing him, which wasn't like her. She teased everybody—except Danny since that night he'd shot the kid.

"The opera *Carmen.* The dazzling man killer."

"There's an opera named after me?" As if she didn't have Carmen the gypsy dancer emblazoned on the side of her helmet. "How cool is that? Dazzling man killer—perfect fit. Are you my next victim? This should be fun."

The guy looked at his watch, typical Delta.

She flipped around until she was upright once again.

"How would you take down a cruise ship?"

Delta operators had no sense of humor.

"Couple-a Hellfire missiles at the waterline?"

The discussion went on for a few minutes, but her thoughts were on why Danny was acting so strangely. She left the Deltas sitting in their rubber boat in the cargo bay talking about it and drifted back forward.

She ended up close behind the two pilots' seats. She didn't usually ride in the observer's chair, but the memory of the two storms—the present one and the one in which she'd met Danny—had drawn her back to the front.

Her last two years aboard the *Calamity Jane II* stood out so much more clearly than the five prior years in the regular Army or the two years of additional training to become a Night Stalker.

No, that wasn't all of it. Each moment *with Danny* stood out. The good and the bad. The smooth perfection of how he'd flown them out of that battle, despite a windshield so star-cracked that he could only fly by peaking out of the bullet holes marking where unfriendly fire had wounded the captain and killed the last person in that seat, despite the shot-up hydraulics that had forced him to wrestle the massive helo by brute force, all while having just shot a kid. The quiet ease with which he sat back at a hangar barbeque: beer in his hand, smile on his face, just watching the goings on, watching her...

Watching *her.*

With the same look as the moment she'd plowed him ass over teakettle into a mud puddle. A look she'd never forgotten, but couldn't understand. Unless...

Her throat was suddenly dry.

She leaned forward and rested a hand on his shoulder.

He flipped to Intercom Channel 4. One, she finally realized, that they'd shared often for privacy. Privacy? They were just on the same crew together, why did they need a private channel? Yet they had one. Sometimes back-enders (her and the other two crew chiefs) shared Channel 2 so as not to disturb the pilots, but usually the whole team stayed on Channel 1. Danny was the only one she had a "private" channel with.

He waited for her in silence as he held tight control of the bucking bronc that was the Chinook in the storm.

"Danny?"

"Carmen," his voice was "normal" Danny. Not substitute Danny Corvo. No joke or humor. Once again her straight man was there.

"Why..." she couldn't quite bring herself to confront her question directly. "...why don't you ever sing?"

He chuckled with the warmth of a caress, accepting the evasion. "Tone deaf. I've been told that I sing like a choking hyena."

"You can't be that bad."

"Sadly, sometime when we're alone, I can prove it. Besides, if I don't sing it lets me hear you better."

And now they were back to the inexplicable attack of nerves she was having. She checked the HUMS again, but the helo's health was just fine despite the thrashing of the wind and rain. It was hers that was in doubt.

"You're still wondering what I did with the real Danny Corvo?"

"Well..." Carmen took a deep breath and plunged in. "You've always been the straight man. Mr. AJ Squared Away."

"That's sailor talk. What would that be in Army-speak? Mr. Shiny Shithook pilot?" A shithook was slang for an Army Chinook helicopter.

"See! That! That isn't the Danny I know."

"But it is," he whispered as she watched him slew their Chinook around a particularly dense cloud that blanketed a whole section of the radar screen. It was so strange to be having this conversation while he was busy and Captain Roberts was sitting about a foot away, oblivious to everything.

"How? The Danny Corvo I know doesn't joke or tease or—"

"Okay. No tease. There's this beach I know, just down from my grandfather's house, called Praia da Marinha, in southern Portugal on the Atlantic. Just a few hundred kilometers from where the opera about you is set. Warm. Soft sand with tall cliffs, sea arches, caves. It is one of the most beautiful places I've ever been. I would take you there. Maybe you'd wear a red bikini. Same color as your beautiful hair."

"Already said, no bikini." It was lame, but it was the best defense she had against such a beautiful vision.

"How about a flamenco dancer's dress?"

She sat back and glared at the side of his helmet. That didn't sound like Danny either—no matter how much she liked the sound of it. Her and Danny off somewhere sunny. They'd—

Her and Danny?

Her personal HUMS system should be flashing red lights and alert sirens.

"Why didn't you ever say any of this before?" She wanted to grab and shake him. Would have if he wasn't flying.

"Tired of waiting."

"For me?"

"No, me. To be brave."

She wasn't sure if she'd ever met a braver man. Heavy gunfire, his captain wounded, rattled because he'd shot an underage terrorist, and *then* started to re-land his helo to retrieve the wounded Delta. "What in the world do you have trouble being brave about?"

"Not yet."

"What do you mean, not yet?"

"Two more minutes."

She glanced at the mission clock on the helo's main console. 2358.

Too stubborn and maybe too unnerved to ask why, she folded her arms and waited in silence.

She could feel Danny smiling as he flew. They reached the edge of the storm closest to the cruise ship where the Delta operators would soon be simulating an attack. He banked hard, out of the interminable pounding of the storm and into clear air. The wind calmed and even the sky above began clearing as they raced away from the storm. He slid back down toward the sea.

They were the two longest minutes of her life.

It finally flipped to four zeros.

"A new day. Now give."

"Not just any day."

"Danny..." she knew she was grinding her teeth.

"June Fourteenth." He waited.

She didn't get it.

"Two years ago today..."

The date was ringing a bell. It was...the day she'd joined the crew of *Calamity Jane II*. It was the second anniversary of... "Oh shit!"

"Yep! Two years ago you bowled me over and I've never recovered."

"Two years," she could barely breathe.

"It's our second collision-anniversary."

"What was the first?" And then she knew and was sorry she'd asked.

"The kid."

She'd made a point of tracking Danny down afterward at the carrier. He'd been sitting on an old tire in a back corner of the hangar deck, just staring out at the dark sea. She didn't remember what they'd talked about, not much of anything. But they'd sat for hours and she remembered his brief hug and his whispered "Thanks" when the sun rose over the Gulf of Aden.

Again his silent patience while she processed things. He understood her. Everyone else she'd been able to brush off with a joke or a flirt.

Not Danny.

He'd stuck by her. Encouraged her. Made sure she knew she was welcome from that first day. In the Night Stalkers you didn't need someone to push you to excel, everyone did that. Everyone set their standards so high that you just wanted to strive to keep up with them. She was no different. Nor was Danny.

One of the Delta couples came up with a change in the deployment for the exercise. They ran it by her and the two pilots. They'd decided to add a maneuver to the simulated attack.

After she told them it was technically possible—though she kept to herself that it was bat-shit crazy, making it perfect for Delta—they cleared the last of the details with Danny before returning to the cargo bay.

Danny had been her quiet place. Somehow he let her know that she was okay even when she was too tired to speak or too sick of the unending supply of terrorist nut jobs.

He was...the man she didn't know how to live without. When she'd hauled the trainee pilot's body out of the copilot seat, she'd only been able to be thankful that he'd been sitting there rather than Danny. It was a guilty thought, but it ran deep. She would step in front of the bullet herself if it made sure he was still in the world afterward.

"Fifteen minutes to target," Danny announced on the PA.

No response. She turned, and could see that the Delta operators were completing their final prep. Silent warriors indeed.

Danny had stayed silent about his attraction to her. So carefully silent that she'd assumed he wasn't attracted at all, making her keep her own mouth shut about how much she'd been attracted to him. Shut enough that she'd almost buried the feeling. Just kept on being Carmen—wild, funny, in your face.

But now she knew, now she understood that smile on Danny's face. He always laughed with her jokes, but he also saw the quiet person inside her too. It wasn't Carmen the flashy gypsy dancer he was attracted to. It was Carmen Parker, lead crew chief of the Night Stalkers' Chinook *Calamity Jane II.*

"Danny?"

"Carmen," he said it exactly the way he had before.

"You really feel that way?" Was if even possible she could be so lucky?

He twisted all the way around to look at her for just a brief moment. "Really."

She wished she could see his eyes behind the visor, but she could see his smile, and that was enough. With Danny Corvo that was everything and it always would be.

He turned back to flying and she hustled back to make sure the Delta team was ready for the drop. She lowered the rear ramp and peeked out into the night.

The sea was calm, twenty minutes and sixty miles from the storm's closest approach.

The sky was clear.

All the flying ahead wouldn't be smooth. There'd be more gut wrenchers, but she knew, she just *knew* that they'd get through it all together.

Justin started humming a song over the intercom. Vinnie picked it up with his low baritone and she found herself joining in on the melody before she caught herself.

"What the hell?"

"Y'all amaze me," Justin Roberts spoke over the intercom, his Texas cranked up to full mud-thick. "Like y'all think that simply going up to little old Intercom 4 makes you private somehow. Rest of us tumbled to that trick about six months back. Let me just say, 'bout time, you two." And then he swung back into the music.

"Does this mean I'm going to have to buy a goddamn bikini?"

There was a mass chorus of, "Yes!" without breaking the rhythm.

"Then all you boys are buying goddamn thongs. Beach wedding."

There were laughs over the channel.

"Love you, gypsy dancer. Since the first day," Danny slipped in quietly between the words.

And he was right. "Since the first day," she echoed back.

Then, as she helped the Delta operators launch their boat out into the night, she joined in the chorus.

The hills (skies, Danny stuck in) are alive, with the sound of music.

"They were right you know," she whispered between the words. "You do sing like a choking hyena."

He only sang louder.

It took an entire chorus before she could stop laughing with joy and join back in.

IF YOU ENJOYED THIS, YOU MIGHT
ALSO ENJOY:

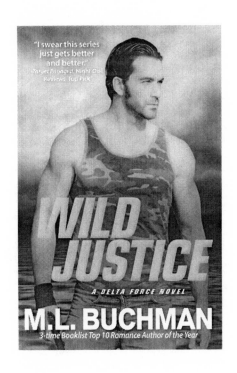

M.L. BUCHMAN

Love in a COPPER LIGHT

A NIGHT STALKERS CSAR ROMANCE STORY

LOVE IN A COPPER LIGHT

*T*he most dangerous mission of all...CSAR.
Combat Search and Rescue.

Pilot Penny "Copper" Penrose *flies into every battle with a can-do attitude—even training missions. If only she could find that confidence off the battlefield.*

Medic Barry Goldsmith *risks his life to help the wounded while under fire. He blew his chances with Penny once—a risk he won't take again, seeking Love in a Copper Light.*

INTRODUCTION

Love in a Copper Light *served several functions for me.*

It was a chance to check in on Noreen and Xavier who got together in my surprisingly popular novella Guardian of the Heart. *Noreen had originated all the way back in 2013 in* I Own the Dawn *as the hero's sister. Fans had been begging me for her story and when I wrote it, it seemed there was more to tell. However, when I sat down to tell it, it turned out it was a short story and not another novella.*

I was puzzled by that for a while. As a writer, I've learned to let a story (or novel) discover its own length. Too long and it feels thin. Too short and it gets crunched and isn't satisfying. So, if this wasn't a novella, what was it?

I didn't know until I'd finished it.

The US military holds massive exercises to maintain combat readiness. Perhaps the most well-known one is Red Flag at the Nellis Air Force Base in the Nevada Test and Training Range. To keep that superlative edge, they are always pushing the limits. And out at that edge is not always safe place to be.

Yes, this is a love story. But it is also an homage to the incredible things our, and probably most, militaries do. Now all we need to do is to find a way to not need them at all. That is a day that most soldiers I've talked to look forward to.

CHAPTER ONE

The Tonopah Test Range Airport tower gave them clearance and they were gone. Control towers didn't want any return response; they just wanted you out of their airspace. So their helo lifted into the airspace of the Nevada Test and Training Range—the NTTR—and raced away from Tonopah without a word.

"This next part always freaks me out."

"And you say that every time, Copper." Vince Jawolski was flying low and fast, piloting their combat search-and-rescue helicopter toward their hold position for tonight's training exercise.

It was true, she did always say it, but that didn't make Penny "Copper" Penrose feel one bit less freaked. Not that she was worried about the battle—real or simulated—but rather that there was one in progress and their job was to *wait*. CSAR aircraft didn't risk their precious medics until someone actually needed help.

In minutes they were circling five miles and ninety seconds outside the primary battlespace deep in the heart of the NTTR— five thousand square miles of blasted-to-hell desert. It was the perfect place to stretch their Black Hawk's rotor blades a little bit. "Blue Helm" was a massive exercise to keep skills fresh and shake the bugs out of new tactics—without having someone shooting live rounds at them while they were doing it.

Five helos. That was their concern in tonight's training scenario, out of the fifty aircraft and fifteen hundred ground troops spread across the Nevada desert.

The two transport birds had already delivered their 75th Rangers elements, to mess with a tank corps from the 10th Mountain, and slipped away.

Two heavy gun platforms—one DAP Hawk and one Little Bird —were circling high above on overwatch.

And one kick-ass CSAR team all set to pull out any injured when the shit—simulated shit—*did* hit the fan. The six of them had been together for a while and she loved what they could do. But circling out of sight of the battle, there was nothing to see in this ass end of the NTTR except the occasional flight of F-35 jets off to test their mettle in some other section of the exercise. Meanwhile, she was getting tired of having the same night-vision view painted on the inside of her visor as they circled behind a low range of jagged ridges of broken rock.

While she waited for the call, she wondered what David was up to tonight. Was he—

Shit!

She'd been rid of that disaster for two months—splattered across the windscreen like an entire fleet of pulped butterflies— and still her mind went there. Why did she naively keep hoping? Civilian men *never* understood military women. It was like strong women just didn't compute in the civvie world; which sucked for her. Strong women didn't really compute in the military world all that often either. She'd seen too many female soldiers who chose to play the slut role to get attention or the little sister role to avoid it. She wanted to play the herself role—and it wasn't getting her crap.

Penny sat in her copilot's seat and tapped her way across the three status screens she was monitoring in a fast rotation. It wasn't quite a nervous twitch—at least so she liked to assure herself— even if it would look that way to anyone able to see what was flashing across the inside of her helmet's visor.

System status. Engine temperature: stable at 1,950 degrees Fahrenheit. Hydraulic and pressure systems online. Fuel: 87%. Twenty-seven different readings.

Flight status. Two-zero feet AGL—above ground level. Slow cruise: twenty knots. Running dark: infrared lights only. Heart of the NTTR. Nineteen different facts.

Battlespace. Still five miles and ninety seconds away. Two gunship helos at three and five thousand feet, and a drone at thirty thousand. The transport birds had returned to base—they had it easy now that they'd survived landing their teams. Easy unless things went badly and they had to extract the inserted Rangers under heavy fire. But the ground elements were holding strong and reporting no casualties.

The whole situation made for one messy tactical readout with every single identified fighter—good guy or bad—represented on a 3D map of the terrain by a symbology that had taken a months to learn but was now second nature.

System status. Twenty-seven readings…no changes.

Flight status…

Penny had never been able to help herself. She'd flown combat for too many of her years in the service. Every nerve in her body, and most definitely her adrenal glands, *knew* they were supposed to be in the heart of the battle. In the zone. Riding the edge.

Just because this battle was simulated didn't change squat.

Since she'd gone CSAR, now she was off to the side, waiting while others fought. Her body was here, but her body's chemistry was deep in the simulated action.

System status. All nominal.

Flight status…

By flicking through them fast enough, she could actually spot anything that changed in real time across all three spaces. All nominal. As if *that* wasn't enough to make her crazy.

She'd done this so many times, she was able to do it automatically and still harass the team. She was a multi-tasking kind of girl.

And one task was *not* going to be thinking about a jerkwad civilian named David. Distraction. Definitely needed one.

"Calling me Copper, that's another thing!" Penny groused over the intercom to her crewmates. She didn't know why she even tried, it was one battle she was never going to win. With the name of Penelope Penrose and copper-red hair, the "Copper" nickname had been inevitable. "Why you're just as bright as a copper penny!" was a pickup line that she usually answered with mere disdain, unless she'd been drinking, then it might be with her knee—she was tall enough to peg most men easily. Fighting battles is what she did.

Too bad everybody on their flight had learned not to answer her now, even if they didn't change their tune. Not her pilot, not the two crew chiefs perched at their miniguns, and not the two medics along for the ride until they got the call.

"Lame-os!" She teased the lot of them.

It earned her a chuckle from starboard gunner Xavier Jones who sat at a minigun mounted close behind Vince's pilot seat.

Unlike normal CSAR birds that went unarmed into battle, the Night Stalkers flew fully armed helos—without a Red Cross emblem—that just happened to carry a couple of medics. The Night Stalkers flew to places no one else could go, so they often had their own CSAR support.

"Long as you get me back in time for my wedding, I'll call you anything you want...Copper!"

"You're no help, Jones." He'd hooked up with Noreen Wallace, one of the crew's two medics. And like several other of their crews in the 5th Battalion E Company, command was letting them serve together—unique in the whole military as far as she knew. "How is it that no one ever tagged you with a nickname, Noreen?" Everyone else had one, though other than hers they weren't used all that often.

"No one dares. I'm a freakin' force of nature, that's why. Or so Xavier keeps telling me."

"It's true. Sure won't catch this boy messing with that." The six-four super-soldier Xavier would be the serious, hardcore pillar in any relationship that didn't have Noreen on the other side of it. If Penny was black, shorter, and a medic, she'd want to grow up to *be* Noreen Wallace. As it was, she had three strikes against that dream.

System status.

Flight status.

Battlespace.

It felt as if she had nothing to do, even if that wasn't true. Copilot on a CSAR Black Hawk helicopter was never a dull seat. One of the many things she loved about flying for the US Army's 160th SOAR Night Stalkers.

"What would you like to be called?"

She blinked and lost track of her screens. Barry Goldsmith, Medic Two, never spoke to her directly. He was always pleasant and had a decent sense of humor, but something in her quashed every comment. No one had ever actually asked her that, so she didn't have a quick answer.

"I'm guessing that 'Red' would be too cliché for you," Barry continued over the intercom.

"I might have hospitalized the last dude who tried to call me that—back in tenth grade. He probably could have used your help."

"Okay 'Red' is out. I probably wouldn't have been able to stabilize his condition for transport; remember I was in tenth grade at the same time."

Actually she hadn't known that. Barry was definitely the "mature one" on their crew; which wasn't actually saying much.

They were all deeply trained pros, had to be to fly with the Night Stalkers, but that didn't seem to stop their bird being loaded up with a bunch of goofballs at heart—herself included. She kept her silence until she had the rhythm of her flashing screens rolling again.

System status.

Flight status.

Battlespace.

System... God the waiting was killing her. David had always —*shit!*

"I've got to have some worthy trademark besides my name being Penny and my hair color. And no, my ex-boyfriend's consistent focus with the shape of my chest doesn't count."

CHAPTER TWO

Ex-boyfriend?

"When did that happen?" Barry clamped his jaw shut, but it had just slipped out of him. He'd totally missed the "ex-" happening, though he *absolutely* remembered them getting together. He'd gone on a bender the night he'd heard about it— then had to report himself unfit for duty when a surprise mission cropped up the next day. He hadn't touched a drink since, not even a beer.

"Couple months back, the misogynistic prick. He couldn't cut the grade. Turns out he thought I was sure to quit during our last tour in the Dustbowl because no woman could possibly hack Afghanistan. He'd also been counting on me washing out—'fired' he called it—because a woman couldn't possibly be good enough to fly big, nasty helicopters."

"What an ass." As if Barry could be so proud of his own actions. His bender had been because he was sick of not being able to speak to the most amazing woman he'd ever met. By the stories she'd told at first, it had sounded like David was the one, which meant he'd lost her. He'd completely missed when her David-stories had fallen out of their helo banter.

Well, if David was dumb enough to mess it up with Penny, Barry wasn't going to fall into the same trap of silence he had before. "Sounds like he didn't deserve you. Too stupid to know what he had."

That had all of the rear-enders—those who flew in the back of the helicopter—twisting around to look at him. Noreen, and the two crew chiefs: Xavier, and Mason "Jar" Buckley.

"What?" he mouthed at them.

He tried not to read too much into Noreen's smile before she turned back to quadruple checking their med supplies—*her* pre-battle habit.

"Thanks, Barry. He *was* an ass. Next time could someone tell me sooner?" Penny answered after a thoughtful silence. "Final fight was him demanding I quit so he'd know I would live long enough to raise our future children."

"You were engaged?" How had he not known any of this about Penny?

"Not even close. He was just that disconnected from reality."

"What did you do?" Women always tongue-tied him, but only the ones he was attracted to. It was a ridiculous curse that thankfully only he knew about. How many stunners had left him an opening in high school, ones who he'd been too awed to speak to, before they'd lost interest and drifted off?

"I did what any Night Stalker woman would do, I dumped his ass. Then I sugared his Porsche 911 Targa's gas tank."

"No way!" Noreen's merry laugh blasted from the intercom.

But it didn't sound like the Penny he knew.

"Way! Well, actually... Turns out that sugar doesn't really do much damage if you dump it into the gas tank, but most people don't know that. So I sprinkled it on the ground by the gas cap, dumped the empty bag on the ground, then sat back in the shadows to watch the fun. Man did it mess with his head. He actually cried—down on his knees hugging his bumper. It was beautiful! More than the bastard ever did over me."

Barry laughed, "You rock it, girl." Now *that* sounded exactly like Penny.

Once again the rear-enders were all looking at him in surprise. He was just glad that Penny was up in her seat facing forward.

CHAPTER THREE

*P*enny was still puzzling over Barry's sudden chattiness when she spotted it.

Flight status.

Battlesp—

"Vince!" Her call was all that was necessary.

Vince carved a turn for the heart of the battle before the official call came in. Full up on the collective, Black Hawk's nose down for maximum speed.

"Little Bird down. Little Bird down," sounded over the radio in that perfect flat voice that battle commanders always had. "Sector Alpha. Three. Fiver."—the "-er" making the number clearer over the radios.

On the battlespace display, Penny had seen the tiny attack helicopter stumble in midflight. It was like it had tripped on something hard.

The problem with CSAR holding safely at ninety seconds outside the battlespace was that they *were* ninety seconds outside the battlespace.

The pilot of the Little Bird was doing a hell of a simulation as he tumbled out of the sky. End-os, rolls, rolling back the other way.

Then a truly chilling, "Mayday. Mayday. Mayday." Nobody called that during a training scenario. She'd had to do it once in the Dustbowl when an RPG had eaten her tail rotor, and the words were almost impossible to speak.

No one was shooting live ammo, so something critical had broken. And it had broken bad.

With her nerves amped up, it felt as if, for that ninety seconds, they were slogging through molasses. The meters flew by at the Black Hawk's top speed, but still the seconds crawled by one at a time.

Sixty seconds...

On the tactical display, the Little Bird wasn't going down gracefully, but it wasn't a dead-stick plummet either. Someone was still fighting to save the bird.

"Medics alert," she called over the intercom. "MH-6M attack Little Bird going down. This is not a simulation."

"Any other helpful news for us?" Barry Goldsmith, the handsome golden-hair boy from Brooklyn, was always looking at the bright side of everything. The more intense things got, the quirkier he got. One hell of a defense mechanism—something she'd always appreciated about him. One of many things.

"Sure. Simulated battle is still in full swing," Penny shot for a light tone, but doubted that she succeeded as she watched the horrifying flight playing out on her display. The thousands of personnel, and billions of dollars of aircraft and hardware in motion for this exercise didn't stop due to one falling helicopter. They probably assumed it was a simulated loss. "We're planting you in a hot LZ on the fly."

"Excellent. My panic response was out of practice anyway. Medic Two ready. Noreen?"

"Medic One. Always ready," Noreen sounded even more ramped up than usual for her. Of course she was marrying their totally studly gunner, starboard-side gunner Xavier Jones in a few days.

Forty-five seconds...

Penny had expected the two medics, Noreen and Barry, to get together. They were always so chummy that they even sounded like a couple. She'd done her level best to not be jealous of Noreen for getting him. Then Xavier showed up and kicked Noreen's feet out from under her—or more likely the other way around.

Just watching the two of them had shown her everything that was wrong with David, and she'd dumped his sorry ass.

But Barry still hadn't spoken to her outside of duties, which had been a bummer. Had to be something wrong with her, if a nice guy like him was avoiding her. Or so she'd thought until just now.

Thirty seconds...

The Little Bird gave a final flinch in the air. Fifty feet above the ground, the pilot managed to halt their plummeting descent by some miracle of piloting that was impressive even by Night Stalker standards. It wavered in the air for several seconds, then simply fell straight down.

A cloud of dust obscured it from view.

"We're staying down for this one," Vince announced. It was a dangerous choice. Normally CSAR dumped off the medics, scooted their twenty-million-dollar bird up to safety, then slid back to ground again when they were ready for pickup. On the ground they were vulnerable, even to simulated forces. Every extra second was a risk for the aircraft, but it was also a second less that it would take to transport the victims.

Penny wondered if anyone else even knew about the emergency other than them. The Mayday had come in on the CSAR frequency—it was standard practice to not disrupt other battle communications.

CHAPTER FOUR

*C*ontact!

He and Noreen hit the ground running before the CSAR bird had fully settled on its wheels.

Barry was first on site, and wished he wasn't. The MH-6M Little Bird, nicknamed the Killer Egg for all the weapons it carried, was little more than a Plexiglass bubble barely big enough for the pilot and copilot. The tiny backseat had been filled with the big ammunition cans for their side guns. Engine behind, rotor above, two skids and a tail boom: that's all there was to it.

Two things had saved the pilots' lives. The nose had plowed into the blown-loose dirt around a crater made during some previous training, and their ammo cans were empty—light-based scoring weapons had been mounted in place of the heavy guns. If the cans had been full, a quarter-ton of ammunition would have slammed into the backs of their seats and probably crushed them.

Impossibly, the Little Bird was still running. Its rotor blades had been broken off, but the rotor head still spun fiercely to the screaming whine of the damaged turbine.

Not his problem.

Noreen circled to help the copilot.

Barry's trained responses were already doing a triage on the pilot. Max Engel. *Shit!* They had breakfast together this morning over a game of backgammon.

Pulse: fast and light.

Breathing: yes, airway clear.

Eyes: still responsive, though he was out cold.

No obvious breaks. Nearside leg and arm appeared okay. Barry reached over to check Max's other arm where his hand was still holding onto the collective control beside the seat.

Except it wasn't. His hand was, but there was no arm attached below the elbow. A chunk of the shattered windshield had sliced it off during the crash landing. If it had happened aloft, Max would already have bled out.

Someone reached in through the missing front windshield and began tapping controls. In seconds, the pained scream of the dying engine began to ease.

It took Barry three tries to get a grip on what was left of Max's arm. Once he finally had a firm hold on it, he managed to yank free a tourniquet, but couldn't get it looped on through the spray of blood. The person shutting down the helo reached in and helped him place and tighten it. Max would certainly never fly as pilot again. Talk about a lousy deal of the cards; Max loved to fly.

Unable to do more inside the crumpled cockpit, Barry popped the release on the safety harness. It would take two people to get him out, but Noreen was busy with the semi-conscious copilot.

"Take his head."

The person tapped three more controls and the helicopter finally fell silent and went dark. All Barry could hear now was the distant *crump* of flashbangs which had taken the place of major explosives. There were light bursts of simulated fire from the helo's two miniguns as Mason and Xavier protected the grounded CSAR bird from "enemy forces."

The person raced around and took careful hold of Max's helmet.

"Keep his neck in the best alignment with his spine that you can."

"I know what to do." Penny. Of course she would be there when needed. He could always count on Penny.

Once they had him prone and Barry had a pair of IVs pumping fluid and blood back into him, Penny turned aside for a moment.

He heard her retching her breakfast out in the dirt, then she was back and helping him with a steady hand.

CHAPTER FIVE

"You did really great."

It didn't feel as if she had. Penny sat in the ER waiting room and stared at the sleeves of her flightsuit, as did most of the other people there. She had washed her hands—scrubbed them hard—but Max's blood had bathed her up to the elbows, and spattered her everywhere else before they'd staunched the flow.

"Penny," Barry's arm came around her shoulders, "you really did. Don't know if I could have saved him by myself."

She shook her head.

"Penny?" Barry was worried.

About her mental state. How in hell was she supposed to explain what was really bothering her?

"Hey, Copper," he made it a tease.

She looked at him.

So close, so kind and worried—she couldn't ignore that.

"It's not the blood that's bothering me. I don't even think it's what happened to Max, though I'm sorry as hell for him. He handled a big part of my training—a damn good man to have at your back."

"Then what is it?"

"Gonna sound stupid."

"Try me."

Penny scraped at a bit of dried blood on the back of one of her fingernails. She'd had friends die before—had worn their blood more than a few times.

"C'mon or I'll start calling you Copper Penny."

"I am…" Penny wanted to look away from his deep blue eyes, "unconscionably glad to be alive. Time is so goddamn precious and I've wasted so much of it. I feel ashamed."

Barry started chuckling. He jostled her with the arm she hadn't noticed he still had around her shoulder.

"What?"

"I *am* sitting next to CSAR pilot Penny Penrose of the 160th SOAR Night Stalkers highly decorated 5th Battalion E Company, right?"

"I know that. That's not what I'm talking about."

Barry squinted his eyes his blue eyes at her. "Then…what's the topic?"

A doc interrupted them. Operation was done, they'd cleaned up the amputation. Max had come out from under the drugs just long enough to show no brain damage from blood loss, but not long enough to know he'd lost both his arm and his career before they'd put him back under. He was stable enough that they were shipping him to the VA hospital near Sacramento so that he'd wake up near his family.

Barry had led her out of the antiseptic hospital and into the clean desert air.

They were out in the cool desert in time to watch the sunrise over the NTTR.

CHAPTER SIX

"*W*hy are you talking to me now?"

"What are you so ashamed about wasting time on?" Barry sat outside himself for a moment and wondered how he was actually speaking to Penny Penrose about something other than a mission. But the opportunity was too precious to waste.

As the sunrise progressed, they walked together across the airfield, headed to the SOAR hangar on the Tonopah Airport. Only a mile away, it wasn't worth requisitioning a jeep. There was traffic associated with the on-going training exercise, but theirs had been the only traffic toward the hospital. No one passed to offer them a lift, for which Barry was grateful.

The sun had warmed the sky to a dusky red that matched the color of Penny's lovely hair.

"Give, Copper Penny. Or I'll call you Red next."

"Like living dangerously, do you, Barry?"

Better to answer with a question than the truth. "Talk to me, Penny."

She stopped and stared out at the desert. The horizon was shifting from red to pink for three-sixty around. He loved the desert sunrises, where the whole sky colored at once so that it seemed the sunrise could come from any direction and surprise you.

This time he gave her the silence to collect her thoughts.

The sun had finally revealed its plan of attack for the day and was a hard yellow glow, not quite cracking over the Kawich Range yet. The light caught in her hair until it shimmered. Her skin was so pale that a brush of freckles across her nose stood out even in this light.

The sun had broken free of the hills and begun its climb into the morning before she finally spoke.

"David is what I'm ashamed of. The men before him. The time I wasted with them. Max almost died last night."

"Is it Max you're interested in?" *Please say no.* That would be awful in so many ways.

"Max? No. He's got a girl in San Francisco. Good one, he says. Hopefully she'll stick when she sees what happened."

Barry had heard the same news, but he'd missed the whole breakup between Penny and David, so he could have missed something with Max as well.

"After last night, I'm just aware that I don't want to waste any more time. I've wanted to be like Noreen Wallace since the moment I met her, but I could never figure out how. Now I know why I wanted to be like her. She's happy. She's honestly and thoroughly happy. On top of that, she's marrying a damn good man and knows it. I want a good man like that. One who makes me smile and feel good about who he is and who I am. Who we are together."

She started walking again, kicking up dust as if to watch it catch the light. Or maybe as if kicking away her past choices. Barry liked the second possibility for himself and he fell in beside her to kick away some of his own dust.

"Now tell me why you've suddenly started talking to me."

"The truth?"

"The truth," Penny nodded emphatically.

"Sure you can handle it?" At the teasing tone, he felt more like himself than he ever had talking to her. Focusing on the upside had always been his goal, and now he truly was.

"I'm sure, Barry," and the quirk of a smile gave him hope. She was a top flier in the best helicopter unit in the world. And the best feature on the beautiful redhead was her smile.

"What the hell," he put his bets all in. This time he was playing to win. "I'm hoping to convince you that I'm that good man."

CHAPTER SEVEN

"*I* know you're a good man. Otherwise—" Then Penny's brain went sideways on her and she stumbled to a halt.

Barry stopped and watched her. At first his eyes were cautious, but soon she could see the humor rising into them. The smile climbing up in close formation.

"What..." but she didn't know what she wanted to ask. "Why..." didn't help either. "But..." she waved her hand helplessly. It might have been toward their CSAR helicopter that they had nearly reached, though now disappearing into the heat shimmer rising off the vast expanse of pavement. Or she might have been waving toward the past.

"Why haven't I said anything before?"

She could only nod.

"Gearing up the nerve to talk to you took a while."

"A damn long while."

"Well, I was almost there, and then you starting seeing David. Seemed like keeping my mouth shut was the right thing to do after that."

"*Almost there? What stopped you?*"

"You're scary as hell, Copper Penny."

"I am? No I'm not. Even if I am, you're a combat medic who just saved Max's life. How can you be afraid to talk to a girl?"

He shrugged uncomfortably, "When it's you. I am."

Penny scrubbed a hand through her thick hair, then began walking slowly toward the parked helo. "Why?"

"Because in addition to being drop dead gorgeous, you're also the most impressive woman I've ever met."

"Me? Maybe the military me. There's a whole me you don't know that's a total mess."

Barry grabbed the shoulder of her flight suit as she reached to open the cargo door. She wanted to see if they'd cleaned it up yet. He turned her away to look at him.

"It's *exactly* the you that *I* know. I've been watching you a long time—on and off the flightline. It's just that I didn't realize until last night that you weren't with David anymore. I wasn't going to miss my opportunity again, even if the answer was no."

"The answer to what?" Penny was feeling all muddle-headed. Maybe it was the heat. Or Max's injury. Or—

"The answer to the question of—will you go out on a date with me?"

"Well, at least you aren't asking me to marry you and have kids."

"Not yet," Barry's smile said he knew exactly what he'd just done to her brain.

"So what's this date going to be?" It was the best defense she could come up with to buy her a moment to think. The screens of her life were changing far too fast for her to focus on. All systems…in flux!

"Well, we're both going to be at Xavier and Noreen's wedding in a couple days, care to be my date?"

"You want our first date to be a *wedding?*"

"Sure." Whatever hesitancy and silence Barry Goldsmith had

always shown to her had evaporated with the morning light. "Breaching unknown territory together."

"Let me guess. You're expecting me to be the one who catches the bouquet?"

"I can always hope."

Penny really didn't know what to do with him. He was handsome as all hell, a great guy, and a top medic with the same elite outfit she'd spent years clawing to get into.

And...she liked him. Liked him a lot. She'd seen his work, his dedication, and his kindness under the very worst of circumstances. And she had no real secrets from him either. He'd had every opportunity to see the good and the bad of her over their last year together.

"A date at a wedding with me catching the bouquet," she repeated, but it didn't sound nearly as strange as the first time she'd said it.

"Uh-huh." His happy tone had her considering various ways she could wipe that smile off his face.

But she didn't want to. So, rather than following her normal pre-flight procedures with men, she'd implement a change of protocol.

"What do you say, *Red?*" Now he was just asking for it.

"A date?" She decided that for Barry she just might want to be the woman catching that bouquet. "But we haven't even kissed yet."

"I know how to cure that, Penny from Heaven."

So did she. And if Barry wanted to see her that way, she was going to let him.

Like the good pilot she was, she didn't bother answering with words.

IF YOU ENJOYED THIS, YOU MIGHT
ALSO ENJOY:

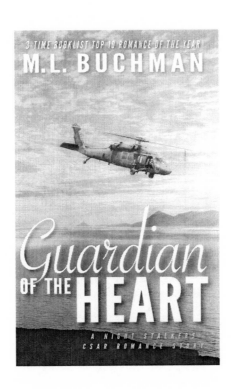

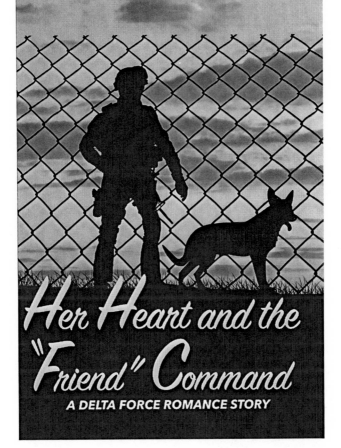

M.L. BUCHMAN

3-TIME BOOKLIST TOP 10 ROMANCE AUTHOR OF THE YEAR

Her Heart and the
"Friend" Command

A DELTA FORCE ROMANCE STORY

HER HEART AND THE "FRIEND" COMMAND

*M*ilitary **War Dog handler Liza Minot** *finally lands her big chance. A Delta Force mission requires her and Sergey's specialty—tracking explosives.*

*When assigned to **Master Sergeant Garret Conway's** squad, her past confronts her. Back in high school days, he ran over her first dog. Rex's old age and failing health made it a cruelty or a mercy—she still can't decide which. However, Conway the boy and Conway the man are two very different problems.*

Only with her war dog's help can they both break free of their past to track down Her Heart and the "Friend" Command.

INTRODUCTION

I've discovered that a lot of the Delta Force short stories have a richness and a depth inherent in their nature. I'm not sure where that comes from, but neither am I complaining. This also makes them run longer than most of my other stories.

Her Heart and the "Friend" Command *(by far the longest story this year) picks up less than a year after the fan favorite* Her Silent Heart and the Open Sky *(2016's longest story). And it follows the same team, two of whom came out of Delta Force #2,* Target Engaged.

This story, as well as tales like Reaching Out at Henderson's Ranch *and the brand new White House Protection Force #1,* Off the Leash, *can all be traced back to a fan who sent me an email three years ago. She asked when I was going to start writing about MWDs, Military War Dogs. We started conversing about it.*

Her family plays foster home for MWD puppies from Lackland Air Force Base—where most MWDs are raised and trained. The dogs typically spend two years with a foster family before they are tested for temperament and skills prior to training. It acclimatizes them to tight human bonds. She sent me a reading list, and it wasn't long before I knew she was right, I had to write about them.

315

That was the real focus of this story. The handler-dog bond runs deep in the field. They depend upon each other for their very lives. They eat together, sleep together, and fight together. And, perhaps most surprisingly —because of the IED-laden battlefields in Afghanistan and Iraq—the dog and their handler lead the way on almost any patrol. It isn't up to the top warrior to take point, but rather the one who will keep the team the safest.

To set a love story in such a harsh environment has always been a challenge that I've enjoyed. So drawing on a dog from the past to shape the relationship in the present seemed like a nice touch and I love the depth it added to this story.

CHAPTER ONE

"Today's the day, Sergey."

He watched her as she lashed on her fatigues, boots, vest, and helmet. His eyes tracked every motion as she stood over her pack in the safehouse bedroom. A grand word for a faded concrete cube, peeling whitewash, and a steel cot that might have once been comfortable, but certainly wasn't anymore. A tiny window let in the last of the day's red light and the occasional whirl of the bitter dust that southern Afghanistan used for soil.

"You'd make me feel crazy self-conscious, Sergey, if you weren't a dog." Her fifty-five pound Malinois war dog popped to his feet as she knelt beside him to strap on his own Kevlar vest. Normally he'd be kenneled rather than curled up at the foot of her bunk but, since the US military had sent her to a forward operating base in Afghanistan hell, such amenities were non-existent. She far preferred having her big furry boy asleep at her feet. They both did.

"Of course, Delta Force never is anywhere normal, are we?" She slipped the vest over his head and smoothed it down his back. Flipping the chest strap between his front legs, she buckled it into

317

the belly of the harness. One more strap farther back and he was fully geared up. She double-checked the feed from the flip-up camera on his back and tested the infrared nightlight. Both showed up clearly on her wrist screen and her night-vision goggles. All set for a little nightwork. The small window filled with the last red of the sunset meant they'd be on the move soon.

Delta Force. We. That was such a cool sound. She'd made it. Sideways, but she'd made it into the most elite fighting force anyway. Even Delta needed MWDs—military war dogs, though she preferred multi-pawed wagging detectors—and dogs for Special Operations needed their Spec Ops handlers. Dogs for the regular forces could transfer from one handler to the next, but it took a very special person to manage a dog trained to Delta standards.

"You are so handsome in your vest, aren't you?" She rubbed his ears then brushed her hands down his legs, an automatic gesture in which she checked for everything from burrs in the fur to the condition of underlying muscle and bone.

"Where do I sign up for such treatment, Minnow?"

She sighed. Of course no world was perfect.

Elizabeth Minot—the nickname had been inevitable despite her family pronouncing it My-not—didn't bother to look up at the male voice; didn't need to turn to know what he looked like.

Garret Conway would have shoved aside the aging drape that served as the room's door with a military disregard for gender. He'd be slouching against one of the jambs, arms crossed over his chest as he glared down at the two of them with his dark brown eyes. He wasn't much taller than she was, Delta selection didn't favor tall and strong, but rather the driven and powerful. Dark hair worn long, a trim beard that eased the hard lines of his face.

So instead, she continued talking to Sergey as she finished checking him over. Pads of his paws...tail. As always, she tweaked the tip for good luck which earned her a doggie smile. All good.

"Maybe if the nasty sergeant promised to love me for a Kong

dog toy and a crunchy biscuit, I'd deign to talk to him." Like she'd give the arrogant bastard the time of day. He'd been an utter twit of a boy back in the blue-collar core of Baltimore—the Dundalk neighborhood being the only thing they had in common. And just because he'd grown up into a seriously handsome soldier didn't make him any less of an SOB. She knew his dark side all too well and it was just one of the trials that the Powers That Be had placed across her path, landing her on *his* team after she'd rarely thought of him for a decade.

The fates were off at a bar crawl somewhere laughing their asses off for saddling her with him as the squad leader of her first-ever deployment with Delta. It had been a rude shock when she'd arrived this morning.

Master Sergeant Garret Conway was going to be a problem.

"Do you think he'd like a dog toy?" She asked Sergey. To make her point, Liza bounced Sergey's Kong toy on the wooden floor of the safehouse they were squatting in.

The hard rubber, shaped like a five-inch marshmallow man, ricocheted in an unexpected direction, sending Sergey pouncing, missing, and pouncing again as his attack sent it off in another direction. A frantic scuffle ensued—which included a brief strike beneath the sad excuse for a bunk—before Sergey sat back, the triumphant winner of the tussle. He smiled up at her proudly with the adoration clear in his eyes. He gave her the Kong and she traded it for a doggie treat from her pouch.

The Kong and treat were why MWDs worked so hard. They didn't care about explosives. They just knew that when they sniffed out the explosives, they got the toy then the treat.

She fished out another treat and held it out to the squad's leader—that's how she'd think of him. Not friend—never was. Not even acquaintance from Baltimore. He'd just be Master Sergeant Conway, her Delta Force squad leader.

"Want one?" Though why she was teasing him, she didn't know.

Garret managed to take the small treat without touching her

fingers. He eyed her as he bounced it in his palm. He'd been the lean and dangerous kid in high school and she could still see it in his narrowed eyes though he'd certainly filled out since then. Nobody had messed with Garret—nobody dared. He'd always had a circle of wannabes, but he hadn't needed them. It was more as if he was a one-man center of dark power and the others had merely been drawn like night moths. No matter where she went in the school, it had always seemed that he was there in the background watching. He missed nothing.

Occasionally, if she'd wanted to track someone down, she'd ask him. That was about the only time they ever spoke, but he always knew. She knew almost nothing about him. His dad was a stevedore down at the port—the kind who drank too much when he got home. Her dad was a machinist who didn't. It bothered her that she couldn't remember more about him.

Garret had always had a hot girl under his arm at every school dance or block party. He'd never been picky on the last count: athlete, cheerleader, from another school (a big social crime that only he could get away with), slut… Never mattered as long as she was built. Liza once again blessed her lean figure that had served her so well in track and field, and in the Army. Surviving her three brothers had developed her strength early and she'd never let that advantage go.

When her dad had slipped a German Shepard pup under the tree for her fifth Christmas, she'd found her calling. The two of them had played and run together until a car had killed him when she was seventeen. By then he was slow, mostly deaf, and blind in one eye.

She'd been walking him home from the vet who had given the worst pronouncement of all—cancer, with only days to live. She often wondered if Rex had known what he was doing when he'd stepped off the curb before she released him. It had been instantaneous, merciful, and utterly horrifying. When she'd looked up from Rex's suddenly lax form into Garret Conway's eyes, she didn't know whether to thank him or try to kill him.

Liza still didn't.

Garret continued to watch her as he fooled with the treat. Then —with no more words than he'd offered on that horrible day while he'd put Rex in her lap in the back seat and driven her back to the vet to arrange for cremation—he held the treat out for Sergey.

Sergey's sharp snarl had him jerking his hand back.

"What the hell?"

"I haven't told him that you're a friend. He's very careful."

"So tell him, Minnow." Half the high school had gone to "Little Fish." At least he'd never done that.

Tell Sergey that Garret was a friend? Not in a thousand years. But the dog only knew the one word. She had no way to explain "asshole from my past but don't attack him" to a dog. There was *friend* and there was *attack*.

Finally, she simply said, "Down."

Sergey lay down immediately, but continued glaring at Garret. *Good dog.*

CHAPTER TWO

*G*arret didn't know which of the two looked more dangerous: the tall slip of a blonde or her damn dog. It was clear that neither was glad to see him.

Of all the possible soldiers command could have sent his way, why did it have to be her? Had someone seen the shared high school in their past and decided they were doing him a favor? No. They'd looked at skills and decided she was the best fit for the job based on skills and availability—meaning she'd already been in the dustbowl rather than having to be shipped in from the States.

He didn't doubt that for a second. She'd always been one of those overachiever types. A top student and the school's star decathlete. After watching her win seven-of-ten events in a decathlon, easily winning the overall event freshman year, he'd tried out for the team. That's when he'd discovered what an amazing athlete she truly was. The coach had kicked him loose after three events: not the first cut, but almost. Thank god she hadn't been around that day to see his humiliation.

The next year, he'd made it through all of the events before being cut. He'd finally made the team the year she went All-State—

the football team. He was fast and knew how to take a hit—but it wasn't enough to shine among the guys who'd caught their first pass as they were leaving the womb. He'd graduated second string and hadn't liked it.

Minnow was the gold standard of women. It sucked that he'd never been able to speak to her. The beautiful, popular, star athlete shone with a brightness that made his life feel even darker and dirtier than it was.

He tossed the dog treat down in front of the Malinois. Sergey didn't even track it to the floor—his attention remained riveted on Garret's face, and not in a good way. His muscles remained bunched and ready for action.

"We've got some chow in the other room," he said to Minnow. "Briefing in ten. Out the door in twenty." Then he turned his back on them and walked back to join the rest of the team.

"It's okay," he heard her speak softly to the dog.

There was a sharp snap of jaws that took all of Garret's training not to react to. Then he heard the quick crunch as Sergey ate the treat he must have snapped up.

The hut's other room was just as disgusting as the sole bedroom he'd given Minnow and her dog. Their safehouse was little more than the smallest of three huts inside a massive ring of HESCO barriers and piles of sandbags. A dozen years of occupancy by a rotating stream of NATO forces hadn't been kind to it. A small firepit, a table covered in his team's gear, wooden pegs driven into cracks in the concrete from which their rifles dangled on their straps. Regular forces were standing security outside, so at least they didn't have to think about that. The other four Unit operators were too quiet and had clearly heard everything.

"Mutt and Jeff," Maxwell and Jaffe, the nickname inevitable as they were two jokers like a comedy routine, ping-ponging remarks back and forth. They could go all day if he let them. One tall and at least a little thoughtful, the other short and quick-witted. They were also both crack shots.

"Both of you load up long."

No need to tell them twice. They opened hard-shell cases and began assembling their preferred sniper rifles. Predictably Mutt favored an old-school Accuracy International AWM and Jeff ran with a hot-rod Remington M2010 that he'd hand-modified—only a true sniper tinkered with a ten thousand dollar rifle. Both were barreled for the .300 Win Mag cartridges, so that they could swap ammo if needed.

"BB," Burton and Baxter on the other hand, could be addressed interchangeably. As different and distinct as Mutt and Jeff were, the BB boys weren't. Both explosive and electronic techs, they were generally quiet but had a habit of finishing each other's sentences. No sign of a sense of humor, it was just something they did. One from Oregon, the other from Idaho and despite three years together he wasn't sure which one. They'd both kicked their pasts to the curb, which sounded good to him—as if he couldn't feel the past and her dog watching him through the doorway at his back.

It still felt strange to be in charge of the team. Chris had just recently opted out after his wife Azadah came down with an incurable condition, becoming mother of his first child. Since when did hard-core Delta operators turn all mushy? The answer: since he'd fallen in love with an Afghan refugee during the team's three-month deployment in Lashkar Gah and taken her home. Just because she'd helped them take down some of the top "most wanted" in southern Afghanistan was no reason to fall in love with her. At least not that he could see.

What had been crazy was that none of them had noticed her while she'd been working as their cook and charwoman—except Chris. Yet when Garret had seen her at the wedding in upstate New York, she was so stunning it was hard to believe. High-born, fallen on hard times during all of the wars, fluent in several languages (including a soft English), she had somehow shifted from being invisible to being impossible to look away from. The woman had glowed and Chris, the lucky asshole, had never looked so happy in the six years he and Garret had served together.

But Garret wasn't going to have any of that. He'd finally found himself in The Unit, as Delta called them themselves. No way was he leaving except if they carried him out and *that* was something no operator really thought about.

It felt even stranger being in charge with Liza aboard. He couldn't imagine that Minnow would be any less than an amazing asset—he just wasn't sure how he was going to survive it.

CHAPTER THREE

*T*here hadn't been time to really meet the others when she'd slipped into Wesh, Afghanistan along with the pre-dawn light. The Unit had been returning from a long patrol and had crashed into their bedrolls. Even less talkative than normal for Unit operators; which was saying something. They'd obviously been pushing hard.

Unsure what to do or how to behave—and totally unnerved at finding Garret Conway in command—Liza had taken his gesture toward the back room as banishment and hunkered down. In the middle of the night she'd decided that there was no way he'd get the best of her and ruin her first chance with The Unit.

So, she entered the main room as confidently as she could.

Sergey was her envoy. She kept him on a tight lead, which was completely for show as she could command him much more accurately and quickly with gestures and voice commands.

She greeted each one the same way, "If you'd hold out your hand for Sergey to get your scent." As each one did, she'd clearly say, "Friend." Each time Sergey would look up at her to make sure, then take a sniff and accept a pat on the head.

"Don't know what your problem is, Conway," tall-and-lean Mutt tickled Sergey's ears. "Looks like a sweetheart to me."

"Just a big old mushball, aren't you?" Jeff, Mutt's short-and-solid sidekick, gave her dog a neck rub.

"I don't know…" Baxter was more interested in checking out the vest with light and camera than the animal wearing it.

"…looks ready for a Spec Ops mission to me," Burton finished. Both were middle-build and Nordic blond. It would be hard not to get them mixed up except that Burton paid some attention to Sergey before checking out the dog's military vest himself. He looked to Sergey rather than her for permission before he reached out to toy with the camera—a gesture Liza appreciated.

The infrared and daylight camera was center-mounted on his back with a flip mount so that it could fold forward or back in case Sergey needed to squeeze in or out of a small space. It also had an infrared light to really illuminate the darkness when needed. A Lexan faceplate protected the lens. The antenna mounted close beside it was a flexible whip rather than a knockdown.

Then they both inspected the feed to the screen on Liza's wrist.

"Very cool!" Baxter noted.

"Thanks!" Burton rubbed Sergey's head in appreciation for his patience.

She had the feeling that she was invisible to the men, as she often did when Sergey was beside her. No complaints from her. Let them focus on the dog, she didn't need their praise, only his.

Then she turned to Garret…no, Conway. Everyone else called him Conway and so would she. Once more he slouched against a wall, sporking his way through an MRE—Meal-Ready-to-Eat—straight out of the bag. Shredded BBQ Beef, with black beans and notoriously soggy tortillas, for breakfast.

She stopped Sergey two steps from Conway. Sergey didn't strain on the leash, but she could feel his tension vibrating up its length. Or maybe her tension vibrating down it.

The dog always knows what the trainer feels, she repeated her trainer's prime axiom. *Always. So only feel what you want the dog to feel.*

Liza took a deep breath to calm herself.

"Friend," she managed. Though it was harder than she'd expected—and she hadn't thought it would be easy.

Sergey and Conway both looked at her in surprise. Here was one man who saw her clearly behind the dog. He lowered his hand for Sergey to smell, but didn't look away from her.

She could feel her dog still looking at her in question.

"It's okay," she repeated, though she wasn't sure for whose benefit.

CHAPTER FOUR

*L*ast night's patrol—and the five nights before that—had narrowed down their mission. Narrowed it down enough for Garret to know they'd need all the help they could get, specifically from a MWD. He'd sent the request up the chain of command and they'd sent back down Sergey and Minnow.

Time to just live with it. Just this one assignment, then she'd be gone back into the vast world of US Army Human Resources Command and wash up on someone else's shore. That knowledge, like so much in the military, was both a relief and a knife to the gut.

He unrolled the map of Wesh, Afghanistan, and the near edge of Chaman, Pakistan, separated by the towering, dual-arched Friendship Gate.

"The Durand Line, the border between Afghanistan and Pakistan, is over two thousand kilometers long from Iran up to India. It is generally named as the most dangerous border in the world—which if you've done time in Korea you know is saying something. The two countries have been fighting over it ever since the line was first drawn in 1893 by the Brits and the Afghan Amir.

Oddly, Pakistan is fine with the line, it's the Afghanis who say they'll never accept the border."

"Whoever would want this stretch of desert is welcome to it."

"Pashtuns, dude." Mutt and Jeff were at it again. "The Pashtun tribes cover thousands of square kilometers on both sides."

"Then why are they killing each other if they're all Pashtuns?"

"Not our business," Garret cut them off. Because there were a hundred layers of answers to that question: some historical, some religious, some about power, and none of it good for the locals.

He could feel Minnow assessing their group dynamics. It made him see himself and all his flaws as a commander as if seeing himself through stranger's eyes. Too rough? Or just holding the team's focus? He couldn't think how to change the patterns even if he understood what they were. Chris had always made it look so easy. How was he supposed to know that leadership was such a pain in the ass.

"Our business is that Wesh-Chaman is the only crossing for hundreds of kilometers in both directions. All through the Afghan War—"

"Which one?"

And again it spun out of his control before he even—

"The one that started with Alexander the Great. That was like three hundred AD or something."

"Three-thirty BC, dude, learn your history. And no, he's talking about the one that started in 1978 with the Communist Insurrection and hasn't stopped since. Next came the Soviets, the communist collapse, the Taliban, and then us. No wonder this place is a disaster area. Did you know—"

"Shut up, Jeff," Garret shut them down harder this time. "I'm talking about the US War in Afghanistan and you assholes know it so give me a goddamn break. This Wesh-Chaman crossing has been our major supply route since Day One for all of southern Afghanistan. Still is, since we haven't really left, and it's coming apart, again. Tonight we're going to put some of it back together, again."

"Good. I was getting bored. How about you, Sergey?" Mutt rubbed the dog's neck where he lay between Mutt and Liza. Sergey just scowled up at him, Garret-radar on red alert. The dog wasn't having anything to do with the "friend" instruction no matter what Minnow commanded.

Garret continued. "They sent in a reinforced platoon of over sixty regular Army, and they found squat. Now it's Delta's turn."

The five of them, a woman, and her dog.

"The US has had constant problems with the Paki gunrunners supplying the Afghanis. In turn, the Pakis have been getting nailed by the Afghani militants who think shelling civilians across the border during a census-taking makes some kind of sense. Just last week they blew up another pair of fuel tanker semi-trucks. Not like the sixteen they got at once back in 2009, but—"

"Can you imagine what..." Baxter joined in for the first time.

"...two hundred thousand gallons was like..." Burton was on it.

"...all at once?" Baxter sighed for having missed such a spectacle.

"Ka-boom!" they said together and both sighed again. They were both explosives techs, so he let them have their moment.

"I'm lead," Garret told them. "BB, you're both hot on my tail. Mutt and Jeff, you alternate sniper overwatch and watching the back doors."

"Where do you want us?" Liza had her hand dug into the dog's fur. He could see that her knuckles were white no matter how calm her voice was.

"You, Minnow, are glued to my hip."

And wasn't that going to be fun.

CHAPTER FIVE

he buildings of Wesh were pitch black—invisible except as dark notches out of the stars. Without her night-vision goggles she couldn't have made it ten steps. No street lights and what electricity the town did have was apparently on the fritz per usual in small Afghan towns. A few windows were lit by the flickering of oil lamps, a very few. It was a town with air conditioning, and one that needed it desperately. She and Sergey had been tramping through Afghan hell for three months now and neither of them were any more used to the heat than the day they landed.

"What are we after?" Liza eased down the narrow street far closer to Garret Conway than she'd ever been to him in high school. Much to her surprise, she'd liked watching him with the men. Whatever else she might think of him, his men trusted him completely. This wasn't some cluster of sycophantic hallway teens; these were top Unit operators.

"Sergey's specialty," Garret kept his voice low. "There is a constant stream of explosives moving in both directions here. Bombs for inbound NATO supply trucks headed into Kandahar and Lashkar Gah. And Taliban and other pissed-off Afghanis going into Pakistan to blow the crap out of shrines and the civilian populace. I don't care which side is holding it, I just want it gone. No matter which way it's headed, it comes through Wesh. We want the bombmakers and their middlemen."

Wesh was laid out differently than most Afghan towns she'd patrolled. Usually they were a rabbit warren of streets which had evolved for donkeys and pedestrians. But the old Silk Road had passed through here since the Romans began trading with the Chinese and probably before that. The town was sliced by the one wide main street that must date back thousands of years. Rather than being lined with haphazard two-story structures that were connected only by the chance of shared walls, the main road was lined to either side with long rows of stone one-story warehouses. Each warehouse was a great V with dozens of storefronts and storage bays facing inward—the open end of the V facing the trade road. They served the only passage between the countries for a long way around.

At the head of the first V, Garret stopped at the corner of the building where they were in deepest shadow.

BB were close behind them.

Jeff had peeled off to go down the back side of the building in case they flushed anyone out that way.

Conway tapped her shoulder then pointed across the street and up. With her night-vision goggles, she could just make out Mutt on top of the only two-story building for several hundred meters around. He then indicated for her to lead the way, pointing close along the line of closed shops.

She turned on the feed from Sergey's camera in one eye of her NVGs. For brightness, she selected a level that didn't distract her, but she could see as an overlay if she concentrated on it. Originally, it had been a vertiginous experience—disorienting dog-style motion fed into the human eye—but she'd learned to use and finally appreciate it. Wherever Sergey went, she could feel the connection between them until they functioned as one.

She knelt next to Sergey, gave him a good scratch, then whispered, "Seek." A hand gesture—that she knew he could see even if it was too dark for unaided human eyes—was all the direction he needed.

In that instant, he transformed. He would no longer react well to anyone trying to touch him, but neither would he be bothered by Garret Conway standing a foot away. He now had only one task in mind—sniffing out one of the thousand-plus explosives compounds he'd been trained to recognize.

Trusting her, he stepped around the corner and began working his way along the line of shops. She swung loose her FN-SCAR assault rifle, double-checked that the flash suppressor was in place and moved in behind him. Sergey trailed his nose along the base of battered wood and steel garage doors that shuttered each bay of the long building.

Fifty meters down, he skipped a narrow doorway, probably leading up a set a stairs to the roof. She snapped her fingers lightly, calling him back. He double-checked where she indicated, but showed no interest, so she waved him to continue.

After the third building with no "alert," she could feel the team's growing impatience.

But she knew she couldn't share that. Couldn't let Sergey know or he'd pick up on it, get distracted or hurry at the wrong moment.

She signaled him along the fourth building and followed in his footsteps.

CHAPTER SIX

*G*arret didn't know whether to be thrilled or worried. If his team had been searching on their own, they'd still be back at the first building, breaking into bay after bay of worthless garbage. Some of it would be household belongings, stored when refugees had been told they couldn't take them across the border—all held in the hopes of returning someday. Foodstuffs, manufacturing supplies, bicycle parts, the list was endless. The locks were feeble at best, easily picked. But each lock took time. Each inspection was visual and usually tedious.

But the dog went by each bay as fast as they could walk.

This was either fast…or useless. What if they'd walked by some major weapons cache?

He'd worked with military war dogs before, but always as point on a patrol, sniffing out buried IEDs. He'd never let a MWD guide the destination of an entire mission.

As they moved to the fifth warehouse, he couldn't help watching Minnow. She moved like her nickname: quick, smooth, hardly disturbing the air around her. In a land where standing still and just breathing could produce a rising cloud of brownout dust, she and her dog barely stirred the air as they slipped along.

Get her out of your head, Conway! Being distracted by anything on a mission was bad news. He thought that had been trained out of him, but apparently not.

Liza could distract a dead man already in his grave. That pleasant, can-do attitude she'd struck with the team this evening had been pitch perfect. She'd won all four guys over with her polite introduction and her ever-so-gentle but obviously dangerous-as-hell companion. He pitied the man who tried to touch her uninvited.

Minnow had also stood out because of how she looked. They'd all been in-country for a week and looked it. She'd arrived from wherever she'd been, looking fresh-showered and poster perfect. Her straight blonde hair swinging just along her fine jaw line. Her blue eyes wide and observant. Her smile easy—for everyone except him. And the way she acted with the dog was just too much.

Like the one that he'd murdered and never been able to apologize for, it was clear that she loved her dog and that the feeling was returned. Together they—

Sergey sat abruptly and Garret almost plowed into Minnow when she stopped as well.

The dog was looking up at her expectantly, his tongue lolling happily.

"What?" He was so close to here that he barely had to whisper. As close as lovers.

Shit! He'd just been in the field too long. Had to be to think such things.

Minnow made the throat-cutting signal with her hand meaning danger, then pointed emphatically at the closed door.

Oh! Pay dirt. Sitting was the dog's signal of a find.

She quickly guided Sergey forward, pointing at the ground. He sniffed the ground, but kept walking. No IEDs. Then she led him to the opposite edge of the door. Once more he sat abruptly.

Garret clicked his mic and whispered, "West side, bay seven."

Jeff was now on sniper overwatch and Mutt was on the ground out back. Mutt would position himself to deal with anyone trying to escape that way.

Burton came forward to pick the lock, but hesitated at the door. He swung his hand forward, the sign for point of entry. Then he made an non-standard gesture like twisting a doorknob. Like—

There was no lock for him to unlock. Garret checked the door edges again. No light leakage. It was a double, wooden door, with handles and a wear line where a chain and padlock had hung. The doors would swing out to either side.

In case it was booby-trapped, or a gunman waited in the dark, Garret yanked out a length of tactical line and tied it to one handle. Burton did the same to the other door. He had them switch sides, which confused Burton, but that was just tough. They each backed up holding the end of the line. Burton stood beside Baxter and, as he'd planned, Garret ended up between Minnow and the dog.

He held up three fingers...two...braced himself, then yanked open the doors.

A heavy sheet of black plastic hung just inside the doors, blocking all light.

"*Tsook?*" a voice asked "Who?" through the black plastic.

Garret held up a fist to freeze the team in place.

Someone pulled aside one edge of the plastic less than two feet from where Garret stood with his back against the now open door. The man was backlit by a kerosene or oil lamp and would be night blind. Like most Afghan men, he was thin, weather-beaten, and wore a thin black beard.

"*Tsook?*" he asked again.

Garret reached out, grabbed him by the throat, and dragged him out through the plastic. As the material flapped aside, he didn't see anyone else inside. He thumped the man in the solar plexus hard enough to make sure he wouldn't be crying out an alarm in the next few moments, then passed him back to the soldier behind him.

That would be Minnow! *Crap!* No choice. He handed the man off and hoped for the best.

He used his rifle barrel to brush aside the plastic as Baxter did the same on the other side. Two women squatted low over an entire array of armament. There were dozens of AK-47s and several rocket-propelled grenades. An old Toyota Land Cruiser SUV was stripped down, ready to be turned into a rolling bomb. Everything would be hidden inside door panels, fenders, and seats. The only thing they lacked was a pile of something that exploded to shove inside the exposed cavities.

In moments, Minnow had handed off her prisoner and had the two women bound. Dealing with another woman, the two Afghani women were surprised, but calm. If a man had done it, they'd fight and scream because no married woman was supposed to be touched by another man. Minnow hadn't missed a single trick. No matter how fresh she looked, she'd clearly spent plenty of time in-country.

He squatted down and began questioning the man, who just kept shaking his head in refusal.

That's when he noticed Minnow. She had Sergey playing his nice-doggie game. Garret never heard the word "friend" but neither was the Malinois poised to rend.

Unable to get anything from the man, he finally gagged him just as Minnow signaled Garret to the other corner.

BB made fast work of completely securing the area and clearing the weapons.

"Couldn't get shit out of him," Garret grumbled.

"The women are waiting," Minnow replied. "They aren't happy about it either, but he's brother to one and husband to the other so they have little choice."

"For what?"

"There's a shipment coming tonight," she waved toward the

partially disassembled car. "A big load of explosives. Coming here. Not for a while, but it's coming."

Now *that* was good news.

He stopped BB before they could burn some thermite and melt the weapons cache. Everything had to look normal. He deployed his team as well as he could, restoring the black-out plastic, closing the doors, as well as arranging a few other surprises. He roamed the room. All the tools of a car mechanic's shop were piled along one wall, but no spare parts—new or used. The man was a car-bomb producer. Pull in a car, receive a delivery of explosives and, presto chango, mass destruction in a marketplace.

The front had been cleared for the pending delivery. A stripped Land Cruiser SUV stood in the middle of the bay. The guy was good. He'd welded steel struts in place of the springs. It would make for a hard ride, but the suspension wouldn't sag—a common indicator of a car loaded down heavy with explosives. Near one back corner, past the stack of dismounted fenders and seats, stood the refuse pile—all the stripped-out metal, springs, fittings, even spare tires from prior car-bomb conversions. There was a small gap along the back wall for access to the rear door. He made sure it was secure. To the other side stood a massive, rusted-out truck's engine block. He stashed his prisoners behind that.

At the center of the back wall he was able to sit with a view of the whole bay. He dropped into place with his back against the wall to do what Delta did best—be patient and wait.

A low growl informed him that he should have landed somewhere other than close beside Minnow and her furry guardian.

CHAPTER SEVEN

"Shush!"

Sergey huffed grumpily then lay his head on her thigh, effectively pinning her in place. That blocked any excuse for getting away from Conway.

"How long until the shipment arrives?" Conway checked his watch for the twentieth time in the last ten minutes.

"I still don't know."

"Right. Sorry."

They sat in silence long enough for Sergey to finally relax with a sigh.

"Doesn't like me much."

"You never gave *me* a reason to," which Liza decided was just the truth. She never had, though she was definitely learning to respect the man he'd grown into.

"Murdering your dog. Guess not." Liza could hear the hard knot of pain and self-recrimination in Conway's voice.

"He was dead already."

Conway glared at the ceiling. He'd rested his HK416 rifle butt down between his legs and draped his hands over the protrusion of the foregrip handle. "You saying that you tossed a dead dog in front of my car for the fun of it? I saw him walking."

Liza could feel that awful day coming back over her. Rex had slowed down the few days prior. He'd been old, but still enjoying his play and his food, then suddenly he didn't anymore. It had been everything she could do to not weep after the diagnosis as she walked him home. "One last walk to say goodbye." They'd spend one last night together in her bed then she'd have to put him down in the morning. And then...

"He was a dead dog walking," her voice sounded like a croaking frog, but she held it together. She certainly wasn't going to lose it in front of Garret Conway of all people. Or on a mission. She distracted herself by telling him about the blindness, deafness, and finally cancer. And not just a little, but riddling his body. "Sometimes I think he stepped in front of your car on purpose, just to spare me having to hold his paw while they injected him."

Now Garret was looking down at her, "He was sick? I didn't know."

She could only nod and look down at her hand buried deep in Sergey's fur.

After a long silence—that she couldn't look up from—she could feel him turn to study the ceiling once more. "Well, ain't that some news. You never said."

"The shock, Garret. It was so big. You hit him less than five minutes after I staggered out of the vet's office. I wasn't ready to lose him. Not slowly, not fast. Dad gave him to me when I was five. I have almost no memories prior to him. Then he was gone. It was a blessing in disguise. But I sure wasn't ready to talk about it that day. And afterwards..." all she could do was shrug. "We never spoke much in school."

She heard a soft *thump*, then another, and looked up to see him banging the back of his head against the stone wall.

"What?"

"You and that dog changed my life."

"No we didn't." It was a ridiculous idea.

Then he looked over at her. The deep brown of his eyes so close that she couldn't look away. They'd been almost shoulder-to-shoulder, and now they were nearly nose-to-nose.

"Trust me," his voice went soft and low. "You and he absolutely did."

CHAPTER EIGHT

*A*nd Garret couldn't believe he'd just confessed such a thing. *Keep it professional.* Yeah, too late for that. He was a Unit operator, not a throwback, useless-shit of a self-absorbed testosterone-laden... But he still couldn't believe he'd told her.

And the apology that he'd rehearsed a thousand times in his head, but never found a way to say through the rest of senior year, he couldn't manage now either.

He wanted to look away, he *needed* to look away. But there she was, looking at him with those wide blue eyes the color of a summer sky and he couldn't move. He'd often hung out at the piers along the Patapsco River, waiting for his dad and watching that sky. She was like the only good part of home.

"How did *my* dog change *your* life?"

"Not just your dog."

Sergey looked up suddenly, inspecting her rather than him. Then Garret noticed her white-knuckled hand buried in his ruff.

"Um, you may want to ease up on your dog there."

At that, she finally looked away and he felt as if he'd been released from some sort of hypnosis ray. She eased her death grip

349

and apologized to the dog. Sergey inspected him with curiosity, but no longer animosity.

Then Minnow looked back up at him and he was trapped again by the eyes that were windows right down into her.

"How is it you're still single, Minnow?" Not a question he had ever thought he'd be asking.

She shrugged. "Why?"

"You—" he stumbled to a halt. "I—" *really need to shut the hell up.* "You—" he tried again. "Shit!" he gave up trying and went back to beating his head against the stone wall. Why couldn't the terrorist bastards just show up already? He'd take 'em down. Maybe get a lead on some arms supplier. Interrupt and destroy a big weapons delivery. He knew how to do those. How to talk to Liza Minot was obviously beyond him.

"Garret, you can't just say something like that and not explain it. How did my poor old dog change *your* life?"

Well, at least she was back to that topic. He had some chance of explaining that without screwing up.

"Because I could never run like you." Or perhaps he couldn't help screwing up around her. Giving up, he explained himself.

CHAPTER NINE

*L*iza could only watch Garret with amazement.

He explained his failed attempts to make the track-and-field team to get her attention. *Her* attention. She was a nobody, just a better than average student who had learned how to run and throw so that she could keep up with her older brothers. She been outfielder at home softball games by seven and pitcher by nine. Though after several "slobber ball" complaints, she'd had to teach Rex that if he wanted to sit on the mound with her, he wasn't allowed to chase softballs. Tennis balls, of course, were fair game. He was a major disruption when neighborhood games of stick ball had spilled out onto the hot summer streets.

"Your dog…"

Liza finally realized that Garret didn't even know Rex's name, so she told him.

"Thanks. Killing Rex made me give up on you. No way you were ever going to talk to the guy who murdered your dog."

"But it wasn't—"

"So you tell me now. I'm still not so sure. Anyway. I knew what

I had to do. Even just to live with myself, I was going to have to get truly good at something."

"And you chose the toughest team in the entire military."

He nodded, "And I chose the toughest team in the entire military. Made it too."

She could hear the pride in his voice. Except he was a guy, so it was more like self-satisfaction. Now that he'd made it, *of course* he'd made it. As if any past doubts (and past failings) had been erased by his actual success.

And maybe they had.

"You're not the Garret Conway I knew in school."

"I'm hoping that's a good thing."

She didn't know how to answer, because she wasn't sure what the question was any more. He'd held some kind of a ludicrous torch for her, which had driven him into Delta. Yet, at the same time, he'd given up that torch, and thrown himself completely into becoming a truly superior soldier.

Somehow she and Rex had changed a man's life. And knowing that brought back all the grief she had shut down so hard all those years ago. She missed Rex all over again like a hole in her heart. Yet his final act had been to change a man's life for the better. And again she wondered if it had been conscious. Or some weird doggie sense of what was needed? It would be just too unlikely if it was merely coincidence.

Her head was whirling and she wondered if she was going to lose the Maple Pork Sausage Patty with Pepper and Onions MRE that had been her breakfast hours ago.

"I'm going to go and check on things," Garret leveraged himself to his feet. But before he stepped away, he rested his hand on her shoulder for just a moment. "It's good to see you, Minnow." Then he was across the room checking nothing in particular that she could see.

CHAPTER TEN

They came at moonset. The darkest part of the Afghan night.

Mutt and Jeff had a brief debate over which of them heard the vehicles first. The trucks were coming from the Afghanistan side, so the targets must be the Pakis—this time. Did this bombmaker service both sides? Probably not. He struck Garret as more the fanatic type.

Three Toyota pickups. Most of the traffic to the Friendship Gate was by foot, bicycle, and burro-drawn carts. The motorized traffic was almost entirely massive trucks. There were the NATO and US supply trucks carrying exactly the labeled load limit. These were accompanied by heavily armed patrols to deter anyone attaching an explosive charge to them. The other trucks were just as big, but loaded ludicrously beyond anything the rigs had ever been designed for. Loose hay, bags of grain or rice, stacks upon stacks of bricks, anything—all piled so high that it was a miracle the trucks didn't tip over every time they hit a pothole. These were driven with reckless abandon and had been a staple of the region since forever.

Small Toyotas were good utility trucks, but they were fantastic field vehicles for roving military. Tough, reliable, four-wheel drive, and able to carry a heavy load. Not armored, but cheap and plentiful.

Mutt and Jeff were both on rooftops now. They reported that two of the three were loaded to past the limits beneath heavy tarps. It was the middle vehicle that was worrisome. Someone had mounted a DShK Russian heavy machine gun on its bed. Its round could punch through an inch of armor. If that's what they had in the open, it meant the men in the cabs would have plenty of automatic weapons.

He yanked the Afghani to his feet and pulled his gag.

"You will say the code words, and you will say them properly."

When the man started to protest, Garret yanked his sidearm and rammed the barrel up under the man's jaw.

"*Pohidal?*"

He decided to take the man's wide eyes as a yes that he "understood."

Until Minnow called out to him, "The woman said that her husband is very stubborn."

"Shit!" He didn't have time for this. Garret swung his sidearm aside, then smashed it back against the man's temple. He dropped like a brick.

Minnow helped him drag the man back into a safe spot where the other two women were tied behind the truck engine block.

BB were front and back on the roof of this long arm of the warehouse's V-shape, ready to fire from above or drop down if needed.

His snipers were on opposing rooftops for maximum coverage —one across the main street, the other looking down from the next block back.

That left him, Minnow, and her dog in the equipment bay itself. Bad planning, but his need to keep her close had gotten them here and it was too late to change their plan. Especially as his goal was to keep some of the bad guys alive long enough to get more information about the supply chain.

He crossed to where she was watching the back door from the same protected corner that held their three hostages.

"You keep low and you stay alive, hear?"

She nodded then, after a long pause, "You, too."

No time to think about what that pause might mean.

CHAPTER ELEVEN

*L*iza was thinking about that pause and wondering where it had come from. It was more than something she'd wish for a fellow soldier. She wanted Garret to…what?

Garret—funny how Conway just wouldn't stick anymore—made it a half dozen paces away before he stopped as if he'd been shot. He spun to face her before rushing back. For half a moment she thought he might be coming to kiss her. What reaction that might call for died before it had a chance to be considered as he brushed by her.

"Help me get this guy stripped!" He whipped out a knife and sliced the Afghani's bonds.

"Get undressed," she told him, because she knew what he was after. She took over removing the unconscious man's clothes. Garret was far more powerfully built, but clothes here were loose to fend off the heat. She had all of the man's clothes off and had re-lashed his wrists in case he woke, before turning to offer the clothes to Garret.

Down to his socks and boxers, he was *very much* not the boy she remembered. Muscle rippled over him with every gesture. His job hadn't left him untouched. A long knife scar across his ribs. A bullet wound through one thigh. A spattering of scars that could only come from being caught by a cloud of shrapnel. None of that showed on his face or hands, but his body could only belong to a warrior.

Garret dressed quickly and she did her best not to blush as she helped him, pulling up his *partug* (the blousy pants) and leaving him to figure out how to tie it tightly across his flat stomach while she re-laced his boots. The *khet* over his head, then she was buttoning the cuffs while he tried to settle the draping shirt so that it fell cleanly to his knees.

They kept bumping together in awkward and surprising ways. He couldn't wear his military vest, but the Afghani's vest of brown linen fell past his hips and she was soon ducked under the edge of it to lash Garret's knife's scabbard around one thigh, reaching between his legs to do the lacing.

"A hundred meters," she echoed Mutt's report for him because he'd had to shed his radio to get the pillbox *kufi* hat to sit properly on his head.

She worked her way up his body, tucking sidearms, spare magazines, and grenades where she could. With each oddly intimate contact she became more and more aware of him. When she finished straightening his collar, he'd made a mess of it, it left her hands holding the narrow collar close about his throat.

Liza leaned in and kissed him for luck. Kissed him for welcoming her in and not holding their past against her. To thank him for giving Rex a merciful death. And to thank him for the man he'd become.

Before he could really respond, she pulled back.

"Fifty meters," she took away his HK416 that instinct had returned to his hands and stuffed an AK-47 into them.

Then she turned him to face the front door.

"Go!" She slapped him on the ass to send him on his way, then she hunkered down in her hiding spot beside Sergey and tried not to laugh at her presumption and his surprise.

"Ready," she whispered to her dog. In moments he was standing and in full alert mode. Nothing would be catching them by surprise.

There were two piles of junk in the back of the long warehouse bay. She shooed Sergey over behind one pile, while she crouched in front of the unconscious man and the two bound women.

Before she could take another breath, Garret had stuck his head out through the black plastic and called out into the night, *"Tsook?"*

CHAPTER TWELVE

$\mathcal{G}$arret felt he did a passable job of explaining that his "good friend" was home sick and had sent him in the man's place.

"Yes, poor Hukam," the man's wife was suddenly beside him.

Even with things happening so fast, Minnow had remembered that the woman was unhappy about the explosives delivery. And now here she was helping him.

"Something he ate," she continued. "It must have come from Pakistan."

In covering his surprise, he glanced away…and spotted his own HK416 in Liza's hands where she peeked around the engine block. It was aimed at the back of the woman's head and Hukam's wife must know it. Okay, maybe she had a couple of reasons to be so cooperative.

Garret turned back and wondered how long the ruse might hold up. Not very long.

"Come. We must hurry. Unload so that you may begin the long drive back. I hope the journey was not too hard."

The leader kept his weapon on Garret, but seemed to agree

with the urgency. "You stand aside. We will unload." And he waved the first pickup to back in.

Garret moved to the side wall and was pleased to see that Liza was out of sight, except for a dog tail. Thankfully Sergey wasn't wagging it, but rather standing stock still. Hopefully no one would notice.

Impossible to still think of her as Minnow after that kiss. If she'd wanted him more alert than he'd ever been in his life, she'd figured out how to get him there. Every nuance of that kiss was implanted on his nervous system which was now running at the full-adrenaline setting. He didn't have time to wonder if there was more to that kiss than making sure he was on point, but it had sure as hell worked.

"See?" He tried to distract the leader—and ignore the AK-47 pointed at his gut. "See? We have the car ready." A glance revealed that the incoming supplies were mostly C-4. This was no diesel fuel and fertilizer operation. A lot of money had gone into this effort and they'd stumbled on it because of Liza and her dog.

And the quantity! This many close-packed bricks of C-4 could take down a Parliament building or a Presidential Palace.

A part of him babbled on as if he was extremely proud of his work. Another wished he knew what the hell his team was doing— the lack of radio contact was making him crazy.

Garret tried to keep between the leader and the exposed length of Sergey's tail while the second truck was being unloaded.

CHAPTER THIRTEEN

*I*f Garret didn't move soon, Liza was going to shoot him.

She squatted behind the engine block with the prisoners, which gave her one good line of sight. She'd positioned Sergey near the back door behind the stack of old metal and seats so that the only thing showing past the pile of the truck's fenders was his camera. The two different angles gave her an excellent view of the whole bay—except for Garret being constantly in the way.

Because she was the only one with any idea of what was going on inside the warehouse, she'd become the operation's leader. The fact that she was wholly unqualified didn't seem to matter to the others.

And she couldn't exactly argue, not without being overheard.

So she was answering tactical questions with one tap for yes and two for no.

No, the trucks weren't unloaded yet.

Yes, that really was Garret in the white *khet partug* with the brown vest.

No, not the gray *khet partug* with the white vest.

Yes, with the *kufi* hat.

Yes, it looked remarkably silly on him.

Yes, she wanted to shout. *I will bang your heads together if we get out of this alive.*

No, she didn't have a clear shot on the leader.

Because Garret, you've got to move your ass out of my way.

She looked to Sergey, but he didn't have any ideas either. They were separated by ten feet behind two different piles of junk. Then she noticed that his tail had light on it. Light from one of the trucks shining past the various debris and the engine block.

Very slowly she signaled him out of the light. The view on her wrist screen was now partially blocked by a spare tire, but there was no revealing light hitting Sergey. And the area of the warehouse that Sergey's video feed revealed allowed her to remain hidden, seeing part of the bay with one eye and the dog's angle with the other. She couldn't maintain the split vision for long, but it was enough.

The next time Garret gestured toward something on the truck he glanced back. Then he very deliberately moved aside.

She wanted to kiss him again. He'd been interfering with her picture, because he was trying to protect her dog. He'd seen Sergey's tail and been very careful to block the leader's sightline. That wasn't something a merely good man did. Only a truly wonderful one did something like that.

"I have an idea," Baxter called over the radio. His Pacific Northwest non-accent was a little flatter than Burton's. "Give me a minute."

She could feel Garret's nerves stretching thin as surely as if there was a lead in her hand but connected to Garret rather than Sergey.

In the midst of a sudden clatter from the unloaders, she risked a whispered, "More like twenty seconds."

The second truck was unloaded.

The leader, whose gun was still aimed at Garret, was looking around as if searching for something.

Then Hukam groaned behind her.

The leader twisted her way.

She rolled out into the gap between her engine block hideaway and Sergey's tire and fender pile, and shot the leader in the face over Garret's shoulder. Twice for good measure.

Garret swung free his AK-47 and between them they dropped the other unloaders. The engine roared to life. Then Garret emptied his magazine through the back window of the pickup killing the driver and another guard seated there. The truck lurched halfway out of the bay, then stalled to a stop.

The other two truck engines racketed to life.

"Let the lead driver go," Baxter called out.

There was a harsh blast from the big DShK mounted on the second truck. Stone exploded over her head as rounds from the heavy machine gun pummeled into the warehouse bay. It fired ten, half-inch rounds every second. Rock dust, machine parts, everything seemed to be flying into the air at once.

Then the big gun cut off abruptly as Jeff declared, "Got him!" Thank god for snipers.

Liza risked looking up from where she'd cowered during the fusillade.

"Feh! That's nothing, dude," Mutt transmitted just moments before all hell broke loose.

The Toyota pickup, along with its driver, the DShK, and its dead gunner lifted upward in a massive explosion. BB had planted IEDs out in the yard on just such a chance. Mutt must have triggered one that happened to be directly under the pickup.

The truck shattered. Shrapnel blew into the warehouse bay. Everything that wasn't nailed down blew in her direction.

Once again, flat on the floor, she just prayed that the recently delivered explosives didn't trigger as well.

"Whoops!" Mutt muttered when the explosion had cleared. The

entire bay was brightly lit by the truck burning just outside the door. Scorch marks ran halfway down the length of both walls from the tongue of flame that had shot at them. Afghanistan was hot, but the space was now as hot as an oven and for a moment it hurt to breathe.

Garret had rolled under the partially disassembled SUV during the worst of it. Now he rolled back out and turned to look at her. He wore a boy-happy grin on a man's face. There was not even a hint of the dour, glowering boy who had haunted the high school's hallways.

The third truck engine ground gears and raced its engine as it tried to make good its escape. Garret grabbed the AK-47 from the leader's body and was scrambling toward the door.

"No!" She shouted, remembering that he didn't have a radio. "Baxter said to let it go."

Garret skidded to a halt and looked at her down the length of the bay.

She might have expected confusion, understanding, or surprise on his face. She never expected to see horror.

In that instant, not two feet behind her, she heard the unholy snarl of an enraged Malinois and the scream of a man the moment before his throat was ripped out. She spun just in time to see the steel pipe that Hukam had raised high to smash down on her head fall from nerveless fingers as he tumbled backward under Sergey's onslaught and died.

CHAPTER FOURTEEN

"Check it out," Baxter climbed up onto the safehouse roof and came over with his laptop.

He held it so that Garret and Liza could see it from where they were sitting side-by-side, leaning back against the roof's balustrade and watching the sunset.

"It worked."

Baxter had dropped down from the roof and ducked out into the open to attach a radio bug under the lead pickup before the firefight had begun—that's why he'd said to let it go. But knowing the Taliban would check for any stray signals, Baxter had set it to turn on after six hours, then deliver only a one-second pulse every ten minutes. Essentially undetectable unless someone was specifically listening for it. The US military had a drone up at forty-thousand feet doing just that.

"Hasn't moved in the last nine hours. Based on the imaging from the drone, I think we have our explosives supplier located."

Garret held up his hand and they traded high-fives. Baxter headed back down the ladder whistling.

Now it was just the three of them, sitting together on the roof of the safehouse—him, Liza, and Sergey with his head happily in her lap. They were just above the line of the protective barriers. High enough to see the great bowl of the Afghan sky, but not high enough to be exposed to any distant snipers on the ground.

Hukam's widow had been very forthcoming on the other caches and local bombmakers she knew around town. She'd hated her husband's fanaticism and had just wanted to live quietly and have a family. With her guidance, Afghan regular forces were going in and clearing out Hukam's former associates.

He wanted to put his arm around Liza. Hold her, pull her in tight. He'd like to—

"Is there a reason you haven't kissed me?" Liza asked the question completely matter-of-factly. She was *so* his kind of woman. Ten years of abandoned, mostly, fantasies and she kept exceeding them at every turn.

"Well, I have to admit, there are a couple."

"What? Do you want your own Kong dog toy and crunchy biscuit?"

"Not so much." He risked putting his arm around her shoulders, because if her question wasn't an invitation to enjoy himself at least that much, he didn't know what was.

Sergey's eyes followed him closely, but he didn't raise his head from her thigh.

Liza leaned into his side and he upgraded to tightening his arm into a one-armed side embrace. Still no squirm.

"First, that world-class kiss you laid on me was enough to give a man performance anxiety. Could I *ever* return that one appropriately?"

"That's crap, Garret. You were never a man to not trust himself around women. Remember I saw you in the high school halls all those years."

"Maybe I changed."

"Ehhhh!" Liza made a harsh buzzer sound of "total fail."

"Okay, caught me. Two, I know that kiss was in the heat of the moment right before a battle and—"

"Had a lot of experience with pre-battle kisses, have you?"

He couldn't help laughing. "Can't say I have."

"Should I check that with Mutt, or Jeff?"

Garret offered a fake shudder in response. "Both have beards. Ick!"

"So do you."

"But it looks good on me."

"It does," she agreed then continued before he could do more than be surprised. "So what's the real reason?"

"Got two actually. First, this mission is over for us. Out team is moving out tomorrow. Going after that explosives supplier."

"Maybe you should take me there."

"It's way into the worst country you can imagine. Through the heart of Kandahar Province into Lashkar Gah. We did three months there and it makes this place look like a Caribbean resort."

"Maybe you should take me *there* too."

Garret opened his mouth, but nothing came out. He began to wonder if he'd ever keep up with this woman.

"Bet you could use a good dog team in Kandahar."

"Bet we could," he said it slowly and carefully to give himself time to think fast. "You were a huge asset here. We'd have still been checking the first couple warehouse rows when that truck bomb was rebuilt and had crossed the border if it wasn't been for you two." He scratched Sergey's head. His hand came back unmangled, which he'd take as a good sign. In all his years he'd never seen anything like Sergey taking down a man three times his size.

"Bet we could think of something to do together at a Caribbean resort too."

The air whooshed out of him. There was no answer possible to that one. The Minnow in a bikini on a tropical beach—no Baltimore boy could be that lucky, but he could sure hope.

"What's the real reason you haven't kissed me?"

Garret smiled at her. He just couldn't help himself. As easily as he could imagine Minnow in a beach bikini, he could imagine Liza Minot in a beach wedding dress. The craziest and best part was that he could imagine himself standing right there beside her, feet planted in the sand, with a dog for a ringbearer.

"The real reason…" he trailed it out.

"Uh-huh," she looked up at him with those perfect blue eyes that he never wanted to look away from.

"I don't think Sergey would like it much."

Liza leaned down and tickled the dog's ears. "What do you think? After all, he's not quite the arrogant master sergeant we thought he was. Maybe we need to come up with a command past 'Friend.'"

Sergey inspected him balefully for a long moment before heaving one of his dog sighs as if giving in to the inevitable. He shifted his position so that his back lay along her thigh, but he was now looking out at the desert. Apparently it was okay with him, but he'd rather not watch.

"Well," Liza looked up at him and Garret could feel his heart pick up the pace. "I guess Sergey doesn't really mind. And I most certainly don't."

As he leaned in to kiss her, Garret still kept one eye on the dog.

IF YOU ENJOYED THIS, YOU MIGHT
ALSO ENJOY:

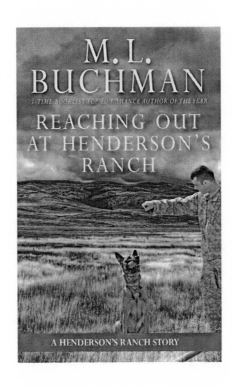

M.L. BUCHMAN

First Day
EVERY DAY

A NIGHT STALKERS ROMANCE STORY

FIRST DAY, EVERY DAY

he heart-warming sequel to The Ghost of Willow's Past.

Helicopter pilot Amy Patterson-James *attacked the future love of her life the day she met him, but those had been special circumstances. She'd punched him out over the remains of a willow tree in the Portland, Oregon rose garden.*

Two years later, on their first day in combat together, she's shot down deep in enemy territory. Wounded and on the run. She banks it all on her love **Chief Warrant Dusty James** *and another old willow tree just as she did that First Day, Every Day.*

INTRODUCTION

Ghost of Willow's Past *was my first-ever short story, my first-ever short story sale, and one of the bestselling ones I've ever had. It was first published in* Fiction River: Christmas Ghosts *and was critically acclaimed by Publisher's Weekly as one of the highlights of the collection. It is the story that launched my short-story career.*

That story had been a challenge because I like connecting my characters to each other—in case you hadn't noticed. And at the time I wrote Ghost, *I was only on my third Night Stalkers novel and had very few characters to spare. So I grabbed Dusty James while he was on vacation in the middle of the novel, gave him a love story, then—if you were to follow the timeline between short story and novel—I wounded him grievously in battle the moment he returned from that vacation.*

I always felt bad about that. In later novels, we see him in the background, so we know he has recovered. We even see him with Amy a time or two.

However, following the timeline and what we know of her career from Ghost, *she has been mostly separated from Dusty and in training since that time.*

First Day, Every Day *is about her first mission as a fully qualified*

377

Night Stalker—*a two-plus year process. It is her life coming full circle to when she almost lost Dusty so soon after finding him. This time it is Dusty who must face that horror. And only that way does he discover the true depth of his love for his wife.*

This story first appeared, like its prequel, in Fiction River: Editor's Choice.

CHAPTER ONE

*C*hief Warrant Officer Amelia Patterson-James felt the jarring impact before she spotted its origin. Standard 9mm rifle rounds would ping off her helicopter's windshield and armor with little effect. The only thing heavy enough to make the *Menace* jerk like this were anti-aircraft rounds, perhaps 23mm. Anything less wouldn't have jarred the helo; anything heavier and they wouldn't still be flying.

The *Menace* was an MH-6M Little Bird helicopter loaded for bear. Twin mini-guns and two seven-rocket tubes mounted outside on stub wings—the coolest office a girl could have. Inside there was room enough for only the pilot and co-pilot, and barely that. The cabin was so tight that the Little Birds were flown without doors, only the large front windshield offering any forward protection and not much of that.

Pilot? Amy felt the controls go loose in her hand. She'd been mirroring Bernie on her set of controls, and learning quite how good he was. It was her first sortie as co-pilot for the 5th Battalion D Company of the U.S. Army's 160th SOAR, day one on the job after two years of training and five prior years of flying for lesser outfits.

Bernie, the pilot, wasn't reacting, which was a bad sign—no time to think about that.

Amy slammed the cyclic joystick that rose between her knees hard to the left and let *Menace* tumble into a sideways roll to get clear of the attack. It would make her harder to hit again; she just hoped that the helicopter was undamaged enough to recover from this roll or she was a dead woman. Her body alternately floated off the seat and slammed back onto it as the helo exchanged right side up for upside down and continued over.

Bernie flopped against her.

A very bad sign.

Pinning the cyclic between her thighs for a moment, she reached up and flicked the setting on his seatbelt harness that attached to the back of his vest. Now it was set to retract-only, like a car seatbelt, locking up during an emergency stop.

Grabbing the cyclic again in her right hand, she gave it a twist during the next tumble. Bernie flopped back against his seat, the harness retracted, and pinned him in place.

A quick glance revealed a hole punched through the left center of his visor. By the size of the hole, her estimate of the 23mm round was right on the money. The ultimate bad news for her pilot.

On your own, girl.

She didn't even have time to add a heartfelt, *Shit!* for Bernie's epitaph.

Amy returned her attention to the sharp granite mountains leading to the narrow mountain pass between Soran, Iraq and Piranshahr, Iran.

U.S. military forces weren't even supposed to be here. This was a classic mission for the 160th Special Operations Aviation Regiment: Get in, hit the target, get the hell out.

Don't be seen.

Something the Night Stalkers of the 160th specialized in...usually.

The *don't be seen* part was easy. It was straight up midnight, two hours before moonrise. The anti-aircraft had caught them as much by chance as anything, firing wildly aloft after the two other helos ahead of her in the flight had roared by. They'd stirred up the hornet's nest and she and Bernie had walked right into it.

The three-bird flight had been flying down the gut of a river canyon. Now Amy was *falling* out of the sky *into* a river canyon and the rock walls were impossibly close through her night-vision goggles, glowing in a dozen shades of dull green in her infrared view.

She stomped on the left rudder and dragged the cyclic back to the right to break the roll.

The roll lashed back the other way and—once her eyes uncrossed from the g-force that drove her against her harness—she was able to focus on the fast-approaching rock of the steep canyon wall.

Menace groaned in protest, but responded.

Her baby wasn't supposed to groan.

Up on the collective with her left hand, craving a right turn through the sky with the cyclic in her right, she managed to skim along the wall with her skids barely a half-rotor diameter above the ground. Ripping along at a hundred-and-thirty knots—with rotor blades only twenty-seven feet in diameter—half a rotor was far too close for comfort.

That's when she spotted the attacker.

Her attacker.

The bastard nasty enough to think shooting her was a good idea.

Guess again, Jerkwad. You messed with the wrong girl.

Racing down the center of the narrow two-lane Iraq Route 3 that followed close beside the river was a white Toyota HiLux, the favorite vehicle of the world's rebels and terrorists. It was reliable as a rock and plenty powerful to carry the ton of weight of the twin-barrel, Russian ZU-23-2 anti-aircraft gun—that was even now trying to get a bead on her as the driver bounced and careened over the rough-paved road. There were two other gunmen in the back of the vehicle firing rifles in her direction. Bright sparks flashed before her as their bullets bounced off her windshield.

Without thought, courtesy of long training, Amy unleashed a pair of 70mm Hydra rockets up their tailpipe.

The first one creased the side of their truck and punched a hole in the hillside above the next curve in the road.

The second one delivered eight-point-seven pounds of high explosive as a direct hit on the tailgate. The rocket punched through the thin metal and delivered its full charge against the substantial anti-aircraft gun.

A fireball bloomed in a blinding green-white flash on her night vision gear, completely overloading the electronics and her optic nerves and obliterating all visibility.

Pull back on the cyclic.

Still dazzled by the explosion, she climbed to clear the aftermath and tried to recall if the thin power lines were on the north side of the road, or south.

North, she hoped, but wasn't sure. After the tumble she wasn't even sure whether she was flying east or west.

Toss the coin.

She pulled up and to the right. South.

Everything came apart at once.

Amy's vision came back in time to see and avoid the telephone pole and line. It was also in time to witness one of her shot-up rotor blades break off at the midpoint. Instead of breaking away free, and giving the other five-and-a-half blades even a slim chance of survival, the titanium leading edge hung on long enough to slam the broken piece into her rear rotor.

With the rear rotor gone and her main rotor compromised, the helicopter whirled into an uncontrollable spin. On the third loop around, catching the power line with one of her skids was the least of her worries as her helmet slammed against a support strut. Knocked silly, Amy's head cleared while the helicopter was still swinging above the ground—upside down. She was dangling a dozen feet above the roadway, bobbing lightly up and down like some inverted carnival ride. The rotor blades, at least what remained of them, still spun below and were now blocking her escape. There'd be no jumping to get clear.

CHAPTER TWO

*T*here was an ominous crack.

The power pole she was caught on snapped from dry rot, not to mention having a ton and a half of helicopter slam into it.

The helo dropped, upside down, onto the boulder field close beside the narrow two-lane roadway. That took care of the lethal rotor at least. *Menace's* last act was to roll slowly onto its side so that her exit was now blocked by the road's surface.

With the death of her console, the information normally projected on the inside of her visor blinked out and took the night-vision gear with it. Amy raised her visor and switched to battery-powered night-vision goggles.

She lay with one shoulder on the ground, still strapped into her seat. Above her, Bernie dangled in his harness. A finger against his throat confirmed what she already knew.

She slapped her chest to assure herself that her rifle and survival vest were still there. Then she punched a fist against the harness release and was free.

Through the cracked glass-laminate of the wide windshield all she could see was boulders and a stretch of road. The canyon was well lit by the blazing truck somewhere out of view behind her. She stood up, impressed that her legs were still working and stuck her head out of Bernie's door to scan around. She felt like a meerkat popping up out of its burrow to scan for danger.

Empty road.

Burning Toyota.

And the sharp, kerosene-bite of Jet A fuel, not something the Toyota would have along. The *Menace*, truly dead, was leaking out her life's blood of highly combustible fuel where a hot exhaust port or turbine engine was bound to ignite it.

With an apology to the dead pilot, she set the timer on the self-destruct charges for thirty seconds and pulled the pin.

Amy climbed out, trying not to step on Bernie as she did so.

She wished she could think of some words to say. Or maybe take his rifle for backup, and any ammo she could grab. Or she could...*Get her ass moving!*

A part of her was counting.

Twenty. Her feet hit the ground.

Nineteen. She started running.

Eighteen and a half—her left leg collapsed beneath her.

"Not good!" she muttered. "Go! Go!" Her leg didn't seem inclined to answer her command.

By twelve she had her FN-SCAR rifle free and by ten the stock extended. *Faster!* It made for a lousy crutch, but by eight she was hobbling away again.

Along the road would be bad. No cover.

Climb the steep canyon wall that began close beside the helicopter?

Height was tactically good, but she didn't have it in her.

Instead she raced across the road.

Almost went down in a pothole the size of Kansas, but recovered.

At three, ignoring pain, she threw herself off the edge and

rolled down the rocky embankment. She crashed into a large boulder close by the water—bad leg first, of course—trying not to scream aloud. The rock was all that kept her from falling into the rushing river.

At zero, the self-destruct charges pre-mounted on the MH-6M Little Bird *Menace* fired off. The charge under the console shredded the electronics and shattered the forward sensor array. The second charge, planted close beside the T63 turboshaft engine, destroyed the engine and the rotor shaft. The last two charges blew the two side-mounted miniguns and the unfired missiles to hell, which in turn ignited all of the missiles still in their housing.

"One kick-ass funeral pyre, Bernie. Sorry, best I could do." Amy spoke from where she'd managed to get behind a boulder and wait out the rolling wave of fire—a scorching heat she could feel through her heavy flightsuit and the transparent helmet visor. Even with her eyes pressed shut and overloaded with stars of pain from her leg, the flash was bright enough to hurt.

When the initial blast was done, she lay there a moment longer.

Five years she'd flown with the 101st Airborne and had never lost a craft. Two more years of intensive training after SOAR had accepted her into the Night Stalkers, still no. And on her first flight as a mission-qualified co-pilot, she was lying wounded along a river in an enemy country where her life expectancy was suddenly very, very short.

And her helo was rapidly turning into charred garbage.

They'd assigned Bernie and her to fly rear guard because it was the safest position for her initial sortie.

Right.

Hell of a first day.

Dusty would laugh himself sick when she told him about it.

CHAPTER THREE

*C*hief Warrant Officer Dusty James was as furious as he thought only Amy could make him.

"That's my wife back there," he snarled at Lola Maloney, the commander of the 5th Battalion D Company. She was flying just five rotors ahead of him.

"It's up to CSAR. Get off the air," she snapped back.

"Combat Search and Rescue, my ass," he cursed at the radio, though without hitting transmit. Lola Maloney had flown CSAR before she went Night Stalkers, so she was biased in their favor.

It didn't help in the slightest that she was right. And that he shouldn't have risked the radio transmission even on an encrypted channel.

Already the spot where Amy had dropped off the tactical data feed on the inside of his visor was miles behind them, and the enemy in front of them couldn't be allowed to gain more ground. He kept his Black Hawk moving at the V-max speed and dove down into the heart of the pass.

They crossed over into Iran at three meters above the rocky soil. He had a fireteam of four U.S. Rangers and pair of Delta operators aboard. They were all headed to cut off the head of an extremist cell that was racing to a refuge in a country where the U.S. didn't dare follow.

Iran had insisted that it could deal with its own problems, but the last few incursions by jihadists from behind the "Hijab Curtain" had gone undetected. Terrorists would strike at the Iraqis, then rush to the Iranian border. There they'd pull on women's clothes including the head covering of a *hijab* complete with a veil. They'd then cross the border—undetected by the male guards who were forbidden by Islamic Law from touching another man's woman.

If the terrorists made it over the last tortuous ten kilometers of road from the border, they would disappear into the quarter of a million people in the city of Piranshahr, Iran.

Tonight they wouldn't be getting away with that. Especially because America's Number Three Most Wanted was in the group.

But Amy—

She had to be alive. No question there, Dusty reassured himself. Too good a pilot, too much of a survivor.

He nosed down and crept a few rotors closer to LaRue's helo.

Get this strike done and then he was going back to find her, no matter what anyone said.

CHAPTER FOUR

*O*nce her hearing recovered from the blast of destroying her own helicopter, Amy paused to assess.

Left leg stung like a son of a bitch. Another reason to imagine Dusty laughing. He was the calm one who seldom swore. He'd hardly even cursed when she'd punched him on their first meeting in Portland, Oregon, and landed him in a bed of thorny rose bushes where an old willow tree had stood.

She was definitely the one with the temper.

First assessment. She heard nothing but the occasional unexploded round cooking off with a bang: two from the helo, one from the truck still blazing a few hundred meters down the road, then another spatter from the helo.

No other vehicle sounds. If anyone was hunting her, they were doing it quietly on foot. She'd thought the night-vision gear had been a write-off, but her final dive had merely knocked it aside. She repositioned the four lens system, three of which were still working.

Rocky valley. Rushing river a dozen meters wide. A lot of rocks and little growth. There were still two heat blooms up over the lip of the embankment.

Second assessment. Her calf still hurt like...*Yeah, Dusty. About like that.* She inspected the hole in her flightsuit. No massive entry hole like the 23mm that had bored through Bernie's helmet.

Only a 9mm. Exit hole the same size behind her calf. No blood pouring out or squishing down into her boot, so it wasn't arterial. She'd been able to walk, which meant the bone was intact. At least before she'd slammed it into the boulder.

Meat shot. A lucky shot that had slid in through the non-existent door while she was maneuvering; too hyped on adrenaline to feel it. Until now! Holy crap it hurt!

She pulled a medical wrap out of her first aid chest pouch. Bright white. She did not need to place a banner on her leg that said, "Shoot me here. Again. Please." But she didn't have time to peel out of the flightsuit and do this properly.

Stuffing away the bandage, she dug out a strip of matte-black hundred-mile-an-hour duct tape and wrapped her calf snugly. A quick check revealed no other signs or twinges of injury.

Okay, time to start surviving.

One. Don't be found anywhere near a burning helicopter because they tended to draw a lot of attention.

Again she listened.

Nothing.

She crawled up to pop her head over the edge of the embankment and scanned through her night-vision goggles.

No one...No one...

There!

A single figure on the road. He was staggering and there were the brighter patches of hot blood on his shirt. He must have been blown clear of the truck by the blast. If one was, another could have been. The odds didn't look good.

So, Amy slid down the rubble bank toward the river that

flowed briskly with the combination of melting snow and a recent spring rain.

She tightened all the cuffs on her flightsuit to keep out as much water as possible and slid down into the water. While she was at it, she flipped the Velcro covers off the infrared reflector tabs built into her uniform's shoulders so that they'd show. They'd reflect back an infrared dot into any night-vision gear, if someone who possessed some went looking for her.

Holy shit it was cold!

Saddle up, girl!

She took a deep breath and let the current carry her away.

CHAPTER FIVE

ocus, Dusty. Focus! You aren't any good to her dead.

SOAR made its living in darkness and so close to the ground that no other pilot would risk the same route, not even in broad daylight. It took immense concentration, a highly trained light touch on the controls, and lightning fast reflexes. He wasn't having any trouble with the latter two.

The first was being a real issue.

CSAR had arrived on the scene behind them. They reported one dead truck, one dead helo burned past recognition, and one dead enemy soldier, still clutching his rifle, bled out in the middle of the road halfway between the two.

The cockpit of the helo only had one body in it, they thought, but it was impossible to tell for sure. No way at all to tell if it was Bernie or Amy.

No other sign.

They collected what scrap they could, had tied the biggest remaining chunks of helo that might be identifiable as American onto a long line, and hauled ass back out to Turkey. The U.S.

forces weren't even supposed to be in this part of Iraq anymore, never mind Iran.

Iran.

Focus, Dusty. Focus!

"There!" he called out a half second ahead of his co-pilot. A trio of vehicles moving fast less than two kilometers from, and closing on, the city's edge.

"Get me alongside the lead vehicle," the Delta Force operator called over the intercom from the rear of Dusty's Black Hawk.

"Let me just shoot a rocket into each of their—" but Dusty was already moving into place.

"Won't achieve the objective," and Dusty knew the Delta operator was right.

The primary objective was to stop these guys at all costs. The secondary was to not let it look like it was done by the Americans. A trio of Hellfire missiles would disintegrate the vehicles in an immensely satisfying cloud of shrapnel. But they would also cut craters several meters deep into the road and probably spark an international incident.

Dusty positioned his Black Hawk alongside the lead vehicle, a hundred meters upslope into the darkness and hugging the terrain. This is why his bird was on this mission. Lola Maloney flew the DAP Hawk, the massively weaponized version of his transport bird. He carried personnel: Delta and Ranger shooters. For the moment, this operation was his.

"Steady," was all the Delta said as Dusty held position on the lead. He chose a line of flight that would not intersect the hillside nor lift him up into Iranian radar and smoothed out on the flight controls.

The vehicles were racing flat-out toward a sharp hairpin curve high on the hillside above the town. Dusty came in as close as he dared, estimating the volume of their roaring engines versus his pounding rotors.

Over the intercom he heard the sharp spit of a rifle. Once, twice, three times.

Each in turn, the vehicles swerved badly, right at the heart of the hairpin. Instead of making the corner, the vehicles launched— one after another—off the end of the curve and out into space. After a long fall, they landed in a single heap, or close enough. One caught on fire and the blaze jumped rapidly from vehicle to vehicle. One of the gas tanks exploded.

Through his night-vision, Dusty could see no figures on the move. No one had survived the crash in good enough shape to escape the fire.

"Oh, shooting the drivers in the head is so much more subtle." He couldn't help harassing the Delta operator. He'd wanted, he'd *needed*, the satisfaction of blowing the crap out of them himself.

"I shot the left front tire as each initiated their hairpin turn," the operator replied. "It is unlikely that will be noticed in the aftermath."

Okay, Dusty had to admit that was pretty slick.

They watched the blaze for another twenty seconds, but still no sign of any survivors.

Without waiting for instructions, Dusty spun the Black Hawk and pounded back toward the Iraqi border. And Amy.

CHAPTER SIX

*A*my rode the icy current, cursed the rocks, especially the ones that kept insisting on hitting her bad leg. With each impact, it felt more and more like ice was invading her blood and soon her frozen bones would shatter.

A stream joined the river and the speed picked up. When it flattened, she swam. When it sped through quick rapids, she did what she could to protect her bad leg.

The CSAR craft shot by close overhead and she grabbed her radio: no lights, no action.

She struggled to the muddy bank and a patch of trees. Pulling out a penlight, she saw they were willow trees. It gave her a moment of vertigo-*how were they here but Dustin wasn't? Hadn't they courted under a willow? But was it this one? It's leaves were yellow with autumn. But their tree had been winter bare, hadn't it?* Amy recognized the signs of impending shock and forced herself to inspect the problem.

The problem was that a second 9mm round—one going for her left breast—Dusty's favorite—had smithereened the radio instead. It was hard to be angry about it. The armor in her vest should have protected her as well, but it would have left one hell of a bruise. And that was if she was lucky.

Lucky.

Two years ago she'd met Dusty in the Portland, Oregon, rose garden. The same week she'd started SOAR training. Best two things that had ever happened to her. Too much luck spent there, perhaps. Not enough left over for now when she really needed it.

Two years married but spent mostly apart, together only when they could both get leave. And finally, assigned together to the 5th Battalion D Company three days ago—the only outfit she knew of in the U.S. Armed Forces that ever allowed couples to serve together.

And now she was wounded and alone in a mud bank along an Iraqi river.

Great honeymoon dear. Just perfect.

CHAPTER SEVEN

*D*ustin tried not to think about the tactical readout. There should only be two helos on it; himself and Lola Maloney.

But the readout showed that behind them the Iranians were already up in the air, climbing out of Piranshahr. Thankfully they were too late to see the Black Hawks. Perhaps they would be distracted by the three burning vehicles off the final hairpin turn above the city and not go looking for American phantoms.

He and Lola had their Hawks across the border before the first Iranian helos had even reached the city limits.

However, he could see that up ahead the Iraqis were also airborne and inbound from the west. No one, especially the President of the United States, wanted to be explaining a multiple helicopter incursion by U.S. forces so close to the Iranian border.

"One sweep of the area," Lola said over the radio. "Then we're gone."

She was right, one sweep was all they had time for.

CHAPTER EIGHT

*L*ying in the mud, Amy calculated her chances and they didn't look good. She'd floated too close to a town and didn't know if she'd survive getting back in the water to float further downstream.

The batteries in her night-vision gear were dying.

It was cold and the seals on her flightsuit were never meant to replace scuba gear. Shivers were shaking her badly, making it hard to think and to use her hands.

She managed to dig out the emergency satellite radio and send off a single squirt. Not knowing who was in the area, she didn't dare do more.

The batteries in the NVGs died and she might as well be blind. She had more batteries somewhere. Or it seemed she should. In her vest? Thigh pouch? It was getting hard to concentrate. She pulled off her helmet and set it in the mud beside her.

Darkness.

CHAPTER NINE

*D*ustin found the last flickers of the burning truck, the dead man in the middle of the road, and the blackened patch surrounded by a wide debris field of tiny bits of Little Bird helicopter.

He spun down to land nearby and took the risk of calling Amy's name over the PA mounted on the undercarriage of his machine.

The two Delta shooters hopped out and scouted the ground, first around the burnout spot then farther afield. They snapped to like a pair of Irish Setters and disappeared out of sight over the river embankment.

Twenty seconds later they rushed back onto the helicopter.

Dustin pulled up into the air—parking on an Iraqi highway where two explosions had just occurred with the Iraqi Army on the way was nuts even by SOAR standards.

"The river," the Delta operator spoke as soon as he was back on the intercom. "Blood close by the bank—"

Dustin felt ill and clamped his teeth together.

"—but probably not arterial. Follow the water."

Dustin dropped down into the canyon and eased forward, trusting Lola to watch his back. He wanted to creep slowly so that he could search more carefully, but he was too aware of the impending arrival of the Iraqi forces. His head commanded his heart, so he pushed ahead as fast as he dared. His hand ached on the cyclic as if it knew it would never again hold—

He slammed the thought aside and watched the river.

Every branch caught in the current startled him, as did every ripple and bend. A deer who had wandered down to the river for a drink shone like a blazing hot neon sign in his night-vision gear and just about shocked Dustin to death.

But it wasn't her.

He edged as close as he dared to a town, but there was nothing except some old willow trees dropping down over the bank.

They were going to have to send in a ground SAR team. The chances of them finding...

Amy had to be alive or he'd be lost.

CHAPTER TEN

*A*my heard a pair of helicopters approaching.

The heavy beat of their rotors was almost as deep as the river's rushing waters.

She tried to dig out of the brush bower she'd gathered over herself beneath the trees. Somewhere along the way she'd lost even that much capacity.

It turned out not to matter. Before they reached her, they turned away and were gone.

Amy curled up half on the brush, half under. Too exhausted to burrow back beneath the protective layer. She used what memories she could of Dustin to keep her warm.

But all she could recall was the gray Oregon rain on the frigid December day when they first met.

CHAPTER ELEVEN

*D*ustin was just ten kilometers north of the river on the way back to Turkey when the call came in, transmitted from Fort Campbell, Kentucky, via satellite.

"Nine Vee," tonight's code for the mission, "we just received a satellite radio burst from your vicinity. We have an approximate location a couple hundred meters east of Drybnd, but can't make sense of it."

Dustin did his best to keep his hope under control.

"It was a single word: Willow."

Dustin slammed over the cyclic. Laying every bit of five thousand horsepower the twin T700 turboshaft engines could throw into ten tons of helo, he ran his speed right up against the Never Exceed limit.

He and Amy had met because of one willow tree being cut down and been married in front of the replacement they had planted together.

CHAPTER TWELVE

*A*my came to as they rushed her from beneath her tree toward a waiting helicopter.

"Dusty?"

"Here, babe," said the man crushing her hand in his.

"You found my willow tree, just like that first day when we met."

"Always will," he promised her as she slid back toward sleep. "Every day."

It was good. Dusty always kept his promises.

IF YOU ENJOYED THIS, YOU MIGHT
ALSO ENJOY

AMY'S AND DUSTY'S COURTSHIP IN:

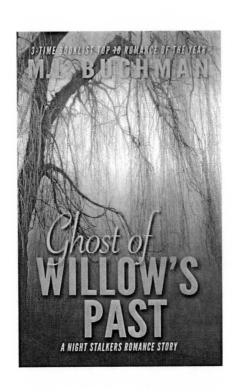

M.L. BUCHMAN

3-TIME BOOKLIST TOP 10 ROMANCE AUTHOR OF THE YEAR

LOVE IN THE DROP ZONE

DELTA FORCE ROMANCE STORY #8

LOVE IN THE DROP ZONE

indy Sue Chavez rocks Delta Force training. However, this
time the instructor drives her more than a little crazy. Almost
as crazy as being called Cindy Sue.

Master Sergeant JD Ramirez believes in pushing his squad, male or
female, as hard as he pushes himself. But Cindy Sue? Her he pushes the
hardest of all.

When the mission calls for the sharpest Delta Force can offer, they
discover Love in the Drop Zone.

INTRODUCTION

I was watching a TV special about the Marine Scout Sniper training. It is generally acknowledged as the toughest sniper course in the military. That got me to thinking. I assume that a Delta sniper probably goes through that same course...but maybe not. What if theirs was even harder?

And because I like writing about strong women, I decided to send a woman through the course.

One of the things I have learned about women is that they think very, very differently from men. Men are linear thinkers, with me being out at the extreme. I spent years working as an efficiency expert, often running massive projects to very tight schedules.

My wife is a very non-linear thinker. We theorize that part of it goes all the way back to hunter-gatherer times. The hunter is focused on the single task. The gatherer is focused on gathering, tending children, keeping a lookout, and a dozen other simultaneous tasks. And in the more modern times, as a career woman with a family, she is juggling even more balls at once. Men think they know what multi-tasking is—in my experience, women live it.

So how would a female shooter's approach to a sniper course reflect that?

That was the simple initial premise of this tale.

This story is really a romance about how men and women think so differently. And also about how formidable they can be when they join those two skills together to face the same task.

CHAPTER ONE

$\mathcal{A}$ shadow loomed over her, blocking out the heat blast of the early morning sun striking across Fort Bragg, North Carolina's Range 37 training area. No question who it was—he blocked out everything good about the quiet morning. Even the chatty cuckoos and the dive-bomber buzz of passing hummingbirds seemed to go silent in his presence.

"Staff Sergeant Cindy Sue Chavez."

"Yes, Master Sergeant JD Ramírez?" Could the man be a more formal pain in the ass? She hated being called Cindy Sue and he damn well knew it, but it wasn't a good idea to talk back to a superior rank—not even when he was being a superior asshole.

Her mother, coming from Guadalajara, had thought Cindy Sue sounded American. But Cindy was Bangor, Maine born-and-buttered and no one in Bangor was named Cindy Sue because it was just too ridiculous—doubly so with her Mexican features and long, dark hair. Her parents had slipped across the border as two starry-eyed sixteen-year-olds seeking the American Dream. They hadn't known any better, but it still rankled. She sighed. America wasn't big on giving out guidebooks to help immigrant dreamers

421

along the way. She should damn well write one, at least on how *not* to name your kids.

Cindy's personal mission to eradicate her middle name had been a success with most of her fellow Delta Force operators. Being a woman in Special Operations did have a few perks. Women were a rare commodity inside The Unit, as well as a reminder of home, most grunts were inclined to treat her nicely and drop the "Sue" after the fourth or tenth time she asked. A rifle butt in the gut often helped the slow learners.

She wasn't about to try that on Master Sergeant JD Ramírez whose dark eyes followed her every move. He positively relished how much she hated her extended name, but he was far too dangerous to risk attacking, at least directly. She loved Mama, so rather than indulging in a bit of matricide for giving her the name in the first place, she was leaning very strongly toward offing Master Sergeant JD Ramírez—from a safe distance.

The heat on Range 37 was already climbing toward catastrophic despite the early hour. Low trees struggled upward to either side of this section of the range. Today's training course lay along the low grassy hillside with scattered scrub and dotted with cheery flowers in yellows, blues, and purples. No hint of real shade anywhere.

Ramírez wore boots, camos, and a tight black t-shirt that had clearly been thought up for men like him. He wasn't exactly Mr. Handsome, but if it was what lay under the clothes that counted, he had Mr. Buff down. His skin had the same liquidy perfect genetic tan as hers, blemished by only a few visible battle scars that served to enhance the image. She'd never dated another Latino and—

Crap!

Some psychotic, "Cindy Sue" personality needed her head examined if she was thinking that about the master sergeant.

The fact that he was a Delta Force instructor standing on a Fort Bragg practice range—perfectly in his element—did help the image right along but she wasn't dumb enough to fall for any girlie, daydreaming trap. Master Sergeant JD Ramírez was magnificent in more than just his looks. He was a hundred percent superior *soldier.* That was what she aspired to. Which was ridiculous for a woman half his size, but it didn't matter. She'd known JD almost as long as she'd been in Delta Force and he was the finest warrior she'd never fought with. They had yet to be assigned to an action team together—merely "rubbing shoulders" in situations like this refresher training.

Ramírez still hadn't spoken, but she was going to wait him out. She wasn't even going to give him the satisfaction of looking up at him. Instead, she began preparing for the day.

His boots took a step away. Hesitated, then took another, unveiling the sunrise's full glare. None of the birdsong she'd been enjoying returned. His attitude had cleared the entire zone.

"Do me a favor," his voice was rough.

She squinted up at him. All she could see was sun dazzle, but she knew from experience that he never quite looked at her when speaking.

"What, Master Sergeant?" *Not choke you to death for being a personal thorn in my backside?* That was almost too big a favor to ask. And why was he haranguing her rather than the other seven operators sitting in the dirt and gearing up to survive today's test?

JD had been on her case since the first moment of the course. She didn't expect him to ease up just because she'd survived her first six months in Delta, hunting Indonesian pirates, but it was way past just being a "thing." His *un*-favoritism was so blatant that the other operators had unwound from their arrogant male smugness of innate superiority enough to comment on it. None had offered to protest on her behalf, of course, but that was fine. As a Delta operator she could take care of herself.

And JD Ramírez was now topping her list of things to be taken care of. Not in a good way. She'd start by stuffing his head inside The Foo Fighters kicker drum. Then have Beyoncé strut her stuff up and down his back while wearing her gold-flecked spike-heel boots. If only.

Today was the final sniper stalking test. It was the last day of a month-long skills refresher. Not a lot of field stalking involved in hunting Indonesian sea pirates. Her shooting precision from a moving platform like a boat or helicopter had certainly been honed, but Delta didn't believe in letting *any* skills go stale. If that meant every deployment ended with a month under the ungentle thumbs of the trainers—who were fellow operators—it was fine with her.

But she was getting a real antipathy for that trainer being JD.

"Don't fuck up, Cindy Sue," he finally managed to grunt out.

"Thanks, Master Sergeant. That's *real* helpful." She didn't need advice on how to get through today's sniper stalking test—especially not from JD Ramírez. She wished she had a few rounds in her rifle to deal with him. Maybe pepper the dirt as his feet to make him dance to *her* tune.

"I'll be your spotter."

Perfect! "Yes, sergeant. Glad it'll be you." So perfect that if she had a spare live round, she just might shoot herself in the foot to get out of it. She could feel the other seven of her teammates risking glances at the friendly little tête-à-tête she was having with the master sergeant. Why wasn't he giving *them* any beef? They'd been working quietly together, preparing for the day.

In stalking tests, spotters were definitely not the helpful guy looking over your shoulder and calling out range-to-target, wind speed, temperature, and all of the other factors required in long-shot marksmanship.

She'd aced the shooting part of the course days ago.

Now, his job was to sit in the target's position with a high-powered scope and try to spot her crawling through the brush to kill him—with a single round. If he could pick her out, catch her even bending a stalk of grass the wrong way, she'd flunk the test and have to start over. Three fails and she'd be bounced back to a full week of stalker training.

In other words, not a chance was she going to let *anyone* spot her. Especially not Mr. Perfect Soldier JD Ramírez.

She continued preparing her ghillie suit. An itchy mesh of burlap and tattered string, it broke the unnatural shape of a sniper slithering toward their target. Once interwoven with local flora, it would drape like a cloak over her head and body, making her into a small patch of slow-moving landscape. An extension of the ghillie would wrap around her rifle. She began lacing in bits of foliage that were native to this particular range. New Jersey tea and sweetfern grew well here. A small selection of the summer grasses, even now shifting from flexible green to August brittle brown, would add to the suffocating layer she'd be spending the next four to five hours underneath.

There was a certain...stench to a well-prepared ghillie suit. It reeked of everywhere it had been. Dragging it along a dirt road for a 10K run had impregnated it with Fort Bragg dust and grime. Trips through reeking mangrove swamps, snorkeling across cow manure ponds, and crawling up the insides of large sewage pipes had added their own head-spinning miasma of awful.

The Marine Scout Sniper Course had a "pig pond" to teach their snipers to go through *anything* to reach the target. The Delta trainers were far less kind. The old Maine saying, "Cain't get the'a from he'a" simply wasn't in a Delta vocabulary.

Ghillie suit smell never truly washed off the skin considering the number of hours they'd spent wearing them. The scent clung until at least a couple of layers of skin had been shed over time. It worked as a high-quality male repellent in any bar—certainly better than Deet against the avaricious mosquitos of the Maine woods on her parents' farm.

The smell formed an impenetrable barrier to anyone—except for a fellow sniper. To them it was the sweet stench of belonging. However, repelling all would-be boarders wasn't much of an issue after the first day into the refresher course. Delta training schedules didn't leave much spare time in an operator's schedule. Going to the bathroom. Maybe. Eating? On occasion. Sleep? Yep, sleep was for SEALs and other lazy-ass wimps.

She sat cross-legged in the hot sun and continued working on preparing her ghillie. She did her best to ignore Master Sergeant JD Ramírez as he glared down at her.

There had been a synergy between them since the first day—an unacknowledged one. She never shot as well as she did when JD was watching her. There was something about his mere presence that drove her to be better. At first, she'd hoped that he'd eventually notice the woman inside the soldier.

After the last thirty days, she figured she could do with a lot less "notice."

CHAPTER TWO

$\mathcal{J}$D did his best to look away from Cindy, but it wasn't working. He had a full, eight-operator squad that he'd been hounding through the course for thirty days. Just as planned, they now looked battered and weary. They were completely in that head-down, whatever's-next-bring-it-on mode that every Delta operator knew to their very core. The battle was mental. The course was partly a skills refresher, but mostly a reinforcement that mere human limitations weren't a part of being Delta.

At least he had seven of them in that mode.

Number Eight, Cindy Sue Chavez, sat calm and collected in the blazing sun, plucking up the local plants for her ghillie as if she was collecting a wedding bouquet. Nothing he or the other instructors had thrown at her made her fade in the slightest. Hell, *he* was exhausted.

Delta instructors didn't slack off—they were on rotation, in from field operations as well. If the squad did a mile swim wearing boots, ammo, and a heavy rifle, the instructors swam right beside them wearing the same gear. His shoulders still throbbed from yesterday's ten-mile hike with a forty-pound rucksack, just before the last test day on the shooting range—an exercise designed to rate ability to shoot after a hard infiltration. He was just glad it wasn't his day to crawl across the field hoping to god that some sharp-eyed spotter didn't pick him out of the foliage and send his sorry ass back to the start line.

"What is it about me that you hate so much, Master Sergeant?" Cindy didn't look up from preparing her ghillie suit. Her voice was a simple, matter-of-fact, want-a-soda tone.

"Hate? What makes you think I hate you, Chavez? No more than the next operator who slacks off."

It earned him a single long look from her dark brown eyes before she turned back to preparing her ghillie.

Yeah, they both knew she hadn't been slacking off and he'd been chapping her ass.

"Just don't screw up today." He walked away before he could say something even lamer.

Delta women were rare, but he'd worked with a number of them and was past being gender-biased in either direction. Except Cindy Chavez belonged in a gender all her own. Delta women were tough, real hard chargers, just like the men—Delta Force didn't recruit anyone who wasn't exceptional.

But there was something about her that blew all his calibrations about operators.

Was it her beauty? The fact that she was a top athlete? The fact that she didn't take shit from anyone—not even him? He especially liked that about her.

He hadn't even been able to think of another woman since he'd first met her over a year ago. It had certainly cut down on his favorite recreational pastime. He'd look at a bar babe with her bright blues and deep cleavage zeroed in on him, and then picture the slender, dark-eyed Cindy Chavez and he was outta there.

Even now he could feel those thoughtful, unrevealing eyes tracking him as if he was her next sniper target.

He walked over the broad, kilometer-long hillside slope that she would be crawling across. It was as ugly as a Kansas prairie—a place he hadn't been able to leave fast enough. He took his seat on the raised platform for the spotter/target—last of the three to arrive. Open to all sides, it had a wooden roof that seemed to focus the heat, even if it blocked most of the sun. From the central rafter dangled a metal target that the snipers would have to hit in order to pass—hit without being spotted.

There wasn't a breath of air. No wind to mask the sniper's traverse through the grass and brush. None that would get in his lungs after standing so close to Cindy Chavez and watch her fine-fingered quick movements of preparing her ghillie.

JD hoped that she made it, he really did. He knew he'd pushed her harder than any of the others. But his next assignment badly needed a woman of Cindy's caliber if they were going to survive it.

CHAPTER THREE

A three-hour skull-drag across the field. *Never bring your head up. Never move two inches when one would do.*

Four of the eight stalkers had been picked off by the sharp-eyed spotters. They'd have another try at it after lunch—by which time the North Carolina heat would be beyond brain-baking and their limbs would already be weary beyond functioning from their first attempt. Fine motor control would be out the window.

Not her.

A Marine Scout Sniper had to start a thousand meters out and crawl undetected to within three hundred meters from the spotter/target. A Delta operator was supposed to get within a hundred: the length of a football field from the best spotters in the business. A fifteen-second sprint away.

The first of the snipers to reach the start line undetected just fired off a blank to indicate he was ready. The three spotters on the platform all focused on finding him. She'd bet it was "Grizzly" Jones. His beard was as unruly as a bear's, which was a fair description of his body shape as well. He was incredibly good.

If the spotters couldn't find him, they'd clear him to fire a single live round at a metal target hanging over their heads. If they still couldn't find the shooter by muzzle flash, or by the blowback suppressor stirring up the grass, then he'd pass the test.

The rule was: no one else moved while they waited for a sniper's second shot.

They were unable to find the shooter. The spotters cleared him to fire.

Cindy heard the hard crack of his live round followed almost instantly by the sharp clang of the metal target mounted in the center of the spotter group.

The spotters continued their efforts, but miscalled his location by a good three meters. A sniper not only had to arrive invisibly, he was also supposed to avoid being shot immediately after making his own kill.

The sniper rose on the all clear signal. She didn't bother wasting time to see who it was.

One thing she'd learned about Delta, rules were for other people.

Since the moment everyone's attention had focused on finding Grizzly—or whoever—Cindy had been headed sideways.

CHAPTER FOUR

$\mathcal{T}$wo more snipers had passed. That meant there was only one left and JD would be damned if he could find her.

The time limit was fast approaching and he didn't want Cindy to time out. He needed her on his next assignment. He wanted this success for her. He wanted her—

The thought petered out there. An unfinished truth.

He rubbed the sweat from his eyes. The air was shimmering at even a hundred meters. The smell of baking grass, scrub, and the unique blend that was Fort Bragg dirt—that he knew so well from crawling across so much of it himself over the years—was distracting him.

What would Cindy smell like? Not in her ghillie, but instead fresh from a shower after a hard day in the field? Or still hot and sweaty, lying back among the five-petaled wood-anemone? He liked that thought. It made a pleasant companion as he returned to scanning the field. The controls on the tripod-mounted scope nearly burned his hand with the late morning heat.

He figured it was okay to think such things, as long as he never showed them. To keep such thoughts about her in check—which was damned hard because she was so incredible—he made a point of keeping her angry at him. Her name had been but the latest of many techniques, but already she was growing immune to it. He was running out of ploys to avoid thinking about her.

Focus on the hunt.

A sniper wasn't just a hunter who could kill at a distance, they were also a countersniper. The very best snipers hunted other snipers. Finding a sniper hunting *him* was eerie…and fun. How he'd stumbled into the best job on the planet, he didn't know. How a woman like Cindy had charged into it simply awed him. He *knew* how goddamn hard it was.

Did that stalk of yellow lupine waver with the blurring heat, or because Cindy had brushed against it? Or was it a part of her ghillie suit? He wouldn't put it past her to put a bright flower in her camouflage, simply because no one else in their right mind would think to do something so likely to draw attention.

Was the dark spot at the right edge of the field and a hundred and twenty meters out just a dark spot in the foliage, or was it the bore of Cindy's rifle aimed his way? There was no glint of the glass of her rifle scope immediately above the dark spot, so he moved on.

There was a directionless snap of someone firing a blank round.

It had to be Cindy, she was the only one left out there. He double-checked his watch. One minute inside the time limit, she was still good. Knowing her, she'd probably been in position for an hour and had simply waited to make him worry.

A glance down the line at the other two spotters. Neither one had a clue.

He felt an itch between his shoulder blades, but couldn't pin it down.

He called out, "Clear to fire."

All three of them had their heads up from their scopes hoping to spot the muzzle flash. Typically, they could pin down the shooter's location within a dozen meters before the shot, then used the scopes to pinpoint for the muzzle flash. Not this time.

Her second round slapped into the metal target. The other two trainers were still scanning the field.

JD glanced up at the battered metal target dangling over their heads and couldn't help smiling. A thousand rounds had scarred the front of the metal plate. There was only one impact splash on the *back* of the target.

He turned to look behind him. He should have trusted that itch between his shoulders.

A quick scan told him that there wasn't a chance that he was going to spot her—there was a line of dense brush behind the spotter's platform.

The other two spotters noted the direction of his gaze. Their protests about the trainee leaving the boundary of the stalking field were immediate, but he didn't bother listening.

He might not be able to see her, but Cindy Sue Chavez was exactly what he was looking for.

CHAPTER FIVE

*I*n the last twelve hours, Cindy still hadn't gotten over JD's knowing smile. It had been erased by the time she was called "clear" and had descended from an exceptionally prickly hawthorn tree she'd climbed into on the wrong side of the range.

There's been no hint of a smile as he'd ordered her to prepare for immediate deployment.

"We have an assignment," he'd addressed her without the derision that had become his standard *modus operandi* these last thirty days. "Deep infiltration. High risk. Masquerading as a couple. Minimum time is anticipated as thirty days. If it goes right, we may be deployed for several months together. You're my first choice and my only choice. We'll leave at sunset. Does that work for you?"

Deep undercover with Master Sergeant JD Ramírez? Not the pain in her ass that he'd been for the retraining, but rather the most impressive and attractive soldier she'd ever met—suddenly addressing her as an equal?

Her surprise was vaster than the hundred and thirty acres of the Range 37 shooting range and she'd barely managed to nod her agreement.

At sunset, they'd hustled aboard a C-17 Globemaster transport jet and staked claim to the steel decking of the sloped rear ramp— one of the most comfortable spots on an uncomfortable plane. It had turned southwest toward Mexico and he had done what all Spec Ops warriors did on a flight—passed out. Headed into a mission, you never knew when you'd get to sleep next, so the jet engine's conversation-ending roar worked better than a general anesthetic on any Special Operations warrior.

Except it didn't for her this time. Maybe it was because she'd spent six months deploying from helicopters; sleeping to the heavy downbeat of the rotors while being rocked in the cradle of a racing Black Hawk was her norm. Maybe the stability of the massive C-17 is what was throwing her off.

She didn't want to think that it might be his enigmatic smile that was costing her precious sleep. She'd expected him to be pissed at her trick—the other two spotters certainly had been —not smile.

JD Ramírez was a classic Delta soldier—nothing about him stood out, at least to the untrained eye. It was the SEALs and Rangers who tended to have the big guys. A Delta had strength and skills like the other teams, but mostly they possessed an irrationally extreme perseverance against all odds. None of that showed on the outside.

While not overly handsome, that smile had completely altered her view of him. After thirty days of hounding after her to outperform every operator around her, his smile—so clear in her rifle scope—had been beyond radiant. And not as if her success was his doing; she knew *that* type of arrogance all too well.

No. It was as if he was proud of her in the way her father had been the day she'd joined up to defend their new country.

Cindy would be damned if she was going to get all sniffly. That wasn't in a Delta's personality matrix, but she still couldn't shake that smile. It was a long time before the engine roar anesthetic kicked in even enough to doze.

CHAPTER SIX

urning his back on where Cindy Chavez lay beside him during the flight didn't help matters in the slightest. JD couldn't believe what he'd seen as she'd crawled out of that hawthorn. Bloody from a hundred thorn scratches—and a smile as big as the sun in the Kansas sky.

He remembered the first day he'd seen her. He'd been the lead range instructor at the shooting test during Operator Selection. A hundred and twenty applicants were down to fifteen before they reached him. His goal was to make sure that every one of the fifteen was also a top marksman. By this point in the selection, a missed target wasn't a black mark, instead it was an opportunity for instruction—right up until too many misses knocked the hopeful back for retraining.

You're not reading the heat shimmer correctly.

Don't hesitate before a heartbeat, instead plan for it. At a thousand meters, the surge of blood driven into muscle by a heartbeat could shift a shooter's aim by several meters.

Of the twelve who made it through the shooting test, there was one he never had to give a correction to, because she never missed.

He'd placed her last on the second day of shooting, by which time the wind was kicking hard and gusty over the blazing pasture of the Range 37 stalking range. Undeterred, she'd finished the test with only two misses—an incredible achievement he was only able to match, not beat.

"How the hell did you do that, Cindy?" Without even thinking, he'd rolled over on the steel decking to face her. She was so close and so goddamn beautiful that he couldn't find the air to explain what he was asking about. He wasn't even sure himself anymore. They were close enough that, despite the dim red nightlight of the cargo bay, he could see every eyelash as her eyes fluttered open.

The Globemaster was transporting a pair of Black Hawks and a half dozen pallets of supplies to Colombia for the never-ending drug war. The crews and equipment crammed the eighty-by-eighteen foot bay solidly. Their vehicle—a totally incongruous Dodge Viper sports car that he couldn't wait to drive—rested on the last pallet in the line. The two of them lay on the C-17's sloped rear ramp close beside it. They'd be getting off much sooner than everyone else aboard.

She blinked at him in surprise.

"You actually talking to me, Master Sergeant?"

"Might be," not that he'd admit to it. And now he was close enough to smell her. The odors of the sniper exercise had survived her shower, but there was another, indefinable scent that almost had him reaching for her. She smelled of wilderness, adventure, and a warm fire on a cold winter night.

"Will wonders never cease," she muttered, little louder than the engine roar. "How did I do what? Climb a tree with no one noticing?"

"You did that by ignoring the rules, which is one of the reasons you're on this mission. By the way, how close were you before you did that?"

"I was inside the shoot line for twenty minutes before Grizzly shot, but once I crawled there it seemed too simple."

"Too simple," he grunted out. The stalking test was one of the hardest challenges there was for a sniper, and she'd shown a level of confidence exceptional for even a Delta by not just taking her victory.

She nodded.

"Where did you learn such patience?" He'd meant to ask where she'd learned to shoot. Her eyes skittered aside strangely at his new question. "Don't lie now. You already cheated on the test this morning. One sin per day should be enough."

Her eyes slowly returned to focus on him. Made even darker by the Globemaster's dim lighting, they seemed to reveal more of her than they ever had before. "Are you sure?"

"Am I sure of what?"

"That one sin per day is enough."

He propped his head onto his fist, with his elbow placed on the steel deck so that he could look at her more clearly. Unsure of what she was referring to, he shrugged and hoped that she'd continue on her own. The engine roar seemed to build during her continued silence until it wrapped around them like a cocoon.

Now it was her turn to shrug before speaking. "What's the real reason you've been pushing at me so hard all month? It's not gender bias. I figured that one out on my own."

"I need you for this assignment. I need a top-performing woman."

"There's your one sin for the day. Now try again, without the half-lie."

"Some day you'll have to tell me how you did that."

She shrugged maybe yes, maybe no.

JD looked at her. Really looked. They lay closer together than he'd ever been to her. As her eyes were telling him nothing, he watched her lips for some hint of her thoughts. He could just lean in and—

Get himself tossed into lockup for sexual harassment.

"I'm pushing you away because..." Because he was an idiot. He should be doing anything he could to bring her close. Though much closer and they'd be in each other's arms.

Her gaze almost skittered aside again, but this time locked and held.

"You a hypnotist too?" he barely managed to whisper.

CHAPTER SEVEN

*C*indy wished she had a US Army Field Manual on men. JD Ramírez had been pushing her away because...he was attracted to her?

"What kind of sense does that make?"

His eyes crossed for a moment as he puzzled at her question.

"You're attracted to me?"

"No," his voice was flat, almost harsh again.

"Then *what?*"

He reached out and brushed a finger along her cheek.

It sent a chill of surprise through her so strong that she couldn't suppress the shudder.

"It's nothing as mild as that," he whispered. Then he blinked hard as if suddenly coming awake.

"Shit!"

He sat up abruptly, leaving her lying on the sloped rear ramp trying to gather her thoughts that had just scattered to the horizon faster than the big jet's turbulent wake.

He didn't go far. JD yanked off his jacket and leaned back

against the charcoal gray sports car's bumper and faced her with his knees pulled up and his elbows resting on them.

She sat up and looked at him. They were toe to toe. Beyond him she could see the 101st Airborne fliers and grunts and a couple squads of 75th Rangers. Some slept, some were joking around. There was a poker game going on in one of the helo's open cargo bays. They were all leaving the two Delta Force operators, their hot car, and their secret mission alone.

Her insides were far less orderly. Everything was tied up in knots. JD didn't hate her, which was news in itself. But he also wasn't attracted to her—it was "nothing as mild as that." What came after that was only too clear.

"You pushed me so hard so that…so that I wouldn't want to be around you?"

He nodded, then shrugged, then shook his head. But he wasn't looking up from his boots either.

"I'm a patient person, JD, but you'd better explain yourself because I suck at guessing games."

"Where did you get such patience?" He glanced up at her, looked away, appeared to realize what he was doing and finally faced her squarely.

"Change of subject."

"I asked first, and earlier."

"No way, José Domingo."

"That's not my name."

"What is it then?"

He shook his head.

She growled in frustration. "Enough shit, Jesús Dominic or whatever your name is. Speak or I'll beat the crap out of you. Right here. Right now. Faster than even any of the 75th Rangers can save you."

His smile invited her to try and she was almost tempted. When she didn't, he studied the ceiling of the Globemaster's cargo bay for a long moment before responding.

"I've never met a woman like you, Cindy Sue," this time it was a friendly tease rather than derision.

So she only kicked his calf hard enough to make him flinch. He held up a hand to show that he'd finally gotten the message.

"The way you shoot. The way you look. Both sexy as hell." He made a point of scanning down her body.

They were both dressed in para-military-civilian-on-holiday mode: well-worn boots, cargo pants with a few too many pockets, black t-shirts, and jeans jackets. She ignored his full-body scan, because she was doing the same. Out of his jacket and frustrated past speech, he looked beyond amazing.

"But it's the way you think that truly knocks me back. I've read your entire record, probably know it better than you do I've read it so many times. You don't just think outside the box—you don't even see it. I should have known you'd hunt me from behind," he laughed with delight.

It should be irritating, but she loved the sound of his laugh.

Then he sobered abruptly. "Look. I never meant to say any of this. If you want out, we'll scrub this mission and I'll find another way in."

A sleek, late-model Dodge Viper sports car. Two Deltas posing as an adventure-seeking paramilitary couple who both looked Latino and were fluent enough in Mexican-accented Spanish to sound local. Pretending to be out of work and looking for fun in the heart of Mexico's drug country.

They were on a kingpin hunt.

Most of the cartels were personality cults run by one or two charismatic individuals. Taking out El Chapo had broken the chokehold of the Sinaloa Cartel. But others had risen in their place to take advantage of the sudden weakness. Time to infiltrate and take down some more kingpins.

It was a fantastic chance for an important and exciting assignment.

And with JD Ramírez, the best soldier she'd never served with. But what if he was more than that?

Cindy liked the way that sounded.

She liked it a lot.

"No. I'll stay." But she couldn't make it too easy on him, or his ego might get out of hand. "I think this mission sounds interesting. I like a challenge."

CHAPTER EIGHT

*J*D still couldn't get a read on what Cindy was thinking. She was not a woman who wore her thoughts on her sleeve. Or on those beautiful lips.

Her smile had either said that's all she thought the op was, an interesting challenge. Or was it some sort of double entendre about himself. He just couldn't tell. He could hope, but he couldn't tell.

Once they were seated side-by-side in the Viper—hot lady in hot car inside a combat aircraft, damn but he was doing *something* right—he reached into the miniscule glove compartment. The car's cockpit was so tight, he was practically in her lap to do so. He still didn't know if that was welcome or not, so he pulled back as fast as he could.

"Here's your ID." He handed her a battered set of Mexican papers.

She riffled them open, "Gloria Chavez."

"I thought it would be easy for you to remember to respond to because you're so freaking glorious." And he really needed to remember when to shut up.

Cindy— No! Gloria, for the duration of this mission, held the papers to her chest as if they were somehow special.

Before he could ask what she was thinking—not a chance she would tell him but he wanted to ask anyway—the loadmaster tapped on the hood of the car. Then he raised a hand as if pulling up the parking brake.

JD made sure it was raised, then gave a thumbs up.

The loadmaster began knocking loose the tie-down chains on each tire.

"What's your name?"

"I'm Juan David Ramírez on my papers."

"What's your real name?"

The loadmaster lowered the C-17 Globemaster's rear ramp. It opened to reveal the dark of night and a remote stretch of a gravel road deep in the Sonoran Province south of Nogales.

He tried to find some way to not answer the question, but couldn't find one.

He stomped down on the brake and started the car's engine. It thrummed to life. He could feel the vibration, but the redoubled roar from the jet and the open cargo bay door completely drowned the sound out.

"Jimmy Dean."

"Like the sausage?"

He sighed, "*Exactly* like the sausage. My parents wanted an American sounding name and didn't know much English when I was conceived."

Her laugh sparkled to life. She reached out a hand and rested it on his arm as if to steady herself. It was the first time they'd ever touched, other than that one stolen brush of his finger down her cheek—the softness of her skin had almost undone him there and then. She'd become a thousand times more real in that moment.

Now, with her fingers wrapped lightly around his bare forearm, energy jolted through him like lightning.

"You asked how I was so patient?" The laugh still bubbled in her voice.

"Yes?" JD responded cautiously. Now he wasn't so sure he wanted to hear her answer.

The loadmaster flashed ten fingers twice. Twenty seconds.

JD slipped the car into third gear, but kept his foot on the clutch. He hit the headlights, and the outside world leaped to visibility. Beyond the open hatch and a dozen meters below, a two-lane unpaved road raced away from them. Off to the side, lay nothing but dirt and scrub brush.

"You kept me at a distance by chapping my ass."

Cin—Gloria didn't make it a question, so he didn't do more than nod.

The loadmaster held up ten fingers. Ten seconds to go. They flew five meters above the road.

"I kept you at a distance with my patience. I made myself learn it so that I wouldn't just fall into your arms."

He risked glancing over at her. "Since when?"

Her smile was glowing. The same smile she'd worn after climbing down out of that hawthorn tree with her face all bloodied. The same smile she'd first shown him after acing the marksmanship test all the way back in Delta Selection.

"Since the first time I met you, Master Sergeant JD Ramírez. I pushed like I never had before—to get you to notice me."

"It worked. Mary Mother of God but it worked."

The loadmaster thumped on the hood and flashed three fingers at him.

Cindy locked her fingers around his arm.

The surge of joy passed into her as he dumped the brake and the car began to roll down the ramp.

The Dodge Viper gathered speed just as the steel ramp struck sparks and whirled a cloud of dust from the graveled surface.

Cindy braced for the jolt of the combat drop.

Her heart was racing, but not with the adrenaline of the tires hitting the roadway at just over a hundred miles an hour. Nor was it the deep throaty roar of the C-17 battling back aloft the instant they were unloaded to continue its journey south. The American military plane had never actually touched wheels in Mexico.

Glorious? He saw her as glorious.

He was right. It had worked. She was attracted, no, drawn to him like no one else in her life. That he felt the same was indeed a fantastic gift.

JD dropped the car into gear and, without slacking off the speed one bit, they raced off into the night. She could feel his muscles as he found the right gear for swooping over the rough road. She kept her hand on his arm because that's where it belonged.

Juan David and Gloria.

Maybe they'd just choose their names permanently, as they'd chosen their careers in Delta.

Maybe, after months of playing at being a couple, she'd choose Gloria Ramírez.

As they raced through the night toward a new adventure, she knew there was no doubt about it.

When she leaned over to kiss him on the cheek, he fishtailed hard on the gravel for a moment. Then he grinned over at her and punched it up another gear.

Together they flew down the road.

IF YOU ENJOYED THIS, YOU MIGHT ALSO ENJOY:

M.L. BUCHMAN

3-TIME BOOKLIST TOP 10 ROMANCE AUTHOR OF THE YEAR

DELTA MISSION:
OPERATION
RUDOLPH

DELTA FORCE ROMANCE STORY #9

DELTA MISSION: OPERATION RUDOLPH

*I*n three days, **Betsy** retires from a decade as a Delta Force tracker and shooter. But a training mission gone wrong—or perhaps gone "strange" is a better word—sets her one last challenge.

St. Nick's lead reindeer, whose name is actually Jeremy, has gone missing. The dangerously handsome **chief herder elf, Horatio,** needs the best tracker in any world.

Is Betsy hallucinating?

Can Christmas be saved?

Is there enough time left for: Delta Mission: Operation Rudolph?

INTRODUCTION

I always try to write my stories with the highest degree of realism I can bring to the page...without ruining the story. For example, I don't try to pretty up war, but I don't show the truly dark side of it either.

But every now and then, I just can't help myself and I get a fit of the sillies

This fit of silliness is actually an homage to J.R.R. Tolkien's The Father Christmas Letters. *They were written from Father Christmas to his nieces and nephews during WWII about his problems with an absentminded polar bear, troublesome goblins, and a wide variety of other North Pole adventures. For a number of years I wrote similar letters to my own kid each Christmas following their continued adventures from where Tolkien had left off.*

I was also writing this immediately after finishing Big Sky, Loyal Heart *set on Henderson's Ranch. Discovering that reindeer and caribou were the same animal—called by separate names on separate continents—gave me a fun and whimsical idea. Like* Since the First Day, *this was a chance to overlap two stories and offer strangely different points of view.*

And the final twist is simply because I so love having women mess with Mark Henderson's head. It makes me laugh every single time.

CHAPTER ONE

*L*ive-fire training.

She didn't need any blasted live-fire training.

Especially not during a freak snowstorm that was inundating Range 37 at Fort Bragg, North Carolina. Betsy's personal thermostat was currently set to Congo jungle, not three-days-before-Christmas blizzard.

Okay, the pretty white flakes fluttering down on the rifle range didn't count as a blizzard—though she'd grown up in Arkansas and it was more than she was used to—but it was cold enough that they were sticking to everything, including her. And her breath showed in puffs. She focused on breathing only through her nose to cut down on the clouds that might give away her position to the instructors.

The fact that she was out of Delta Force and the Army in three more days didn't matter to them. She'd done her decade in the field and Christmas Day would mark her release from service. But when command said you did a training, you did one. She was theirs to order about until the moment she walked out the gate.

Betsy kept low behind a stone wall and pondered the enemy's

next move. She'd barely had a glimpse of the artificial town that was the core of the training range's purpose. The Fort Bragg training squadron was always rearranging it in unexpected ways. She'd been in the field for a full year on her latest deployment, so the hundreds of hours she'd spent here over the years were now irrelevant.

The hundred-plus acres of Range 37 was a 360-degree, live-fire shoothouse. Some parts were modern urban, others Kandahar Province-low-and-crammed-together.

What kind of idiot training scenario sent a solo soldier on a snatch-and-grab mission? Minimum for that type of operation was a four-man team: two to grab, two to guard. Instead, they'd sent her in on her own without any explanation.

The only way out is through. Old axiom.

Of course solo was the story of her life. Dad gone from the beginning. While her high school classmates had been discovering friends and sex, she'd been caring for her mother through a fatal bout of cancer. Delta Force, the true loners of the US military, had been as natural to her as breathing. One of the only women there? Sure. Whatever.

But a one-woman snatch-and-grab operation? She was probably the best they had for that—no matter how stupid an idea it was. Perhaps they were using her to test some crazy scenario just to see how it worked.

Fine! Time to show them just what she *could* do.

She lay down in the snow and fast-rolled across the gap between the stone wall she'd been crouched behind and the brick building next over. As she rolled, she kept her rifle scope to her eye. Her best moving shot for rooftops was actually on her back, not her stomach—an unlikely trick she'd learned by accident in Mosul. Head tipped back, HK416 at the ready, she spotted two hostiles atop the wall on the far side of a broad courtyard. She hit both from her back, rolled onto her stomach, double-tapped an armed bad guy target crouching by a plywood maple tree, then two more into the mannequins on the roof from her back just to make sure the targets stayed dead.

The six hard clangs of bullets striking metal targets registered only after she was safe behind the red brick.

She held her fire as two children mannequins peeked at her from a nearby window. A dummy woman rushed across the street, her form gliding on a hidden track. A rough-painted man close behind her, using the woman figure as a shield, had an AK-47. Two harsh rings of metal echoed between the buildings as Betsy shot him twice in the face—all she could see of him—and one more as she hit his knee through the fluttering back of the woman's dress.

A particularly large snowflake plastered itself across the lens of her shooting goggles. It left a wet smear when she brushed it aside.

Betsy had tracked her quarry off the edge of the map somewhere, slipping out of simulated Afghanistan into a quaint French village setting that she didn't recall ever seeing before.

The next building over, probably just painted plywood, was an exceptional imitation of rose-and-gray stonework, medieval arches, and cobbled streets barely wide enough for two donkeys to pass. It would make a resting place for the Merovingian French kings back before the Dark Ages. With the snow, it looked perfect for finding a little Provençal bistro with a mug of mulled wine and a cozy chair by a stone fireplace.

Of course the best that would be waiting for her after this would be a hot cup of coffee and a burger at the SWCS DFAC—the Special Warfare Center and School Dining Facility. If she didn't freeze to death first.

A glance back the way she'd come to make sure no one was behind her and—

Betsy blinked hard, as if that would clear away the obscuring snow.

There was no longer an Afghan town behind her, though she knew she'd just been through one. She was at the center of a French village that looked too authentic, even for Range 37. Alleys twisted. Yew trees, so old and gnarled they truly might have been planted by some ancient French king, rose before a two-story, stone, row house. A cluster of dormant rose vines climbed a nearby wall, some of the stems thicker than her arm. They'd been there a while…a long while.

An actual donkey, pulling a tiny cart bearing a large wine barrel, clopped along, his unshod hooves muffled by the fallen snow. The hard rattle of the two ironclad, wooden wheels sounded from the cobbles.

She spun back to look down the street where she'd just shot the target with an AK-47. More people flowed across the courtyard now, but not gliding on any hidden rail. Some carried gigantic woven baskets, others wooden platters of food—all hurrying this way and that as if preparing for some event. Their clothing was loose and broadcloth.

And puffs of breath were coming out of their mouths.

There weren't supposed to be any real people in a live-fire training except the attackers—in this scenario, just her. If she made a mistake, she could kill an innocent, not that she ever had. She'd always scored perfect marks in target discernment. A man came out a doorway close beside where she lay in the snow and almost stepped on her.

"Excusez-moi." He definitely spoke before hurrying down the road. Not a mannequin.

She sat up carefully, keeping her eye out for potential shooters. All of the people on the streets—and there were more with each passing moment—were dressed for some form of medieval village reenactment like the Norwegian Folk Museum in Oslo, only more French-Grand-Master-painting-come-to-life than simplistic-Nordic.

Not a one looked at her. She glanced down at herself to be sure that she hadn't changed as well. Army boots, camo pants, Kevlar shooter's vest filled with spare magazines for her rifle and a Glock still in its holster. She indeed still held her HK416 rifle and could feel the helmet on her head. Another blink, and she could feel her eyelashes brushing on the inside of her shooter goggles.

"What the hell?"

Even the air smelled different. Baked breads, wood fires, roasting meat that made her stomach growl.

Only one man was out of place now. He stood in the exact center of the courtyard and was looking directly at her.

Out of place! The alarm went off in her head. Instinct kicked in and she aimed and fired, only at the last moment realizing that he held no weapon. She tried to shift her aim, but knew it wasn't enough.

The man leaned slightly to one side and the bullet missed his cheek by a hair's breadth, smacking into a stone arch behind him and releasing a puff of rock dust as it pulverized itself.

Then, as calm as could be, he looked back at her.

Nobody, but nobody dodged a round fired from an HK416.

CHAPTER TWO

*B*etsy could only stare at him as the villagers continued
to mill about without paying any attention to either of
them. By now the donkey had drawn even with her position. She
reached out to touch it. Though she wore thin gloves, it felt real
enough.

The man, however, didn't look real. Six feet tall, but slender as
a willow branch. He didn't look unfit or misproportioned, just
impossibly slender. He had glorious black hair that fell to his waist,
whereas her own blonde was short-cropped and barely reached
her jawline. He had a long face with high cheekbones, pale skin,
and the bluest eyes she'd ever seen. He was dressed in form-fitting
black leather that might be appropriate for a chick on a
motorcycle calendar. It did look very fine on him, so maybe she
finally understood why guys went so ape over those kinds of
calendars. A little. Not much really.

One thing was for certain, though. It made him look even more
out of place in Medieval France than she did.

She couldn't react, couldn't find it in her to move as he stepped among the hurrying townsfolk until he was standing just an arm's-length away. A thin red line scored his cheek.

He noticed the direction of her attention and raised a hand to brush at it.

"I'll have to remember to move faster in future encounters."

"Move. Faster." People didn't step aside from bullets moving at 890 meters per second.

His smile was brief, but dazzling and she could only blink in surprise.

"But..." She didn't know "but" what, but it was the only sound she could make.

"I'm Horatio."

"Horatio?"

"Yes," his voice was impossibly deep and sounded more like flowing water than spoken words.

"Is that like 'Go West, Young Man' Horatio Alger? Or 'Alas, poor Yorick' in Hamlet?"

"Nor Captain Horatio Hornblower. Just Horatio the Herder."

"The herder of what? Who..." No. "*What* are you?" She forced herself to look away from his dazzling blue eyes. Her gaze landed on a prominently pointed ear where the chill wind blew aside an elegant length of his hair like some runway model's. He was both the handsomest and the prettiest man she'd ever seen, even if he wasn't one.

A group of children, ones she'd have labeled as beggars, gathered together in a group and began to sing in Latin. As a child, she'd chosen to do her confirmation into the Roman Catholic church in Latin. As an adult, she could only wonder why she'd bothered with any of it.

Orientis partibus
adventavit asinus,
pulcher et fortissimus,
Sarcinis aptissimus.

"From the east, the pretty Advent donkey carries the sacred baggage?" Maybe not so much with her Catholic school Latin.

"It is an ancient Latin Christmas carol, popular in twelfth-century France," the man waved his long-fingered hand negligently about as if that was somehow where they were. "In your language it is called *The Friendly Beasts* and relates the legend of the animals who helped with the birth of Jesus. That verse is the donkey telling of carrying Mary to the manger."

"Oh." What else was she supposed to say to such a crazy statement. She considered for a moment. This *definitely* wasn't Range 37. She rose to her toes and tried clicking the heels of her Army boots together three times.

Nothing changed.

Maybe it only worked for ruby Army boots.

Horatio smiled at her as if he knew exactly what she was doing.

"Allow me to escort you elsewhere," he turned sideways to her and offered his arm. At a loss for what else to do, she shifted her rifle to her other hand—in shooting, all Delta operators were ambidextrous— left the safety off, and slipped her fingers about his elbow. He felt as thin as he looked, but he felt as strong as a seasoned operator who could hike fifty kilometers with a full pack, just to get *into* battle.

He led her down the street to a doorway that had a wooden sign hung above it depicting a cluster of grapes, and led her inside. The smoke from the big, ill-vented, stone fireplace stung her eyes and there was a rank smell like an entire Delta platoon that had been in the field for a month without bathing. But beneath that, the cinnamon and nutmeg of mulled wine and the richness of mutton stew filled the air.

Horatio sat with the elegance of a powerful man at a small, rough table close by the warm fire. She propped her rifle against the wall close to hand and sat across from him. Their knees brushed together comfortably. He didn't draw away, but neither did he press. It was merely comfortable, friendly even. Not something she was used to with men. For the most part they either wanted sex or wanted her to get the hell out of the boys' club military unit. Horatio the Herder was harder to read and she rather liked that bit of mystery.

In moments, they were served with clay mugs of wine—enough to plow her under the table if she tried to finish it—and a steaming bowl of stew.

"The wine is quite acceptable, but I would exercise a degree of caution regarding the stew," Horatio winced as if it was bad memory.

She sipped at the wine and decided that if *this* was good wine, she'd definitely be avoiding the stew.

Betsy pinched herself, no change.

"Any chance that you'd know how badly I was injured or when I'm getting off these drugs? Or are you just a gorgeous hallucination named Horatio?"

Horatio hid a smile with a big draught of wine, but his blue eyes twinkled. They *actually* twinkled. It made him look very merry. If he really was in full elf-character, which his pointy ears indicated was likely, maybe it was part of his job to be merry. But that didn't explain how he'd made those pretty blue eyes twinkle. Of course "Elf: identification and interaction with" wasn't in any part of Delta Force's Operator Training Course.

Maybe she didn't want off these drugs, whatever they were. She'd had morphine after being shot up in Nigeria once and been completely loopy but calm as well. She still remembered portions of that helo ride while the combat search-and-rescue medics struggled to stabilize her. An incredibly handsome stranger, even in a seedy medieval pub, was a far more interesting reaction.

"I can place you back in Range 37 at any moment you should choose to request it. But I would like to discuss a special mission with you prior to such an eventuality."

"A special mission?" She tried the wine again while considering where he might have learned such speech patterns. British sitcoms came to mind. The second sip of wine slammed the back of her throat with its tannic bite. This time it only made her want to gag rather than rip her throat out, which was an improvement. She could also taste the high alcohol content. That, she decided, could be a good thing in the current situation and managed to brace herself through a third taste, but couldn't manage a fourth.

"Yes," Horatio spooned up some of the stew, apparently ignoring his earlier warning—at least until he put it in his mouth. Then looked as if he didn't know where to spit it out.

"In the fire."

He did so, creating a brief flurry of sparks.

"Back to my question," Betsy nudged her own stew bowl a little farther away as a safety precaution. "What *are* you and why am I hallucinating you?"

Not finding anywhere to wipe his mouth, he used his fingers, then wiped them on the edge of the table. "You are *not* hallucinating."

"Just what I'd expect a hallucination to say."

Horatio sighed before forging on. "This is real. Or mostly real. We see each other, but the locals merely observe a pair of strangers in locals' clothing."

"Uh-huh." Betsy could only assume this was one of those accidents that was bad enough for amnesia to kick in. Most of this she wouldn't mind losing, though Horatio himself was a real pleasure to look at. She'd been in the field a long time and dallying with a squad mate just wasn't an option. Horatio however... He looked far yummier than the wine.

What *had* happened?

Maybe a stone wall of Range 37 collapsed onto her? Or perhaps one of her shots at the metal targets had ricocheted back. At this point it wouldn't surprise if one of the targets had *shot* her back. Talking to a reindeer herding elf in a twelfth-century pub made anything seem possible.

"And as pertains to your earlier question, I am an elf—of the

Christmas variety. The one entrusted with the care of Santa's reindeer, if I may be specific."

"Hence, Horatio the Herder," Betsy didn't think her imagination was strange enough to cook up this one, which was tipping the scale—impossibly—toward the side of this experience being somehow real.

"Precisely. My dilemma lies in the fact that it is only three days to Christmas and I can not find the lead reindeer anywhere. I have need of aid from a professional."

"Me?"

"You."

"You need me to track down…Rudolph?"

"Well, his name is Jeremy, but essentially yes."

"Jeremy the red-nosed reindeer. Doesn't exactly have the right ring to it, does it?"

"Robert L. May was prone to agreeing with you, which is why he changed the name for the Montgomery Ward children's book he wrote regarding Jeremy's tribulations as a young reindeer."

"Wow!" Betsy managed a large swallow of wine to fortify herself. "You actually delivered all that as a straight line. I'm impressed." Then she stared down at the wine and wondered what exactly was in it that she almost believed him.

CHAPTER THREE

"So, lay it out for me."

"Lay *it* out? What needs laying out of it?"

Betsy pulled out her Benchmade Infidel knife, thumbed the release, and the four-inch, double-edged blade snapped out the front of the handle. She began carving the Special Operations Command shoulder patch into the wooden table with the point—a stylized arrowhead with a knife up the middle.

Horatio eyed her carefully. "I expect that you are a hard woman to buy Christmas presents for. What's your Christmas wish?"

"I gave up on wishes a long time ago."

Horatio looked at her aghast.

She held up the blade. The black-coated D2 steel appeared bloody in the dim firelight. "This one did nicely as a gift to myself. Start talking, Elf." She returned to her carving.

"We permit the reindeer to run wild during the summer season."

"I could do with a little running wild myself." Betsy could feel her inhibitions slipping away. She hadn't had that much wine. But knowing that you were injured and in some drug-induced dream made it difficult to care much about propriety. And if she was going to run a little wild, who better to do it with than a gorgeous man-elf-herder-thing.

"They always return when the fall lengthens the wavelengths that leaves reflect."

"Lengthens the wavelengths? Oh, reds and golds. Never mind. Keep going." Keeping her gaze averted from his intense eyes didn't help much. His slightly hoity-toity way of speaking didn't diminish the fact that his voice was just as beautiful as he was. She couldn't be so shallow that a beautiful man with a liquid voice was getting to her, even if he was.

"Jeremy has failed to return."

"That was the fall. And you're just contacting me three days before Christmas? That is not what we'd typically call adroit mission planning." She began digging the arch of the upper tab of the shoulder patch. What if she carved in the word "Airborne" as it should be and the table was discovered eight hundred years from now? Cause a hell of a stir. Perhaps she should drop into wherever this village was in the real world and find out for herself.

"Actually, yesterday was the final day of fall. We have now traversed the threshold of the winter solstice and such matters are suddenly come to a head."

"Maybe a hunter got him."

Horatio actually flinched. His oddly light complexion paled even further.

"Sorry, but you have to consider all of the possibilities."

"That is one I shall not be considering until all other hope is lost."

"So, where do we begin?" It wasn't often that an impossibly beautiful man asked her to do something so highly unlikely. Usually it was requests for sexual favors, which wasn't something she doled out to any Tom, Dick, or Horatio.

"At the stables, I suppose."

"Of course. Because why wouldn't Santa's reindeer have

stables. Are you nuts, Horatio? I was thinking it was me, but maybe it's you."

"I have not considered the possibility," Horatio's beautiful brow actually furrowed for a long moment as he studied his wine, then shook his head, causing his hair to flutter attractively. "No, I find your premise unlikely."

Could she ever be with a man prettier than she was? If he looked like Horatio, in a heartbeat.

"Do elves kiss?" It was amazing what could be done within a drug-induced haze.

"We do," the color returned to his cheeks, brightly.

"Do they marry?"

"Is that a proposal, Betsy?"

Now it was her turn to scoff. "I just don't like my fantasies to already be married before I kiss them."

"Then you may do so without further concern if that is your wish." The bright color high on his cheeks wasn't going away, which was rather cute.

It would be a little like kissing a movie star. He was too perfect. But that wasn't exactly a complaint worth filing with the Fantasy Dream Department—a division of the US Army Personnel Services Branch she'd never thought of submitting a requisition request to before.

Betsy reached across the table to snag the lapel of his body-hugging black leather suit and pulled him closer. She leaned in and briefly tasted the mutton stew on his lips. Thankfully, she was past that before it could put her off completely. Past that, he tasted of cinnamon and the wild outdoors of a snowy night. Of luscious hot cocoa and a crackling fire.

Horatio's kiss was warm, attentive, thoughtful…and masterful.

If she hadn't been dreaming before, she most certainly was now. Dreaming of how fast they could go somewhere there weren't any other people, just the two of them and a big, warm bed.

Her pulse was soon chattering faster than an M134 Minigun on full auto, yet Horatio was still only exploring the first steps of a kiss.

"Get me out of here," her own voice sounded desperate and needy.

"As you wish."

CHAPTER FOUR

*T*he cold slapped her so hard that she lost her breath—as
well as her lip lock on Horatio.

"What the hell?"

"The stables."

"You brought me to a freezing cold barn?"

"I brought you to the source as you requested. These are the
reindeer stables of St. Nicholas of Myra."

Betsy could only look around in astonishment. A long line of
stalls appeared to be made out of living yew trees, all trained into
walls and stable dividers. Their roots were lost beneath a luxuriant
layer of living grass—the brightest green she'd ever seen. The
stables were lit by fireflies swarming among the branches.

And the sky.

The ceiling was of glass so clear that she could hardly tell it was
there between her and the magnificent night sky. As she blinked
away the worst of the pub's smoke and her eyes adjusted, she
began picking out constellations.

"That's the North Star."

Horatio looked up as well. "It is."

"It's directly overhead."

"Point six seven degrees from directly overhead to be precise. We are at the celestial north pole rather than the magnetic or geographic one. Nice, isn't it?"

"But the North Pole isn't over land. It's over sea ice."

"It is, in most planes of reality."

Betsy couldn't think of what else to do...so she hit him. Not hard—it had been a very nice kiss after all. Just squarely enough in the solar plexus that he wouldn't be able to speak for a few moments so that she could do some thinking.

Horatio dropped to his knees and wheezed a bit.

North Pole.

A missing reindeer named Jeremy.

An elf, a very handsome elf who could kiss better than any human—a kiss that also left her wondering what else he could do better.

St. Nicholas beneath Polaris the North Star in some very adjacent reality.

Real? Surreal? Digital? Drugs?

No way to tell.

She sighed, and helped Horatio back to his feet.

The only way out is through. Old axiom. There were times she hated old axioms.

"Last spring. Did anyone see which way Jeremy went?"

CHAPTER FIVE

$\mathcal{I}$t had taken the CIA years to find bin Laden. And another half-year to actually get around to taking him down after "Maya" had found him.

She had three days to track a reindeer. Her total assets? One elf who didn't want it to be known that he'd lost Santa's most famous reindeer, Jeremy.

The first break came when they were questioning the other reindeer. They didn't like having her around and were very standoffish, until she dug around in Horatio's larder and found a bag of carrots. They warmed up to her quickly after that. Who knew that reindeer had a major weak spot for carrots.

A small portion of St. Nick's deer herd—mostly the younger set —had gone south and west last spring, rather than south and east to their normal habitat in Finland. It turned out that reindeer had a particularly low-brow sense of humor—even worse than most Delta operators. They liked spending their summers mingling with the Finnish herds and teasing them about not making the cut to become a Christmas reindeer. They also weren't above tripping them into mudholes and the like.

The breakaway herd had crossed down over the Canadian tundra, mingling with the caribou herds in some sort of convention. But they quickly grew bored as the Canadians had even less of a sense of humor than their Finnish counterparts.

That had led to any number of fights and endless head butting. The younger members of the herd whined about it no end.

"Teenagers," she scoffed to Horatio after he'd translated that for her. "Hard to deal with."

"Gift cards." Apparently that was his harshest epithet. "It is the only way St. Nick has found to deal with them at Christmas."

Betsy had been such a good girl as a teen, of course taking care of her ailing mother had made that an obvious choice. She'd even been well behaved as an Army grunt then a Delta operator. And now, just three days from freedom, she'd been injured and was drugged up in some Fort Bragg hospital. It didn't seem fair.

She tossed out some more carrots to get the rest of the story. Most had continued west to roam with the big herds in Alaska. But Jeremy had turned south once more, toward the heat and bright sun. He'd said he was headed to a place called Mont-a-land or something like. None of them had ever heard of it.

"Montana?"

Some of them thought that sounded right, but were more interested in carrots than answering questions. She took the bag with her when she left. When they protested, she simply made a show of resettling her rifle across her shoulders...which proved most effective. About time they did some growing up.

She and Horatio started in the Canadian Northwest Territories at a place with the unlikely name of Reindeer Station. Eight or nine houses located along the edge of the sprawling Mackenzie River delta less than fifty miles from the Arctic Ocean. It wasn't all that much warmer than the North Pole with just two days to Christmas. The river was iced over and was crisscrossed with snowmobile tracks. She'd borrowed a brilliant red parka with a white sheepskin lining to keep her warm.

It took most of the morning to track the region's sole remaining reindeer herder to his remote cabin. It was a gruesome affair. Not merely well away from even the hamlet of Reindeer Station, it was also the butchery for bulls thinned from the herd. Reindeer meat was stacked outside in the Arctic chill and quick-frozen beneath hides. Inside the hut, the tools of the trade dangled from hooks on the wall. Yet the herder also had a young reindeer on a leash as a pet.

Horatio was shivering even more than the temperature could account for.

Betsy held his hand tightly to calm him, which she didn't mind doing at all, while she was talking to the man. Even while shivering from disgust or distress, Horatio's hand was as warm as a handmade quilt. He appeared perfectly comfortable in his body-hugging leather despite the Arctic temperature.

The herder's English was limited and apparently Horatio was only fluent in English, French, and reindeer, so he was of no help. The herder, speaking mostly in some Inuit language, allowed as he might have seen a rather curious animal that had stood aloof from his herd of three thousand reindeer. A magnificent bull with more points than he could count. He waved south.

"Inuvik?" That was the next town, some twenty miles away.

He shook his head and waved again.

"Fort McPherson?" It was the only other town she knew in the Northwest Territories.

Again the wave south, "Mont-a-land."

CHAPTER SIX

*B*ut going directly to Montana was too big a leap. It would take forever to pick up Jeremy's track again. So they worked south in stages following the rumors of an aloof, many-pointed bull reindeer.

"I thought Jeremy was supposed to be a cute little guy."

"Indeed he was, seventy-five years ago when Robert L. May wrote about him. He has matured somewhat over the years. He is still a sweetheart though as he never allowed the success to go to his head."

"How long do reindeer usually live? Maybe he died of old age."

"Fifteen to twenty years, typically, unless they are in the employ of St. Nicholas. Then their lives are rather extended."

Betsy eyed him carefully. There was an agelessness to Horatio's clear features. He would have been as classically handsome a thousand years ago as he was now. Perhaps there were some questions that it was better not to ask.

Besides, time was running too fast.

"Can't you slow it down?"

"Not even St. Nicholas can do that."

Thirty-six hours remaining.

Jeremy wanted her to eat something after they'd chased leads all the way down the frozen Mackenzie to the small town of Yellowknife on Great Slave Lake. From there, they'd run the ice road over to the hamlet of Detah and were now sitting in a small barn. The owner had told the story of the most "magnificent bull" he'd ever tracked while hunting. Best he'd ever seen, but apparently his shot had gone wild.

"Jeremy is very wily," Horatio's whisper had tickled her ear like a warm breeze.

She tried a carrot, but they'd frozen hard. "Give me an MRE and let's get going."

So, he gave her a pre-heated Meal-Ready-to-Eat. She didn't ask how. Next time she'd ask for a roast beef dinner with Yorkshire pudding and see if her friendly neighborhood hallucination could deliver.

"Maybe you should rest." The small barn had a hayloft, and the hunter had returned to his ice fishing on the frozen lake. It was tempting. So very, very tempting. She couldn't remember the last time she'd been this tired.

"When the mission is done." She chowed down on the Southwest Beef and Black Beans while Horatio massaged her shoulders. Now that was something she could become very used to—far better than the cold, lack of sleep, and the utterly ludicrous situation.

His fingers were strong enough to ease even her soldier-hard muscles until she felt ready to melt against him. She tossed aside the empty MRE package and decided that a little melting wasn't completely outside the mission profile.

She'd forgotten—mostly—about the kiss in the ancient French bistro. The memory did nothing to prepare her for what happened next. Horatio felt luscious as he pulled her tightly against him. In mid-clench, she tried to rub herself even more tightly against his incredible body.

Horatio grunted, and not in a good way.

"Your vest," he managed to gasp.

Betsy paused and looked down between them. She wore her Glock sidearm, as most Delta did, front and center for a fast draw. Above that, pockets of ammo and emergency supplies made hard edges that had left scrapes on his smooth leather.

"Sorry." Vest. Mission. Ludicrous scenario.

The only way out is through.

She sighed, sat up, and patted Horatio's cheek. He had the decency to look disappointed despite the gouges she'd been digging into his chest.

"Your colonel," Horatio nodded to the south, "said that you were the hardest-driving scout in his entire team."

"You spoke to Colonel Gibson about finding one of Santa's reindeer?" She tried to imagine how the stern colonel took it.

"Perhaps I may not have asked him quite directly, but he was very impressed with your skills."

That was news to her. She hadn't known that Delta Force's commander even knew who she was.

She sighed to herself that some overwound inner drive wouldn't even let her enjoy a hallucinatory snuggle.

They left the tiny Detah barn and they turned south across Alberta.

CHAPTER SEVEN

*T*hey had pizza in Banff and she spent three delicious hours mostly passed out in the curve of Horatio's arms in a snowed-in hiking cabin high in Glacier Park. She didn't ask how Horatio moved them from place to place. It seemed that they flowed, glided, perhaps simply morphed from one destination to the next. It was a dream, so it was easy to not question the transitions.

But she would miss her time with Horatio. No, she'd miss Horatio himself. Even strung out on whatever narcotic was giving her this extended dream, she was becoming very attached to him.

Yes, he'd started out all strange and mysterious and mostly concerned about a missing reindeer. But he had shifted. More slowly than their jumping from one place to another, but just as steadily.

Still wrapped in her parka, she lay in his arms in the chill cabin and felt…right. As if it was where she was supposed to be. Perhaps "content" was a better word, though it was not one that had ever come up before in her life.

He hadn't asked about her past, which was just as well. She

didn't want to talk about it. But neither had he talked about his. Did elves have pasts? Did elves have regrets? She hoped not as she had enough for both of them.

"What is an elf's life like?" She could feel him shift as if he was looking down at the top of her head in some surprise.

"Normal enough. The reindeer usually do a good job of taking care of themselves, that's why I didn't think to worry. Generally I spend but one month a year tending them. It's a good life for them as well." And he began telling her about their grazing habits, and the practical jokes they liked to play.

One year they'd started at the South Pole rather than the North, forcing St. Nicholas to act like a Dumpster-diver as he dug out successive presents from the bottom of the sleigh's pile instead of working top-down. Or the year they'd switched all of the rabbits' stockings with all of the squirrels'—the rabbits had ended up have a grand game of ice hockey with the acorns and walnuts but the squirrels had never figured out what to do with the sudden bounty of cabbage.

It was only as they were trekking south into the Flathead Wilderness of Montana that she realized he'd told her nothing of himself. Perhaps it was fair, she'd said nothing of herself either, but it rankled. Of course, with his voice, she'd happily listen to him reading the naughty and nice name list—especially the naughty if he gave some of the details.

Dawn broke hard.

She couldn't think of how else to describe it. While traveling through Canada, they had been in and out of snowstorms beneath gray skies. This morning, they'd left the cabin in Glacier Park beneath the last stars of the night, almost as brightly perfect as those from Santa's reindeer stables. It had been a relief that the North Star had shifted well down the sky, so they were indeed well to the south.

But standing atop the Castle Reef ridgeline and looking down at the Montana Front Range in one direction, and up into the heart of the snow-capped Rocky Mountains in the other, dawn began with a snap as sharp as the cold.

The sun lanced over the flat horizon from impossibly far away and the entire world was catapulted into a limitless blue bowl of sky.

"I take it this is why they call it Big Sky country," Horatio sounded breathless.

"I guess." Betsy also couldn't catch her breath. It might be the eight-thousand-foot elevation or the slicing cold of the morning wind driving ice crystals into her face like blowback from Barrett .50 cal sniper rifle.

It might be the view.

But it was more the realization that this was December 23rd. One way or another, their quest would be over today. As soon as sunset hit the International Date Line in roughly twelve hours, St. Nicholas would be flying off to do his job—with or without the errant Jeremy.

Yet she could feel that he was close. Some instinct, honed over the years by Delta training, told her their quarry was nearly in sight.

She flagged down a rancher passing by in his helicopter, who settled it neatly atop the peak. Clearly ex-military by how he flew, despite the fact that he now commanded a small Bell JetRanger with a herd of horses painted along the side.

"How can I help you, ma'am?" He drawled it out in a Texas accent so fake that it would get him lynched in certain states. "Need a lift off this here hilltop?"

"No, we're fine."

"We?" He tugged his mirrored sunglasses down enough to squint at her strangely.

She glanced aside at Horatio who just shook his head.

Fine. Whatever. So he was invisible or something. Had he shown up for anyone else, or had she just crossed Canada as a solo crazy lady talking to herself? She'd bet on the latter, but didn't have time to deal with it now.

"Have you seen a reindeer that—"

"Reindeer? We have moose and elk in these parts. Even a few caribou, but no reindeer."

"Reindeer and caribou are the same animal," Horatio prompted her.

When the pilot didn't respond, she repeated the information.

"Wa'll, ain't that a wonder."

"Have you seen a particularly impressive one lately?"

He rubbed his chin thoughtfully. He'd have been the handsomest man in any crowd that didn't include Horatio.

"Might have heard mention of one. Over to a hot spring up along the North Fork Deep Creek. My wife said she saw one when one of our guides and a guest shot—"

"Shot?" Betsy grabbed the pilot's arm in a panic.

"Shot two *young* bulls," the man looked down at his arm in some distress and tried to shake her off. At least the awful Texas accent was gone.

She shook him by his arm to keep him talking.

"She said it was the biggest old bull she'd ever seen. Had himself a couple of does and a fawn. Guess they didn't want to break up the family. Ease off, lady." He wiggled his arm a little and grimaced.

"Jeremy has a family?" Horatio's blue eyes were almost as wide as the Big Sky. Then he looked at her and his gaze shifted as if asking if she also had a family.

She had no one. No one on the outside, and in just another day, she'd be out of Delta and have no one on the inside either. This definitely was *not* the moment she wanted to be thinking about her future.

"Do you know where that hot spring is?"

Horatio nodded.

"Of course I do," the pilot looked at her strangely. "I'm the one who just told you about it. Are you okay all alone up here?"

"Not really." She let go of the pilot who began massaging the arm she'd had a hold of. She was hunting for one of Santa's reindeer and absolutely falling for a hallucination named Horatio, but she didn't want to talk about it with some rancher pilot. "But I can find it on my own."

"I can't just leave you here, lady." The pilot looked around. There was nothing to see from the summit of Castle Reef except snowy mountains, dusky plains, and the biggest blue sky ever.

"Fine, *I'll* leave *you*, then. Thanks for the help."

She walked past Horatio. For the first time, she could feel one of his spatial shifts slowly wrapping around her before it actually happened.

"What the hell?"

She liked that she left the pilot with his own hallucination to figure out. Misery loves company.

CHAPTER EIGHT

*T*he hot spring was unoccupied, but it didn't take her long to pick up the fresh tracks through the snow.

"By the tracks, it's a big bull, two does, and a half-grown fawn."

Horatio let her lead the way. It was a hard slog through the deep snow, even though the herd had broken the path.

At one point, an avalanche had erased their tracks. It took them several anxious hours to pick them up again on the far side of the damage path.

It was barely an hour to local sunset—and only four or five to Global Flying Time—when she found them. The small herd was grazing near a copse of Douglas fir that had blocked much of the snow. They were kicking aside the little snow that remained and eating the frozen grass.

"Jeremy!" Horatio's shout of joy shook loose an entire cascade of snow from one of the trees that she barely managed to dodge.

The two of them—elf and reindeer—ran to each other and were soon chattering away in reindeer which sounded like grunts and squeaks to her untrained ear.

Betsy ducked under the low-hanging branches and found a

small spot clear of snow where she could lean back against the trunk and wait.

Exhaustion rippled through her as it always did after a hard scouting job. But it wasn't just that. She was leaving Delta because she could feel that she was losing the edge and, with how far past it Delta normally operated, that was an unacceptable change. One far too prone to death. For the first time since she'd joined the Army, she didn't belong anywhere. Yet over the last three days…

Betsy watched Horatio as he was introduced to the rest of Jeremy's family.

For the last three days, Betsy had started to belong. Not merely due to her skills either. When she was with Horatio even something as crazy as searching for Santa's missing reindeer made sense. Anything…*everything* somehow made sense when she was with him. She hadn't truly belonged somewhere that she could ever recall, but she could see herself belonging with a fantasy named Horatio.

She must have dozed, though the sun had barely shifted when Horatio kissed her awake. That gained her undivided attention, but he was too excited for it to last more than a moment.

"He has a family. But he couldn't get them back to the stables on his own. He needed an elfin herder to transport them the first time. Jeremy is a good man—"

"Reindeer," she corrected him.

"Reindeer," Horatio readily agreed and kissed her on the nose. "He didn't want to abandon his family, but didn't know any of the locals who could send me a message. Apparently love at first sight happens for reindeer as well."

As well? Is that what had happened to her? It didn't seem very likely, but neither did anything in the three days since she'd last stood on Range 37.

Now Horatio was looking at her very intently. "You're the most amazing human I've ever met, Betsy."

"Human?" But that said nothing of the amazing elf women he'd surely known. Why was she pining for a drug-dream fantasy?

"Woman. Of any breed or species. I've been watching you for days and can't believe your tenacity and skill. Or your beauty. Can all human women kiss the way you do?"

Betsy could feel herself becoming overwhelmed by his compliments. But nothing overwhelmed a Delta soldier. They were trained to keep their thoughts under control in any situation.

She slipped her fingers into his magnificent mane of hair and tugged it lightly to pull him closer.

"Perhaps I won't give you any excuse to find out."

"Mmm," he made a happy sound as he leaned into her kiss.

She could feel it supercharge her, ramp her up even the way a decisive victory couldn't achieve. There was a feeling of vitality, of joyous triumph at being alive at the end of a hard battle.

Horatio made her feel that ten times over. His kiss filled her thoughts until they overflowed and radiated back to him. She wanted him to take her right here, right now. Under the trees. In the snow. Even with the reindeer watching. She didn't care.

She opened her eyes to look up into his amazing eyes the color of the Montana Big Sky, just as a particularly large snowflake plastered itself across her shooting goggles she didn't recall putting back on.

It left a wet smear when she brushed it aside.

And once again she was in the heart of a mock Afghan village, dusted with North Carolina snow.

A mannequin bearing an RPG leaned out of a doorway.

Only habit had her shooting it twice in the face and once in the chest.

CHAPTER NINE

*B*etsy finished the Range 37 course with the same high marks she always did, but felt none of the victory at the score—even though she'd managed to snatch-and-grab the bad guy on her own.

The next two days were a slow slog through the bureaucracy of leaving a service she'd given a decade to. Quartermaster this. Housing that. Personnel records the other thing.

She couldn't equate the Range 37 exercise and the two days of bureaucracy involved in leaving the service with the three days she'd spent with Horatio the Herder tracking a stray Christmas reindeer.

At each step she took through her Fort Bragg reality over the same three days, she could feel the other reality fading into memory. The three days with Horatio had passed so quickly and now time crawled.

December 21st: Quartermaster this. Horatio's strong hands resting on her shoulders a moment longer than needed as he helped her into a red-and-white parka while they stood in the most magnificent stables she'd ever seen.

December 22nd: Housing that. Holding each other close in a small hayloft in Detah on the frozen shores of the Great Slave Lake. A feeling of belonging she'd never known.

December 23rd: Personnel records the other thing. Waking in his arms in a Glacier Park cabin and knowing she had never been anywhere so safe or so...important before in her life.

December 24th: nothing but a blur. Horatio the elf would be with his reindeer, making sure they performed their annual flight, preparing the stable for their return. Bedding them down when they were done.

No one that she'd served with was currently rotated into Fort Bragg from abroad, so she passed her final days in the US military in silence. Alone.

The snow had melted and new teams were working their way through Range 37. No twelfth-century French village with bad wine and poisonous stew would be awaiting them any more than it was awaiting her. She'd go back if she could, just to see Horatio once more. Once she was out, maybe she'd take her motorcycle to Europe and go searching for a French pub with an Airborne shoulder patch carved into one table's surface.

But there wouldn't be. Hallucinations didn't work that way. It had taken a long and lonely Christmas eve to convince herself that was all it had been.

Early Christmas morning, she turned in her firearm, was issued her DD 214 Honorable Discharge form, and was issued a temporary visitor badge that would see her to the front gates. She bundled up against the chilly day, missing the warmth of the North Pole parka, though she didn't really feel the cold anymore. Climbing on her Yamaha YZF superbike, Betsy rolled out the Manchester Gate by Pope Airfield.

Maybe she'd swing south and see a bit of the country. She had no real plans until summer. But then her course would be certain. This summer, she'd be chasing the melting snow north, starting with the Flathead Wilderness. Even if it hadn't been real, she'd retrace the path as far north as she possibly could, right up to Reindeer Station on the banks of the Mackenzie River.

Perhaps there would be a reindeer, a small fawn grown into the grand bull that would at least remind her of Jeremy and she could pretend that he would lead her north to a stable made of yew trees.

At the Fort Bragg gate, the corporal took her temporary pass, and saluted her smartly. She returned the gesture for the last time, then rolled out the gate. Out Manchester Road, she'd pick up North Bragg Boulevard and punch south.

For now.

Then she'd—

Betsy slammed on the brakes and tried to make sense of what she was seeing.

Just off base, along the wooded lane, stood Pyrates Sports Bar. It wasn't much of a place: pool, beer, and a decent burger.

And leaning against one of the big maples stood an impossibly thin man with black hair down to his waist and eyes the color of the Big Sky.

She couldn't release her death grip on the handlebars as Horatio strolled up to her and reached out to raise the visor on her helmet.

"Hi."

"Hi? *Hi!* That's what you have to say for yourself? I've spent three days convincing myself that you were just a hallucination. What are you doing to me? Is this some kind of weird drug experiment or—"

Horatio leaned in and kissed her.

She dropped the clutch. The Yamaha lurched then stalled, and broke the kiss. She'd already forgotten his taste of cinnamon and the great outdoors. How had she possibly forgotten that?

"Does that feel like a hallucination in your consideration?"

Betsy could only shake her head.

"I know this is a little abrupt, but how would you like a job?"

"No way, Horatio. You evaporated at the end of the last one."

"I would not this time."

"And I'm supposed to trust an elf hallucination on that?"

"Absolutely," and Horatio's smile lit his eyes to a merry twinkle, just as they did every time.

"Why?"

"Because I could use the assistance of a skilled reindeer herder."

"You want me to live at the North Pole with you?"

"We would travel a lot. I only tend the reindeer around Christmas. An elf's main job during the year is rather global: spreading good cheer wherever he can."

"Can you promise me that you're not a hallucination? I really want you to not be a hallucination." Even if he was, Betsy had the feeling that she wasn't going to care.

"I've been wracking my brain to find an appropriate Christmas present for you. That wish will do nicely. I promise you that I am completely real."

She hadn't thought about a Christmas wish in a long time, but if there was ever one she wanted to come true…

Betsy kissed him lightly, then nodded toward the back of the bike.

"Climb aboard, Horatio. We've got some good cheer to spread."

CHAPTER TEN

*B*etsy leaned against the yew tree that made one side of the stable's main door and pulled her red-and-white parka more tightly about her as she watched Horatio with the herd. It was Christmas Eve and once more the excitement practically shimmered through St. Nick's stables.

Harnesses with bright polished bells were laid upon well-curry-combed backs as the reindeer pranced with delight. A small elf choir stood up in the hayloft singing about Good King Wenceslas, Little Drummer Boys, and Friendly Beasts. She noted that Rudolph was nowhere in the repertoire—Jeremy was *not* a fan of Robert L. May. He'd grown to be a very dignified reindeer.

"Especially now that he has a family to look after," Horatio had whispered softly in her ear one night.

And his nose was definitely not red, his main point of contention.

Before Jeremy was harnessed into the lead position, he clopped over to her and faced her silently.

Betsy's grasp of reindeer language still sucked, though she was improving.

But he didn't say a word.

Instead, he tipped his head down, and shifted his face gently against her chest and simply rested it there. His great rack of antlers framed her protectively to either side.

She hugged him, wrapping her arms around his head.

"Merry Christmas to all," she whispered to him. "And have a good flight."

He snorted a soft laugh at her twisting of the last line of Rudolph's story before pulling away to stride over to his position to be harnessed in.

With a stamp and snort and a prance and a paw, the herd was soon aloft, towing St. Nick and his sleigh on their merry rounds.

The silence seemed to be a long time settling over the stables once they were gone. But in time, even the fireflies had settled and only the quiet stars of the Arctic night lit the stables.

Jeremy slipped close beside her and wrapped his arms about her. She rested back against him and marveled at how her life had changed. How she would never be alone again.

Last Christmas, Horatio had given her a gift beyond imagining, she was no longer alone in the world.

She rested her hand on her own belly.

Tomorrow, Christmas morning—after the reindeer had completed their flight, then gone to bed for the night—she would tell him the news.

Her gift to him would be—she tried not to think it in the same rhythm as the Rudolph poem, but being married to a Christmas elf was changing her in many wondrous ways—that quite soon they'd be three.

IF YOU ENJOYED THIS, YOU MIGHT ALSO ENJOY:

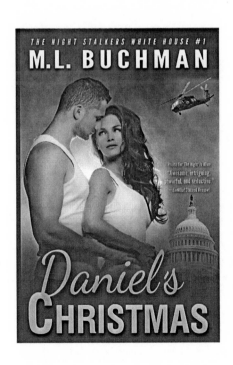

M. L. BUCHMAN

3-time Booklist Top 10 Romance Author of the Year

The Christmas Lights OBJECTIVE

a Night Stalkers 5E romance story

THE CHRISTMAS LIGHTS OBJECTIVE

*K*elsey *"Killjoy" Killaney can track down the worst drug
lord of a Mexican cartel. But of all stupid days, why
must it be on Christmas? Her least favorite day of the year.*

*Jason Gould flies with the very best, the Night Stalkers 5E helicopter
company. Christmas ranked as his best day every year, until this one.*

*When the mission comes to take out a drug lord on Christmas Eve,
maybe they can both track the Christmas Lights Objective.*

INTRODUCTION

I decided that I wanted to end the year with the Night Stalkers. And this story was for December, so another Christmas story seemed appropriate. We're once more aboard the *Calamity Jane II,* which is fast becoming my favorite heli-crew. (Of course, *every* team is my favorite when I'm writing about them.)

I felt bad for Jason, because for several books and short stories now, he's been the quiet guy hanging out alone at the far rear ramp-gunner position. I felt that Christmas was high time for him to finally get his own happy-ever-after adventure.

The problem with a helicopter is that it is a fairly static world. Hard to bring in an excuse for adventure, danger, romance, *and* Christmas. So I sent them out into the world on a "kingpin" mission.

The heart of this story though, is Christmas.

The challenge for a writer is getting "truth" on the page. It doesn't have to be factual or reality-true, but it must be some part of the writer's own personal "truth." I had to wrestle hard with this story, both the planning and the writing.

My childhood family was the one that saved up all of the year's fights to have a massive, multi-month one over the Christmas tree. Not Christmas itself, just the poor tree. Once I was grown, it took years before I could accept a friend's invitation to spend Christmas with them.

And on the other side of the coin, when I finally met the lady who is now my wife, she showed me that Christmas is also a celebration of joy and family. It came straight from her heart and I'm glad to say straight into mine.

Why do I write romance? Because she taught me to believe in it that too.

CHAPTER ONE

"*T*his sounds as much fun as an air raid at Christmas... Wait, that's what it is." The guy in the goofy Santa hat cut Kelsey off after her opening line of the mission briefing: *This mission flies tonight.*

"Dashing through the air," the senior crew chief of the Night Stalker Chinook helicopter team began singing in her bright soprano. "In a two-rotor heli-sleigh."

"Over the jungle we go, a-fighting all the way," another joined in—an off-key tenor.

The various members of the operation's primary helicopter crew began adding in verses. Soon both pilots and three crew chiefs were rocking to the beat just as if they were in their massive, twin-rotor Chinook.

Sergeant Jason Gould—loadmaster on the *Calamity Jane II* and the man wearing the goofy Santa hat—joined in with a rich baritone. She didn't know why she should be surprised.

But she *was* surprised. He looked like a New York Jew from her own Brooklyn neighborhood. His speaking voice, while pleasant in the few words she'd been willing to exchange with someone in a

Santa hat, hadn't foreshadowed the bone-melting baritone that quickly became the anchor of the song.

She could almost like him, except his hat sported a blinking-nose Rudolph on it. In her book, it was a target saying, "Please shoot me here." Though since they'd just met, and they were both US Special Operations, she left her sidearm in its holster.

They sat in a meeting room in the team's residence building. It stood beside a large hangar—labeled as abandoned. Abandoned deep in the woods of Fort Rucker, Alabama. She'd been directed down a tiny access road that was marked as closed and had looked disused. The gray afternoon, dripping with December rain, made both the building and hangar appear even more sad and weather-beaten. She'd almost turned around—until she noticed the cutting-edge surveillance and security system tucked in the corners of the structures.

The inside of the residence, once she'd gained admittance, was immaculate and comfortable with all of the latest conveniences. She hadn't seen the inside of the hangar yet.

The meeting room's walls were covered in brilliant travel posters—so many of them that they were starting to overlap: Costa Rica, Honduras, and Venezuela were understandable. But there was also Afghanistan, Iraq, Somalia, Libya...

It was the strangest briefing room décor Kelsey Killaney had ever worked in.

"It's my Christmas, too. Not my call." She grimaced as her protest cut off the singing. *Killjoy Killaney.* Once again, the old high school nickname was definitely her. If it *had* been up to her, she'd have scheduled the flight for Christmas Eve anyway, just so that she didn't have to think about "the happy season" for one more millisecond than necessary. But it had been circumstances, not orders that had brought them together on Christmas Eve afternoon.

This morning, everyone at her office in Fort Belvoir, Virginia had been buzzing with the "Best Wishes" and merry yeah-whatever. She'd wanted to lie on the floor and throw a tantrum as if she was nine, not twenty-nine—the little girl wanting everyone to just shut up. Her worldview was more mature now. Now, she was a grown woman who just wished everyone would go away.

Another Christmas wish gone bust. Not that any of the ones as a child had paid off.

This morning, Michael Gibson, the commander of Delta Force, had appeared at her desk inside The Activity's headquarters without warning—not even from security who were there to make sure such things didn't happen. The Intelligence Support Activity worked in one of the most secure buildings on a fort made up of twenty major intel agencies. The Activity's sole purpose was serving the Special Operations Forces, but that didn't mean they were supposed to be able to just walk in.

"There's a jet waiting for you at Davison Army Airfield," had been his idea of a pleasant Christmas Eve morning greeting—which actually worked for her. "Here's your team and mission file to read on the flight."

He'd handed her a slim folder that she wanted to handle as much as a live snake. It had a yellow fly sheet with a dark red border. In large type it only had an identification number and two of the scariest words in the intelligence business: Eyes Only. She'd checked the back of the fly sheet. Her name had been added in the second position, countersigned by Colonel Michael Gibson himself. Theirs were the only two names on the file.

She'd looked back up at him, but he'd been gone. If not for the file clutched in her white-knuckled fingers, she'd have doubted he'd ever been there. One look at the first page and she was on the move. On her way out the door to grab the scram kit from the trunk of her car, she'd stopped off at the front desk. Just as she suspected, he never *had* been signed in...or even seen—Delta Force guys were just creepy sometimes.

Reading the mission portion of the file Gibson had given her, made her the obvious choice for the operation. Actually, the only choice.

Reading the portion about the 5E was just...headshaking.

The 5E had an unprecedented number of missions with an unlikely success rate—even by the Night Stalkers' stratospheric standards. Yet the details of most of their missions had been redacted from the file now sitting in the locked briefcase at her feet.

With their song cut off, they were all sitting and waiting. Waiting and ready for their latest mission assignment. That's when she looked at the posters again.

"Duh!"

Jason, happy in his Santa hat, looked over but she just shook her head to ward him off. She hoped he would look away before she was forced to attack Rudolph's blinking nose. The last thing she needed was to explain herself to a Night Stalking Christmas elf, no matter how nice a voice he had. Why was a New York Jew singing Christmas carols anyway?

Except he wasn't a fellow Brooklynite. According to the file, Loadmaster Jason Gould was from Florida no matter how much he sounded New York.

Kelsey understood now. She didn't need the list of redacted missions—they were right there on the walls. These people collected travel posters of everywhere they'd ever had an operation. Now she could start putting some of the pieces together.

Each poster was a snapshot of a mission file.

"Find Beauty in Honduras." A black ops Honduran mission last year that had shaken the corrupt banking-military cooperative to the core. It had significantly stabilized the duly-elected government—but no hint of who had done the mission. The answer sat in this room.

"Surf Kamchatka." The 5E had done the Russian drone mission.

"Hike the Negev." The disastrous Negev Desert, Israel, mission that had shaken The Activity itself to the core, somehow salvaged by the field team. By this team.

She tried to catch her breath, but wasn't having much luck. No wonder she hadn't heard of the 5E, though they were the logical extension of Henderson's and Beale's D Company. The 5D had been hugely innovative in their approach to military tactics. The 5E, however, were the tactical equivalent of Delta Force—silent and dangerous as hell...or Christmas.

"Damn it!" Jason complained. "Christmas Eve! Shit, man! And I was going to get my nails done tonight." That earned a laugh around the table. The team was apparently unflappable.

Despite her clumsiest efforts, their spirits remained high.

She got along with data, not people.

Activity agents were rarely in on the final mission. They might go out into the field a dozen times themselves gathering intelligence, but operations were generally left to the action teams. But tonight there was no choice.

Kelsey couldn't stop herself from glancing down at Sergeant Jason Gould's hands as he made a show of inspecting his nails critically. They were cut short, uneven, and showed that he made his living with those hands—which made sense for a ramp gunner on an MH-47G Chinook. As one of the three crew chiefs, he'd have a dozen roles to serve—all of which said competent and strong. He was several inches taller than her own five-seven with an attractive leanness. She knew from his file that his family had a sportfishing business out of St. Petersburg, Florida. Curly dark hair and nearly black eyes.

She'd almost been attracted—if not for her hopelessness with attractive men. And the stupid hat.

"We'll go together, Jason. I need a mani-pedi anyway." Carmen. Dark red hair. Crew chief of the Chinook. Married to the co-pilot on the same craft. What a crazy outfit.

Five aboard the Chinook and four more aboard each of the two DAP Hawk gun platforms that would be flying protection. With her that made a total of fourteen flying tonight, plus two assets who had yet to arrive.

As Kelsey had no more control over the crew selection than the mission, she started the briefing. They might appear carefree, but the moment she began laying out the details of the mission, she had a hundred percent of their attention.

CHAPTER TWO

*I*t was still mid-afternoon by the time the short briefing ended and they were into the hangar. The soft rain had turned downright wet.

Jason had been searching for an excuse to talk to Kelsey Killaney since the moment she'd hit the pavement at the 5E's compound. He found it when they stepped into the hangar.

"Stealth, ma'am. Every last bird." Their big Chinook, two DAP Hawks—Black Hawks turned into the world's most advanced gun platforms, and two Little Birds. The last wouldn't be on this mission, and the crews hadn't been called.

"I see that," she sounded a little breathless. "I've simply never heard of them."

"Must admit that we like it that way."

"It explains how," she looked at him puzzled for a moment, as if surprised to find herself talking to him. "How you do what you do."

"That, and the best crew flying." He still couldn't believe that he was here. He supposed it was just being in the right place at the right time. After the Negev Desert disaster, they'd needed a new bird. The Army had provided them with the stealth configured *Calamity Jane II* and shipped them down to the 5E's team at Fort Rucker. Their mission pace had doubled and the complexity as well. He'd always simply been glad to be flying, but in the 5E he'd become more than he'd ever imagined.

And now, with Kelsey Killaney standing so close beside him that he could smell her fresh scent, like a strange winter flower, he started to understand just what he'd achieved. He was a goddamn flyer on the best bird in the sky, anywhere. Maybe, just maybe, he was good enough to stand next to a woman like her and not feel out of place.

They were following the rest of the crew up the rear ramp of the *Calamity Jane II*, prepping it for the first leg of the flight.

Her light brown hair was back in a severe ponytail that emphasized her large eyes. She was fair-skinned and had one of those smiles that looked as if it was always ready, even though she hadn't used it yet that he'd seen. The fact that she worked for The Activity said she was screamingly intelligent—an assumption borne out by the concise style of her briefing. If smart was the new sexy, she was a chart breaker—not that she wasn't by the old measure as well.

He'd truly done his best to pay attention at the briefing, but it had been hit and miss. He'd managed to sit next to her, by the simple stratagem of holding out a chair for her. But, no matter what he did, he couldn't get her to laugh. That hint of a smile hadn't even shifted when he'd started a whole riff about personal grooming tips off Carmen's mani-pedi remark—which was more Zoe the drone pilot's thing than Carmen's anyway.

Danny and the Captain were already in their seats running through checklists. Carmen and George were still outside pulling off pitot tube and air intake covers. So he had a moment and intended to use every second of it to his advantage.

"You need anything, ma'am? If so, I'm your man." He tried not to wince. Smooth as descending staircase on a tricycle—a trick he'd only tried once, but possibly where he got his taste for flying. He was getting no points for subtlety on this effort.

"Do you have a reality check somewhere?" Her question caused him to do a doubletake. So she did have a sense of humor behind her ever-so-serious facade.

"Somewhere, sure." Jason began patting the pockets of his flightsuit, peeked inside a couple of the pouches on his survival vest, and finally pulled a small pack of candy out of his medical supplies. "Will these do?"

Her expression turned into a dangerous scowl, "Hell no!"

He looked down to see if he'd mistakenly pulled out a grenade or a breaching charge, but he hadn't. "Who doesn't like Skittles?"

She sighed and rested a hand on his arm a moment as if apologizing.

Her fingers were almost delicate, but he could see a strength to them. She was so fit that he'd have guessed she was the sort who went to the high-end gym three times a week with a gaggle of girlfriends and had an impossibly handsome aerobics trainer named Julio—*except* that she was Activity. The agents from The Activity were just as likely to go into the field to gather their own intel from behind enemy lines as they were to work at a desk in Fort Belvoir. They were known for being ruthlessly competent. Another thing he liked in a woman. If competence was the new sexy, then—

"Thanks for the offer and, yes, I do like Skittles. I just have this thing about Christmas, so thanks but no thanks."

He looked down at the little pack. It was clearly labeled Holiday Mix and showed only red and green flavors rather than the normal rainbow.

"Seems like you're putting a lot of weight on a little bit of seasonal packaging."

She nodded, "No argument from me. It's the one topic I'm a complete lunatic on."

"Christmas?"

"Christmas," she confirmed as if it was an incursion by an entire battalion of Taliban.

"Completely rational about everything else?"

"Everything!" Kelsey's tone was dry enough for him to laugh, which had several of the crew turning to look at him.

He squinted at Carmen, who had just come aboard and was checking over the internal systems, and mouthed, "What?"

Carmen shook her head, keeping her thoughts to herself, as she continued the pre-flight check.

Fine!

He tried to turn to give Carmen the cold shoulder, but she gave him an I-caught-you wink that blew his timing, even if he didn't know what she was on about.

"Even rational about men?" Jason turned back to Kelsey.

"Always," then she grimaced, "for what good it has ever done me."

"I'm not sure if I should ask if that's a good sign or a bad one for me."

"As long as you're wearing that hat? Bad sign."

He looked up enough to spot the white, furry trim just above his eyebrows and remembered the blinking Rudolph.

"Nope," he looked back down at her and made a point of shaking his head hard enough to make the little bell at the end tinkle brightly. "Even being a gorgeous Activity agent, I'm not giving up my hat for you."

"Your loss," and finally that smile of hers came out. She did a quick turn and hair toss worthy of any disdainful supermodel, then strode up the cargo bay. But it was the smile that slayed him. From pretty to radiant faster than a heat-seeking missile.

He could only wonder what it would take to make her smile

like that again. Taking off his hat? No. She'd smiled while making a joke because he had it on. He'd stick with a winning hand, no matter what she said about Christmas.

There had to be a reason behind it, but he wasn't sure how comfortable he felt digging for it with a complete stranger, no matter how attractive. It wasn't just her beauty. Something in her drew him—deeply. Not a feeling he was used to.

Done with the exterior inspection, George boarded as well and began checking his Minigun just as Carmen began going over hers. His own M240 hung out of the way in its bracket close by the rear ramp.

Kelsey sat in the observer's chair just behind the pilots' seats. That should be safe, they were both married: the Captain to the unit's hot Italian drone pilot and quiet Danny—impossibly—to the vivacious Carmen. The only other crew member was the portside gunner and George was too British to try poaching where Jason had showed interest.

Out of excuses, Jason started his own preflight checks of the *Calamity Jane II* for a mission. Ammo full-stocked after the last mission was still fully stocked. Emergency supplies of food, water, and first aid were fully stocked and inside the refresh date. Enough to feed the whole crew for a week if they went down hard somewhere.

Then he started in puzzling on Kelsey. She must have her own reasons for being so *Bah Humbug!* But it didn't fit her. She seemed...happier than that.

Quiet. Which among the screaming extroverts of the 5E must be a shock. But there was something more. As if—

A high whine of fast-moving tires was all the warning he had to dodge out of the way before a pair of Polaris MRZRs came racing up the rear ramp. He jumped aside, clinging to the inside of the Chinook's hull to stay clear. The MRZRs were four-seater ATVs on Special Operations steroids. Tough, lightweight, fast, electric-quiet, and able to carry a thousand pounds of soldier and gear at sixty miles an hour or scramble over rough terrain at twenty. Except instead of the usual Army tan, they'd been painted like blue and red hotrods. Blinking Christmas lights had been wound around the bars of the roll cage which didn't make much sense unless...undercover as civilian hotrod dune buggies.

Right. Low profile mission. But had the woman who hated Christmas thought of the Christmas lights? Jason suspected that she was the sort of woman who thought of everything and left nothing to chance.

The way the MRZRs raced aboard told him it was either SEAL or Delta at the helms.

Once they were in, he dropped back down. Both drivers wore clip-on fuzzy antlers.

"Duane? Dude! Haven't seen your ugly face since you left the Rangers for that wimp-ass Delta outfit." They'd stayed in close touch, but in four years had never managed to be in the same place at the same time.

"Jason, you Night Stalker piece of shit!" They thumped each other's backs hard enough to hurt.

"Cool antlers. Too bad they aren't half as cool as my hat." Then he spotted the gorgeous Latina stepping out of the other rig. She looked *very* cute in her antlers.

"You must be Sofia. I can't believe that you fell for a lump of coal like this one."

"He is all mine," she said in a happy, lushly Spanish accent, as she gave him a hug. "I have heard so many good things about you. I would know you anywhere by your so very silly hat."

"And if it hadn't been Christmas?"

"By your *very* good looks," she didn't hesitate to laugh.

Then she turned to Duane but kept an arm around Jason's waist so he kept his around her shoulders.

"I do not know," Sofia said thoughtfully. "Jason is *so* handsome.

Why didn't you ever tell me this. Maybe I should be with a Night Stalker man and not a Delta boy."

With all the speed Jason would expect of a Delta operator, Duane hip-checked him into the emergency fire extinguishing system and separated Sofia with a quick hand about her waist—a move so smooth that it had all three of them laughing.

CHAPTER THREE

*K*elsey sat at the far end of the helicopter's shadowed cargo bay and tried to look away. What would she give to be a part of that laughing circle of three? They looked so easy together, so effortlessly happy. That was a part of working for The Activity—she and the other analysts were a collection of loners, brought together by a fascination for the intricacies of information and an ability to turn it into actionable intelligence.

The folder that Colonel Gibson had provided was a perfect example. The first page had contained just three lines of information that suddenly brought her last six months of work into sharp focus.

Delta Team and 160th SOAR 5E, Ech Stagefield, Fort Rucker
Juan Zavala, Christmas Eve
(and an address in Cozumel)

IT WAS Christmas Eve Day and Colonel Gibson had given her the first actionable lead on the elusive Juan Zavala that she'd seen in six months of hunting for him.

Zavala was one of the kingpins of the ultra-violent Jalisco New Generation cartel that she'd been tracing. The Jalisco were the former armed wing of the Sinaloa cartel and were rapidly gaining precedence in the Mexican drug scene. Under the kingpin theory of "take out the top and the internecine battles will do the rest of the cleanup," Zavala was a prime target.

She even recognized the address. It was a beach house that she had researched as one of his likely safe houses, but had never been able to trace him to.

Then the woman separated herself from the two men as they turned to arranging the two MRZRs more carefully and tying them down for flight. She moved through shadows until she was almost at Kelsey's side.

"Sofia?" She'd never expected to see Sofia Forteza again since she had left The Activity.

"Kelsey!" And Sofia gave her a hug as well which surprised her completely. Sofia had been one of her few friends at The Activity before she'd made the unlikely shift to Delta Force. But they'd never had a hugging kind of friendship.

"You seem happy."

"Ecstatic! I didn't know how much I loved being out in the field. Actually, I did know that. I know it better now. And Duane certainly helps," she was practically glowing as she aimed a happy look back down the bay.

"How do you know Jason?" Kelsey wasn't sure why she was asking. She'd watched them hug and felt... She didn't know. As if she wished it was her instead?

"I don't. It is the way that Duane talked about him, I seem to already know him. They served in the US Rangers together. They've stayed very close."

Another skill Kelsey didn't have. She'd lost touch with Sofia the moment she'd headed over the horizon.

"Is this mission yours?" Sofia's effortless manners didn't give Kelsey enough time to feel uncomfortable.

She nodded.

"Good," Sofia nodded her head emphatically in return as the APU screamed to life and then the twin turbines began spinning up. "Then I know everything will go fine."

"You do?" Kelsey must have heard wrong over the building noise. A backwash of hot exhaust rippled through the cabin—it would clear as soon as they were moving. She'd been worrying about the mission every second since Colonel Gibson had handed her the file then evaporated or dropped through a trap door or whatever he'd done.

Sofia dug into her pocket and pulled out a pair of earplugs as the engine noise escalated. She shouted as she slid them in. "You were always the best planner we had when the terribles hit the fan. Except for me, of course. We all knew it and it made you a little scary to work with."

"I was?"

Past words, Sofia simply nodded before heading back down to rejoin the men.

People were scared of her?

Actually, that explained some reactions she'd observed. Rooms did seem to go quiet when she stepped into them, as if she was checking up on everybody. Except the 5E's briefing room. They were so skilled that maybe nothing daunted them.

What would it be like to work with them more? On occasion, an agent was permanently embedded with an elite team to facilitate operational communications more tightly with The Activity's specialties regarding human and signal intelligence. To be embedded with the 5th Battalion E Company would be both a challenge and...fun. Fun? That wasn't something she was very good at and erased the thought from her mind.

But she couldn't help glancing back down the cargo bay. Jason in his blinking Rudolph hat hadn't been afraid of her—just the opposite. He'd continued talking to her even after she'd snapped at him for offering her Christmas candy. Killjoy strikes again.

CHAPTER FOUR

Kelsey Killaney's plan sounded simple on the surface. Jason now knew that the surface appearances had nothing to do with one of Kelsey's plans.

She'd only outlined the basic approach strategy back at Fort Rucker: length of flights, refueling stops, necessary equipment. Per her instructions, beneath his flightsuit he wore slacks, a dress-shirt, and running shoes, though she hadn't explained why at the time. Under his shirt he wore a vest of lightweight Dragonskin armor for a bit of invisible protection.

She'd laid it out on the four-hour flight down to Naval Air Station Key West and refined it on the three-hour crossing to Cozumel after they'd eaten a hurried dinner while refueling. He'd never been to the small resort island off the Yucatan coast. Bringing a hot babe down here for a winter vacation had definitely been on his bucket list.

He'd never imagined that when he did it, he'd be unloaded after nightfall onto an empty stretch of beach ten miles across the island from the city of San Miguel de Cozumel. The weather was perfect. They'd left the storm somewhere over the Florida Keys and now drove out beneath a canopy of stars. Shirt sleeves were just right for the warm evening, though he could have done without the extra layer of the Dragonskin.

Night Stalkers usually didn't deploy on the active part of the mission, that's what Ranger door kickers and Delta operators were for. His job was to get them there, then shuffle away and hide until it was time to come fetch them.

Not on a Kelsey Killaney mission.

"I need an expert in flight operations on the mission team in case something goes wrong."

He'd considered arguing, until she said she was going as well.

"There isn't time to sufficiently brief everyone on the layout. We only have tonight, so I have to be there. I've spent too long hunting Zavala to let him slip away."

Which explained why she'd only requested two Delta operators rather than a full team.

"Can you drive?" Kelsey had asked as they were releasing the tie-downs on the vehicles.

"Sure." Of course he could.

"I mean really drive?"

"Dad ran sprint car races for a hobby. If he paid the entry fee, then got a sportfishing client, I'd drive the race for him. I was a much better driver than I was a fisherman." Then he climbed into the driver's seat of the MRZR and buckled in to settle the point. An MRZR was a close relative of a sprint car. Four seats instead of one, no airfoil on the top, and an MRZR had an engine that could only go sixty, not a hundred and sixty. But those were the differences. In common, they both had: an open metal frame with a serious roll cage, a very low center of gravity, demon-like cornering abilities, and were made for running in the sand and dirt and being fast while doing it.

In the far back, an MRZR had an extra space like a miniature pickup. It could carry two extra soldiers or a pile of gear. Right now, they had massive tourist drink coolers—coolers that were loaded with all of their tactical gear and most of the weapons they had just illegally smuggled into a friendly country. Due to corruption, the results on these types of missions were often better if the foreign government wasn't notified. The challenge was to not be caught in the process as that tended to upset them badly.

It was only as they rolled off the back of the Chinook and onto the deserted beach, that the truth clicked in.

"You already knew that I could really drive. That's why you didn't get a second driver for this mission from Delta."

"Maybe I just like your hat," Kelsey said it as if she was all innocence. No, she said it like a tease—like maybe the first tease she'd ever made.

He drove up the beach and over the berm onto the Quintana Roo road, then waited for Duane and Sofia to join them in the second MRZR. How had that lucky bastard gotten a woman like that? Sofia was beyond beautiful, right up there in Kelsey Killaney's category. And she was a Delta Force fighter. As far as he knew, they had like three women in the entire unit, yet somehow Duane had won her heart. And not just a little. Married if that didn't beat all. The only man less likely to get married in their Ranger platoon than one Jason Gould.

That got Jason thinking about why he himself was that way. Because he was stupid? Or because he'd never met the right woman? He'd take answer B any day. Any day before now. He wasn't sure why she fascinated him so much, but that was a question he was willing to pursue.

"You hate my hat," he reminded her.

"You're right. I hate your hat."

"And how important is it that we go low profile undercover here?"

"Why do you think we repainted the MRZRs in hotrod colors and are wearing civilian clothes?"

"But you hate my hat."

She glared over at him.

"That's too bad." He wasn't quite sure why he'd grabbed the extra accessory when getting civilian clothes out of his room, but he had.

"Why? Because you so *love* your hat?"

"I do, but that's not the problem," he tried to shake his head as if she was pitiful.

Duane and Sofia cleared the berm and pulled up beside them on the empty highway as the helos disappeared back into the night: the big Chinook and the two guardian DAP Hawks. They'd fly out well beyond radar range and refuel from a circling C-130 tanker while they waited.

"Then what's the problem, Jason?" Kelsey's guard was down just enough that if he was quick...

He pulled out his second hat, triggered the flashing nose, and pulled it onto her head. Her hair was impossibly sleek, so smooth it might have been ice, but was so warm and human that it seemed to burn his hand. He yanked his hands away before he could do more.

"There," he declared. Stomping on the gas, he unleashed the MRZR. It leapt down the road with Duane and Sofia close behind. "Now you're low profile."

"I'm going to have to kill you, Jason," she shouted over the racing wind.

"Wait until after the mission, okay?"

CHAPTER FIVE

Kelsey tugged the hat down against the speed-generated wind and hated herself for it. Hated that she hated Christmas. Hated that she still didn't know how to be nice to Jason when he'd been nothing but nice to her. Wearing his stupid matching hat was the first concession she'd managed.

He looked over and grinned at her as he turned left onto the Carretera Transversal to cross the island.

"So, tell me why you're irrational about Christmas?" He shouted over the wind noise. The electric MRZR itself was quiet, but there was roaring wind and the tire noise as they raced the 9.3 miles across the island in a vehicle with no windshield. The wide two-lane road ran straight as an arrow between two uninterrupted walls of green—their headlights well-focused on the road ahead so that they'd be hard to spot from any distance.

Not a chance. "Tell me why you're so crazy for it that you have not one but two Rudolph hats."

They covered a mile in silence before he spoke. He slowed a little, but the road noise barely changed.

"Mom bought them for Dad and I last Christmas. This one is his," he tapped his forehead. "You're wearing mine."

"Why do you have *his* hat? Thief!" She was suddenly very conscious of having Jason's hat on her head. It was so...personal. As if they were together—somehow a couple.

Again the mile-long pause.

"The cancer killed Dad by Valentine's Day. Mom followed him, of a broken heart by July Fourth."

Kelsey felt as if she'd just been punched. She reached out and clamped a hand over his arm in sympathy. Could feel his muscles rippling beneath the surface as he drove. His strength a comfort, when she should be the one providing that.

"Sorry," he steadfastedly stared ahead without a glance toward her. "It just slips out sometimes. When I'm not being careful."

Kelsey could only look at him in amazement. His ridiculous hat and teasing her about it had more meaning than should be possible. In an instant he transformed from a ridiculous man who had been kind to her, to a kind man who didn't mind being perceived as ridiculous—even if he wasn't.

How was he so comfortable in his own skin that he could do that?

She was on the verge of asking, but knew that wasn't right. He'd just laid his heart out on the cross-Cozumel road. His honesty demanded the same.

"My parents hated each other. I still don't know why they stayed together."

Kelsey's hand still rode lightly on Jason's forearm, but she was reluctant to take it away. Through it, she could feel a listening stillness come over him.

"But they didn't fight all year. Instead, they saved all of their bitterness for one 'special season,'" she wished she could do this softly rather than shouting it in short choppy sentences with no ability to gauge her listener's reaction. "The Christmas tree. Mom thinks they're pretty. Dad hates them as a waste of money, space, time... I don't know. It's not like we were poor. Maybe he hates them because Mom likes them. Dad would pick the fight starting in October. Stretch it into February when he was on a roll."

Jason's stillness continued as the lights of San Miguel de Cozumel city began to light the road ahead of them.

"Christmas is nothing but bad memories."

Jason slowed as they entered the outskirts of the city. He hadn't said a word as she'd told him something that she'd never told anyone. She'd always managed to keep her *Bah Humbug!* to herself before. Somehow was never dating anyone when Christmas came around, always opting out of Secret Santa at work. She'd stressed herself into actual illness before any number of Christmas parties.

And Jason just drove.

"Look."

She was looking, to see what his reaction to her was. For some reason it seemed to matter, but she couldn't read it.

Then he nodded to either side of the road.

She looked. There were breaks in the trees. Houses that were little more than hovels were tucked in among palm and avocado trees. And each one had bright Christmas lights. Sometimes just a doorway, sometimes a spiral climbing a palm tree, and frequently a lit creche of the birth in the manger in gaudy plastic. The closer they got to town, the more extravagant the displays.

They turned southwest on the Avenida Rafael E. Melgar.

The waterfront was a wonder of lights. To her right lay the sea. Cruise ship docks jutted out into the dark ocean—the ships lit like cities of their own. Hundreds and hundreds of people strolled along the seawall. Most holding hands or in close groups chattering happily together.

The street was divided by a narrow median with a palm tree every hundred feet or so, and each was brightly wound in Christmas lights. The one- and two-story whitewashed shops along the inland side of the street were a bounty of Christmas displays.

Jason continued to drive in silence.

People waved at them in their two colorfully lit MRZRs, dressed up so that they looked like high-end dune buggies. She waved back.

They passed a tall lighthouse close by the cruise terminal. It cast no light. Yet even from here, in the brightest heart of the promenade, she could see the tall beacon to the south that had replaced it—two white flashes every five seconds.

Was that herself? A decommissioned lighthouse amidst an abundance of light?

She turned back to Jason as he continued easing along in the southbound traffic. Was he the beacon that now flashed so brightly ahead? Somehow he was holding onto the joy that his dead parents had taught him while she was still wrapped up in the darkness that her parents had tried to teach her.

It was a crappy metaphor, especially if it was true and she was the decommissioned lighthouse.

Up ahead there was another light, far taller and flashing brightly. That looked like a much happier metaphor, if she could figure out how to live it.

CHAPTER SIX

"*I* don't want to feel decommissioned any more." Kelsey slipped her hand off his arm and he missed it. He missed the comfort. He missed the connection.

"What?" Jason wondered where that had come from. He was still trying to shake off the memories of last Christmas, his dad already past being able to speak, but smiling as he wore his goofy hat. Meager presents opened on a hospital bed because no one could find the energy to shop for more.

"The lighthouses," Kelsey pointed upward.

Jason hadn't even noticed them. He could barely see anything other than the withered man who took up so little space on the vast bed.

"You think you're a decommissioned lighthouse?"

"Can't prove otherwise by me."

He'd heard her story, about her idiot parents. Had they somehow pounded into this beautiful woman's head that she wasn't worth better?

Jason had asked Sofia about her, when it was clear they knew each other.

"Not much to tell. Brilliant, driven, the very best in very tough crowd. But she really keeps herself to herself, if you understand what I am meaning. She never talks about anything outside of the missions. So it's not as if I'm giving anything away because neither will she."

But Kelsey just had. To him.

"Kelsey?"

"Uh-huh."

"How could you get something so completely wrong?"

"What? I know where Zavala is. I know the layout of the house. We are the perfect assets to do this fast and quiet." She was back on the mission, and she was right. They'd rolled past the flashing lighthouse, leaving behind traffic, another cruise terminal, and once more were into the outskirts of the rapidly disappearing town.

"There," she pointed. They dropped down onto the narrow shore road past the big resorts, the Chankanaab Beach Resort being the last of them. He had a quick glimpse of a quiet lagoon and thatched huts. It was the sort of place he'd imagined bringing a woman, though not with a load of weapons, rather with a bikini and a lot of time with nothing planned.

They continued south along the shore. The low beach and berm were usually close by, except when lush estates pushed the access road inland.

"Here," Kelsey pointed again.

He turned off into a vacant lot. It made a gap through the scrub trees and palms connecting the road to the beach. He stopped before they reached the sand. The electric MRZRs were silent and he could hear the gentle splash of the waves picked out in the headlights. He and Kelsey here, together. It was very easy to imagine.

Duane and Sofia rolled up quietly behind them, but Jason ignored them.

Instead, he turned to Kelsey. Her face was randomly lit by the blinking Christmas lights on the roll cage. The shifting shadows made it hard to read her expression.

"It's Christmas Eve," he said, for lack of any better ideas.

"It is," she looked down at her folded hands.

"Got a present for you."

"Better than this hat?" Then he saw her bite her lower lip because she now obviously understood the importance of the hat. He'd only been teasing when he put it on her, but it had gained so much meaning in the last half hour.

"Well, okay, it's not *that* cool, but I'm making this up as I go."

She only nodded, but it was quick, accepting. Then she appeared to brace herself.

He dug in his pocket and pulled out the bag of Christmas Skittles, handing it across solemnly.

Kelsey stared down at it for a long time before taking it gently from his hands.

"To hell with your past," he told her. "To hell with mine. New beginnings. Though I figured I was safer to start small." It was also the only thing he had to give at the moment.

She looked up at him with her dark eyes so wide that they seemed to catch all of the colors of the Christmas lights at once.

Then she clutched the little packet of candy to her chest with both hands, and nodded for him to continue down the beach.

The plan was fiendishly simple—he wondered if all of Kelsey's plans were like that. If so, she absolutely belonged in the 5E. It was beyond stealth…it was cool! And so much better than the home invasion that was their backup scenario.

They drove the two Christmas-decorated MRZRs slowly down the beach. In front of each beach house before Zavala's, they stopped and sang Christmas carols. When her clear soprano joined in, it really brought it to life. The owners came out, offered punch and apple fritters at one house and orange sugar cookies at the next. Each stop drew out the owners of the next residence along the beach front.

At Zavala's, the last in the row, the pattern held. Zavala came out to hear them and brought a bottle of rum. On the last stretch of darkened beach, they knocked out his two guards with dart guns they'd stashed under the seats, drugged Zavala and his equally dangerous brother as well before tying them in back of the MRZRs, and continued on their way as if nothing had happened. His capture only took seconds.

Just inland was the little-used Aeródromo Capitán Eduardo Toledo. A small field used for tourist flights during the day, and nothing at night. The Chinook slipped in and they drove up the cargo bay ramp so fast that the helo barely stopped.

Once they were aloft and clear of Cozumel, Kelsey came to find him where he was leaning against the angle of the raised rear ramp —his normal post as tail gunner.

She still wore the hat.

And she opened her joined hands for just a moment to show that she still clutched the little packet of candy, before once more holding it to her chest. And her eyes, those wide, lovely eyes looked ready to take on the world.

Then she leaned in to kiss him. Not some quick thank you peck, but soft, lush, so full of warmth that for a moment he felt as if he was indeed lying on a sunny Cozumel beach with her.

"Thank you," she whispered from mere inches away.

Jason tried to come up with some quip. Something to ease the moment for the lady in the blinking Rudolph hat. But all he could think to whisper back was the same, "Thank *you*."

He'd assumed this Christmas would be hell, because of the memories of the last one. Instead, she'd given him the gift of hope as a present.

When she kissed him again, this time letting herself curl up against him, he had hope for the many Christmases to come as well.

IF YOU ENJOYED THIS, YOU MIGHT ALSO ENJOY:

THANKS FOR READING ALONG!

*A*nother year has gone by, another baker's dozen of tales have been told.

I hope that they brought some joy, some escape, and a few happy sighs.

If so, I feel that my goals were well achieved.

See you next year!

DON'T MISS THESE PRIOR GREAT COLLECTIONS!

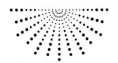

AVAILABLE AT FINE RETAILERS EVERYWHERE.

A SHORT STORY COLLECTION

The IDES
of MATT
2015

M.L. BUCHMAN

"Buchman's work has catapulted him to the top, and the honor is well deserved." —RT Reviews

A SHORT STORY COLLECTION

The IDES
of MATT
2016

M.L. BUCHMAN

"Thrill-Ride: The 10 Romantic Novel of the Year" —Booklist

ABOUT THE AUTHOR

M.L. Buchman started the first of, what is now over 50 novels and as many short stories, while flying from South Korea to ride his bicycle across the Australian Outback. Part of a solo around the world trip that ultimately launched his writing career.

All three of his military romantic suspense series—The Night Stalkers, Firehawks, and Delta Force—have had a title named "Top 10 Romance of the Year" by the American Library Association's *Booklist*. NPR and Barnes & Noble have named other titles "Top 5 Romance of the Year." In 2016 he was a finalist for Romance Writers of America prestigious RITA award. He also writes: contemporary romance, thrillers, and fantasy.

Past lives include: years as a project manager, rebuilding and single-handing a fifty-foot sailboat, both flying and jumping out of airplanes, and he has designed and built two houses. He is now making his living as a full-time writer on the Oregon Coast with his beloved wife and is constantly amazed at what you can do with a degree in Geophysics. You may keep up with his writing and receive a free starter e-library by subscribing to his newsletter at: www.mlbuchman.com

Join the conversation:
www.mlbuchman.com

Other works by M. L. Buchman:

The Night Stalkers
MAIN FLIGHT
The Night Is Mine
I Own the Dawn
Wait Until Dark
Take Over at Midnight
Light Up the Night
Bring On the Dusk
By Break of Day
WHITE HOUSE HOLIDAY
Daniel's Christmas
Frank's Independence Day
Peter's Christmas
Zachary's Christmas
Roy's Independence Day
Damien's Christmas
AND THE NAVY
Christmas at Steel Beach
Christmas at Peleliu Cove
5E
Target of the Heart
Target Lock on Love
Target of Mine

Firehawks
MAIN FLIGHT
Pure Heat
Full Blaze
Hot Point
Flash of Fire
Wild Fire
SMOKEJUMPERS
Wildfire at Dawn
Wildfire at Larch Creek
Wildfire on the Skagit

Delta Force
Target Engaged
Heart Strike
Wild Justice

Where Dreams
Where Dreams are Born
Where Dreams Reside
Where Dreams Are of Christmas
Where Dreams Unfold
Where Dreams Are Written

Eagle Cove
Return to Eagle Cove
Recipe for Eagle Cove
Longing for Eagle Cove
Keepsake for Eagle Cove

Henderson's Ranch
Nathan's Big Sky
Big Sky, Loyal Heart

Love Abroad
Heart of the Cotswolds: England

Dead Chef Thrillers
Swap Out!
One Chef!
Two Chef!

Deities Anonymous
Cookbook from Hell: Reheated
Saviors 101

SF/F Titles
The Nara Reaction
Monk's Maze
the Me and Elsie Chronicles

Strategies for Success (NF)
Managing Your Inner Artist/Writer
Estate Planning for Authors

SIGN UP FOR M. L. BUCHMAN'S NEWSLETTER TODAY

and receive:
Release News
Free Short Stories
a Free Book

Get your free book today. Do it now.
free-book.mlbuchman.com